A
BOLLYWOOD
AFFAIR

A
BOLLYWOOD
AFFAIR

SONALI DEV

KENSINGTON BOOKS
www.kensingtonbooks.com

For Mama and Papa for living Happily Ever After

ACKNOWLEDGMENTS

Writing your first acknowledgments page has to be a lot like giving your first acceptance speech at the Oscars. You've practiced it in your head so very many times and yet when the moment arrives, it's so huge, such a culmination of your dreams, of your immense good fortune, how can you ever articulate it sufficiently?

I would love to say that this book was hard labor, that my path to publication was riddled with sacrifice and tears. But I can't. Writing Samir and Mili's story was pure joy, and my path was riddled with the incredible generosity and support of so many people I could never name them all or ever thank them enough. But I'm going to try anyway.

First, my incredible husband for knowing exactly how to walk the tightrope between needing me and giving me space to chase my dream and for all that delicious dal, clean laundry, and faith.

My children for being as undemanding as two teenagers can ever be expected to be. If there are other children in the world who say to their mother, "You go write. We'll make us some ramen noodles," the future of our race is bright indeed.

My parents for never being more than a phone call away from dropping everything and rushing to my aid when I need them.

My best friend for being my sounding board, my springboard, my storyboard, not to mention my periscope into Bollywood. She believed in my writing long before anyone else did and it has been the most priceless of gifts.

My beta reader girls, Rupali, Kalpana, Gaelyn, Robin, India, and Jennifer, for the most insightful reads and for being my champions.

My friends, Advocate Pallavi Divekar, for letting me pick her legal eagle brain on Indian Marriage Laws and Village Panch Councils, and Smita Phaphat for an insider's view into Rajasthani culture. Without them there would be no story.

My sisterhood of writers, who are without a doubt the best part of this business. The Aphrodites—Robin, Savannah, Cici, India, Clara, CJ, Sarah, Ann Marie, Denise, and Hanna—for holding my hand every single day. The Windy City RWA chapter for never letting a plea for help go unanswered. The Chicago North RWA chapter and the Golden Heart Lucky 13s for their unconditional support, and the RWA community at large for being the best example of feminine power in the entire world.

My agent, Jita Fumich, for a million questions answered, and my editor, Martin Biro, for being my Right Time and Place and for leading me through my debut with such kindness, and the entire team at Kensington for making this so very easy.

And lastly and most importantly to each and every one of you for taking the time to read my words, to you I owe my deepest thanks. Without you all these people would have supported me in vain.

PROLOGUE

❧⟡❧

A sea of wedding altars stretched across the desert sands and disappeared into the horizon. The celebratory wail of *shehnai* flutes piped from speakers and fought the buzz of a thousand voices for attention. Hundreds of red-and-gold-draped children sat scattered like confetti around auspicious fires ready to chant their vows. The Akha Teej mass wedding ceremony was in full swing under the blistering Rajasthan sun.

Lata surveyed the scene from the very edge of the chaos. Her father-in-law had pulled some hefty strings to obtain this most coveted corner spot, where it should've been relatively quiet. Only it wasn't, thanks to her son's chubby-cheeked bride, who bawled so loudly Lata couldn't decide if she wanted to slap the child's face or pull her close. What kind of girl-child cried like that? As though she had the right to be heard?

Lata's older son, the twelve-year-old groom, spared one disinterested glance at his bride's ruckus before strolling off to explore the festivities. Lata's younger son twisted restlessly by her side. Even hiding in the folds of her sari, his foreign whiteness made him stand out like a beacon against the sea of toasted brown skin and jet-black hair. Unlike his older brother, he couldn't seem to bring himself to look away from the crying bride.

Finally, unable to contain himself any longer, he reached out and gave her fabric-draped head a reassuring pat. She whipped around, her wet baby eyes so round with hope Lata's heart cramped in her chest. The gold-rimmed bridal veil slipped off her baby head, revealing a mass of ebony curls forced into pigtails. The boy tugged the veil back in place. But before he could finish, the girl lunged at him, grabbing her newfound ally as if he were a tree in a sandstorm, and went back to wailing with intensified fervor. Her huge kohl-lined eyes squeezed rivers down her cheeks. Her dimpled fingers dug valleys into his arm. Her soon-to-be brother-in-law winced but he didn't pull away.

"You whoreson!" Lata's father-in-law shouted over the bawling girl. He'd just finished up the wedding negotiations and he turned to the boy with such rage in his bushy browed gaze that Lata rushed forward to shield him. But she wasn't quick enough. The old man drew back his arm and slapped the boy's head so hard he stumbled forward, finding his balance only because the tiny bride gripped him with all her might.

"Get your filthy hands off her!" The boy's grandfather yanked the girl away. "Get him out of here," he hissed at Lata, spittle spraying from his handlebar mustache like venom. "Ten years old and already grabbing for his brother's wife. White bastard."

Anger ignited the gold in the boy's eyes and swam in his unshed tears. Lata squeezed him to her belly and pressed her palm to his ear. He fisted her widow's white in both hands, his skinny body trembling with the effort to hold in the tears. The girl's gaze clung to them even as the old man dragged her away. Her chest continued to hiccup with sobs but she no longer screamed.

"Why does Bhai's bride cry, Baiji?" the boy whispered against Lata's belly, his Hindi so pure no one would know he'd spoken it for but a few years.

Lata kissed his soft golden head. It was all the answer she would give him. She could hardly tell him it was because the child had been born a girl, destined from birth to be bound and gagged, to never be free. And she seemed to have sensed it far sooner than most. Sadly, the poor fool seemed to believe that she could actually do something about it.

1

All Mili had ever wanted was to be a good wife. A domestic god-dess-slash-world's-wife-number-one-type good wife. The kind of wife her husband pined for all day long. The kind of wife he rushed home to every night because she'd make them a home so very beautiful even those TV serial homes would seem like plastic replicas. A home filled with love and laughter and the aroma of perfectly spiced food, which she would serve out of spotless stain-less steel vessels, dressed in simple yet elegant clothes while mak-ing funny yet smart conversation. Because when she put her mind to it she really could dress all tip-top. As for her smart opinions? Well, she did know when to express them, no matter what her grandmother said.

Professor Tiwari had even called her "uniquely insightful" in his letter of recommendation. God bless the man; he'd coaxed her to pursue higher education, and even Mahatma Gandhi himself had said an educated woman made a better wife and mother. So here she was, with the blessings of her teacher *and* Gandhiji, melt-ing into the baking pavement outside the American Consulate in Mumbai, waiting in line to get her visa so she could get on with said higher education.

Now if only her nose would stop dripping for one blessed sec-ond. It was terribly annoying, this nose-running business she was cursed with—her personal little pre-cry warning, just in case she was too stupid to know that tears were about to follow. She squeezed the tip of her nose with the scarf draped across her shoulders, completely ruining her favorite pink *salwar* suit, and stared at the two couples chattering away over her head. She absolutely would not allow herself to cry today.

So what if she was sandwiched between two models of newly wedded bliss. So what if the sun burned a hole in her head. So what if guilt stabbed at her insides like bull horns. Everything had gone off like clockwork and that had to be a sign that she was doing the right thing. Right?

She had woken up at three that morning and taken the three-thirty fast train from Borivali to Charni Road station to make it to the visa line before five. It had been a shock to find fifty-odd people already camped out on the concrete sidewalk outside the high consulate gates. But after she got here the line had grown at an alarming rate and now a few hundred people snaked into an endless queue behind her. And that's what mattered. Her grandma did always say "look at those beneath you, not those above you."

Mili turned from the newlywed couple in front of her to the newlywed couple behind her. The bride giggled at something her husband said and he looked like he might explode with the joy the sound brought him. Mili yanked a handkerchief out of her mirror-work sack bag and jabbed it into her nose. Oh, there was no doubt they were newlyweds. It wasn't just the henna on the women's hands, or the bangles jangling on their arms from their wrists to their elbows. It was the way the wives fluttered their lashes when they looked up at their husbands and all those tentative little touches. Mili sniffed back a giant sob. The sight of the swirling henna patterns and the sunlight catching the glass bangles made such longing tear through her heart that she almost gave up on the whole nose-squeezing business and let herself bawl.

Not that all the longing in the world was ever going to give Mili those bridal henna hands or those bridal bangles. Her time for that had passed. Twenty years ago. When she was all of four years old. And she had no memory of it. None at all.

She blew into the hankie so hard both brides jumped.

"You okay?" Bride Number One asked, her sweet tone at odds with the repulsion on her face.

"You don't look too good," Bride Number Two added, not to be outdone.

Both husbands preened at their wives' infinite kindliness.

"I'm fine," Mili sniffed from behind the hankie pressed to her nose. "Must be catching a cold."

Both couples took a quick step back. Getting sick would put quite a damper on all that shiny-fresh newly weddedness. Good. She was sick of all that talk over her head. Being just a smidge less than five feet tall did not make her invisible.

The four of them exchanged meaningful glances. The couple behind her smiled expectantly at Mili, but they didn't come out and ask her to let them move closer to their new friends. The couple in front studied the cars whizzing by with great interest. They weren't about to let their position in line go. The old Mili would have moved out of the way without a second thought. But the new Mili, the one who had sold her dowry jewels so she could go to America and finally make herself worth something, had to learn to hold her ground.

There's a difference between benevolence and stupidity and even God knows it. Her grandmother's ever-present monotone tried to strengthen her resolve. She was done with stupidity, she really was, but she hated feeling petty and mean. She was about to give up the battle and her place in line when a man in a khaki uniform walked up to her. "What status?" he asked impatiently.

Mili took a step back and tried not to give him what her grandmother called her idiot-child look. Anyone in uniform terrified her.

"F-1? H-1?" He gave the paperwork she was clutching to her belly a tap with his baton, doing nothing to diffuse her fear of authority.

"Oy hoy," he said irritably when she didn't respond, and switched to Hindi. "What visa status are you applying for, child?"

The flickering light bulb in Mili's brain flashed on. "F-1. Student visa, please," she said, mirroring his dialect and beaming at him, thrilled to hear the familiar accent of her home state here in Mumbai.

His face softened. "You're from Rajasthan, I see." He smiled back, not looking the least bit intimidating anymore, but more like one of the kindly uncles in her village. He grabbed her arm. "This way. Come along." He dragged her to a much shorter queue that was already moving through the wrought-iron gates. And just like that, Mili found herself in the huge waiting hall inside the American consulate.

It was like stepping inside a refrigerator, pure white and clinically clean and so cold she had to rub her arms to keep gooseflesh from dancing across her skin. But the chill in the room refreshed her, made her feel all shiny and tip-top like the stylish couple making goo-goo eyes at each other on the Bollywood billboard she could see through the gleaming windows.

She patted down her hair. She had pulled it tightly into a pony-tail and then braided it for good measure. Today must be an auspicious day because her infuriating, completely stubborn curls had actually decided to stay where she had put them. Demon's hair, her grandmother called it. Her *naani* had made Mili massage her arms with sesame oil every morning after she combed Mili's hair out for school. "Your hair will kill me," she had loved to moan. "It's like someone unraveled a rug and threw the tangled mass of yarn on your head just to torture me."

Dear old Naani. Mili was going to miss her so much. She pressed her palms together, threw a pleading look at the ceiling, and begged for forgiveness. *I'm sorry, Naani. You know I would never do what I'm about to do if there were any other way.*

"Mrs. Rathod?" The crisply dressed visa officer raised one blond eyebrow at Mili as she approached the interview window. The form she had filled out last night while hiding in her cousin's bathroom sat on the laminated counter between them.

Mili nodded.

"It says here you are twenty-four years old?" Mili was used to that incredulous look when she told anyone her age. It was always hard convincing anyone she was a day over sixteen.

She started to nod again, but decided to speak up. "Yes. I am, sir," she said in what Professor Tiwari called her impressive English. The ten-kilometer bike ride from her home to St. Teresa's English High School for girls had been worth every turn of the pedal.

"It also says here you're married." Sympathy flashed in his blue eyes, exactly the way it flashed in Naani's eyes when she offered sweets to their neighbor's wheelchair-bound daughter, and Mili knew he had noticed her wedding date. Another thing Mili was used to. These urban types always, always looked at her this way when they found out how young she had been on her wedding day.

Mili touched her *mangalsutra*—the black wedding beads around her neck should've made the question redundant—and nodded. "Yes. Yes, I'm married."

"What is your area of study?" he asked, although that too was right there on the form.

"It's an eight-month certificate course in applied sociology, women's studies."

"You have a partial scholarship and an assistantship."

It wasn't a question so Mili nodded again.

"Why do you want to go to America, Mrs. Rathod?"

"Because America has done very well in taking care of its women. Where else would I go to study how to better the lives of women?"

A smile twinkled in his eyes, wiping away that pitying look from before. He cleared his throat and peered at her over his glasses. "Do you plan to come back?"

She held his stare. "I'm on sabbatical from my job at the National Women's Center in Jaipur. I'm also under bond with them. I have to return." She swallowed. "And my husband is an officer in the Indian Air Force. He can't leave the services for at least another fifteen years." Her voice was calm. Thank God for practicing in front of mirrors.

The man studied her. Let him. She hadn't told a single lie. She had nothing to fear.

He lifted a rubber stamp from the ink pad next to him. "Good luck with your education, Mrs. Rathod. Pick up your visa at window nine at four p.m." *Slam* and *slam*. And there it was—

APPROVED—emblazoned across her visa application in the bright vermillion of good luck.

"Thank you," she said, unable to hold back a skip as she walked away. And thank you, Squadron Leader Virat Rathod. It was the first time in Mili's life that her husband of twenty years had helped his wife with anything.

2

This was what Samir lived for. Drinking himself senseless with his brother was a thing of such comfort that Samir couldn't think of a single other situation in which he felt so completely and wholly himself. Samir took a sip of his Macallen and scanned the crowd divided equally between the glass dance floor suspended over the swimming pool and the bar that overlooked it. He'd much rather be at one of his regular city bars with his brother, but when the wife of one of Bollywood's biggest superstars invited you to her husband's "surprise" fortieth birthday party, you showed up. And you acted like you wanted to be here more than anywhere else in the world. Especially when you needed the birthday boy to act in your next film.

The good news was that the hideous parts were over. The stripper had jumped out of the cake, the champagne fountain had cascaded down a tower of crystal flutes and been consumed amid toasts, tears, and flashing cameras. Now the frosted-glass hookahs were bubbling at tables and the smell of apple-flavored tobacco mingled with the smell of weed and cigars. Samir actually enjoyed this relatively mellow part of the evening, when the pretense was mostly over and everyone was too high to care about how they looked or how quotable what came out of their mouth was. Plus, the combination of the sapphire-lit pool shimmering beneath the glass dance floor and the blanket of stars above was quite beautiful. Not to mention the fact that his brother was here with him to enjoy it. He took another slow sip of his drink, leaned back on the low lounge-style sofa and let out a deep sigh.

Virat threw his head back and laughed. "Bastard, you're sighing. I swear, Chintu, you're such a chick."

"Shut up, Bhai. That was a man-sigh."

"Is that like one of those 'man purses' you carry?" His brother pointed his all-Indian Old Monk rum at the Louis Vuitton messenger bag leaning against a plush silk pillow next to Samir.

Samir shrugged. Given that he was a brand ambassador for Louis Vuitton, he could hardly carry anything else. It was the only modeling gig he did anymore. The money was fantastic and he liked the rustic flavor of the campaign. Truth was he had never enjoyed modeling. Too static for him. But thanks to his half-American genes and the white skin that had made his childhood hell, assignments had fallen in his lap far too easily to turn away. India's postcolonial obsession with white skin was alive and well. And modeling had led him to the camera so he couldn't begrudge it. Even after ten years, bringing a film alive from behind the lens still gave him his best hard-on.

Virat shook his head as if Samir was a lost cause. "Seriously, you drink that fancy shit, you color-coordinate your closet, and you actually fucking know the names of things you wear. Did I teach you nothing?"

Actually, Virat had taught Samir everything he knew. His brother was just two years older, but he'd been a father to Samir, their real father having had the indecency to die without either one of them ever knowing him. The bastard.

"You tried, Bhai. But who can be like you?" Samir raised his glass to his brother. "You are, after all, 'The Destroyer.' " They said that last word together, deepening their voices like they had done as boys, and took long sips from their glasses.

"The holy triumvirate," their mother had called them—the creator, the keeper, and the destroyer. Their mother was the creator, of course. The boys had fought for the title of destroyer. Virat had gone to the National Defense Academy at sixteen and become a fighter pilot in the Indian Air Force and Samir was writing and directing Bollywood films. There was no longer a fight about who was "The Destroyer."

"You boys don't look anywhere near done." Rima, Virat's wife, returned from her third ladies' room visit of the evening.

The brothers stood, weaving a little, and grabbed each other's arms to steady themselves.

"Are you tired? Do we need to leave?" Virat's rugged, big-man face softened to goop. He rubbed his wife's shoulder. Her belly was starting to round out just the slightest bit and the angles of her face had lost some of their sharpness, but the rest of her was as slender and graceful as ever.

Rima ran her fingers through her husband's hair and they shared one of their moments. The kind of moment that made Samir feel like a rudderless ship with no land in sight. Not that he was looking for what they had. Neha was on location for a shoot and he was actually relieved that he didn't have to share his time with his family with his girlfriend.

Rima turned to Samir, went up on her toes, and ruffled his hair. Virat might still call him Chintu, which meant "tiny" in Hindi, but at a couple inches over six feet Samir had a good half foot on his brother.

"*We* don't need to leave." Rima gave them one of her angelic smiles. "But *I* am tired, so *I* am going home. You two try to save some liver for later?"

"Don't be ridiculous. We'll take you home. Bhai and I can finish up there. The party's winding down anyway." Samir reached for the jacket he had slung over the couch.

"Yeah, we're not staying here without you, baby," Virat said before wrapping his arms around Rima and breaking into a seriously tuneless rendition of "I Don't Want to Live Without You." Usually Samir wouldn't mind anyone murdering that particular Foreigner song, but there were still a few journos hanging around at a nearby table and the thought of Virat and Rima's private moment mocked in some bitchy film magazine column made Samir positively sick.

Rima, genius that she was, stroked Virat's lips with her thumb, silencing him. Samir loved the woman. He mouthed a thank-you and got another angel's smile in return. "No. You boys continue. I'll send the driver back." She tapped Virat's chest with one finger and gave Samir a meaningful look. "Samir, he's definitely not getting behind a wheel like this, you understand?"

"Yes, ma'am," both brothers said in unison.

Samir watched Virat follow Rima with his eyes as she let the hostess air-kiss both cheeks and walk her out. "*I'm* a chick, Bhai? You should see how you look at her."

"A real man isn't afraid of love, Chintu." A line of dialog from Samir's biggest Bollywood blockbuster. And Virat pulled it off in an almost perfect impersonation of the hero's theatric baritone.

Samir laughed. "Hear! Hear!" He downed the rest of his scotch in one gulp.

"But seriously, isn't she the most beautiful woman in the world?"

"Undoubtedly, and you're the luckiest bastard."

"Hear! Hear!" Virat downed the rest of his drink too.

A waiter promptly brought them two new glasses. Samir signaled him to stop after this one.

"I don't deserve her but I love her so damn much." Virat raised a hand when Samir tried to interrupt. "No, I don't. I'm a lying bastard, Chintu. You know I am."

"No, you're not. Where is this coming from, Bhai?" Samir picked up his drink. But something in Virat's expression made him put it down again.

"You don't think my wife needs to know I was already married once?"

Seriously, where was this coming from? It had been twenty years since their mother had taken them and fled their village home in the middle of the night. After that none of them had ever mentioned that abomination of a marriage their grandfather had forced Bhai into. It was easy to forget that their grandfather's hand had marked more than just Samir's back.

Samir gave his brother a hard look. "You were *not* married. That was not a marriage. You were twelve years old, Bhai. In case you've forgotten, underage marriage is illegal in India. And if that's not enough Baiji had it annulled a long time ago."

Virat pulled his wallet out of his pocket. The leather bulged over tightly stretched seams. With so much shit stuffed in there how did Virat ever find anything? Samir's own wallet was, like the rest of him, impeccable. Two credit cards, a driver's license, a black-and-white picture of himself squeezed between Virat and Baiji at a village fair before they moved to the city, and a wad of crisp notes.

After a few moments of fumbling, Virat pulled out a folded piece of paper and handed it to Samir. It was a letter handwritten in Hindi.

"Read it." Virat signaled the waiter for another drink. Samir caught the waiter's eye and signaled him to water down the peg before he started reading.

> *Dear Mr. Viratji,*
> *Namaste.*
> *This is the first letter I am writing directly to you. I hope you will forgive my boldness. Although I have never communicated with you, as is appropriate in our great culture, I was in constant contact with your grandparents through their living days—may the gods rest their souls. Your grandfather was a stalwart among men. As your grandparents must have informed you, like any good daughter-in-law should, I took care of them over the course of the twenty years that we have been married. The entire village is witness that I am the best daughter-in-law in all of Balpur.*
> *While I consider it my most humble duty to take care of your family—our family—I think it is time that you give me the opportunity to take care of you also. I have recently completed my graduation in sociology and I have been groomed by my grandmother to be the perfect officer's wife. I know that when you come for me, you will not be disappointed. There are those in Balpur who believe I am something of a beauty. But I never say that because I have been taught modesty.*
> *Your grandfather promised my grandmother every day*

*for the past five years that you would come and take me
home and every year we have waited patiently. Now that
your grandfather is gone, I am at a loss as to what to do.
If you are the man your grandfather boasted of, I know
that my wait is now coming to an end. As you know, my
grandmother—who has raised me with the very best values—is my only remaining support and she makes herself
sick with worry.*

*And one last thing before I take your leave. I have per-
sonally seen to the upkeep of our family haveli for the past
three years. The old house is now in need of more serious
repairs than I alone can handle.*

*My grandmother sends her blessings. I lie prostrate at
your feet. Please come and take your bride home.*

Yours,

Malvika Virat Rathod.

Samir looked up. The letter hung limp from his fingers. "You've
got to be fucking kidding me."

They both burst out laughing.

"I lie prostrate at your feet?" Laughter clenched and un-
clenched Samir's belly, but he couldn't believe he was laughing.
This was sick.

"But I never say that because I've been taught modesty." Virat
laughed so hard he choked on the words.

"Shit, Bhai, what are we going to do? The village girl thinks
you're still married to her. How the fuck did this happen?"

Virat's laughter dried up. "It has to be our grandfather. The bastard clearly lied to Baiji when she petitioned to annul the marriage.
Evidently, he never submitted the papers. I did talk to a lawyer
and basically, even though underage marriage is illegal for a bride
under eighteen and a groom under twenty-one, the fact that the
marriage took place in the village of Balpur complicates things.
Thanks to the Village Panch Council laws, the village council gets
to decide whether marriage vows that were performed under their
jurisdiction are valid or not. And it seems like the Panch Council

has deemed this marriage legal. Which means, Rima and I—" He slumped into the couch.

"That's crap, Bhai. How can a marriage you were forced into at twelve be legal?"

Virat stared at his drink, the usual self-assured sparkle in his dark eyes dull with despondence. "The lawyer says that if we can get the girl to sign papers saying the marriage hasn't been consummated, and that it happened without her consent, then the marriage is considered void. Our grandfather is actually punishable by law for doing this. To think we could've sent the old bastard to jail."

"Fuck, there's a missed opportunity." Samir raised his glass and finally took another sip. "To the old bastard. May he rot in hell."

Virat drank to that. "I'm still screwed, Chintu. I need to take care of this before the baby comes. I want no legal doubt about my child's legitimacy or about Rima's rights as my wife. What if I go out on a sortie and my plane goes down and I never come back?"

The words kicked Samir in the gut. His buzz disappeared. "Shut up, Bhai. I'll hook you up with my lawyer. Peston will eat these people for lunch if they give us trouble." Something about the mention of the *haveli*, their ancestral home, in the letter had made discomfort jab at him. The property was worth a few million rupees, at least. These rural types sounded all innocent but they could be really devious.

Not that he would think twice before crushing anyone who threatened his brother and sister-in-law in any way. No amount of deviousness was going to do the village girl any good if she dared to mess with a Rathod. *Malvika Virat Rathod* indeed.

3

Mili was dying—a slow painful death by drowning in soap suds. She'd been scrubbing dishes for four hours straight. She felt like one of those cartoon characters, with only the top of their heads visible behind a mountain of dirty pots and pans, from those *Chandamama* comics she used to inhale as a child. Over the past three months she had done battle with so much grime, so much greasy muck, she might as well be a scouring pad herself. A sharp-edged warrior against a world of sticky stir-fry grease.

She plucked one long-stemmed ladle out of the water-filled sink and spun around, slashing the air as if it were a sword in her yellow rubber-clad hands, and found herself staring right into the face of her bug-eyed boss, the illustrious owner of Panda Kong, Eastern Michigan University's only on-campus Chinese restaurant, where Ridhi and she spent four evenings every week. Of course he would make his entry at this precise moment. Because Mili could never ever do anything remotely mental without being caught.

Egghead contorted his bitter-medicine face even more than usual and threw her some eye darts. She tried smiling at him in a fashion that suggested flailing utensils while scrubbing them gave them that extra shine. But he turned away, unamused, and left the already freezing kitchen ten degrees cooler with his disapproval. She stuck out her tongue at his retreating head and did a little shoulder wiggle to shake off the chill.

"LOL!" Mili's roommate, Ridhi, squeezed past Egghead into the kitchen, another tower of dishes teetering precariously in her arms. Ridhi thought all conversation was essentially an exercise in text messaging. "OMG. Did you see his face?" She dumped the dishes into the sink Mili had just about emptied.

"You mean the expression that told me exactly how desperately he wants someone to answer the Help Wanted sign on the door so he can get rid of the crazy Indian girl?"

"No way. Egghead would never let you go. He'd handcuff himself to you if he could. You work too hard. If anything, he's wondering how to take that sign down so he can get you to do even more work."

Mili groaned from the depths of her soul.

Ridhi grinned. "Girl, how will you ever keep a secret for me with that expressive face?"

Mili's heartbeat sped up. She turned on the hand spray and started to hose the muck off a giant wok. "Did you hear from *him?*"

Ridhi's face got instantly dopey. One mention of "him" and Mili could picture the sweeping romantic Bollywood number swirling inside Ridhi's head—dancing choruses and all. Ridhi lived on planet Bollywood along with her friends Action, Emotion, and Romance.

"Well." Ridhi threw one surreptitious glance over her shoulder as if Daddyji's spies might be hiding in the Panda Kong kitchen at eleven p.m. "Ravi is totally freaked out after I told him Daddy was trying to set me up with Mehra Uncle's doctor son. He doesn't want to take any chances. He thinks we should—"

Egghead decided to demonstrate Mili's impeccable timing once again and walked in just as Mili put the pot down and turned to Ridhi for the rest of the drama.

"I lock up outside. You think dishes get done sometime tonight?" he snapped with complete disregard for the Mt. Everest of gleaming dishes on the draining board, not to mention the fact that he was interrupting a conversation.

Ridhi glowered at him. Mili picked up a pan and directed her anger at it instead.

For all the glamorous fantasies Mili had harbored about America, none had involved being buried in dirty dishes in a foul-smelling kitchen or being sucked into a supporting role in a full-on film-style elopement.

When she had first met Ridhi, Mili had wondered how she was ever going to carry out a conversation with her. Ridhi had spoken only in monosyllables. But the disadvantage of starting in the spring semester was that the campus was as isolated as a crematorium at midnight and Mili desperately needed a roommate. And a deathly silent one who looked ready to throw herself off a bridge was better than none at all. There was no way Mili could afford the five-hundred-dollar rent out of the six hundred dollars she made as a grad assistant. The eight dollars an hour she made for scrubbing the life out of these pans was reserved strictly for sending home to Naani.

Suddenly, after two weeks of skulking around the apartment while Mili attempted desperately to push food and cheery conversation in her direction, Mili's sad-sack roomie had magically blossomed into Ms. Bubbly herself thanks to a phone call from the hero of her story—Ravi. They'd met last year when Ridhi had been a freshman and Ravi a grad student heading up the computer lab. He'd made every one of Ridhi's bells gong in unison like a temple at worship time. But even though Ravi was Indian he came from South India, while Ridhi's family hailed from the North Indian state of Punjab. Ridhi's father took such pride in his Punjabi heritage that the idea of his daughter associating herself with a South Indian boy had quite literally given him a heart attack.

Lying in his ICU bed, plugged into life support, he had made Ridhi promise she would stop her "rebellion" and free herself from the influence of "that South Indian boy" and marry a good Punjabi boy like a good Punjabi girl. It was your classic movie plot—from three decades ago.

"Daddy's stuck in the seventies," Ridhi had told Mili. "That's when he first came to America. He refuses to believe the world has moved forward. If he saw the clothes my cousins in India wear or the stuff they do with *their* boyfriends he'd have so many heart attacks he'd have to rent space in the ICU."

It hadn't taken Ridhi long to realize that all the ICU promises in the world couldn't keep her away from her hero, and Ravi and she were planning to ride off into the sunset together. Only Ridhi's family was very well connected. Her uncle worked for the Immigration people and all manner of threats to deport, dismember, and generally destroy Ravi had been freely tossed about in full-on film-villain fashion.

Mili was terrified but Ridhi was "so overplaying the victim," and here they were, walking to their apartment, leaving a sparkling Panda Kong in their wake while Ridhi filled Mili in on her grand elopement plan.

"So Ravi's accepted the job offer," Ridhi said, leaving out the details like Mili had begged her to. "He can support us now. And I refuse to let Daddy keep us apart for a moment longer." She threw another glance over her shoulder, scanning the night, and dropped her voice to a whisper. "Ravi's going to pick me up and we'll drive to—"

Mili plugged her ears and shook her head.

Ridhi smiled. "We'll drive to his new place. Then as soon as Ravi's parents get their visa and come down from India we'll get married and this nightmare will be over." Her smile suggested it wasn't so much a nightmare as the adventure of a lifetime.

But it didn't feel like an adventure to Mili. She was terrified of turning it into a nightmare. She had never been able to lie outright so there was no question of letting Ridhi tell her any specific details. Because if Mili knew something and Ridhi's family found Mili, she didn't know how she would keep them from tracking Ridhi down. And there were two things Mili would never ever allow to happen—one, she would not be deported before her course was done; she had worked too hard to get here, and two, she would not be the reason for messing up a love story. Because although Mili had never known what having your love returned felt like she had been in love for as long as she could remember.

She had prayed for her husband's success and safety every day of her life. She had fasted at every Teej festival so he would have everything he ever wanted. She had dreamed of him and yearned for him and although she tried really hard not to care about having those feelings reciprocated, she believed in love with all her heart.

If Ridhi was lucky enough to be loved back, Mili would do everything in her power to make sure it didn't slip through Ridhi's fingers.

Samir did a quick rollover and maneuvered himself to the top. It wasn't easy. He was still inside her. But he could tell from the look on Neha's face that she was going to say it. *Fuck.* Tangled in his eight-hundred-thread-count sheets, with that spent, thoroughly pleasured look on her face, she looked like a fucking schoolgirl, dying to spill her secrets.

If he moved fast enough, he might still get away. He shoved his palms into the bed, trying to push himself off her.

She moaned and wrapped her legs around him, trapping him in place. "I love you."

Fuck.

The words hung in the air between them like claws poised to dig into flesh. Why did they do this—every single one of them? Why did they have to ruin a perfectly good, perfectly mind-numbing fuck this way? Why?

He manufactured a smile. But it came moments too late. Her face deflated, her legs slid off him and the dreaded wetness rose in her eyes and pooled along her lids.

He yanked himself out of her, slumped on his back, and closed his eyes. The crumpled condom flopped against his thigh. He needed to get cleaned up but that would have to wait. This wasn't going to be quick. It never was.

"Aren't you going to say anything?" Her voice was so small. If he were capable of guilt he'd have drowned in it. But all he could muster was raging restlessness. He wanted to kick himself. He'd missed the signs. Again. Letting Little Sam do his thinking for him had to stop.

Although Little Sam was *very* happy right about now. Neha had turned out to be even better than he'd expected. The perfect combination of a hot body, up for anything, and a cool heart that didn't get in the way and make things messy. It had been almost like finding a female version of himself. Until now.

"I said I love you, Sam." A nasal whine slipped past her practiced huskiness.

Samir made the effort not to wince. He propped himself up on his elbow and faced her. His biceps, his delts, his pecs responded to the studied move and bulged obligingly. Neha's eyes followed the movement, lingering hungrily on skin still slick with massage oil and sweat. Little Sam stirred.

"I mean like really *love-love* you." Her words were a full-blown accusation now.

The stirring stopped dead in its tracks. *No, you don't. You really love-love what we just did.* But telling her that would dial up the drama and Samir saved the drama for his films.

Women never accepted horniness for what it was—horniness. He'd never understand it. Why had he thought she'd be different? With all that ambition a commitment should've been the last thing on her mind. Where were all those users the film industry was supposed to be full of? Why couldn't he find himself one for a change?

He placed one finger on her lips, using all his strength to keep his impatience out of his touch. He had to get on with his day. He was going to hear back on the Shivshri Productions project today. It could be the biggest fucking day of his life. Or the worst fucking disappointment. And he had no idea which it was going to be. Just like now. Fucking story of his life.

"Shh, sweetheart. Don't. You know how much I like you. But I would never—"

"You *like* me?" Dear God, could she please dial down the nasal. "We've been together six months, Sam. Six months! And you—you *like* me?" She shoved him hard and sat up, clutching the silken cotton to those lovely breasts.

He let his eyes turn smoky—sincere, willing to sacrifice his own needs for her. "Listen, baby, look at you. They're calling you the next big thing. You can go all the way to number one. You know that. I would never take that from you."

The anger flashing in her eyes diffused a little.

"You know how it works. Now's the time to focus. Producers won't touch you if they think you're settling down. You think I don't want all your attention? I'm a man, Neha, you think this is easy for me?"

He must've done the hurt look really well because the stubborn set of her jaw softened. She stroked his face. He pulled her fingers to his lips. "I won't do that to you. I won't be responsible for letting you waste all that talent."

"You're Sam Rathod—being with you can't possibly damage my career."

"I'm Sam Rathod—a fling with me is great publicity. But if they even suspect a long-term relationship, producers won't touch you. I'm the Bad Boy, remember? I'm trouble with a capital T. You've just had your first hit. It's a huge one but you know this business. You can't lose your focus if you want to get to the top."

"I don't care, Sam. I never thought I'd feel this way about anyone. I don't care about success, about being number one. All I want is to be with you."

Holy. Fuck.

Indian women and their need to go all domestic on you. Once they got into that space there was no reasoning with them. The familiar *click* that signaled the end of his patience snapped in his head. He pushed himself off the bed and dumped the condom in the trash. He swept up the robe laid neatly on the leather recliner and belted it around his waist. "Listen, Neha, can we talk about this later? It's a big day for both of us." He turned around and headed toward the double doors, caressing the carved panels salvaged from the ruins of the Jaipur palace, letting the solidity of the five-hundred-year-old wood calm him.

"Sam!" Neha called after him.

He ignored the panic in her voice. "Eggs okay for breakfast?" He grabbed the post that held up the spiral staircase and spun himself onto the stone treads. He loved this staircase, loved the unencumbered openness of it. He'd spent weeks with the architect getting the lines just right. He flew down and landed with practiced ease on the marble floor.

He heard Neha get off the bed upstairs. Heard her scream and come tearing out of his room. He spun around just in time to duck away from the ceramic vase that came flying at his head. It missed by an inch and crashed against something behind him. Good, he'd been wanting to get rid of the ugly-ass housewarming gift for years. But if anything happened to one of his paintings, he was going to kill her.

"You bastard," Neha shrieked as she rushed toward the railing-less staircase, tangled up in his sheets like a careening Venus de Milo.

"Shit, Neha. *No!*"

Before he knew what was happening, she tripped. Her body twisted around the fabric and toppled sideways onto the stone stairs. One end of the sheet hitched on the top step as she fell over the edge and rolled out of the sheet like Cleopatra rolling out of the carpet. He ran to her but didn't make it. She landed on her face with an ungodly thump, the white sheet flapping like a flag over her motionless, naked body.

"Neha! Fuck, Neha?" He fell to his knees next to her, his heart hammering. A trickle of blood seeped from her mouth and Samir thought he was going to vomit.

"Neha?" He stroked her face. She coughed, opened her visible eye for a second, mumbled something, and then closed it again. *Thank you, God.* "It's okay, sweetheart. I'm here. You're going to be fine."

He flew up the stairs, grabbed his cell phone and their clothes and ran back down, pulling on his jeans with one hand and punching the number for the ambulance with the other.

A busy signal. Fuck.

He dialed his doctor and prayed for better luck.

"Sam? What's wrong? It's six in the morning," a groggy voice answered.

"I know what the fucking time is," Samir barked into the phone, pulling his T-shirt over his head. "Neha fell down my stairs. Long story. She's conscious, I think. Can you get to the clinic?"

"Yeah. I'm leaving now. See you there."

He rolled her over, being as gentle as he could. "Neha, sweetheart?"

She moaned. With quick movements he dressed her, keeping up a steady stream of words. A house full of servants and today there wasn't a soul to help. But he always gave his staff the night off when his girlfriend slept over. His housekeeper's granddaughter lived in his home, and Neha wasn't exactly the kind of person who could handle a child like Poppy.

He lifted Neha's limp body and carried her down to the building lobby. His driver wouldn't be in until eight. He was going to have to drive himself. Except he found a ten-ton water tanker blocking the building gates. Fan-fucking-tastic.

"Get the damn tanker to move. Now!" Samir yelled at the watchman and headed for the car.

The man fluttered about like a headless chicken, opening and closing his mouth, and did absolutely nothing.

"What?" Samir snapped.

The watchman jumped back. "Sir, the tanker driver went off to get some chai."

This day just got better and better. "Go get a taxi or a rickshaw. I need to get to a doctor." Samir raised Neha higher, just in case the nitwit had missed her, whimpering and half-conscious in his arms.

The nitwit didn't move.

"What?" Samir snapped. The man jumped back as if Samir were about to put Neha down and tear him limb for limb. "What?" Samir gentled his voice.

"Sir, today is the thirteenth."

"So?" It took all Samir's strength not to shout. He wanted to shake the guy until his teeth rattled.

"Sir, it's Mumbai *shutdown*. The opposition party has called for a citywide public transport strike. No taxis. No rickshaws. No nothing."

"Fuck. Fuck. FUCK."

Neha convulsed in his arms. The watchman made a squeaking sound and mopped his forehead with his elbow.

Without another word, Samir walked past him, past the chugging driverless water tanker blocking the gate, and stepped onto the dusty, dug-up street. The roadwork had been going on for over six months. The good news was that Mumbai didn't wake up until eight a.m. The street was isolated. Samir pulled Neha close and started to run.

4

Mili loved the mile-long walk from her apartment to her office in Pierce Hall. Truth be told, she loved everything about Ypsilanti, the quiet university town in Michigan she had called home for four months, except maybe the tongue-twister name. She loved the neat roads, the redbrick facades, the rolling expanses of lush green grass. But most of all she loved the wide-open blue sky with perfect white clouds that looked like they had been drawn with a crayon.

Back home in Rajasthan the sky was a more purple blue and the clouds were more feathery brushstokes than distinctly etched curves. And yet it was the sky that eased Mili's ache for home. Ypsilanti was the only place other than Balpur where she had seen so much sky. In Jaipur the buildings lining the lanes cut the sky in half. As for the few days' worth she'd seen of Delhi and Mumbai, you'd have to fall over backward to get even a glance of sky through all that concrete.

As she neared Pierce Hall she had the strangest feeling, not quite as if she were coming home but as if she were going to a dear friend's house. She swiped her card in the reader and took the half flight of stairs down to the basement. The musty old wood scent filled her nose. Everyone in the office complained about the smell. But the painted timber pillars that lined the open courtyard at the center of her grandparents' house had this exact smell. Mili had spent so many afternoons with her cheek pressed against a pillar while her *naani* dispensed advice to the village women that the smell was infused with all the warmth of her childhood.

The office was empty. The rest of the graduate assistants and the professors who ran the Applied Research Unit wouldn't start to arrive for another thirty minutes. But it was Tuesday and on Tuesdays Mili came in early to use the office phone to call her *naani*. She used her own calling card of course and she had cleared it with Jay Bernstein, her boss. She hung her mirrorwork sack on the coat hanger and dialed the number. Her *naani* would be waiting at the village post office for her call. Naani had steadily refused to have a phone installed in her house. "There's no one I want to talk to whom I can't talk to on the face," she always said. And now her granddaughter had run off where she could no longer talk to her "on the face."

"Did you eat your dinner?" Always the first question.

"Yes, Naani." Except it had been breakfast.

"How much longer before you come back home?" Always the second question. "He called, you know?"

Mili pulled the phone away from her ear and groaned. "No, Naani, he didn't. No one is going to call." At least not yet. But she was here and she was going to make something of herself, make herself so worthy no one in their right mind would turn her away. And then she'd call him, instead of waiting. Maybe.

"He's going to call. You mark my words," Naani said with so much conviction Mili wondered what scheme she was cooking up. "Have I ever been wrong?"

"No, Naani, you're never wrong."

"Do they feed you well? I've heard horrible things about hostel food. The other day at the Delhi University hostel thirty students died because a lizard fell into the dal."

"There's no hostel, Naani. I told you, I have a flat and a kitchen of my own." No point mentioning that soon she wouldn't have a roommate. If she told *naani* she lived alone, her grandmother might not need to pretend a heart attack like she'd done when Mili had decided to leave for college in Jaipur three years ago. She would have one for real.

"How much does dal cost there? The price of dal went up to

eighty rupees a kilo yesterday. And unless you're rich you can't even think about onions, let alone put them in your mouth."

Mili hadn't eaten dal in four months. She had seen a bag of dal marked "yellow split lentils" in the grocery store last week. She had picked it up and held it to her cheek when no one was looking. But it cost twelve dollars, so buying it was out of the question. She practically lived on potatoes. French fries cost a dollar in the union. And chocolate was really cheap too.

"It's a good thing onions give you gas then, Naani. Are you taking your blood-pressure medicine on time? Are you making sure you don't eat too much salt?"

"*Hai*, what's the point of living like this? Don't eat salt, don't see your granddaughter. Take care of myself at my age when I raised an able-bodied granddaughter with an able-bodied husband. An officer no less." Naani started to sob and Mili had to squeeze her nose to make sure she didn't start.

"Naani-*maa*, please. It's just another four months. Before you know it I'll be back to take care of you."

"Your *naani-maa* will die in that time."

"No, you won't. You'll outlive me."

"*Hai hai*. Let the witch take your tongue. What a horribly inauspicious thing to say. Let your enemies die. Is this what they teach you in that America?"

"I'm sorry, Naani, I shouldn't have said that. It's been fifteen minutes. I can't talk anymore. I'll call again next Tuesday, okay?"

Naani let out another sob. "Go, go, learn your books. Make me proud."

This was why Mili came in half an hour early on Tuesdays. It would take another fifteen minutes for the tears to stop. Every time she spoke to Naani, Mili had an overwhelming sense of having run away from her duties. Did everyone who left their country feel this way—ground between the millstones of courage and cowardice? Or was it just her?

Mili often wondered if other people felt the same way about things as she did. She was perfectly aware of the fact that there was nothing normal about her life. Even in her village, she was the youngest girl to have been married. And she had to be the only girl on earth who had no idea what her husband looked like after twenty years of marriage. She had never left her village until she was twenty years old, except for a school trip to New Delhi when she won an essay contest at fifteen. And until she was twenty-four she had never even left her home state of Rajasthan.

College in Jaipur had opened up a whole new world to her. A world where girls competed shoulder to shoulder with boys in the classroom without apology. And here in America her classmates wouldn't even understand what that statement meant. There was no fear in the women here. None at all. And Mili loved that. Sometimes when she watched them in class, the way they stood, their spines erect and proud, their chins up, their laughter loud and unencumbered, she wanted the women at home to have what they had. And she wanted it so badly it made tears burn in her eyes.

No, no matter how much it hurt to hear Naani's sobs, being here felt too right to be wrong. And this was only going to bring her closer to what she wanted, what Naani wanted. Mili was sure of it.

"I'm not running, you bastard, and that's final. And don't fucking give me that look."

But DJ being DJ continued to skewer Samir with his patronizing gaze. If the bastard wasn't half his size, Samir wouldn't think twice about pummeling his agent's face.

"Listen, Sam. The scandal from the bar last month isn't cold yet. This is going to look really bad." DJ leaned back in the hideous red velvet chair that totally fucked up the richly wood-paneled conference room at the studio. The ugly chairs were one of the updates the owner's son had put in, undoubtedly to prove to the world that running the studio he'd inherited from his erstwhile superstar father involved some actual work. Samir wished he'd leave the décor alone and focus on upgrading the recording and editing equipment instead.

"I thought my trusted agent likes that my scandals keep me in the news."

DJ gave him that look again—as if Samir-the-brat was throwing a tantrum and swami DJ in all his patient glory refused to indulge him.

But Samir wasn't in the mood for this bullshit. He had to get back to the editing studio and finish up the edit on the ad film, which by the way he'd done only as a favor to one of DJ's other clients. A fact the bastard seemed to have conveniently forgotten. "Being accused of punching a few hundred-kilo fuckers is different from being accused of hitting a woman. And just to jog your lazy-arse memory, I only pounded their ugly faces because they were dragging a struggling kid into the bathroom. I was actually rescuing her. So much for fucking heroism."

DJ's face softened. Oh, *now* he cared. "The girl's parents called again, by the way. They wanted to thank you for keeping it out of the press. Her dad just made another donation to the Tirupathi temple for your long life and success."

Samir waved away his words. Whatever. Now DJ wanted to go all hero-worship on him. Last week he couldn't push hard enough to use the girl to make Samir look good. *This is your chance to salvage the Bad Boy, Sam.* But no way was Samir going to ruin some teenager just because she was too stupid to know what kind of bastards guys were. He didn't need to give her any more life lessons. Those bastards in that bar had done the job well enough.

"Those pictures in the *Times* today are really god-awful, Sam." His trusty right-hand man could always be counted on to gnaw off all the sugar coating from every bitter pill.

"She fell down my stairs and landed smack on her face, naturally she looks bad. And before you look at me like I'm a bastard, let me remind you that I ran two kilometers with her in my fucking arms. Fuck, I have to stop being such a hero. For all the good it does me."

Someone pushed the door open and both DJ and Samir turned to see the errand boy poke his head into the room. One look at their faces and he started to back away.

"Hey, Ajay, come on in, boss." Samir pulled the door open and the boy limped in with two glasses on a tray, his polio boot thunking on the ceramic tile.

"No sugar, all black, Sam-Sir. Just way you like." He handed Samir a glass of what had to be the strongest coffee in all of Mumbai. "They asked me to tell you they're ready for you in the studio."

"Thanks, this is perfect." Samir took a sip and ruffled his hair.

"I'm going to look at the final cut of an ad film and Ria Parkar's in it. I know you're her biggest fan. So give me ten minutes and you can come and watch, what say?"

The boy's face split into the widest grin. He nodded furiously and hurried away.

DJ's jaw worked as he took a sip of his coffee. Twenty years ago DJ had been an errand-boy at this exact studio. "At least make a statement telling the press what happened, Sam."

And they were back to the inquisition.

"Sure, I'll run right along and tell them: 'I didn't hit my girlfriend. She tripped and fell down the stairs.' They'll have no trouble believing me. And while I'm at it why don't I tell them 'we're just good friends.' They should lap that up too."

DJ opened his mouth.

But Samir had had about enough. "Before you start your broken record again, no, I won't run and I won't lie low. I've done nothing wrong." His phone vibrated in his pocket. "Neha is just being vicious. She'll clear the record with the press when her anger dies down. I'll talk to her."

"Sam, you know how conservative Shivshri Productions are. The whole playboy image is one thing, but an abuse scandal and they could drop you like a hot potato."

"They're not going to drop me. I've worked my ass off giving them three hits in three years. And I spoke with Shivji this morning. Unlike my agent, he had no trouble cutting me some goddamned slack."

DJ rolled his eyes and raised his hands in surrender. Good. About time the harassment section of the meeting was over and they got some work done. Except DJ chugged down some more coffee and jumped straight to uncomfortable topic number two. "How's the script coming along, by the way?"

He fucking knew how it was coming along. It wasn't.

His phone vibrated again. Samir reached for it. No way was he telling DJ he still hadn't been able to write one single word. It had been half a damn year and nothing. He didn't need another lecture on finding someone else to write his script for him. Samir always wrote his own films. And that was never going to change. Usually he could pull scripts out of his ass at two weeks' notice. Now he had the green light for the project of his heart and he was frozen. Frozen. Hours at the laptop and not one word to show for it. He tapped his phone.

It was his mother.

He pulled the phone to his ear. "Yes, Baiji?" he said in Hindi, holding up his hand at DJ, asking for a minute.

His mother didn't answer. He heard a sob, then silence.

The room went completely and utterly still around Samir. "Baiji? Hello?"

Another muffled sob. "Samir . . . Samir, *beta* . . ."

His mother never lost her cool. She rarely even frowned. The only time he'd ever seen her cry was when she'd held him that last time his grandfather had made like Charlton Heston in *Ben Hur* and whipped his back to shreds.

He wanted to ask her what was wrong but nothing came out.

The voice on the line changed. It wasn't Baiji anymore. It was Rima. Only it sounded nothing like his sister-in-law. It sounded like a dead woman with Rima's voice. "Samir?" she said.

Of course it's Samir. What the hell is wrong? He wanted to scream, but he said nothing.

"Come home," the hollow voice said. "Your brother . . . Oh God, Samir . . . Virat's plane went down."

5

"You know, Mill, sometimes I think about Ravi, and I feel like my heart is going to explode. There are no words, no words to describe what just thinking about him does to my entire body." Ridhi popped another square of the Hershey bar into her mouth and closed her eyes.

They were sitting cross-legged on Mili's mattress on the floor of their shared bedroom, the chocolate bar dwindling rapidly in its glossy brown wrapping between them. Mili broke off another piece with the reverence it deserved and popped it into her mouth. *Oh. Heavenly. God!* Whoever discovered chocolate was a genius and this Hershey person—may all the gods from all the religions in the world bless him ten times over—was a divine angel. Pure pleasure melted through her entire being. Surely there was no other sensation quite like this in the world.

Ridhi grinned at her like a fool and gave her one of those looks that indicated she had done something "adorable" again. "If I were a man, I'd want to eat you with a spoon, Mill. I don't know how your Squadron Leader let you out of his sight."

Mili stuck out her tongue at Ridhi. "Is that what your Ravi does, use a spoon?"

Ridhi made a face but the deflection worked and her eyes grew instantly dopey again. She threw herself back on the mattress. "You know, the first time Ravi touched me, I thought I was going to burst into flames. I think I had an orgasm even before we got to the good stuff."

Mili sucked furiously on her chocolate and squeezed her eyes shut.

Ridhi giggled. "How was it for you the first time with your Squadron Leader?"

Mili's cheeks warmed. She had told Ridhi she was married. The truth. But she hadn't mentioned that she hadn't met her husband in twenty years, so to have had a first time with him would have been magical in more ways than one. "Unreal," she said, her eyes still closed. The truth wasn't as hard as people seemed to think it was. You just had to phrase it right, so it wasn't a lie.

"Get out!" Ridhi yanked Mili's arm so hard she fell back on the mattress, laughing. "I mean if he's a military man, he must be all aggressive in bed, ha?"

Mili's cheeks went so hot they had to have turned maroon again. What was the point of being dark if you couldn't even hide a stupid blush? Ridhi said a very American "aw" and went up on her elbow next to her. "You know what the sweetest thing about Ravi is? He's so unsure of himself. I feel like I'm totally corrupting him. But it's also so annoying. Sometimes I want him to just lose his head and totally come at me, you know."

Oh, Mili knew all about wanting someone to come at her, come to her, come for her. Anything but neglect her as if she were a crumb on the verandah no one bothered to sweep up.

"So, is your Squadron Leader going to come see you while you're here or are you going to go without sex for a year?"

Mili tried not to choke on her chocolate. Every single person she'd ever known would have swooned in a dead faint before asking a question like that. "You know, I used to believe he would come for me, but now I'm starting to think he might wait until I go to him."

"OMG, Mili, I just realized we're both waiting for the men in our lives like good little Indian women." Ridhi burst into giggles.

Mili's heart did a little twist. *Yes, but yours can't wait to be with you. Mine . . . well, he doesn't have that problem. Yet.*

Ridhi popped the last remaining chocolate piece into her

mouth. "I can't wait a moment longer to finally be free of Daddy. He has never let me make one single decision for myself. He chose the courses I took in high school, tried to choose my career. 'Medicine is the most gratifying, most lucrative profession in the world. Why would you want to do anything else?' "

She did a pretty authentic male falsetto with a Punjabi accent and Mili giggled.

"The first time I had my way was when I did badly on my SATs and he couldn't do a thing about it except rant and shut me out. I wish I had figured out sooner that there are things he can't control."

Mili sat up and pushed a wispy strand of hair behind Ridhi's ear. "Ridhi, do you ever wonder if—"

"No. I've thought about it—whether wanting to be with Ravi has to do with getting back at Daddy. But no. Ravi is—you have to meet him. He's the most handsome, the kindest man I've ever met. And Daddy can't keep me away from him by marrying me off to some Punjabi doctor. I'm not marrying anybody just because he's Punjabi and certainly not just because he's a doctor." Her eyes shone like bright lights.

Envy swirled in Mili's chest, hot and heavy. What must it feel like to have that kind of freedom? The freedom to forsake everyone and everything, to break every bond and reach for the man you chose for yourself. For a moment she wanted it so badly it burned a hole inside her.

Then just as quickly it was gone and guilt flooded where it had been. She smacked her forehead. "I'm sorry, Ridhi, I don't know what I was thinking asking a question like that. Ravi and you are going to be so happy. I just know it."

Just like she knew Virat and she were going to be. She would make it happen, whatever it took. So what if she hadn't chosen him? She had vowed to be his forever, body and soul, and in the end that's all that mattered.

A horrible, bottomless feeling settled inside Samir. Not just the sadness that had squeezed around him like shrink-wrap ever since he'd picked up the phone. This feeling was layered on top of that sadness, under it. This feeling he had carried inside him for as long as he could remember in that unforgiving hollow that held up his ribs. It had woken him up on countless nights, screaming, drenched in sweat. As a child Baiji had held him, rocked him back to sleep. In adulthood he had simply learned to silence the screams.

This feeling was the reason he avoided shooting in America. One film in New York—that's all he'd done. New York he could handle. The choked-up concrete jungle he could handle. It was this open-earth, open-sky America that made his insides cave in. He didn't need a shrink to tell him exactly where that came from. This icy hollow inside him was the only thing he'd taken from here—from the country of his birth. The country he'd been tossed out of like so much garbage. The country where mothers could just pick up their children and give them back like clothing that didn't fit.

He gave the Corvette some juice and she purred under him like the sweetest lover begging for more. He was going to drive to the chick's house, hand over the papers, get her to sign and then get the hell out of here. And if she happened to be in need of some persuasion, well, it was a good thing persuasion was one of Samir's best talents. He had never had an actor refuse him a role, no matter how big of a star, and he had yet to meet a woman who wouldn't give him exactly what he wanted.

Already she had been too much trouble. Talk about being hard to find. Thank God for DJ and all those damned contacts of his. From Balpur to America. If finding her hadn't caused him such heartburn he'd be impressed. The vaguest memory of a chubby-cheeked girl bawling amidst wedding fires flashed in his mind. And like all memories from his childhood, it blew the raging hole in his gut open.

He forced himself to think about the letter instead. About laughing with his brother. About Rima's tears.

If Rima isn't my legal wife, that makes our child a bastard, Chintu.

Those had been Bhai's first words when he came out of his coma. God, what if no one ever called him Chintu again? He still couldn't believe Virat had escaped with two broken legs and a few broken ribs. But the weeklong coma had left Samir as terrified as the child who'd been thrown into a well in a fit of rage. Who'd been branded a bastard and then beaten for it. It had been Bhai who had jumped into the well after him and pulled him from the darkness. It had been Bhai who had thrown himself across his back to shield him when their grandfather's belt came out to play. If anything ever happened to Bhai, there would be no one to pull Samir away from the terror. Horrible hot anger rose inside him and a desperate need to do something, anything, to make it go away.

The GPS showed ten miles to Ypsilanti. Where had she found a town with a name like that? *Ip-sea-lan-tee.* That's how the car-rental lady had pronounced it. He repeated the ridiculous tongue twister under his breath. And why did it have to be Michigan? Fifty states in this godforsaken country and she had to pick the one where he'd first felt the burn of hunger in his belly, felt the horror of finding the woman who'd given birth to him lying in her own vomit, her white cheeks sunken, her eyes rolled up in their sockets, blood trickling from her nose and mixing with the acrid yellow liquid pooled under her head. He had crawled through the snow on bare hands and feet, unable to stay upright in the waist-deep snow, absolutely sure she was dead, absolutely sure he was going to die too. Even today, when he woke from the worst of the nightmares, he couldn't feel his arms and legs.

He let go of the steering wheel and rubbed his hands on his jeans. This was fucking bullshit. Ancient history that had no place in his life anymore, thank you very much. He rammed his foot on the accelerator. How long would it take the chick to sign the papers? If only Bhai were here to make a wager. Not that Samir had much choice but to get it done in a few days and get his ass back to Mumbai. If the script wasn't completed by the end of this month he was going to need a new career. This was his biggest budget yet. International-market big. With what they were giving him, he could actually make the kind of movie he'd been dreaming of since the first time he touched a camera. But if he'd had trouble writing before Virat's plane crashed, after the accident it was as if his brain had forgotten what it took to make words, let alone make stories. He had spent the entire plane ride from Mumbai to Detroit staring at his open laptop with nothing but buzzing white noise inside his head.

It was another strike against the girl. Not only had she piled worry and guilt on his brother's head when he should've been focused on his recovery, but she had also dragged Samir from his work. Away from doing what he should be doing—writing, taking care of Bhai, doing anything that did not involve coming back to this godforsaken country and being sucked inward into the hollow that was suddenly too close to the surface.

Next to him the legal notice she had sent the day after Virat's accident taunted him from inside his messenger bag and set his blood to boil. What kind of sick bitch sent a wounded soldier a legal notice demanding a share of his ancestral property? He'd made damn sure his lawyers wouldn't let her get her greedy little paws on anything. But he didn't trust anyone but himself to make sure she didn't come anywhere near Bhai and Rima ever again. He would carry the expression on Rima's face, as she sat by Virat's side waiting for him to wake up, to his dying day. Bhai was right in keeping this from Rima. Some chick who crawled out of nowhere was not going to subject Rima to any more pain. At least not until the baby came.

Samir switched gears and caressed the sweet spot with his foot. "Would you prefer an automatic, sir?" the lady at the rental counter had asked. Who needed the flat lifeless ease of an automatic? What he needed was to feel the throb of each one of those four hundred and thirty horses as they pounded beneath his foot and he harnessed them into submission with his bare hands. If the village girl gave him any trouble she better be ready to have her life turned upside down. He was in no mood to suffer gold-digging opportunists. Hunger for vengeance against every injustice that had ever made him helpless raced through his veins. Maybe he wouldn't let the sneaky little bitch off that easy. Maybe he'd turn on some Sam charm and make her fall so hard she'd be panting to sign the annulment papers. The thought calmed the fire a little. But not nearly enough.

6

Mili's heart thudded as Ridhi and Ravi backed out of the parking lot. She waved madly until Ridhi's beaming face disappeared from sight. Ridhi looked so happy that the flutters of nervousness bouncing about in Mili's belly seemed pointless. Even so, she joined her palms together and said a quick prayer for their safety before turning around and heading back to her apartment building. Ridhi called it a rundown shitpot but with its red bricks, white balconies, and sloping black roof Mili thought it was the most beautiful building on earth—after her home in Balpur, of course. She would never disrespect the home that had sheltered her all her life. But she sent up an apology anyway. Things were going so well she didn't want to jinx fate by appearing ungrateful.

Life was wonderful. Ridhi was going to have her happily ever after, Mili had aced her midterms, and her boss had asked her to coauthor a paper with him. There was the small problem of the rent. Of course Ridhi wanted to keep on paying her half, but how could Mili make her pay rent for something she didn't rent? Not that any of that mattered right now. Ridhi and Ravi were finally together and in this moment Mili couldn't bring herself to care about anything else.

It was just so incredibly romantic. Slightly crazy, awfully scary, but insanely romantic nonetheless. Mili jiggled her hips in a little *thumka* dance. She'd find a way. She'd made her way from Balpur to America. She could make the fifty dollars in her purse last until her paycheck came in next month.

Please, please keep them safe. And please don't let Ridhi's family find me. She repeated the plea for the hundredth time that day. No matter how hard she tried she hadn't been able to stop worrying about ruining Ridhi's love story if Ridhi's family found her. She did a quick sweep of the parking lot with her eyes, 007-style. Then followed it up with a full 360-degree spin. There wasn't a soul in sight but one could never be too careful. Better get inside. Considering Ridhi had just taken off, chances were it would be at least another day or two before Ridhi's family caught on and came after Mili. Even so she planned to stay out of the apartment and hide out in Pierce Hall and the library until she knew that Ridhi and Ravi were safe.

Something rustled behind her and she jumped and spun around. A man was parking a bicycle too close to the huge green refuse tank across the parking lot. Oh no, today was the day the collection truck came.

"Sir!" She ran after him. "Hello?"

Clearly, he didn't hear her because he sauntered off in the opposite direction. She raced to catch up with him and tapped him on the shoulder. He turned around and looked down at her as if she had just broken out of a mental asylum. Had to be her hair. Her grandmother always said she looked a little mad when she left it loose. She pushed it back with both hands. It bounced right back and spilled all over her face.

"You parked your cycle too close to the dirt," she said, panting slightly.

Almost lazily, he pulled a headphone from one ear and gave her a look that suggested she wasn't worthy of being listened to with both ears.

"They'll take your cycle away if you leave it there." She pointed at the bright yellow bike.

The poor fool just stared at her. Maybe it was her accent. They often didn't understand her English. A sharp stab of homesickness pierced through her followed by an intense urge to hear the familiar tones of her mother tongue. Yes, big fat chance of that happening here.

She slowed down and tried to speak more clearly. "The big truck, it comes to take away the dirt today. They'll take away your bicycle if you leave it there." She swept her hand from the bike to the huge green tank in which everyone dumped their trash bags.

More blankness. Maybe he didn't speak English.

She tried again. "They collect it on Friday—you'll lose your bicycle." She walked up to the bike and rattled the handle.

Finally understanding sparked in his eyes. "You mean the Dumpster? Are you trying, to tell me they collect the garbage today?" He laughed, but it wasn't a kind laugh.

She refused to feel small or stupid. Dumpster. Garbage. Not "tank." Not "dirt." It was just a matter of getting the terms right. Next time she would.

She nodded but couldn't get herself to smile at him anymore.

"Yeah, I know," he said really slowly, enunciating each word as if she hadn't just spoken to him in English. "Why do you think I put it there?"

She gaped at him. "You don't want it?"

"Well, duh. Why would I like throw it in the Dumpster if I wanted it?" He jammed the headphone back in his ear. "You can have it if you want it." And with that he walked off.

Did she look like someone who picked up things other people threw away? *You can have it if you want it*, indeed! What was she, a trash picker?

But instead of heading home she found herself standing in front of the *Dumpster* inspecting the bright yellow bicycle. The paint had scraped off in a few spots but other than that it was beautiful. If she had a bike she wouldn't have to walk around campus or make the mile-long trek to the grocer on foot. She darted a furtive glance around to make sure no one was watching, then grabbed the bike and quickly backed it away from the Dumpster and walked it to the bike rack just under her balcony, unable to stop smiling. There were several other bikes there. She parked hers in the one remaining spot and gave in to the urge to wiggle her hips in another little hip-wiggling dance. Naani was right. When a door closed, a window always opened. You just had to have the good sense to stick your head out of it.

Samir hated slowing the Corvette down. It was a damn shame. But once he got off the highway he ran into red light after red light until the insanely sexy growl of the engine started to taunt him. He revved it. An uppity looking blonde swept a sideways glance at him from her giant SUV. Automatically, he counted under his breath. One . . . two . . . three . . . And there it was, the double take. *Not looking so bored anymore, are we, missy?* He burned her with his smolder just as the light turned green, then drove off, leaving her gaping in his wake.

Slowly the buildings got closer together and older and more decrepit, going from the set of a rural saga to a period film. Redbrick bungalows with steeple ceilings and snow white trim lined the gravelly, rundown street. He sped past a concrete sign that said EASTERN MICHIGAN UNIVERSITY EST. 1883 and the GPS started to go crazy. *Turn left, turn right, turn left. Make a U-turn!* Reluctantly, he reined the engine in, listened, and the tinny electronic voice led him to a dingy little parking lot that smelled as if the world had rotted and gone to hell. A garbage truck was digging up a Dumpster. Impeccable timing, Sam!

Samir screeched to a halt as far from the Dumpster as humanly possible, pulled himself out of the convertible without bothering to open the door, and stared up at peeling trim on the deserted redbrick building. It was lights, camera, action time.

Mili was in the middle of peeling the wrapper off her last remaining chocolate bar when she heard the knock. She took a quick bite and put the rest of it back in the empty fridge. Her stomach growled in protest. She hadn't eaten anything all day. There were some noodles from Panda Kong in the fridge but she needed those for dinner. Who could be knocking on her door? No one, and she meant no one, had ever knocked on that door in the four months that she had lived here. Except that one time those Jesus Christ people had stopped by and tried to give her a Bible. Another forceful knock. Too forceful. The Bible people had been too polite to knock this hard. Something about that knock made her defenses bristle.

It couldn't possibly be Ridhi's brother, could it? Ridhi had said they'd send him first.

Another knock.

Oh Lord. Oh Ganesha. Oh Krishna. What now? Ridhi was gone only about half an hour. If Mili let anything slip they would find Ridhi and Ravi before they got away. A complete tragedy-style ending to their love story. Mili could never let that happen. Never. Never.

She tiptoed to the door.

"Hello? Anybody there?" A deep, authoritative man's voice shouted from the other side. A deep, authoritative *Indian* man's voice. She looked through the fuzzy peephole. All she saw was a blurred outline of a large figure. *Oh. Lord.* She tiptoed backward and tripped over the shoes she'd left in the middle of the floor, and landed on her bum with a thud, knocking over the lone chair that stood in the middle of the room. Oh no, she had probably broken the one piece of living room furniture she owned.

"Hello?" the voice called again, sounding a little confused. He'd heard her. *Oh Lord.* She hurried to the balcony. No way was she going to be the reason for Ridhi taking on her monosyllabic-slash-near-suicidal avatar again. She leaned over the white spindle railing and saw her new bike on the bike rack just below her. It wasn't much of a jump. Just about seven feet to the grassy mound below. She jumped.

She landed on her feet and then toppled headlong into her bike, which in turn crashed into the three other bikes next to it. Metal tore through her shirt and jabbed her shoulder. The crash made her ears ring. "Shh," she hissed at the bike she was lying on and tried to straighten up.

Samir heard a loud crash. He ran to the open stairwell and leaned over the railing. Some sort of crazy creature with the wildest mass of jet-black curls was dusting herself off and trying to grab a fluorescent yellow bike from a jumbled heap. Was she stealing it? In her rush to pry it free she stumbled backward and her eyes met his. Something in the way she looked at him set alarm bells gonging in his head. His eyes swept from her panicked stance to the low-hanging balcony. Had she jumped? *Damn it.*

"Hey! Wait a minute. Are you Malvika?" he yelled at her.

Her eyes widened to huge saucers, as if he'd accused her of something truly heinous. Was she crazy? She had to be because before he knew what to do next she yanked the bike free, hopped on it, and took off as if he were some sort of gangster chasing her with a gun.

He ran down the stairs, taking almost the entire flight in one leap, and saw her desperately peddling away from him. The rickety piece of shit she was riding wobbled and teetered, looking even more unstable than she did. She turned around and gave him another terrified glance. What was wrong with the woman? Just as she was about to turn away again the bike's handle jerked at the most awkward angle as if it had a mind of its own and she went hurtling into a tree at the end of the street.

"Holy shit!" He ran to her.

By the time he got to her she was lying on her back, her butt pushed up against the tree trunk, her legs flipped over her head like some sort of contortionist yoga guru and the bike intertwined with her folded body. Through the tangle of hair, limbs, and fluorescent metal he heard a sob and a squeak.

"Hello? Are you all right?" Leaning over, he lifted a long spiral lock off her face. It bounced against his palm, soft as silk.

One huge, almond-shaped eye focused on him.

"Teh thik to ho?" he repeated in Hindi. He had no idea why he'd spoken it or why he had used that rural dialect he now used only with his mother, but it just slipped out.

The tangled-up, upside-down mess of a girl, looking at him from behind her legs, literally brightened. There was just no other way to describe it. Her one exposed eye lit up like a firework in a midnight sky. He pushed more hair off her face, almost desperate to see the rest of that smile.

"You can speak Hindi," she said, her surprisingly husky voice so filled with delight that sensation sparkled across his skin.

For one moment the almost physical force of her smile and the uninhibited joy in her voice stole his ability to speak.

She squinted those impossibly bright eyes at him. "Sorry, is that the only line you know?"

"What? No, of course not. I know lots of lines." Wow, that must be the stupidest thing he'd ever said in his life.

She smiled again.

He gave his head a shake and forced his attention on her mangled situation instead of that smile. As carefully as he could he pulled the bike off her. "Can you move?"

She bit down on her lip and tried to push herself up. But instead of her body moving, her face contorted with pain and tears pooled in her eyes.

He dropped down to his knees next to her. "I'm sorry. Here, let me help you." He ignored the absurd shiver of anticipation that kicked in his gut as he reached for her.

No man had ever touched Mili like that. Ridhi's ridiculously handsome brother wrapped his arms around her and tried to ease her into a sitting position. Pain shot through her back, her legs, through parts of her body she wasn't even aware she possessed, and all she could think about was the warm bulges of his arms pressing into her skin. So this was what a man's touch felt like.

Yuck. She was an awful pervert. *You're a married woman,* she reminded herself.

But then he gave her another tug and she forgot her own name. Pain buzzed like a million bees in her head. She tried to be brave but she couldn't stifle the yelp that escaped her.

"Shh. It's okay. Let me look at that." He propped her up against his chest and reached out to inspect her ankle. His face faded and blurred and then came back into focus. His skin was almost European light and his hair was the darkest burnt gold. If he hadn't spoken Hindi the way he had, she might have mistaken him for a local.

He touched her ankle and she was sure something exploded inside it. She sucked in a breath and her head lolled back onto his chest. A very bad English word she had heard only in films rumbled in his chest beneath her head, which suddenly weighed a ton. Her stomach lurched. She heard a pathetic whimper. It had to be her. He didn't look like the whimpering type.

"Shh, sweetheart. Try to breathe. There, in, then out." His breath collected in her ear. His voice had an almost magically soothing vibration to it. He slipped a cell phone out of his pocket. "Is there anyone I can call? We need to get you to a hospital."

At least that's what Mili thought he said, because her ears were making funny ringing sounds. She leaned back into his wall-like chest and tried to focus on his face, which started spinning along with the fading and the blurring. "Snow Health Center is around the corner. I can walk."

"Right," he said. "Or why don't you ride your bike?"

She was about to smile, but he made an angry growling sound and scooped her up in his arms. How could a flesh-and-blood body be so hard? Like tightly packed sand, but with life. The buzzing in her ears was a din now and she had to fight to keep her eyes open. He jogged across the parking lot to a very shiny action-film-style car.

"I'm going to put you in the backseat, okay?"

She nodded. As long as he kept talking to her in that soothing voice of his, she didn't care what else he did. "Your car is yellow," she said. "Just like my bike."

He grinned and laid her down on the backseat of the roofless car so slowly, so very gently, she felt like she was made of spun sugar. Her ankle hit the seat and she felt like a sledgehammer on an anvil. She dug her fingers into his arm to keep from screaming. He didn't pull away. He just kept talking in that magical voice until finally he faded out. The last thing Mili remembered was asking him to put her bike in the rack. No, the last thing she remembered was his smile when she asked him to do it.

7

The first thing the girl did when they entered the clinic was throw up. She had passed out in the car but when Samir lifted her slight body and carried her into the building she started mumbling incoherent words into his neck. And when he put her on the gurney like they asked him to, she leaned over and threw up—on his shoes. His custom-crafted Mephistos. Super.

It was all downhill from there. The receptionist kept asking him all these questions and for some reason he felt compelled to make up shit on the fly. And since he did such a bang-up job sounding like he knew what he was talking about, thanks to DJ's research on the girl, they gave him a clipboard crammed with forms to fill out while they rolled her away to get some X-rays.

"Sir, you put her name down as Ma-la-vai-kaa Sanj-h-va—" The perky redhead behind the counter was going to hurt herself saying the name.

"Maul-veeka Sungh-vee." He enunciated it slowly and tried to put her out of her misery.

She fluttered her clumpy lashes at him for his effort. "Yes. Um. There's no one by that name in our database." She looked at him like she expected him to help.

He shrugged.

"There's a Malvika Rathod—a Malvika Virat Rathod."

Exactly what he needed to hear. His anger came back in a choking surge. His brother's comatose body, Rima's hands clasped in prayer, Baiji's silent desperation—the nightmare flashed in his mind. *Keep your mind on why you're here, asshole. Get her to sign on that line and get the hell out of here.*

"Yes, that's her," he said.

"You put your name down as Samir Rathod. Are you related?"

"No. No, we're not related. I was confused when I filled the form out. I thought you were asking for her last name, not mine. Let me change that." Samir gave the clumpy-lashed girl his patented smolder and watched as she, like the rest of her sex, melted in a puddle at his feet. She pushed the clipboard back toward him, batting away with those eyelash clumps.

Samir scratched out the name Rathod and put down Veluri. His agent's name would have to do.

"You can see her now," a nurse said, coming up behind him as he handed the clipboard back.

She led him to a large ward separated into sections by curtains with the most hideously girly pink flowers. What was this, the Victorian tea-party ward?

"She needs to stay the night. She doesn't have an emergency contact listed and she said there's no one we can call." The nurse's tired eyes searched his face, as if she too expected him to help.

"No one?"

The nurse nodded.

Shit.

"I'll stay." What else was he supposed to say? He could hardly leave her here to crawl back to her apartment on her hands and knees. And it wasn't like he had anywhere else to be.

Mili had no idea what she was going to do. There was a huge window behind her, but it was sealed shut. Not that she could move if she tried. The nurse had put her ankle *and* her wrist in splints but it still hurt like a *Deghi* red chili in her eye. How had she been so stupid? Her stupidity was going to cost Ridhi her happily ever after. At least she had bought time. This entire mess had to have taken at least an hour. By now Ridhi and Ravi were definitely

far enough from Ypsilanti to have a chance. The thought brightened her. Plus, she had no idea where they were, so she couldn't
give them away. Also, maybe after having her throw up on his
shoes, Ridhi's brother-slash-cousin had left and decided to chase
Ridhi down on his own.

He walked in. He lifted the floral curtain with one bulging arm
and filled up the tiny space it enclosed. Mili blinked. She didn't
think she had ever seen anyone who looked quite like that before.
At least not in real life. Not only was he as perfectly chiseled as a
statue, he was also impeccably put together like one of those models in ads who tried to look oh so casual about wearing perfectly fitted, shiny new clothes around the house. But who were they trying
to fool? Except this one was barefoot.

She swallowed guiltily and he followed her gaze to his feet.
"They couldn't find hospital slippers in my size."

Her eyes nearly popped out of her head. "Good Lord, what size
feet do you have?"

"Fourteen." One side of his lips quirked up as he watched her
reaction.

For once she couldn't find a thing to say. Her own feet were a
size four and a half.

"How are you feeling?" His golden eyes moved from the cast on
her leg to the cast on her arm.

"It's not too bad." Or at least it wouldn't be once the medicine
they were pumping through the IV started to work. "I'm sorry
about the shoes. I didn't mean to do that. But I swear I don't know
anything." Oh no, why had she said that? It must be the stupid
medicines.

He blinked and raised his eyebrows. He looked so genuinely
surprised she wanted to slap his face. The one thing she couldn't
stand was people playing games.

"Seriously, no point pretending, I know why you're here and
you're wasting your time. I'll never tell you anything."

He opened his mouth to say something but it seemed she had
completely stumped him and he shut it again.

"What kind of brother are you anyway? How can you stand in

the way of love? Separating two people who are meant to be together is a sin of the worst kind. Don't you see that?"

Anger darkened the translucent brown of his eyes. He glared at her as though she was the one who had done something wrong, not him. "How can you love someone you've never met?"

"What do you mean never met? Did you think a little separation would kill the love? I know you're playing the heartless film-villain type right now. But don't you understand how it feels to be in love?"

Samir just stood there opening and closing his mouth. For the umpteenth time in the short while he'd known her, he wondered if the girl was completely crazy. And she wouldn't stop talking long enough for him to get his thoughts in order.

"You seem like such a nice person. See how you helped me. No one who can be so gentle, so—" Suddenly her pitch-black eyes lost focus and her lids drooped as if they had turned too heavy. She seemed to drift off.

"Did they give you something for the pain?" he asked. She looked like she'd taken a hit of something potent. "Do you want me to get the doctor?"

Her eyes fluttered open, then shut, then open, then shut. Incoherent sounds came from her mouth. Her lids kept fluttering as if she were fighting to stay awake, until finally her lashes fanned out against her cheeks.

He'd never seen lashes like that. They made him want to touch them just to make sure they were real. He'd never seen eyes like that. Her irises were the size of small coins, the color of onyx mined from the remotest deserts of Rajasthan, and they harbored an innocence from some long-bygone era. Except it was all just pretense. He imagined those fake-innocent eyes skimming the legal notice she had sent his brother and they turned beady in his head.

In the event of Virat Rathod's death his entire pension fund, insurance monies and his share of all ancestral property belong to Malvika Rathod. The words seared like brands on his brain.

In the event of Virat Rathod's death.

Her eyes fluttered open again, pain and narcotics playing up the wide-eyed innocence just the way diffused lighting did in still shots. Samir reminded himself who she was. The woman who'd cared only about getting her hands on the *haveli* when they didn't know if Bhai was going to live or die.

"Sleep now. We can talk later."

"See, so nice." Those were her last words before her breathing evened into sleep.

Samir woke up to find his face pressed into a paper-covered mattress. Damn jet lag. He straightened up and noticed her fingers clutching his, her touch cool and soft. She had the smallest, most delicate hands he'd ever seen. Her entire hand from fingertips to wrist spanned a little more than his palm. The way her eyes had widened when he'd told her his shoe size flashed in his mind and he smiled. When he pulled his fingers from hers she stirred, but when he patted her forehead she calmed back into sleep.

All night she had tossed and turned and moaned in pain. And a tiny piece of him had been glad she wasn't alone. No one should be alone in this state. Finally it had been easier to pull his chair close to her bed and pat her head when she winced. It seemed to be the only way to calm her down.

He looked at his Breitling. It was almost midnight. They had both been asleep for hours. He stood up and stretched and separated the blinds to look out the window. The sky was an endless black. He was wide awake. And he had absolutely nowhere to be. He was supposed to have checked into the hotel yesterday, but with Malvika's accident, all his plans had turned upside down, quite literally.

He glanced around the room. His washed and ruined Mephistos were drying in a corner. Fluorescent red numbers flashed on some sort of monitor on one wall. Plastic tubes and medical contraptions covered every surface. Amidst the clutter, on a rollaway cart, lay a yellow notepad and a pen. Samir walked up to it and picked them up. Before he knew what was happening, he found himself sitting down by her side, and writing.

* * *

When Mili came to, for the first few moments she had no idea where she was. Then she tried to move and the pain that ripped from her ankle to her wrist almost split her in half and dragged everything back. She must've moaned or screamed or something because the man sitting by her bedside frowned and leaned closer. She forced the painful fog in her brain to clear.

Oh no. It was Ridhi's Greek god, male-model brother-slash-cousin-slash-whatever relative he was. They must have really drugged her good because despite his hair standing up on one side and bedsheet wrinkles on his cheek he still looked as perfectly put together as he had before she fell asleep.

He studied her with honey brown eyes that belonged in those ultra-fancy magazines Ridhi loved to read. " 'Morning."

Oh God, his voice sounded exactly the way he looked. Golden, impeccable, as if the creator had paid special attention while crafting it. She frowned. As a rule Mili disliked pretty people. They reminded her of that girl Kamini in her village who always got what she wanted just because she looked like some sort of Bollywood star with marble white skin. *Ugh.*

He leaned closer and patted her forehead with far too much familiarity. Good Lord, he even smelled the way he looked, like that perfume they folded into Ridhi's magazines. Mili narrowed her eyes and gave him her fiercest look. How dare he get so overly familiar anyway? And act as if he were doing her some sort of favor. He was the reason she was here in the first place. He was the reason her new bike was broken. Her beautiful bike. She suppressed a sob.

"What's wrong?" he asked as if he'd known her for years. And why was he grinning like that?

"I'm sorry, do I know you?" she snapped.

That threw him. Good. "I believe I haven't introduced myself. I'm Samir Ra—Veluri."

"Raveluri? What kind of name is that?"

"Not Raveluri. Veluri."

"Then why did you say Raveluri?"

He closed his eyes, swallowed, and then opened them again. "Can we start over?"

"Sure, but first please take your hand off my head."

Greek God looked utterly offended, as if no one had ever had the gall to ask him to stop touching them. "Sorry, it seemed to calm you down when you were in pain, so I thought—"

"You stayed here with me all night?" The heat of her temper fizzled like water on a hot *tavaa* pan. Then flared again.

Through all her mind's acrobatics, he remained as calm as the Buddha himself. Which made her temper flare some more.

"You told the nurse there was no one she could call," he said with utmost patience, "so I thought—"

"You chased my only friend away. Now you want me to be thankful?" Everything that had happened after he knocked on her door flashed in her mind and she wanted to slap his perfect face.

"Who said anything about being thankful?" His hands tightened on the yellow writing pad he was clutching and the muscle in his jaw twitched the tiniest bit, but other than that he kept his smile as serene as ever.

"You had that look, like you expected gratitude." Just for walking the earth, just like that stupid cow Kamini.

"Can I ask you a question?"

She shrugged.

"Are you crazy?"

See, she was right. All pretty people were horribly rude. That's when it struck her. It was morning. Ridhi had to have left Michigan.

"Why are you smiling?" he asked.

"Because I just realized that you won't find Ridhi now. She got away."

He looked completely dumbfounded. "Who's Ridhi?"

"Who's Ridhi?"

After they'd both repeated the phrase "Who's Ridhi?" over and over again an absurd number of times, Samir had to find a way to exit the loop. This girl was certifiable, no doubt about it. If he had to hunt down a girl halfway across the world, why couldn't it at least be someone who bordered on sane? Someone nice and nor-mal. Yeah, right, when was the last time he had met a nice and nor-mal girl? At least she was easy on the eyes. And sitting next to her, after a year-long dry spell, he hadn't been able to stop writing.

Holy. Fuck. Talk about complicating the plot.

"Okay, listen, if I knew who this Ridhi was, would I have asked who she was?" He tried logic. Although from what he'd seen thus far logic didn't stand much of a chance with this one.

"What kind of man doesn't know his own sister-slash-cousin-slash-whatever you are?"

Did she just say "sister-slash-cousin"? Who used the word *slash* in a sentence? "So you think this Ridhi person is my sister-slash-cousin?" Not that he knew what that even meant. Could she speak Sane, please? He continued to smile at her with that utterly ab-sorbed look that made chicks go all gooey in the head.

Her onyx eyes narrowed, then widened in shock. "You're not Ridhi's brother?"

Now they were getting somewhere. He nodded. "Not her brother-slash-cousin-slash-any other relation."

Her flawless chocolate skin went the oddest shade of maroon. He didn't know how she did it but her super-tiny form shrank into itself. "Oh. Then why were you chasing me?"

Great question. And the perfect cue.

He reached for his messenger bag with the papers that had brought him here, playing the lines he had to say in his head: Virat's plane. The annulment.

The yellow notepad slipped from his hand and fluttered to the gray linoleum floor. He squatted next to it. It was more than half-filled with closely scrawled words. He picked it up and stroked the ink-filled lines with his thumb. The words had burst from him all night like water from a hose. And man, had it felt good.

"What's that?" Her onyx eyes skimmed the pad and met his as she tried to sit up. Pain exploded in her eyes and she folded over on her side.

He sprang up and leaned over her curled-up body. "Shh, it's okay."

Hair spilled over her face. He pushed it aside to reveal wet cheeks and a face scrunched up in pain. "Try to breathe. I'll call the nurse."

By the time the nurse had pumped her full of pain meds again, Samir found himself firmly in the middle of a classic good news–bad news scenario. The bad news was that he was stuck playing nurse-maid for the next few weeks. For one, there was no one else to do it. For another, he just couldn't bring himself to serve her annulment papers while she lay there doped out of her mind. The good news was that when he went home in a few weeks not only was he going to have his brother's annulment, he was also going to have a completed script.

"Thanks." It was the first thing she said when she opened her eyes.

Samir looked up from the yellow pad—it was almost out of pages—and found a shyness on her face that hadn't been there before.

"How are you feeling?" he asked.

"I'm afraid to move," she said, barely moving her lips, but her eyes smiled. "You didn't answer my question earlier. Why were you chasing me?"

"I wasn't. I just moved into your building. My uncle is from your village, Hari Bishnoi. He gave me your address. I was just trying to stop by and say hello when you took off. I just followed you." His writing mojo was definitely back. In all its genius.

"Well, that was stupid."

So much for genius.

Seriously, she jumped off a balcony and rode a bike into a tree and *he* was stupid? But instead of telling her that he gave her one of those made-just-for-chicks smiles he had honed to an art form during his modeling years.

She frowned. "So, you're just my new neighbor?"

"Yup." Or at least he would be as soon as he got DJ to find him an empty flat in that shit-smelling building of hers.

"And you sat here all night watching over me when you don't even know me?" Her eyes filled with tears.

What the fuck?

She squeezed her eyes shut, then opened them again and met his eyes with such directness he felt it all the way in his gut. "I think it's time we started over." She touched her heart with her unhurt hand, a one-armed namaste. "Hello, Samir. My friends call me Mili and I'm honored to make your acquaintance."

8

The sound of Samir moving about in her kitchen woke Mili. She had been home for almost a week and Samir had planted himself by her side so firmly she was reminded of her neighbor's goat in Balpur. The goat had shadowed Mili so insistently Naani had named him "Viratji" in a bid to move the fates along. Except that unlike the goat or his namesake, Samir had actually saved Mili's life. If not for him, surely she would have died either of starvation or an exploded bladder.

She sat up on the mattress on the floor. Samir had moved Ridhi's mattress to the living room for her. For the hundredth time since she had met him, she sent up an apology for comparing him to Kamini. The only thing Kamini had ever bothered to save was her marble-white complexion from the Rajasthan sun. Mili had always marveled at her impressive collection of umbrellas and her diligent use of them. The only thing Samir was proving to have in common with Kamini was said white complexion but with none of the proud awareness of possessing it. He might strut around in that way of film heroes with overly bulky arms—as if he were lugging buckets of water in both hands—but he had carried Mili up and down the stairs to her doctor's appointments, fed her, and made sure she took all of her thousand medicines before the pain killed her.

As usual, he had propped up the crutches against the wall so they were within easy reach. Frustration tugged at her mouth and she frowned at the blasted things. What was the point of those crutches anyway? She'd been brilliant enough to hurt her wrist and her ankle at the same time, so she had no real way of gripping the stupid things to push herself anywhere. Add to that the fact that she was the most uncoordinated fool in all of Balpur and those crutches were going to stay propped against that wall until one of her broken parts healed.

"Why are you glowering at the crutches again?" Samir grinned his toothpaste-model grin and it was almost as beautiful as the sandwiches in his hands. "Do you need to go?" He indicated the bathroom door with a flick of his head and Mili wanted to die.

His stupid grin widened. It was a good thing her medication turned her into a drooling, groggy loon who dropped off into la-la land without warning. If it weren't for being drugged and half-conscious she didn't know how she could have handled letting a complete stranger help her to the bathroom and then wait outside while she struggled to do her business. And he usually did it without any hint of that amused grin he was flashing at her now.

He nudged her with the plate and she realized she was staring at her hands to avoid meeting his gaze. She gaped at the twin pieces of art he had piled on the two plates Ridhi had left behind. Her mouth watered like a starving street urchin's. Every kind of vegetable was stacked up in layers of color between two brown pieces of bread.

At first she'd been embarrassed to let him into her kitchen, given that the sum total of her food supply included one half-eaten Hershey bar, a carton of milk, and stale, greasy noodles. But he had gone out and picked up bags full of groceries, and all her medicines, and a heating pad. He'd insisted the groceries were really for him, because he needed to eat too and apparently there were no utensils in his apartment.

He had let her use his cell phone to call the Institute, Panda Kong, and her professors to let them know that she needed to stay off her ankle for two weeks. Professor Bernstein at the Institute had told her to take four weeks if she needed to. "I'll remember to exploit you once you get back on your feet," he'd said with so much kindness she had spilled tears onto Samir's super-fancy phone.

Egghead at Panda Kong had been far less gracious. "Don't know if can keep job whole two weeks," he'd said. But at least he hadn't fired her like she'd expected him to. She'd been prepared to beg if needed, but a promise to return to work as soon as she could had been enough. How on earth was she going to send money to Naani this month with two weeks of dishwashing wages gone? And there was still the little issue of the rent. Not to mention paying Samir back for her medicines and the groceries.

Samir handed her a plate. "See, you can already sit up by yourself. In a few days you'll be using the crutches with ease."

Only someone who had no idea how clumsy she was would say such a thing.

"This is beautiful," she said reverently, and picked up the top slice to study the riot of color inside.

"Don't worry, Mili, there's no meat in it." He raised an amused eyebrow at her as she poked the innards of the sandwich.

"Sorry, I have to check. It's just a habit. I had a horrible incident at the union last month." She thought about how awful *that* stuff had tasted and wiggled her shoulders to ward off the memory. "I told the person 'no meat' and he tells me: 'It's not meat, it's fish.' Yuck!" The memory almost made her lose her appetite. But who was she fooling? With a sandwich like this in her hands there was no real danger of that happening.

Samir laughed that low, understated laugh that didn't belong on a pretty boy at all and took a bite of his own sandwich.

"Are you a vegetarian or a nonvegetarian?" she asked him, carefully laying the slice back in place.

"I do eat meat, but if you mention that in front of my mother, I'll deny it. And then I'll have to kill you for breaking her heart."

Mili bit into the sandwich and almost passed out again. "What on earth did you put in this?" she said, chomping with all thirty-two teeth and thanking all the gods for every one of the ten thousand taste buds in her mouth. "This is delicious!"

He watched her eat, his smile disappearing behind a guarded expression, and pulled two envelopes out of his pocket. "Your mail." He crossed his legs and settled into the mattress next to her.

Both envelopes had the university logo on them. Mili's heart sank.

She took another bite before forcing herself to put the sandwich down and picked up the one from Snow Health Center first. Despite the flavors dancing on her tongue, nervousness trembled in the pit of her stomach. So much for being able to stretch the fifty dollars in her pocket.

She had tried to ask the nurse how much all those splints and medicines were going to cost but all she'd said was, "We'll send you the bill in the mail." At least Mili had assumed she was talking to her, because the nurse's eyes had been glued on Samir. Just like the doctor's eyes and the receptionist's eyes. Just about every woman who'd walked into her room had had eyes only for him. He seemed perfectly comfortable with the attention. He gave every one of the drooling females the glad eye, and soaked up all the adulation without the least bit of an apology. How must it be? To be worshiped because of the way you looked. She glowered at him. Then felt like a terrible person because he had just fed her the best food she'd eaten in days, in months.

He chomped at his sandwich and tipped his chin at the bill, coaxing her to open it.

Mili squared her shoulders and ripped the envelope open. Her mouth went dry. The amount under the "To be Paid by Patient" column made it hard to breathe. He handed her a glass of water and she repaid him by almost choking to death on it.

He moved closer and rubbed her back. "What's the matter, Mili?" Gentle up and down strokes.

She sidled away and glared at him. "You're trying to choke me to death, that's what's the matter." Dear Lord, she was an awful, terrible person.

Instead of rising to her bait, he took the paper out of her hand. "Is that your hospital bill?"

She thought about snatching it back but what was the point? She was letting a complete stranger practically live in her home and he had taken care of her more than any human being other than Naani ever had. There really was no point in standing on ceremony.

But then he looked at the figure on the paper and smiled. He smiled!

"It's just a hundred and twenty dollars," he said.

Samir kicked himself. Of all the dumb-assed things to say. Mili's face deflated right before his eyes, as if he had taken a pin to that ridiculously upbeat spirit of hers.

"I'm sorry. I didn't mean for it to sound like that. It's just that with everything one hears about hospital bills in America I was expecting to see a larger amount."

Her eyes widened in horror. But just for one second.

What was wrong with this girl? She had enough money to pay for a ticket to America and an education here and a hundred-and-twenty-dollar bill was giving her palpitations? He looked around the apartment. Shit, he was an idiot. Baiji was right, his brain totally shut everything out when he was working. There was no furniture, no food in her apartment. A sick sort of feeling twisted in his heart.

She took the bill back and looked at it again. Muscle by muscle she pulled herself together. God, if he could get his actors to show each and every emotion like this he'd be the best fucking director in the world.

"You're right, it's only one hundred and twenty. I must've misunderstood the number of zeroes. You must think I'm so stupid." She topped off the act with a perfect self-deprecating grin and a smack on the forehead with her bandaged hand. Pathos, anyone?

And he thought he was the grand master of backtracking. She was totally kicking his ass in that department. "Not at all, an extra zero would scare me shitless too," he said, and took a bite.

Her shoulders slumped. She looked absurdly relieved, her filter-less, expressive face at work again. Then suddenly she remembered the avocado-tomato-carrot-and-green-pepper sandwich on her lap and the tension evaporated for real. She dived into the sandwich. There really was no other word for it. Each bite seemed to make pleasure wash through her being. Her lips, her throat, her eyes, all of her got involved in the experience. Got lost in it.

He stood and backed out of the living room. He put the dish in the miniscule sink and glanced around the kitchen. Truly, how had he missed this? The entire apartment was marginally larger than his closet back home. Maybe all of four hundred square feet. The living room was the size of a large passageway with a niche to one side that served as a dining space and led into a kitchen that housed one noisy fridge, a cruddy cooking range, and two feet of counter space. At the other end of the passage-slash-living room, as Mili would call it, was a bedroom that could hold two mattresses, a crappy old dresser and desk, and enough space to tiptoe between those. The bathroom was the size of Samir's linen cabinet, a stand-up shower that he would never fit in, a pot that had his knees knocking against a wall when he sat on it and a sink he could wash his hands in while sitting on the pot.

Okay, so the girl wasn't exactly loaded and he should have seen it sooner. And if he hadn't been writing like a crazed genius he might even have. He rinsed off the plate, letting steam rise from the sink, and forced himself not to think about the bliss on her face when she ate. He had to be careful, real careful with this one. For all her guileless innocence, for all her wretched condition, he had to remember that nothing justified sending a legal notice to a man lying in the hospital fighting for his life. Especially when that man was Bhai.

"DJ, this apartment is really and truly a piece of shit. Warm and fresh-from-the-ass shit. It smells like shit, it feels like shit, all the stuff in it is actually the color of diarrhea." Samir looked around "his" apartment. Just the thought of calling it that made him cringe.

But for the next month it was his. He had made DJ rent the shithole because it was two doors down from Mili's. Apparently it had been easy. Apparently more than half the building was empty. Big surprise.

"There's a Hyatt two miles from you. I've had a suite booked there for the past week. Either get your ass over there or stop whining like a little baby."

"I can't go to the Hyatt, genius. Mili can't leave the house. Someone needs to keep an eye on her. She doesn't even have a cell phone. It's like she's living on Gilligan's Island, only with no friends."

"She has at least one friend, it would seem." Swami DJ laced his voice generously with meaning.

"Yeah, I'm doing this for friendship, asshole. Not because my brother is lying in bed with both legs in casts and a pregnant wife who may not be his wife at all. You think I like playing nurse-maid?"

DJ answered that with some loaded silence. Whatever.

"Listen, there's really no one else here to help her. Her room-mate eloped the day I arrived."

"The girl seems to have quite a penchant for drama."

"No shit."

"You still writing? You think you'll get it in by the deadline?"

"I might just." Truth was he was damn sure nothing was going to stop him from meeting his deadline. And it was a fucking mira-cle. They'd been back from the hospital just six days and Samir had already written more than he had in years.

Except he hadn't written one single word of it in this shit-colored haven. All his writing had happened around her. He'd typed the words from the yellow pad into his laptop in her apartment the day they got back and then written like a madman all night and all morning while she slept. And then written some more for the past few days while she slept some more.

His laptop sat open on the battered carpet that naturally was the color of bacterial diarrhea. He'd tried to write before he called DJ but he'd been able to do nothing more than stare at the damn screen.

"I'll let you know how things go. Can you at least find out if there's an option in this building with less excretory accents?" After all, Mili's apartment was smaller but not as hideous.

"Of course I will, boss. It's what I do."

Samir thought about giving writing in his own apartment an-other shot but he knew he would be wasting his time. He'd been pushing away the realization but he couldn't anymore. By some damn trick of fate it had turned out that after that night in the hos-pital, being around Mili helped him write.

Fuck.

Someone up there was on her side. Until the script was done, he had no choice but to help her so he could keep writing. By the time the script was done she'd be so in his debt she'd sign the papers without so much as a whimper. Maybe someone up there was on his side too. Who was he to argue with a win-win situation like this?

He grabbed the laptop and headed back to Mili's apartment.

Mili stumbled out of the bathroom on her crutches. This was the first time she'd been able to get to the bathroom by herself, thank heavens. But it had been more a combination of luck and momentum than any real skill. Samir had spent an entire hour that morning trying to help her figure the blasted things out, but with both a wrist and an ankle gone and her natural tendency to trip over thin air, it was a lost cause. He, on the other hand, seemed to possess enough strength in one powerful leg to support his own substantial bulk, balance her and her crutches on his head, and pull off a one-legged bhangra dance with his eyes closed. Maybe it had something to do with having feet the size of boats.

She tried to hop to her bedroom, teetering between the cursed aluminum prongs that somehow became tangled with one another and flew from her hands. One crashed to the ground and the other bounced off her bedroom door, flew back at her, and thwacked her on the head.

"Stupid donkey-faced piece of junk." She clamped it grudgingly under her armpit and quite literally willed herself into the bedroom where she realized that the armpit in which she had shoved the poor crutch smelled pretty sour. She pulled her maroon T-shirt off without falling to the floor, which was nothing short of a miracle, and pulled a blue T-shirt from the drawer.

She had found the T-shirts at a street vendor outside Borivali station in Mumbai the day she got her visa. It had taken a marathon bargaining session but she'd badgered the shopkeeper into letting her have all six colors of the T-shirt for the price of three and then she'd seen the lace underwear and gathered the guts to make him throw it in for free. She had no idea what had got into her, but something about the black lace had made her feel hopeful and ready for her husband and she'd had to have it. Just her luck that the street vendor had turned out to be from her neighboring village and she had bought two pairs of jeans for full price to keep from dying of embarrassment.

Before that all she had ever worn were traditional Indian *salwar* suits, the long tunic blouses worn over loose flowing pants or tights. After buying the T-shirts she'd left all her *salwar* suits behind in a bid to make a true fresh start here in America. She loved the freedom her shirts and jeans gave her. No *duppata* scarves, no ironing and starching. And when she had the use of all her limbs they were really easy to get on and off.

Now, however, nothing was easy. Between balancing on the crutches and getting her arms into the armholes, the stupid shirt twisted around her head. She tried to yank it down, but her bad wrist snagged in the fabric and blinding pain shot through her. Even though, thanks to the shirt wrapped around her head, she was already as blind as an ostrich with its head in the sand.

The door clicked open. Mili froze in place. "I'm not decent," she shouted as the door creaked open. Why-oh-why had she ever given Samir a key?

There was complete silence. She scrambled under the stretchy fabric, ignoring another jolt of pain, and tried to twist around. "Samir? Hello?"

No answer.

Oh no. It wasn't Samir.

"Samir?" she shouted and yanked at the T-shirt. But the crutches and cast knotted her up even tighter. "Who is it?" She twisted around, struggling to stay upright. Her heart slammed in her chest. *Oh God, please.* "Who is it?" she tried to shout again, but it came out a sob.

"*Shh.* Mili, it's okay. It's just me." His arms went around her, adjusting the T-shirt so it freed her shoulders and cleared her head.

Tears streamed from her eyes. Breath hiccupped in her lungs.

"I'm sorry, I should've knocked." He tucked a loose curl behind her ear and had the gall to give her a calming, steadying glance as if he hadn't just scared the life out of her. He wiped her cheek with one finger. She'd never seen his eyes so dark, so alive. His hands moved lower and he pulled the zipper of her jeans in place.

Anger exploded in her chest. She shoved him away, hard. But instead of budging him, she flung herself back. He caught her but her crutches crashed to the ground, leaving her with no support but his huge powerful body that radiated heat like a bonfire. Helpless anger surged through her, heightening the pain and making her tremble. He tightened his grip around her, his stupid, bulging arms so gentle she wanted to claw at them.

"Let me go." She tried to throw off his arms but her hand hurt too much. She tried to scramble back but her foot wouldn't take her weight.

"Mili. Relax. What's wrong with you?" She hated the calm in that voice of his.

"You idiot!" She had never screamed at anyone in her life. "You scared me half to death. I thought someone had broken in. I thought . . ." A stupid sob escaped her.

"I'm sorry," he said again. Color crested his cheeks. His arm was still too familiar around her, too possessive. His eyes were too gentle when they met hers. "I didn't knock because I thought you were sleeping. I had just given you your painkiller. It knocks you out."

How dare he use that against her. "I needed to use the bathroom. Can't I use the bathroom in my own home? Why do you have to be here all the time anyway? Why can't you just leave me alone?"

His arms stiffened around her. The liquid heat in his eyes iced over. "Maybe because you can't even pull your own damn clothes on by yourself. Excuse me for trying to help."

Her heart was slamming again but it was with anger this time. "I didn't ask for your help."

"Of course you didn't—there's such a line of friends outside your door just waiting to help you."

Shame slid like oil over the flames of her anger. "I can pull my own clothes on just fine when I'm not scared out of my mind." His hands burned her skin. She wanted them off. "That doesn't give you an excuse to touch me."

His head snapped back. Anger so intense sparked in his eyes, she sucked in a breath. Very deliberately he removed his arms from around her. "Why the hell would I want an excuse for that?"

Her good leg wobbled, but she locked it in place and willed herself to stay standing. Not that it mattered. Without a backward glance, he stalked out of the room, out of the apartment. The door slammed behind him. The second the door shut Mili realized she couldn't move. He had left her standing in the middle of the room on one leg, with her crutches on the floor, and not one blessed thing she could hold on to.

9

Samir wasn't fuming. He wasn't even remotely disturbed. The world was full of ungrateful people. If ten years in the industry had taught him anything it had taught him that. *An excuse to touch her?* Of all the ungrateful, presumptuous things to say to him. Who the fuck did she think he was?

He slammed his laptop shut. There was no point glaring at the words. He'd formatted the damned thing to death. Tagged all the characters, put in all the settings, titled all the scenes. But not one word of real writing. He put the laptop on the floor next to him and went to the kitchen to get a drink. But of course the shit-colored apartment was empty as an idiot's head. Not a fucking thing in there. His stomach growled. He needed to get something to eat too. Real food, not just the cold sandwiches he'd been eating at Mili's for a week.

He refused to recall the expression on her face when she ate. Refused to think about the warmth of her skin on his fingers, or the feel of her hair, or the way her waist had fit in his hands.

Shit.

He slammed the door of the empty fridge shut.

What was wrong with him? He had never touched a woman who didn't want him. Not to mention she was the last person on earth he should ever want to touch. For more damn reasons than he could count. Not the least of which was that she was an ungrateful, self-righteous prima donna. Who would have thought it?

I didn't ask for your help. She had some gall for someone who couldn't even stand on her own—

Holy shit.

Holy. Fucking. Shit.

He ran out of his apartment and down the hall, fumbled in his pocket and found the keys. He was about to push the door open when he remembered to knock. He did it lightly. There was no answer. Shit. *Shit.* He had left her standing in the middle of the room without her crutches. Something squeezed in his chest. He wanted to ram the door open, but he stilled his hand, and as gently as he could, he pushed it open.

"Mili?" he whispered into the empty living room, then walked to her bedroom.

The sight he saw body-slammed him so hard he reached for the wall to steady himself.

Mili lay in the middle of the floor, curled into a ball on the stained and discolored carpet, her eyes closed, her lashes wet. Perfect shining curls spilled from the band that attempted to restrain all that wildness. Spiral strands trailed across the clumping pile of the carpet, across her shoulders, around her neck, across her cheeks. Why did she have to be the most beautiful girl he'd ever laid eyes on?

Wetness glistened like moonlight on her cheeks. Her pert up turned nose was red and wet. He sank down on his knees next to her. Her fingers were curled around one of her crutches. The other crutch lay a few feet from her. Her sprained arm was pulled to her chest as if she were trying to stop it from hurting.

He removed the crutch from her fingers, brushed her hair from her face. She was passed out cold. It was the Demerol he'd given her earlier, before he'd scared her shitless and then abandoned her on one foot with nothing to lean on.

She took a shivering breath that drew her brows together in a pained grimace and Samir felt something he had never felt before. He felt an actual physical ache in the region of his chest, absurdly close to where his heart was supposed to be.

As gently as he could, he lifted her up. She was so tiny, so warm. Her body fit perfectly in his arms. The memory of her breasts in the thin cotton of her ridiculously sensible bra, and the impossibly deep curve of her waist disappearing into her unzipped jeans, flashed in his mind one more time. Of course she was right. He had wanted to touch her. The sight of her half-undressed body had felled him when he'd let himself into her apartment. She had been terrified and he had lost his ability to speak at the sight of her.

Little Sam was at work again. And as usual that meant nothing but trouble for Samir.

He carried her to the lumpy mattress that served as her bed and laid her down. Her lush, wide lips trembled as she took another sighing breath and he refused to acknowledge the urge to know what those lips tasted like.

She's sleeping, you bastard.

She's in pain.

And you left her lying on the floor to cry herself to sleep.

Samir wiped her cheeks and pulled the rough plaid blanket over her and tucked it under her chin. He threw one glance at his watch. She would be out for another two hours at least. He knew exactly what he had to do.

Mili awoke to the most incredible aroma. Fresh garlic and cilantro being fried with stinging hot green chilies and ground cumin. And the smell of heaven itself—wheat rotis being roasted on an open fire. Her stomach growled so loudly, if she weren't awake, it would definitely have woken her up. She had to be back home in Naani's house. No other place on earth smelled like this. She opened her eyes and found herself in her own room.

The blanket she had used since she was three years old was tucked all the way under her chin and her crutches were propped up against her mattress within easy reach. The sight of her crutches brought back a bitter memory and anger pooled in her stomach. He had left her standing on one foot. With no support and no dignity. After struggling to stand for a few minutes she'd fallen to the ground like an orphaned cripple. She had tried to pull herself up, but her wrist and her ankle had both hurt too much and despite her resolve the tears had flowed until her eyes drooped shut.

She remembered the thunderous look on his face when he had

walked away and grimaced. She had no idea why she had been so angry, why she had said those things. All she knew was that she had needed to push him away. And she certainly had no idea why it hurt so much when he had let her.

That couldn't possibly be him cooking, could it? He could make the most delicious sandwiches, which kind of went with his whole city-boy persona. But this aroma suffusing her apartment, *this* was the very smell of her village. Good Lord, but it smelled good. So incredibly, maddeningly good, she was going to go crazy if she didn't get her hands on it right now.

Maybe Ridhi was back? But Ridhi had burned the chai the first time she used the stove. Ravi then? God knows *someone* had to feed them when they were married and it wasn't going to be Ridhi.

Mili sat up and pulled the crutches toward her. They were light and strong and she was going to figure out how to get off the floor and on them if it was the last thing she did. She used her good hand and managed to push herself off the mattress onto her good foot with one crutch tucked under her arm. But the other crutch was still on the floor and how was she supposed to get it? If the hurt arm and foot were on the same side this would actually be doable. Oh, forget it—she decided to go for it and lunged for the crutch on the floor. But the one under her arm slipped from her grip and flew forward and she followed suit.

Strong arms wrapped around her before she hit the floor. They pulled her up and held her in place until she caught her balance, caught a handful of his sleeve and caught her breath at the feel of hard muscles under her breasts.

Hair spilled around her face, mercifully hiding her flaming cheeks from his sight.

"You okay?" he asked against the curls covering her ear, his voice so tender, goose flesh started at the nape of her neck and dotted tiny bumps down her spine. For a few moments neither one of them moved. Then he pulled away. "I didn't plan that. I swear."

She twisted her head and looked up at him. "I'm sorry. I should never have said that."

He turned her around and held her at arm's distance. He was about to say something when she noticed rough, sticky dough where his hands cupped her elbows.

"Is that dough on your hands?"

"Difficult to make rotis without getting dough on your hands." He lifted one hand up for display.

"You can make rotis? I don't know any man who can make rotis."

"I doubt you know any man like me, sweetheart." His smile was teasing but there was that liquid heat in his eyes again. And it tipped her slightly off balance.

He slipped his hand back under her elbow and steadied her. Warmth rose from his doughy palms and spread down to parts where warmth had never until now ventured. She swallowed. She didn't know how it happened, but suddenly they were standing so close she could hear his heart thudding in his chest. Unless that was her own heart.

This was wrong. Dangerous and wrong in every way. She wasn't free to do this. But the strange heat spreading through her slowed her reflexes. She was about to push away from him when her eyes started to sting, something burned in her throat, and a shrill siren burst through the air.

Samir pulled away first and tried to push her onto the mattress. But she clung to his sleeve, refusing to let go, so he scooped her up in his arms and ran into the living room.

The kitchen was filled with smoke. The smoke alarm was going crazy. "Shit, I left a roti in the pan." He turned off the burner under the roti, or at least it must've been a roti before it had turned to the tissue-thin scrap of charcoal emitting smoke into the room. He put her on the countertop, ran to the living room, and opened the windows.

The smoke started to clear but the alarm wouldn't stop shrieking.

"Get that magazine and fan it." Mili pointed to Ridhi's *Cosmo* magazine lying on the floor. It's what Ridhi had done when she'd burned the chai.

He fanned frantically and finally the din stopped. Mili peeked over his shoulder at the cinder roti. He turned and followed her gaze. "I hope you like your rotis well done," he said.

And they both started to laugh.

Samir had never met a woman who ate like this. Come to think of it, he had in recent years never met a woman who ate, period. Neha treated food like it was evil incarnate. She was in constant conflict with any little morsel she had to force into her mouth.

Mili ate as if she were making love to the food. Fierce, hungry love. Slow, sultry love. Every bite sent her into raptures, the pleasure of the flavors bursting on her tongue palpable in the tiny peaks of bliss flitting across her face. What would it be like when this woman orgasmed?

They were sitting cross-legged on the floor and eating with their hands in traditional Indian fashion. Samir was glad to have the plate in his lap because for all his pleasure at the sight of Mili eating, Little Sam was paying the price.

"This is truly the most amazing potato *sabzi* I've ever eaten and the dal is perfect and the rotis make me feel like I'm sitting in my *naani*'s kitchen in Balpur." She kept a constant string of compliments going as she ate. They bubbled from her as if she couldn't contain herself. Samir, who usually found all forms of flattery oppressive, never wanted her to stop.

"Seriously, I'm starting to doubt your manhood."

Samir choked on his roti. Was that a coquettish look she threw him?

Nope. False alarm, because she ruined the effect by following it up with a furious blush. She took another bite. "I meant, how can a man cook like this? Whoever taught you must be a magician."

"She is. When I was little I had a hard time letting go of my mother's sari. So I spent a lot of time with her and she spent a lot of time in the kitchen, so I learned."

"A mummy's boy." She spooned some dal into her mouth and her eyes went fuzzy with delight.

"Most definitely."

"But if these are the results, every man should be a mummy's boy." Damn it, if she kept saying these things with that artless smile he was going to push her into the mattress and show her other things he was really good at.

"I'm glad you like it." He reached over and wiped a tiny splatter of dal from her chin.

"Is that what you think? That I like it? I don't like it, Samir. I, oh good heavens, I . . . I love it." She popped a piece of seasoned potato into her mouth and said *love* so lustily that the plate in Samir's lap almost flipped over.

Fortunately Mili seemed completely clueless about his painful condition. Because suddenly her eyes got serious and warm. "Why did you do it?" she asked in that husky, breathless voice of hers.

"Well, I used to be sitting around while my mother did all the work, so I figured I might as well help her out. She kept teaching me, so I kept picking it up."

Her impossibly dark eyes softened and got even more serious. "I meant, why did you cook today?"

"I was desperately hungry."

She kept skewering him with those flashlight eyes. For some reason he knew she wasn't going to stop until she had her answer.

"Because I was sorry."

That signature blush danced up her cheeks.

It was his turn to drill her with his eyes. Her turn to look away. "I'm sorry I left you like that, Mili. It was a horrible thing to do."

She lifted her heavy fringe of lashes, and met his eyes again. "Samir, I was a complete stranger and you've done nothing but take care of me from the moment you met me. You have nothing to apologize for."

"So you weren't mad at me for leaving?"

She colored some more and he couldn't help but smile.

"Just a little bit." She pinched the air with her thumb and forefinger.

"See."

"But not because you were horrible. I was mad because . . . because . . ."

"Because you were helpless and dependent and because you expected me not to be such a bastard." She cringed at the word and he felt like an even bigger bastard. "Sorry. Because you expected me to have more decency than that."

She opened her mouth but no words came out. She put her plate on the floor. "Samir, you've been more than decent."

"Mili, there's something you should know about me. The one thing I'm not is a decent guy."

"That's not true." She shook her head and her mad curls danced about her shoulders.

"No, seriously, there's a lot you don't know about me. But that's one thing you should know. And while I'm not a decent guy, even I know that leaving you like that was an awful thing to do. And I truly am sorry."

Her clear-as-morning-sunshine gaze shimmered with moisture. She gave the food he had cooked another worshipful glance. Her words made her lips tremble before she spoke them. "Samir, it's not the fact that you left that's important. What matters is that you came back and made it right."

10

The only movement Mili allowed herself was to crack open one eyelid. Just enough to see that Samir was still slamming away at his laptop as if he were pounding his heart into those words the way he'd done almost nonstop for over a week. She couldn't believe she was lying on a mattress on the floor a few feet from a man she barely knew. A man who looked like *that*. If her *naani* ever found out, there was no avoiding that heart attack she kept threatening. And yet Mili felt, if not entirely comfortable, utterly safe. Especially now that he knocked and diligently announced himself every time he came over.

"How long have you been up?" He only half looked up from his laptop, that one-part-amused, two-parts-arrogant smile diffusing the concentration on his face.

"What are you writing?"

Both amusement and arrogance dissolved behind a wall. "Just something."

"That's a long something you've been writing. I thought you said your workshop didn't start for a few weeks?" He'd told her he was here for some sort of special month-long writing workshop.

He stared at the screen, a frown crinkling his forehead. "It doesn't. But I came in early to finish up my script before it starts."

"Script?" She tried to sit up. "Like a movie script?"

He moved his laptop aside and helped her up. "You don't read film magazines or watch much TV, do you?" The arrogance was back full force.

Much as she loved movies, those film magazines made her sick to her stomach and she had never found the time to go out and buy a TV. "Why? Are you some sort of big, famous star?" she teased.

He gave a sheepish shrug and went back to typing.

Oh God, was he really famous? And she hadn't even recognized him.

"Don't look so embarrassed. I'm not that famous. I am a director. But I write my own stories and I've always wanted to take a screenwriting workshop. So here I am."

"Seriously? You're a director? Like a real director director? What have you directed? Anything I've watched?"

"I don't know. Do you watch films?"

"Do I watch films?" Mili flattened an outraged palm against her chest as if he'd just accused her of stripping for cash in her spare time. "I'll have you know I watched every single movie they showed at the Balpur theater—first day, first show." Her eyes went all nostalgic and Samir found himself hungry for a glance at the memories flashing through her mind.

"I mean *hello!* Doesn't the name Mili sound familiar? I'm even named after a Hindi film. *Mili* was my mother's favorite film."

"Your mother named you after a girl who dies of cancer?"

"She does *not* die!" She looked so appalled he had to force himself not to smile. "The love of her life takes her to America at the end and vows to fight for her recovery. Did you even watch the film?" Were those tears in her eyes?

"You mean the nasty drunk who's horrible to her throughout the film?"

She gasped and narrowed her teary eyes to slits. "He is not nasty! He's hurt and disillusioned. His heart is as sick as her body is. And they heal each other." She waved her hands about, making healing sound as simple as making rotis, a few swipes of the rolling pin and you had nice, perfectly round dough circles.

"Have you watched anything that was made in this decade?"

She pulled a face at him—one that told him exactly how much of an arrogant jerk he was. "I watched whatever our Balpur theater showed. After I moved to Jaipur, I never had much time to go to the theater. Pandey, the theater wallah in Balpur, was an Amitabh Bachan and Shah Rukh Khan fan, so that's mostly what we watched. My favorite is *Sholay*, and I've watched *Chandni* eight times and *Darr* five times."

None of those films were made in this decade, but she looked so excited he didn't correct her. Plus, if she hadn't watched movies in the past few years the chances of her knowing who he was were slim. And that was a stroke of luck he wasn't about to question.

"You don't like these films?" she asked as if she were asking if he had a soul and any taste at all.

"No, they're great films. *Sholay*'s one of my favorites too." God, he'd die for a script like that. "But the other two, well, they aren't exactly the kind of films I make."

Ah, so he made those artsy-fartsy films. Pandey had shown one of those once, about this honest cop who goes around killing all the corrupt politicians. It was all so dark and depressing the public had started shouting in the middle of the show and beaten the projection man so badly he had to be taken to a hospital in Jaipur. After that it was only Amitabh and Shah Rukh again.

She stuck out her hand and beckoned with her fingers. "Come on, give me some names. Let's see if I've heard of any of your films. And, you know, so I can name drop."

He smiled. "Have you watched *Boss*? It's about the clash between the boss of the Mumbai underworld and the head of the Mumbai police and how they destroy each other." Pride shone in his eyes, as if he were a parent bragging about a favorite child, and she wished they had let Pandey show those *off* films once in a while.

She shook her head.

"*Love Lights?*" Another proud, expectant look. "It's a dark love story."

She crinkled her nose. "How can love be dark?"

He raised a patronizing eyebrow at her. As though he couldn't believe anyone could be naïve enough to ask such a question.

"Well, it's set in Kashmir. They get separated and she gets involved in a terrorist group and when he finds her again she's training to be a human bomb."

"Good Lord, that *is* dark." Maybe it was a good thing she hadn't watched his movies. They sounded positively morose.

He smiled and picked up his laptop again.

"What are you working on now?" Although after what she'd just heard she was afraid to ask.

He searched her face for a few moments. Just when she thought he wasn't going to talk about it, he spoke. "It's the story of this boy from a small village who comes to Mumbai and makes a name for himself."

"You're writing about yourself?"

"Myself?" He looked startled. "You think I'm from a village?"

"Aren't you from near Balpur?"

All the color drained from his face.

"Don't worry," she said quickly, laying a soothing hand on his arm, "you're a very authentic city boy. It's just your Rajasthani dialect. You sound like you're from near my village." She'd never forget how amazing it had felt to hear that perfect accent of his that first time they'd met. "Have you ever visited your uncle in Balpur?"

His already clenched jaw tightened some more. "A long time ago. When I was very young."

It had been close to twenty years since Samir had been back. You couldn't drag him back to that hellhole with a crane. None of them had ever gone back. Not Baiji. Not Virat. Not even for the sadistic old bastard's funeral. Samir tamped down on the reflex to reach behind him and touch the welts that were no longer visible on his back. He willed the swish of the belt not to sound in his head. But it did.

"Samir, are you all right?" Mili moved closer to him, her eyes wide and limpid with concern.

"I'm fine." What the fuck was it with all these flashbacks suddenly? He lifted Mili's hand off his arm, meaning to remove it, but her fingers were so soft, so warm, he hung on.

She pulled her hand away and didn't push for more. "Tell me

about this boy," she said instead, her voice so gentle his heartbeat calmed.

"He has a gift. He can see the future. Only when he uses his gift for his own gain something catastrophic happens to someone he loves."

"That's awful." She looked horrified again. "Are all your stories this sad?"

"Not all of it is sad. It's set against the backdrop of the Mumbai bomb blasts. And he's able to save thousands of lives."

"But he loses someone he loves? Forever?"

"Yes, but he learns to use his gift to benefit others, learns how that's a gift in itself."

She pushed her mass of curls back with both hands and didn't say more. But she didn't meet his eyes.

"What?" Something was bothering her and, idiot that he was, he had to know what.

She let her hair go and it sprang back around her face. "You can't learn anything from losing someone you love. Any lesson you learn from that isn't a lesson. It's a compromise with life. A lie you tell yourself."

"Our mistakes cost us those we love all the time. We can't stop living, can we? We have to find meaning in something else and keep going."

"See, that's cynicism. Not growth. If you wanted him to truly learn that helping others is a gift in itself then he has to lose things he thought were important, not things that *are* important, like someone he loves." Her brows drew together over eyes that shone with sincerity and idealism. Which in his book was no different from stupidity.

"It's not cynicism. It's reality. What you're talking about is a tidy little happy ending. Have you ever known life to be like that?"

She met his eyes, in that way she had. As if there was nothing separating them, as if there was nothing in the world to be afraid of. "It doesn't matter what my life has been like, Samir. What matters is hope. If you don't believe in a happy ending, what are you living for?" The hope that sparkled in her onyx eyes was so intense, so absolute that dread clamped around Samir's heart, and squeezed.

"I'm sorry," she said after he had been silent too long, and lay back down. "It's your story. I shouldn't have said anything." She turned on her side and closed her eyes.

He stared at the words he'd spent a week pounding out. Damn straight it was his story. And he was determined to write it his way.

Samir had never rewritten a script in his life. Stories came to him whole and he wrote them down. But once Mili got inside his hero's head the bastard started to do all sorts of weird shit and rebel until Samir had to capitulate and let him have his way. But that just meant less sleep and more watching Mili sleep while he worked.

In her waking hours, they talked. Mostly about her school and her years in Jaipur and the women she worked with, at the Institute where they provided a safe house to abused women and trained them in skills to make them independent. Apparently, he wasn't the only one who lost himself when he worked. Watching Mili talk about her work was like experiencing the power of a tiny tornado—she became hungry and focused. It consumed all of her, made her lose track of time.

Made him lose track of time.

So much so that when Samir knocked on Mili's door and turned the key to let himself in, the two weeks he'd spent with her felt like a moment that had sped by too fast.

"Come in," Mili shouted from behind the door and beamed at him as he entered and put his laptop down on the mattress. She chugged down the contents of her teacup with a bandaged hand. The doctor had changed the cast on her wrist to a crepe bandage yesterday and she was able to use both hands now. Her ankle cast would take another week to come off but she had talked them into letting her carry a cane instead of those crutches she hated so much.

"What are you doing?" Samir asked as she hobbled to the kitchen on her cane. Her wet hair was all scrunched up and even curlier than usual. The water dripping from it painted midnight stains on her blue cap-sleeved tee. The only clothes she seemed to own were that exact T-shirt in all sorts of colors, and jeans. That's all he'd ever seen her wear. She was also probably the only woman on earth who looked so distracting in an ill-fitting T-shirt.

She leaned over the counter and poured another cup of tea. Okay, so the T-shirts weren't all that ill-fitting. She hobbled back to him with a cup in her hand. Something about the way the cotton clung to her curves gave the impression of poetry, of softness and strength threaded together in perfect cadence. The kind of perfect melding you had to witness, to feel to believe. Only he wasn't going to be doing any feeling anytime soon. Not anytime ever.

She pushed the teacup at him and flicked her chin up as if to ask him what he was thinking.

Yeah, right, like she needed to share in that cesspool of thoughts. "Thanks," he said and took the tea from her. "You going somewhere?"

"Yes, as a matter of fact I am. It's this thing called school, and this other thing called work. Missed both for two weeks, so I'm hoping they'll both still have me. And you heard the doctor yesterday. I need to get back on my feet now. Otherwise awful things could happen to my body."

"Oh, we could never allow awful things to happen to that body," he said before he could stop himself.

Her eyes turned to saucers again and he wanted to whack himself upside the head.

He took a long sip of the tea. "Are you going to walk to college then?" he asked lazily.

She unfroze. "Nope. You're driving me." She smiled and pushed the teacup to his lips to hurry him up. The moment he was done, she snatched the cup away, put it in the sink, and dragged him out of her apartment.

"Hold on, Mili, my laptop's still in your apartment."

"Don't you want to write in there?"

"Well. Yes. But—"

"Drop me off and then come back here and write." She handed him her cane and let him help her into the car. "You get your writing done in my apartment so you might as well just do it there, right?"

"Right." He gunned the engine. "And this has nothing to do with the hot rotis or dal you might find waiting for you when you return."

"*Oy*, what kind of girl do you think I am?"

"I don't know. You tell me. How far are you willing to go for hot rotis?" Seriously, what the fuck was wrong with him?

Again that look. Wide eyes, dark irises opening up to expose even darker pupils that left her bare. And that furious blush.

He settled into the driver's seat, refusing to let his face reflect the stupid wide smile in his heart. "So where to, *memsaab?*"

Her fingers relaxed in her lap. "I need to go to the office first. From there I can walk to class and then to Panda Kong."

"And then?"

"And then . . . could you please come and get me?" She joined her hands together in a pleading *namaste*.

He grunted. He knew she was teasing him but he still hated the hesitation in her voice. "What time do you get off work?"

"Five-thirty."

"And class?"

"Seven-thirty."

"And Kung Fu Panda?"

That made her smile. Good.

"Around midnight."

His grip tightened on the wheel. She was going to wash dishes with that hand for four hours? Over his fucking dead body. But no point in arguing with her now. He was going to drop her off and then pay Kung Fu Panda a visit. Good thing she'd pointed it out to him on their way here.

"There it is," Mili said, and Samir pulled up to a squat, ivy-covered building with wide steps leading up to heavy wooden double doors. An embossed concrete slab jutting out of the lawn proclaimed it Pierce Hall.

Samir pulled himself out of the convertible and jogged around the car to help Mili out. He handed her the cane, then leaned into the car door and watched her make her way up the concrete path.

Suddenly she turned around. "Samir?" she said softly, as if she were throwing his name into the wind. Her forehead crinkled under the wet curls. She looked so serious.

He didn't respond. Just stared at her, afraid of what might come out of her mouth.

"Can I tell you something? You won't be angry?"

Again, he didn't respond, but his entire body hummed with anticipation.

"You are the most decent guy I've ever met." She gave him that sunshine smile. "Thank you." And with that she limped the rest of the way up the stairs and disappeared into the building.

Samir did a U-turn in the parking lot, spinning so fast the tires screeched. He loved the way this baby took curves. He turned around and threw one last glance at the spot where she had stood and declared him decent before jamming his foot into the pedal.

When he pulled the Corvette into the Panda Kong parking lot it was isolated. The fluorescent red sign was missing a *g*, making it sound like "Panda *Kon?*"—Hindi for "Who the heck is Panda?"

He smiled. Mili would've found that funny too.

Walking in, he found the lights turned low. It was three in the afternoon. Obviously they weren't open for dinner yet. A few Chinese women sat huddled in a circle at the back of the restaurant, singing. Not loud jamming kind of singing. Not even the women gathered around the *dholki* drum kind of singing at festivals and weddings back home, but more a barely audible chorus of lilting melody as their hands worked on piles of green beans.

It took them a few moments to figure out someone had entered the restaurant.

"Not open for dinner yet," one of the women said. The singing stopped, and Samir felt oddly sad.

"Can I talk to the manager?"

The woman gave him a worried sort of look and shouted something in Chinese at the door that led to the back of the restaurant.

"I wanted to talk to him about Mili."

"Ah, Mili!" the woman said much more cheerfully. The women behind her repeated it in unison, looking at each other like the nuns in the abbey in *The Sound of Music*. Samir almost expected them to break into a Chinese rendition of "How d'you solve a problem like Mi-li."

"How is she?" The woman who'd been talking to him pointed to her wrist and her foot. Then turned to the door again and this time bellowed something in Chinese in a substantially stronger voice. The only word Samir recognized was *Mili.*

"She's much better, thank you," he said.

"Mili very nice." She peeked at his left hand, patted her own ring, and asked with some alacrity, "You husband? You new one?"

Now there was a question. No, he wasn't the new one and he certainly was not her husband. She didn't have a fucking husband.

"I'm a friend." Samir found his hands in fists and tried to relax.

"Ah, *friend!*" Another chorus of whispers rose behind her amid scoffing giggles and disbelieving glances. How many times had this happened to him? *Just good friends, ha?* Nudge nudge, wink wink.

A man with a rather nasty frown entered the room and snapped something even nastier at the women snapping beans in a circle. His head was curiously egg-shaped.

"Can help you?" he asked Samir with a look that was anything but helpful.

"Yes, I'm a friend of Mili's. Can we talk for a moment?" Samir threw a glance at the circle as if they were in a Bond film from the Roger Moore days. "Privately."

The man looked suddenly interested. He beckoned Samir to follow him into the kitchen. "Mili good dishwasher. No lazy like friend. Ridhi." He made a face as if he had swallowed something foul. "She no good. Think too much like American brat. No notice before quit."

Of course Mili would be a good worker. Groucho Marx was just going to have to live without his trusty little elf for a few more weeks. "Actually, Mili can't come back to work for another two weeks."

"Why?" The guy looked crestfallen, as if Samir had just told him a family member was on her last leg. "She say she come today. She say she fine."

"But she isn't fine," Samir said. And she was too damn stubborn to admit it.

"Why she not tell me herself, then?"

Because she needs the money, you idiot. "Because she doesn't want to leave you hanging. But if she hurts herself while working here when she shouldn't be, she can sue you."

The man jumped. "No, no. Don't need her. Tell her she no need come back."

Fuck, wrong thing to say. "Listen, relax. She's not going to sue you. All she needs is for you to give her two more weeks."

"No, no. Too much trouble." He pulled out a handkerchief from his pocket and dabbed his egg-shaped head.

The man was at least a foot shorter than him. Samir stepped closer and loomed over him. "Listen, how much do you pay her?"

The man cowered and studied Samir with beady eyes.

It didn't take Samir much to convince him to give Mili two weeks with full pay and a bullshit explanation about the laws requiring her to be paid when she was hurt. All it took was twice Mili's two-week salary. One half for Mili, the other half for Egghead.

When Samir walked out of the darkened restaurant a few hundred dollars lighter, he felt better than he had in a very long time.

11

Of course Mili believed in miracles. But there were miracles and then there was what Egghead had just done. For someone who had never so much as strung two kind words together for her, he had lectured her about taking care of herself because health was wealth and so forth. She'd been contemplating throwing herself at his feet and begging him to let her work—she needed the money, no point in hanging on to her dignity—when he'd informed her that the law required him to pay her since she was missing work because of an accident. She had thrown her arms around him, taking them both completely by surprise. Her appreciation for this great country was growing by the day.

She started down the path that led from the restaurant to her apartment. Samir wasn't going to pick her up until midnight. The mile-long walk had seemed like nothing when Ridhi and she had made the journey every day. Now she seemed to be moving so slowly she might as well be walking backward. Her ankle weighed her down and refused to move the way ankles were supposed to. But the cane was so much easier than those cursed crutches. In fact the cane was kind of fun. It made her feel like a retired colonel in an old film. Grinning at her own silliness, she spruced up her gait. But then it struck her that Egghead might find someone else to do her job and not want her back in two weeks and she didn't feel like smiling anymore.

She could say with the utmost honesty that she had done every-thing in her power to do her job well, scrubbing every utensil until it shone, wiping down every counter after Egghead had wiped it down himself. And she'd done all this while keeping her mouth shut and her eyes down. Her ideal-woman act would have made her *naani* proud, right down to no answering back and plastering a patient smile across her face. She'd even helped Egghead's niece with her homework.

She just could not lose this job. She needed the two hundred dollars to send to Naani. Although this month she was going to need the money to make her rent, if she ate nothing.

The thought of food made her stomach growl and the sound of her growling stomach brought Samir's Greek god face blazingly alive in her mind. His face and his body and that presence of his that swirled around him like a sweeping Rajasthan sandstorm everywhere he went. Her mouth watered. Not because he looked like a minty-fresh toothpaste model but because he cooked like the goddess of domesticity.

He'd solved some of her food problems by stocking her fridge with groceries. She could go a good month on that food. But he ate like a bull—or was it a pigeon? She could never remember which one of those animals ate twice their weight in food every day. Maybe she could steal food out of her own fridge and hide it in the office fridge to use after he was gone. Was that stealing from him or stealing from herself?

It didn't matter. Tomorrow she would start to take some of the food he bought and cooked and put it in the office for after he was gone. Desperate times did call for desperate measures. She was not going to feel guilty about wanting to feed herself. And that was that.

She came to the end of the parking lot. All that effort and all she had done was cross it. Her ankle was starting to throb and she had that trembling, weepy sensation in her belly from the rising pain. Maybe she should go back to the restaurant and ask Egghead to drive her home. She turned around and gauged the distance and noticed a tall, bulky man watching her. Something about the way he was looking at her raised her defenses and she turned and started scrambling away.

The man broke into a run. She had no chance. Before she knew it, he was upon her.

"Wait, Malvika Rathod?"

She acted like she hadn't heard him and kept on half walking, half hobbling along on her cane.

"Excuse me, ma'am, I asked if you were Malvika Rathod."

"No," she said and kept walking.

"Are you sure?"

"I would know if my name was Malvika Rathod, wouldn't I?" She clenched her jaw and tried to keep her panic levels down. There wasn't a soul in sight but it was still bright and she was on campus. She had nothing to worry about.

"Then what's your name?"

"If you don't stop following me I'm going to scream."

"Listen, I'm Ranvir, Ridhi's brother. I've been looking for her for a week. Everyone at home is sick with worry."

Mili spun around. Ridhi's brother didn't stop in time and almost ran into her. She took a step back, stumbled, and fell on her bum.

Before she knew what was happening, a yellow convertible screeched to a halt next to her. Samir leapt out of the car and ran at Ridhi's brother like some action-film superhero.

"Samir, wait!" Before her voice left her mouth, Samir's fist connected with Ranvir's jaw and he went flying back into the pavement.

Samir lifted the horrified boy, for all his chubbiness, like a bag of feathers, and pulled his fist back for another punch.

"Samir, stop. Stop!" Her voice finally seemed to reach him. He dropped the guy and ran to her. His eyes travelled over her body as she sat on her bottom on the sidewalk and his breath seemed to catch. He threw one desperate look at the cane lying next to her and his gaze met hers. His eyes softened with something so tender, so helpless she couldn't breathe.

"My God, Mili, are you okay?" It was the first time she'd seen Samir like this. She had a clear view all the way inside, no filters, no fronts. He fell to his knees next to her.

"I'm fine." She reached out and touched his knuckles. They were bleeding. "He was just asking me a question."

"By pushing you off your cane?" His voice trembled.

"He didn't push me. I fell. I didn't realize how unstable I was."

"Your leg's in a cast and he assaulted you and you're protecting him?"

The guy groaned behind them and Samir sprang up. "I'll kill you, you bastard."

"Samir, stop. At least hear me out."

But Samir already had the guy pulled up by his collar. Ranvir had seemed so large and threatening when he'd approached her only minutes ago. Now, hanging from Samir's hands, he looked like a pudgy little schoolboy.

"He's Ridhi's brother. My roommate's brother. He was just asking me where she is."

"I've been looking for her for weeks," the guy squeaked. "I just want to know if she's safe."

"Samir, you're choking him. Can you let him down? Please."

He did. Then he scooped her up and carried her to his car with all the glowering finesse of a caveman.

Beating the shit out of the poor fuck might have been a more humane way to deal with him. As it turned out, Mili had different plans for her absconding roommate's brother. Five minutes after delivering a neat right hook to his jaw, Samir was carrying the man a café latte—complete with a frilly cloud of whipped cream and chocolate sprinkles.

Mili sat by the huge mullioned windows in the university food court and dispensed her lecture as if she were Mother Teresa while the idiot stared at her openmouthed like a zealous devotee. She was sending him on a guilt trip so long he could've circled the globe by now. He looked ready to weep. Fucking bozo.

"She's in love. Don't you understand? If you force her to marry someone else, she could kill herself. You know Ridhi. She's so *filmy*, she'll do it just to prove her point. And you know who would have to live with it for the rest of his life?"

The idiot actually shook his head.

Samir slammed the latte in front of him. "You," he said, because, really, the guy needed help. "The correct answer is *you*."

Mili gave Samir a congratulatory look, using both hands to indicate his brilliance to the nincompoop. Suddenly Samir felt like an insider. He put Mili's mocha in front of her and took a sip of his black coffee. He flipped a chair around, straddled it, and watched as Mili proceeded to empty one . . . two . . . three . . . four packets of sugar into her cup. If he had picked up more packets, she might never have stopped. It was a mocha, for fuck's sake. Wasn't the thing already sweetened for a diabetic coma?

She took one long slurping sip and looked like she was having another one of those food-induced orgasms. Dumbass drooled at her as if she, and not her mocha, were the sweet treat. Fan-fucking-tastic.

"Haven't you ever been in love?" She skewered Dumbass with those sugar-softened eyes. He whimpered.

"You think it's easy to find someone who will risk everything for you? Go on the run in a foreign country, jeopardize a career, risk deportation? You think it's easy to find love like that?"

The guy stared at her, then turned to Samir for help.

"No. The right answer is *no*." Samir was nothing if not helpful.

"No," the guy repeated with a dazed but not entirely ungrateful expression.

Samir raised his coffee in salute and took another sip.

Mili waved another hand in Samir's direction, indicating yet again his unarguable brilliance. "Look at Samir. Even with those looks, he still hasn't found anyone. Can you imagine that?"

Samir choked on his coffee. Sprayed a goodly amount on the poor guy's white shirt and earned a good beating on the back from Mili. But a little choking wasn't going to stop her. She was on a mission. She continued to pat Samir's back and skewered Dumbass with another glare. "You're her brother. You. Are. Her. Brother. Her brother." She gave the word *brother* so many nuances, such heartfelt emotion, that moisture danced in the guy's eyes. "You should be fighting for her. Helping her and Ravi become one. You should be talking to your father, to your uncles. You should be *helping* your sister."

Samir knew what was coming next. He rested his chin on the back of the chair he was straddling and watched. *She is your sister. Your sister. Your. Sister.* Samir said the words in his head as she spoke them aloud. He was grinning like a fool when she turned her eyes on him. He hadn't had so much fun in years.

She narrowed her eyes and he gave her a big beaming smile for her effort. She shook her head at him and turned back to the brother. *The. Brother. The bro-ther,* who had tears spilling down his doughy cheeks now.

Samir had to work so hard not to laugh, his shoulders shook.

"I'm sorry. Will you help me find her?" the guy said and burst into sobs. Mili pulled him into a hug. Her arms went comfortingly around the idiot's hiccupping shoulders. He took full advantage and completely let loose. Mili patted his back and winked at Samir over his head.

The laughter died in Samir's chest.

All he wanted to do—with an intensity that sucker-punched him in the gut—was pull the bastard away from her.

Instead Samir gritted his teeth and watched as she pushed him away gently and asked Samir to drive them home. It wasn't easy, but of course he did as she asked, without tearing the sniveling idiot's limbs out like he wanted to.

How could anyone be so smitten in such a short period of time? The asshole hadn't pulled his jaw off the floor and shut his mouth once since he'd seen her. Even when they were back in her apartment, waiting for him to finish speaking to his parents, his eyes kept darting in Mili's direction as he mumbled into the phone. Oh, and suddenly Dumbass was her best bud. No, make that Dr. Bestbud. Apparently med school wasn't as important as hunting an errant sister down in full-blown seventies-film fashion.

"You're muttering to yourself, you know." Of course Mili, in her all-seeing wisdom, caught him being even dumber than Dr. Dumbass Bestbud.

"I am not." As dialog went, brilliant!

"And now you're glaring." Her tone was soothing but it only made him angrier.

"The guy attacked you. Excuse me if he's not at the top of my love list."

She matched his glare. "Samir, he's trying to do the right thing."

Dr. Right-Thing came up behind Mili—standing a bit too close for decency if you asked him. "I just spoke to Mummy and Daddy. They were just getting ready to call the cops. I've asked them to hold off until—"

Samir cut him off. "This is all very touching, but how is it that your sister has been missing for two weeks and your family hasn't called the cops yet?"

Both Mili and Dr. Dumbass turned to Samir as if he were from another planet, from Pluto, in fact, not even worthy of being assigned a real planet.

Mili spoke first. Of course Mili spoke first. "How can they call the cops on Ridhi?" Her tone suggested Samir was hanging from a stupid tree on non-planet Pluto.

"Yeah, how?" Dr. Glib added.

They looked at each other and nodded in mutual understanding of Samir's endless thickness.

"Okay, enough with the how-can-he-be-so-stupid looks. Any normal person, any normal family would have called the cops first. *Then* pulled all the relatives out of their respective colleges and jobs to send them off in hot pursuit. I'm just saying."

"Samir," Mili said, drawing his name out even more than she usually did and making it sound like she was saying "you imbecile." "*Honor!* How can you risk public humiliation by going to the cops? It's a family matter. Family has to resolve it."

You've got to be fucking kidding me. He was stuck in a fucking seventies film.

"We're Punjabi, man," Dr. Dumbass-Ten-Times-Over chimed in because what Mili had just said wasn't bizarre enough.

I know plenty of sane Punjabis, Samir wanted to say. But he didn't think it would register with these two seventeenth-century escapees.

"You know what the problem with people like you is?" Mili said. "You live in your own little bubble and you have no idea what the real world is like."

"And in the real world you only call the cops when it's time to look for a body?"

"See?" Mili turned to Dr. Punjabi-Pride, who nodded, all knowing, all understanding. They started a side conversation, because "people like him" weren't worth talking to.

He didn't need this shit. He stalked into the kitchen and yanked the fridge open and wished he had picked up the six-pack that had been calling his name the last time he was at the store.

"I've asked Mummy and Daddy to wait until we get there before they take any action," the newly minted, brave keeper of sisterly honor said behind him.

Samir spun around. "Hold on. Did you just say *we?*" That earned him another one of those non-planet Pluto looks from both of them, which he ignored. "Mili's not going anywhere with you."

"Of course I'm not, Samir." She turned the full power of that sneaky innocence on him. "We both are."

Mili had no idea what was wrong with Samir. But he had slipped into a full-on angry-young-man avatar straight out of an Amitabh Bachan film.

"Can I see you in the other room for a minute? *Now.*" His face thundered like a stormy night and that pulse in his neck was definitely going to pop.

"Sure. But first I need to get Ranvir another bag of ice for his face."

Without a word, Samir snatched the bag of melted ice water from Ranvir's hands and stormed to the fridge. He emptied it into the sink, yanked an ice tray out of the freezer, and dumped ice in the bag—amazingly it didn't melt at his touch.

He thrust the bag at Ranvir. "Don't move until we come back." He gave the poor boy such an intimidating look he might never move again. Mili had no idea why he was being so rude to him.

"Anything else you need done before you give me a moment of your time?" When he looked at her like that, his eyes locked on her as if she were the only person in the room, in the world, she had the strangest sensation in the pit of her stomach.

She followed him into her bedroom.

"Are you crazy?"

So much for only person in the world. "My *naani* says I am, just a little bit. Why?" She tried to give him her sweetest smile but it didn't work.

He looked like he wanted to shake her. "Because I thought the point was to keep your roommate's family from finding her. Not to go off on a quest with them to hunt her down."

"The point is to make sure Ridhi and Ravi end up together."

"But they're together now, Mili. And if you leave your long nose out of their business they might stay that way. Why can't you just stay out of it?"

Because sometimes love needed a tiny push. A little help. Maybe if she'd had someone in her corner, someone to help her meet Virat just once, he'd have seen how much she loved him and she wouldn't be here pining away for him and trying to make herself worthy of him.

"Because Ridhi is my friend and everyone deserves someone in their corner." She touched her nose. Nobody had ever called it long before.

"And you've done great. You've stayed in her corner by not betraying her confidence. Hel—Heck, you jumped off a balcony for shi—God's sake."

"Samir, haven't you ever needed help? Haven't you ever wanted something so bad you wished the entire universe was in your corner? Haven't you been in a place where you've done everything you possibly can and still it's not enough? You need just that slightest bit more. Just that one helping hand?"

His face did that thing it did when he slipped behind his wall. It always reminded Mili of those photos of the Italian town of Pompeii when the volcano Mt. Vesuvius erupted. People in poses stuck in the middle of doing some everyday task—pouring water into a cup, stirring a pot on the stove. Frozen in the middle of life. She'd always imagined how the lava might have slipped over them, so fast they didn't even pause in what they were doing. Samir's face had a way of freezing over like that, as if a molten mask slid over his face so fast his very essence changed from human to stone in an instant.

"No. I always rely entirely on myself. At least I have ever since I became an adult. Ridhi and Ravi are adults. It's between them and their families. Why should we get in the middle of it? Besides, don't you have this thing called a job and this other thing called school?"

"It's Friday today. I don't work at the Institute on Mondays so I have the next three days off. I have school under control. And I don't have to worry about Panda Kong." She still couldn't believe how well things had turned out at Panda Kong. She smiled. "Oh God, Samir, I just thought of something. It's fate that we help Ridhi and Ravi. You won't believe what happened today. I don't have to go back to Panda Kong for two weeks. It's a sign."

Samir swallowed and squeezed his eyes shut. He looked like he might be sick.

"Are you okay, Samir?"

He didn't respond, but he opened his eyes and looked at her with the strangest expression. He looked almost helpless.

"If you're worried about my wrist and ankle, don't be. I can hardly feel it anymore. I'm a really fast healer. I mean, in Balpur I was famous for it."

Suddenly the helplessness was gone and he looked angry again.

"Oh no. You're upset because I assumed you would go with us. See, this is what my *naani* says, that I get carried away. It's just that I—I'm sorry. Of course, you don't have to come. You have all that writing to do. I'll just go with Ranvir."

He grabbed her shoulders, took a step closer, and glared down at her. "You're not going anywhere with that guy. You've known him all of two hours. What's wrong with you, Mili? For all you know he might be a serial rapist." His hands were as gentle as ever, but she felt the weight of his fingers as if they were brands on her skin.

"I had no idea you city boys were such drama queens." She removed his hands and took a step away from him.

He narrowed his eyes at her, not so much drama queen as brooding film hero.

She hated seeing him this way. "I've known you all of twelve days, and you've done more for me than any friend I've ever had." Suddenly she wished she hadn't removed his hands.

Another tortured look flashed across his face. She wanted to reach out and wipe it off. "Samir, I should have said this sooner, but you have to know how much what you've done means." She sniffed back the drop that trickled down her nose. "You took care of me when I had no one else." Oh, forget it. She wrapped her arms around him. "Thank you."

She had meant to give him a quick hug. But his arms went around her, pulled her close and held on. One huge hand pressed her head against his chest. She had forgotten how hard and warm it was, how wild his heartbeat under her ear.

"Mili." Her name rumbled in his chest. She felt the sound rather than heard it and warmth melted through her like molten gold filling a mold at the goldsmith's. It slid into her heart and into the deep dark crevices of her body.

She pushed away from him with both hands. Her wrist hurt and she winced. He reached for her hand, but she took two quick steps and backed away from his touch. She couldn't look at him. A loaded silence wrapped around them. She couldn't let it stretch into awkwardness. "Seriously, Samir, you've done enough. You really don't have to come along. Look at Ranvir. Do you really think he could hurt anyone?" Something else struck her and she smiled. "You can still use my apartment to write. Just make sure I have some dal to come home to."

He didn't respond and she was forced to look up at him.

Instead of his usual arrogant grin she found that his face had darkened again. With a golden face like that, with those honey eyes and that marble-light skin, he could get darker and stormier than anyone she knew.

"I told you you're not going anywhere with him by yourself."

"So you'll come along?" She was an idiot for sounding so relieved, but at least it made his frown go away.

"Yes, but you owe me big time."

"Yes. I owe you. Anything you want. All you have to do is ask. Good enough?" She grabbed his arm and tugged him toward the door.

"Anything I want?" He stopped under the doorway and filled it up next to her. Something about the way he searched her face made more liquid warmth spread in her belly. She swallowed. "Anything I'm in a position to give," she said carefully.

"So now there are conditions?" His arrogant grin was back. And her relief at seeing it made her touch the wooden door frame for luck. The thought of losing his friendship, of ever letting it go, made her heart ache.

She knew she should step away from him, but she couldn't. "Not conditions. What is not mine to give, I cannot give, Samir."

"Fair enough. But I'm warning you, you might regret having ever said those words."

She already regretted them, and felt oddly wild for having issued the offer. What was it about Samir that made her want to take chances? She wasn't in a position to take any chances. She had a mission and she had her *mangalsutra* marriage beads and her bright red *sindoor.* And the bonds in which she was tied were ancient and sacred and unbreakable. And above all else the love in her heart was forever pledged to her husband.

12

Samir knew he should whip out those papers and finish this right now.

Mili looked like she already regretted her promise and it made her look so small, so trapped, his heart did that tight tugging thing again. When they were standing this close she had to lean her head all the way back to look up at him. Her curls cascaded down to her waist as she met his eyes.

An awful feeling of running down a path as it crumbled behind him swirled in Samir's chest. What an idiot he had been to think this would be easy. If he weren't this close with the script—if he weren't terrified that the words would dry up without her. If this weren't about Bhai and Rima, he would've laid everything out in front of her. Right here, right now. She trusted him, he had felt her trust in her body when she hugged him. But trust was the most fragile of things. And what he had to lose was too precious.

No. No matter what he wanted to believe, he knew she would throw him out on his ass if she knew who he was, what he wanted. Something twisted in his gut, and he pushed it away as nothing more than the fear of failing at what he had come for. What he needed was to find the right time to do this. To wait until he was sure she couldn't refuse him. The time to do it any other way was gone.

He let her pull him out of the room. Ranvir's slack baby jaw drooped even lower when he saw Mili clinging to Samir's arm.

Samir pulled her down next to him on the mattress and Slack Jaw settled across from them with the awkwardness of someone who had never sat his princely butt down on a floor.

"So, Ridhi hasn't called you even once since she left?" he asked, making puppy-dog eyes at Mili.

"No, she'll call me when Ravi and she are safe from you people."

Puppy Dog had the gall to look hurt and dial up the goo-goo eyes.

Mili didn't smack him upside the head like Samir wanted to, but she looked angry enough to want to and it made him ridiculously happy. "Ridhi was really afraid you would hurt Ravi."

Ranvir shrugged. Samir had no doubt they would throw Ravi under a speeding train and walk away without a backward glance if they thought they could get away with it. These bastards moved across continents and got all refined, but the veneer of civility was paper thin. When it came to their daughters, their special brand of family honor stripped their facades down in a jiffy and turned them into the Neanderthals they really were.

"It's not like we want to hurt her. Mummy hasn't eaten since Ridhi left. Daddy hasn't been able to get out of bed, he's been so sick. All we want is for her to come home. They are even willing to get them married off. There has to be a way to find out where she is. Can you call her from your cell phone? She won't answer my calls."

"I don't have a cell phone," Mili said without a whiff of self-consciousness.

Ranvir's eyes virtually popped out of his head. The idea that human beings could survive without a cell phone seemed outside the grasp of his pea brain.

"So how do you call people?" This guy was a serious insult to dumbasses everywhere.

Instead of putting him in his place, Mili gave him her most patient look. "I have a phone in the office that I use to make calls and I use a calling card to call my *naani* in India. There really is no one else I need to call."

"What about him?" Ranvir pointed to Samir.

Mili looked up at Samir. He watched her, waiting for her response.

"He's always here, so I never really have to call him." She gave Samir a cool I'm-so-glad-you're-my-friend smile. But her fingers twisted together in her lap. She wasn't quite as unaffected by him as she wanted to believe.

Bastard that he was, he pushed his advantage. He held her wide-eyed gaze and let the moment stretch. Mili colored. Ranvir shifted uncomfortably in his chair. Good. He didn't need the bastard complicating the plot any further. Come to think of it, he didn't want the bastard anywhere near Mili.

He stuck out his hand toward Ranvir without taking his eyes off Mili. "Give me your cell phone."

Ranvir handed the phone over.

"Do you have your sister's number in here?"

"Of course. But she's not answering my calls." He tried to give Samir a superior look but thought the better of it. The first smart thing he'd done since they'd met.

"Have you texted her?"

"Yes. But she's not responding to my texts."

Samir slid open the phone, punched in a message and read it aloud. "Ridhi, Mummy and Daddy have relented. They are willing to get you and Ravi married. I am with Mili. Please call her office phone at nine p.m."

He hit send.

Ranvir looked at Mili. "You think she'll call?"

But Mili had eyes only for Samir and a small fire burned in their onyx depths. "We'll just have to go there and see, won't we?"

The phone in Mili's office rang at exactly nine o'clock. Samir was perched on her desk next to the phone and Ranvir was slumped in her chair.

"Ridhi? How are you?" Mili heard the breathless worry in her own voice. She still wasn't entirely certain she hadn't been sucked into setting up some sort of trap for Ridhi.

"Mill, Oh God, Mill, are you safe? Did they hurt you?" Ridhi said loud enough for everyone to hear even without a speaker phone. She was in full-on Drama Queen mode. It was so good to hear her voice.

"I'm fine, Ridhi. Are you and Ravi okay?"

"Oh God, Mill, it's been fantastic. We've been doing it like bunnies. Everywhere. I'm in heaven, girl!"

Mili's cheeks burned. She turned away from Samir's grin, unable to hold his gaze. She wanted to tell Ridhi to keep her voice down, instead she said, "Ridhi, I have your brother here with me."

Ridhi sniffed into the phone. "Very good. I hope he heard me. Just so he knows there's no *honor* left to save."

Samir gave the phone a thumbs-up.

"Ridhi, I think he's really worried about you."

"Yeah, right. That's why he's been leaving me threatening messages. He's not threatened you or anything, has he? I swear I'll kill him if he has."

Mili glared at Ranvir. With his chubby, dimpled face he looked like he barely even knew what the word *threaten* meant.

"I'm sorry. I was desperate to get her to come home," Ranvir said, hanging his head in shame.

Samir rolled his eyes.

"He says he's sorry," Mili said into the phone, and Ridhi sniffed again. "Ridhi, I think he's worried about you. So are your parents. I don't think they are going to hurt Ravi. They want you to come back."

"Have you talked to my parents?" Ridhi tried to sound scoffing but Mili heard a thread of hope in her voice and her heart twisted.

"No, but I can if you want me to." She turned to Ranvir. "I need to talk to your parents."

It took Ranvir two seconds to get his mother on his cell phone and hand it over to Mili.

Loud sobbing exploded from the phone even before Mili could get it to her ear. "Oh God, *beta*, bless you, bless you. You have no idea what we have gone through. Oh, my Ridhika. Oh, my baby. Is she okay?" No wonder Ridhi was so dramatic.

"Auntie, she's fine. She's just scared."

"What 'scared'? What does she think we will do? What did I do to deserve this from my own daughter? Tell her to come home. Tell her Mummy will die without her."

In the other ear, Ridhi spoke. "Is she on? Is she shrieking in your ear?"

Samir made a noose with his hands and pretended to hang himself. He looked so amused with himself Mili whacked his thigh with Ranvir's phone, then pressed it against her jeans. She spoke into the office phone. "Ridhi, your mother is really very upset."

"Mill, Mummy is always upset. Tell her I won't marry anyone else."

Mili moved the cell phone back to her ear. Ridhi's mom's sobbing had taken on a note of hysteria. "Auntie. Please calm down. Ridhi is okay."

"Don't"—Ridhi's mom shouted into her right ear before making the effort to lower her voice—"tell me to calm down. My pride and joy has run away with some boy."

"Is she calling Ravi names? If she calls Ravi names, I'm never coming home." This was Ridhi in her left ear.

"Auntie, Ridhi says she won't marry anyone else."

"Oh God, but Dr. Mehra's boy is a cardiologist." She said the word *cardiologist* with such reverence she forgot to cry. "*And* he's Punjabi."

"Ravi is a software engineer," Mili said into the phone.

"I know what Ravi is. Why are you telling me that? What did she say about Ravi? How dare she? I'm hanging up."

"Ridhi, wait, please don't hang up."

It was taking all of Samir's strength not to take both phones and toss them out the window. It had been amusing for the first five minutes. But now these two were killing Mili. She was wound as tight as his Breitling. If the conversation ended badly, and how could it not, he had no doubt she would blame the entire debacle on herself.

Ranvir was opening and closing his mouth like a hapless fish and doing absolutely nothing to help the poor girl out. So much for "Ranvir." It meant "the victorious warrior." Who the fuck had named him that?

Samir pulled the landline phone out of Mili's hand. "Okay, listen, Ridhika," he said in the voice he used on his junior artists when he needed them to take him seriously, fast. "Your parents want you to come home. They are going to pay for your wedding— in full Yash Chopra splendor. Then they are going to send you on a honeymoon to Switzerland, just like in Bollywood movies. All they want in return is that you come home and act like all this nonsense never happened. Either you take the offer, or you go to the registrar's office, sign on a ledger, and act like you don't have a family. It's your call."

"Who the hell are you?" this Ridhi person asked in a terrifyingly nasal American accent, completely ignoring the real question at hand.

He said a little prayer for the poor fuck who had signed up for this for the rest of his life. "It doesn't matter. We're calling you from this number in ten minutes. Have your answer ready." And with that he clicked off the phone.

Mili stared at him, openmouthed, as if he had sprouted a third eye. Shrill shouting came from the cell phone hanging from her hand.

"Tell Auntieji her daughter's coming home and to start making wedding arrangements."

Mili pulled the phone to her ear. "Hello, Auntie?" The shrieking stopped instantly. "Ridhi is willing to come home if you promise to treat Ravi with respect and if you give them your blessings."

"So she'll come home and get married at home?" The hysteria evaporated from the voice like magic.

Mili's shoulders dropped a good two inches. "Yes, and she'll even let you plan the wedding and invite as many people as you want. As long as she's the bride and Ravi's the groom."

Nicely done, Mili.

There was some excited shrieking over the phone and Mili couldn't stop grinning. Then Ridhi's mom said something and Mili's face fell. Great, now the woman chose to speak in human decibels.

"Thanks," Mili said in a small voice. "Yes, I'll try."

When she hung up she was smiling again but the joy was gone from her smile and Samir wanted to strangle the woman.

He redialed Ridhi's number and handed Mili the phone. At least the ear-splitter roommate would bring her smile back. It did.

As expected the runaway couple was all set to go home to Ohio and let Mummy and Daddy get them married. There was much sobbing and laughter and then the nasal voice dropped to a whisper. Color slid over Mili's cheeks and she looked away from him.

"We'll talk later," she mumbled into the phone.

And Samir knew without a doubt that Ridhi had asked Mili about him.

Three days after Samir had pulled off that incredible phone rescue Mili waited outside Pierce Hall for him. The yellow convertible screeched to a halt in front of her and Samir sprang out of the car in his usual style, like Ali Baba springing from his earthen urn. He ran around the car and let her in, then he waited until she was settled in her seat before jumping in next to her. She could get around without her cane now but Samir refused to let her walk back and forth from the university. He dropped her off at Pierce Hall in the afternoon and then picked her up and took her home in the evening after class.

"Did you speak to the crazy roomie today? Is she back at her parents' house?"

Mili nodded. Ridhi hadn't been able to stop talking about the wedding. Her mother and she had flown to New York for a day to shop for Ridhi's wedding *lehenga* and jewelry. "Yup, auntie and she are trying to plan the wedding of the century in one week."

Samir groaned. "That sounds painful. So when do you leave for the wedding?"

"I'm not going."

"What do you mean you're not going?"

For obvious reasons Mili didn't exactly love weddings, but that didn't stop her from being heartbroken that she couldn't go to Ridhi's wedding that weekend. For one, she had no way of getting from Ypsilanti to Columbus. As of today she was three days behind on her rent and she felt like a full-fledged criminal, living in a home she wasn't paying for. So buying a bus ticket was out of the question.

"Mili?" Samir made his signature screeching turn into their parking lot and she grabbed the dashboard and squeezed her eyes shut.

"I have schoolwork to finish."

"You told me that you had school under control when you were all set to go traipsing off with Ranvir."

"What are you, some sort of wedding-guest policeman?"

"Far from it. I find weddings hideous. But I thought Ridhi was your best friend. And I thought weddings meant more to you girls than the air you breathe."

"I think air is definitely more important than weddings." Unlike marriage, which was definitely more important than the air you breathed.

"So you're one of those rare girls who actually accepts that weddings are just a waste of money?"

"I wouldn't go that far."

"But they aren't special enough to attend when your best friend is involved?" Samir helped her out of the car.

It was hard to be furious with someone who was so nice to you, but he got her there with such ease. "I just don't want to go, okay?"

His brows drew together but he had the good sense to say no more. When they reached her door he did a two-fingered wave and turned to go to his own apartment. "Later."

"Aren't you coming in?" Was that disappointment she heard in her own voice?

"Not today. Will you be all right by yourself?"

"Of course." She followed him with her eyes as he walked away.

In the three weeks that she'd known him Samir had never left her at the door and not come in. Usually he was harder to get rid of than a scabies itch.

She turned the key and entered her apartment. The aroma hit her first.

A small round table sat in the middle of her dining room draped in a white tablecloth. She walked toward it. Laid out on the table was her favorite meal—yellow dal, perfectly round rotis, and spiced potatoes topped with green chilies and cilantro. Two plates sat in front of two brand-new chairs that matched the brand-new table.

She turned around and saw him standing in her doorway, his big body filling it up, his hip leaning on the doorframe, his arms crossed across his chest. He raised one questioning brow at her, and that's when she realized she was crying.

All his life Samir had hated the sight of women crying. Baiji never cried. Rima had steadfastly refused to shed tears when Virat's plane went down. All the women he knew who did cry used tears as a weapon to get what they wanted.

Already he had lost count of how many times he'd seen Mili cry. But until this moment he hadn't quite grasped how often and how very easily she cried. And he had definitely forgotten how much he hated tears. Because Mili's tears were a thing of beauty. They crashed against his heart like waves, at once turbulent and calming, and shook something free in the very deepest part of him. Her crying was silent, soulful. It spoke all the things she couldn't say. Sometimes it was comical, because her nose watered as much as her eyes did. But there wasn't a smidge of artfulness in it. She cried because she couldn't *not* cry. When emotion filled her up, it spilled from her eyes.

He walked up to her, careful to keep his stride lazy. He reached out and touched her tears. Her cheek was velvet beneath his fingers. "If you're upset I'll put it away. You don't have to eat it."

She sniffed and tried to glare at him through the flood. "Don't you dare!"

He pushed her into a chair and waited for her to say something about the new furniture, but she was too mesmerized by the food. He had wondered if he was going too far with the dinette set, but he had seen it at the huge grocery store that seemed to carry everything from milk to construction tools and he hadn't been able to help himself. He was tired of eating on the floor. Plus, he'd seen her rub her ankle when she sat cross-legged on the floor and he knew it hurt. He had almost bought the matching rattan couch too. But something told him that even with this tiny table and two chairs he had a fight on his hands. Except that until she was done eating she wouldn't be fighting any battles.

Somewhere between her fluttering eyelashes and blissfully raised eyebrows, somewhere between the sensuous working of her jaw and the insanely satisfied smile, it struck him. "You're not going to the wedding because you don't have any way to get there." How had he not figured it out sooner?

She stopped eating and he regretted not waiting until she was done. "That's not the only reason."

"But that's the main reason?"

She shrugged. Fortunately she went back to eating.

"Let me drive you. Your Panjab's favorite son invited me, so I'm on the guest list too."

"Thanks, Samir. But I can't." She didn't look surprised that he had offered to take her and it made him absurdly happy. "You're already doing too much. All that picking up, dropping off"—she waved a spoonful of potatoes around—"all the cooking. You're spoiling me." She gave the potatoes a caressing glance and popped them in her mouth.

She might've thanked him again, but he didn't hear one word because she was in the throes of whatever those potatoes did to her and his mind took off to places it definitely had no business going.

Suddenly she stopped and put the spoon down. "And the furniture." She caressed the white tablecloth with her forefinger. "We have to take it back. I can't afford it."

He opened his mouth but she shook her head. "No, Samir, I can't take this from you."

He tried to swallow, but couldn't quite manage. "Not even as a thank-you for letting me write here? Thanks to you, I'm almost done with my script." Although thanks to her he'd practically had to write the damn thing twice.

She grinned widely. "Is it really almost done?"

He nodded and she picked up the spoon again and dipped it in the dal. "That's wonderful. But the dining table has got to go, and forget the wedding. This"—she pointed at the dal with her spoon—"this is the way to thank me." She scooped some of the yellow liquid into her mouth and licked her spoon with such feeling Little Sam gave up on decency and reared to life. And Samir knew he could no longer talk himself out of the crazy plan that had been brewing in his head all day.

13

When Samir picked Mili up outside Pierce Hall she looked ready to drop dead with exhaustion. She sank into the car seat and held her hand cautiously across her belly the way she always did when it hurt. He handed her a pill and a bottle of water and even the grateful look she threw him didn't have its usual fierceness. Good. He hated that look with a vengeance. Before they were out of the parking lot, her eyelids started to droop shut.

The moment he drove past their street, she sat bolt upright. "Samir, you missed our turn." Of course he was a fool to think it could've been that easy.

"Did I? I'll take the next one."

She narrowed those tired eyes. "There is no next one. You need to make a U-turn."

"Okay, we'll make one. No worries." He patted her knee and tried his best smoldering smile.

She rolled her eyes. "What are you doing, Samir?" she asked as if he were a child about to eat his fifth cookie.

"I'm driving a car."

"But where are you driving your car to?" More of that enunciation.

"We are going on a little trip."

"I don't want to go on a trip. I want to go home. Turn the car around. *Now.*"

"Sure. I'll turn it around and take you right home on Sunday."

"This is insanity, Samir. It's illegal. It's called kidnapping. You could be arrested. The laws in this country are very strict." She sounded like she was threatening a three-year-old. Nevertheless, he shouldn't have smiled, because she jumped straight from annoyed enough to scold him to livid enough to poke his eyes out.

She twisted around and started searching for something. "Let me see your phone." She shoved her hand under his nose.

He laughed. He threw his head back and laughed louder than he'd laughed in a very long time. How could he not? "Wait three hours. I'm sure Ridhi will be happy to let you see her phone and have me arrested."

Instead of a response she gave him her back. Okay, so he didn't have to be a genius to know she was furious. But she was also touched and grateful. She just didn't know it yet. Her pert little nose went up in the air and she wrapped her arms around herself. But her bravado didn't stand up to her exhaustion and within ten minutes of silent fuming she was fast asleep, the wet spikes of her lashes splayed across her velvet cheeks, ribbons of hair cascading from her ponytail.

He tried not to focus on the warmth the sight of her suffused in his chest, not to mention other parts of him. But the only other thing to focus on was the open road and the endless fields and the roaring vacuum it blasted open in the pit of his stomach. Here he was again, driving through his oldest nightmares, the wind blowing open those stubborn ancient wounds. And the only thing that made the restlessness recede was the woman who believed she was married to his brother huddled next to him with those damned wet cheeks. Trusting him enough to be fast asleep in his car even when she was furious at him.

Earning her trust had been disturbingly easy. Not that he had ever had trouble getting women to trust him. Even when he wished women mistrusted him, they chose not to. But it had never bothered him before. Never made him wonder how a woman would survive after he'd moved on. And every woman had survived just fine.

Only Mili was unlike any woman he'd ever met.

An intense urge to turn around and look at her overwhelmed

him. He kept his eyes on the road. But he didn't have to turn around. His mind saw her with high-definition clarity. One long spiral curl sprang free from her ponytail and skimmed her mocha skin still tinted pink with the remnants of anger, those high cheeks a barometer of her endless wellspring of emotion. He gripped the steering wheel tighter. Not because the desire to tuck that errant strand behind her ear was unbearably strong but because a bizarre impatience clawed at his insides. A red barn danced in the distance across a cornfield. The bottomlessness that had made him rise screaming from his nightmares blew open in his chest and cut off his breath.

The welts on his back burned. Fire and tar. The smell of his own blood charred his nostrils, mixing with the smell of coal and wheat husk. The storeroom was darker than the coal. Darker than the well.

"Hold on, *beta*, I'm right here." Baiji's voice was as wet as his back. He lifted his head off the cement floor and reached for it. His fingers searching for the soft muslin of her sari. But there was only the dusty air. And her voice. And Bhai's.

"Chintu? Chintu, come on, champ, wake up. If you get to the window, I can pull you out."

But he couldn't move. He couldn't feel his legs.

"There's snow everywhere," he said. "I can't stand in the snow, it burns, Bhai. Bhai?" His voice rose. His terror tearing through the silence.

"Shh. My precious boy, shh." Baiji's voice. "We'll get you out. It's over. No more. We're going to the city, we're going away. Just you, me, and Bhai. Just stand up one last time. Just this one time."

His back tore, but he pushed off the icy cement. Pushed.

His eyes were puffed shut from tears. He pried them open.

Bhai's shadowy form stuck up from the window. Just his head wrapped in gray sky.

"Are you flying?" he asked, almost smiling. Bhai could fly, Bhai could do anything.

He tried to crawl to the window but his hands slipped on the slickness that dripped down his arms.

"Chintu, come on, champ, you're strong. I know you are. I'm standing on Baiji's shoulders. You know how heavy I am. Come on."

His back disappeared. Dadaji's belt disappeared. Everything disappeared but Bhai's voice and the need to get to Baiji.

Bhai grabbed his hands, and pulled him over. Baiji's sari was in his hands, pressed against his cheeks, twisting between his fingers.

Mili shifted and a blast of wind caught her ponytail. Her hair slapped against the headrest and wrapped around it like ropes. He reached over and set it free. The silk tangled about his fingers. He clutched it, squeezed it. The fist around his throat eased. The slamming in his chest eased. He sucked in a breath, let it fill his lungs, and rammed his foot into the accelerator.

Waking up in a speeding car was the strangest feeling. As if you had been flying in a dream and then you continued to fly after you woke up even though you didn't know how.

" 'Morning," Samir said, his warm honey eyes sparkling brighter than the sun slipping into the horizon behind him, setting his gold-flecked hair ablaze. The familiar possessiveness in his voice sent a thrill down her spine before she could stop it and that made all her anger come raging back. She squeezed her eyes shut and turned away from him.

He swung the car into an exit at full speed and entered the parking lot in his signature screeching-tires fashion. Mili was proud of herself for not grabbing the dashboard or showing any sign of how much his driving acrobatics terrified her.

"Maybe a little coffee will improve *memsaab*'s mood?" He walked around the car and held her door open.

She got out. What kind of man didn't realize that she was perfectly capable of opening her own car door? She stepped around him, her stupid ankle sending a jolt of pain through her from having been in the same position too long. Fortunately she didn't stumble. She just stuck her chin up and started walking, ignoring the pain and refusing to limp.

The sky had started to darken, but the building was lit as if it were Diwali, the festival of lights. One glance around the parking lot told her that the yellow convertible was the only car there. She looked over her shoulder to make sure he was close by.

He placed a hand on her elbow. And something about the gentle, possessive way in which he touched her made her yank her arm away.

"So it's going to be the silent treatment, I see." He stepped past her and held the heavy glass door open, not a bit of remorse on his smug face.

How could he be so completely unaffected by how she felt, by how much she hated what he had done? "You don't see anything. You see only what you want to see. You do only what you want to do. You don't care what anyone else wants. It's called being a bully, a big, selfish, pigheaded bully."

Without waiting for a response she stormed to the ladies' room. Or at least she wanted to storm. What she managed was a pathetic hobble. Once inside the bathroom, she leaned against the wall and bent over to squeeze her ankle. She had to bite down on her lip to keep from crying out. The stupid thing throbbed but it didn't hurt badly enough to warrant tears. One huge drop of moisture clung to the end of her nose and dripped to the floor in front of her.

She squeezed her nose the entire time that she used the toilet and then scrubbed her face with soap and water. Her ponytail was beyond salvaging, so she yanked off the band and pulled the tangled mass into a bun at her nape, shoving the stubborn curls that popped free in place, and waited for the tears to stop.

When she stepped back out, Samir was leaning against a wall across from the ladies' room, one knee bent and resting on the roughened bricks behind him. His heavy burnt-gold hair shone under the fluorescent lights. An unfamiliar flash of raw pain and exhaustion flared in his honey-brown eyes when he looked up at her. But he blinked it away before pushing himself off the wall and walking toward her.

"Quite a temper you've got there," he said, searching her face in that way that made her want to look away. And it brought the anger back full force.

She headed toward the exit without responding.

"Slow down, Mili. You're limping." He grasped her arm. The same possessive familiarity of his gaze heated his touch.

She pulled her arm away and kept walking.

"Mili, seriously, you can't possibly be such a hypocrite. You know how badly you wanted to go to the wedding. How can you be this mad at me for helping you?"

"Helping me? You've known me, what, all of three weeks? What makes you an expert on what I want? How dare you call me a hypocrite, you . . . you . . . arrogant donkey!"

He looked startled. His mouth quirked. She wanted to dig her nails into those shoulders of his and shake him until his perfect white teeth rattled. She opened her own car door and sank into the seat.

"So, you're saying you truly were not dying to go to Ridhi's wedding?"

"For someone who thinks he knows what I want, can't you figure out I don't want to talk to you? Leave me alone."

His lips quirked some more as he turned the key in the ignition. "So you aren't going to answer the real question?"

Why would she? She didn't owe the big, kidnapping bully answers.

Not that she had an answer. Her opinion about weddings, about marriage in general, was getting more and more turbulent by the day. And it made her so angry, so incredibly sad, she felt like she couldn't go on. Stupid wetness pushed at her eyelids, and her nose, her stupid nose started dripping. If she stayed very silent, maybe he wouldn't notice she was crying.

"Mili?" She hated the tenderness in his voice. He made one of his racetrack maneuvers and pulled into another spot instead of leaving the parking lot. "Are you crying?"

"No, it's raining, but only on my face."

Again that quirking of the lips. She glared at him, daring him to laugh at her.

"I thought Ridhi was your best friend. I'm sorry. Listen, we'll turn around." He killed the engine and turned around to face her.

She swiped her cheeks with her wrists. "Ridhi's not my best

friend, you . . . you . . . idiot, she's the sister I never had. Here in this foreign country she's been my family."

"In that case, we really shouldn't go to her wedding."

She smacked him hard on his shoulder. "You think you are so funny, don't you?"

"I'm the one being funny?" He looked so incredulous that if she weren't so livid she'd smile.

"Of course I'd give anything to go. But I can't go to a wedding like this. And you can't just kidnap me and whisk me off somewhere without asking me what I want. I am not a child. I'm wearing jeans and a T-shirt. You can't show up at a wedding with nothing to wear, with nothing to give the bride. I don't even have a toothbrush. And I have the world's worst morning breath."

He threw his head back and laughed. He had been doing that a lot lately. "Well, I kind of knew that. So I packed your toothbrush."

"You packed my toothbrush?" Mili couldn't remember the last time she had been so angry with someone. "How dare you? You dug through my private things? Who do you think you are?" She pushed the door open. She needed to get out of the car.

He jumped out of the car, ran around to her side and squatted in front of her. His arm rested on the car door, making his biceps bulge a foot from her face. He shone one of his intense looks into her eyes. "Hey, Mili, I didn't go through your things. I would never do that. I found your bag packed and sitting in your living room when I went in there to write. And your brush was sitting right there on your sink."

Her stupid nose started running again. After last night's conversation, she had wanted to go so badly she had decided to take him up on his offer and packed. Then she'd realized how stupid she was being. But she'd forgotten about the bag.

"I saw the bag. That's how I knew how much you wanted to go."

"And you thought it was okay to make that decision for me? To do my thinking for me? Just because you took care of me doesn't give you the right to control me, Samir."

He was leaning too close to her now. She pushed him away. He didn't budge. "Control you? What are you talking about? I've never seen you this angry. What is your problem, Mili?"

"Let me think. Oh yes, maybe being kidnapped is my problem. Maybe being treated like your private property is my problem. Maybe not being allowed to make my own choices is my problem." Her voice cracked and the frown between his brows deepened.

"The only reason I did this is because I thought it was what *you* wanted. I never meant to take away your choices. This was about what you wanted. Cross my heart." But he crossed her heart instead. One tentative finger traced a cross exactly where her heart suddenly and inexplicably started thudding out a frantic rhythm. He trailed the finger to her chin and lifted it up so she stared into his golden eyes. "Do you really want to go home?"

Now she felt even more stupid. Very warm all over and very stupid. And very embarrassed. He had tried to do something nice and she had thrown the biggest tantrum of her life. She wished he would just stop trying to pay her back for his precious script. She wished she didn't see in his eyes what she saw.

His finger turned warm on her chin and trailed her jaw. She tried to pull his hand away, but the closeness of his huge, warm, perfectly sculpted body emanated so much comfort she felt drugged, unable to break the contact between them. Her fingers rested on his. "No, it's too late to turn back," she said, and he smiled his golden smile.

How could a creature this glorious, a soul this beautiful possibly smile at her as if . . . as if . . . No. He felt sorry for her. That's all it was. It couldn't be anything more. Because if it was, they couldn't be friends anymore. Of course he felt sorry for her. She had been in perpetual need of rescuing ever since she'd met him.

In that case, why let him off easy?

The funniest thought struck her. His eyes narrowed as he watched her.

"We're halfway there," she said. "You really should meet Ridhi. In fact, I can't wait for you to meet her."

Her big bully was about to be taught the lesson of a lifetime.

14

Samir had never in his life heard a more terrifyingly nasal, a more earsplittingly high-pitched voice. "Mill! I can't believe you're here, Mill!" The shrieking girl flew down the wide granite stairs of the colonnaded mansion like a squawking bird and flung herself at Mili. Substantially taller and bigger than Mili, she picked her up and spun her around like a rag doll before plunking her down on the sweeping driveway.

Samir watched in horror as Mili tried to land on her good foot, but she couldn't quite manage it and stumbled backward. Fortunately he was close enough to catch her. She turned around and gave him one of those grateful looks he despised. He couldn't find the generosity in his heart to acknowledge it. He was too distracted by the screaming banshee, who wouldn't stop jumping up and down like a two-year-old.

"Mummy, Daddy, come, look, see. Mili's here."

A veritable caravan of people materialized in response to her shrieks. They were all dressed in shimmering gauzes and silks in colors almost as jarringly loud as she was.

Mili beamed as if this was the exact kind of craziness she had been missing in her life.

"Mill, this is Mummy, Daddy, my *maasi*, my *chachi*, my *chacha*, my *taaya*." The list of uncles and aunts went on and on.

How so many people had gathered in a span of one week boggled his mind. Mili bent over and touched the feet of every one of the elders she was introduced to, in the traditional gesture of re-spect, and it was a substantial number. They all hugged her and ruffled her hair as if she were the long-lost daughter of their heart.

Mummyji held her the longest. She pressed Mili's flushed face against her ample satin-clad bosom and wiped her eyes with the chiffon scarf draped around her shoulders. "Oh, *beta*, what we owe you! Oh, how much we owe you!" she kept repeating between sobs. Suddenly she grabbed her hapless son by the sleeve and pulled him toward her. "See who's here. The girl who saved your family's honor."

Ranvir blinked and at least twenty distinct shades of pink flashed across his doughy cheeks.

"She's dark but she's pretty," one of the army of aunties said from behind Samir.

Samir ground his teeth. Ridhi started laughing, an astounding neighing sound that made her shrieks sound like music in compar-ison. Samir plugged the ear closer to her with his finger.

"Mummy, you can't set Ranvir up with Mili." More neighing laughter. "At least think before you start your matchmaking. Mili's ma—"

Mili yanked Ridhi away from her mother, blushing even more furiously than Doughboy. She pointed at Samir, her look exactly that of a child caught with her hand in a cookie jar. "Ridhi, this is—"

Before Mili could say anything Ridhi let out another glass-shattering neigh. "Oh my God! Ohmygod! Oh. My. God. Mili, you didn't tell me *he* was going to be here. Oh my God, you were so wrong. He came!"

Mili looked like someone had stabbed her in the chest. Color drained from her face.

Ridhi ran up to Samir and threw her arms around him. "Oh my God. I have been dying to meet you. Oh my—"

"Ridhi, this is Samir, our new neighbor. He drove me here." Mili cut the madwoman off and Samir wanted to hug her. If that horrendous voice formed the words *Oh my God* one more time, he would have to dump Mili in the car and head back to Ypsilanti right this minute.

Ridhi jumped out of Samir's arms as if he suddenly oozed pus and glared at him. "This is the guy who punched Ranvir?" She planted one hand on her hip and gave Mili one of those loaded woman-to-woman looks that women thought were so subtle.

Fortunately, one of the aunties dragged her into the house. "*Arrey*, enough of your *tamasha*-drama. Come on inside and act like a bride for a change."

He had no idea who the white-haired woman was, but despite being blinded by her parrot-green sari and fuchsia lips, Samir wanted to hoist her on his shoulders and give her anything she desired.

Ridhi grabbed Mili's arm and yanked her into the house behind her. The next time she handled Mili like a rag doll Samir was going to kill her with his bare hands, bride or not.

Samir looked so tortured when Mili grabbed his arm and pulled him into the house behind her she wanted to laugh. Served him right for being such a bully. But one step into the house and Mili knew she would never ever be able to repay him for bringing her here.

It was like stepping over the chasm of time and distance and landing right back home in India. They had arrived just in time for the Ladies' Singing program that was such an integral part of Punjabi weddings. Mili had never actually been to a Punjabi wedding, but this looked exactly like the dazzling affairs she'd seen in films. The entire brightly lit house vibrated with music, and the sound of people shouting over the music. Someone pulled Ridhi away and started doing a bhangra dance with her in the middle of a gigantic hall, which literally was the size of the entire university union.

Mili spun around a full circle, taking the house in. It was even larger than her husband's ancestral *haveli*. And that home was built for joint families. For generations, three to four brothers and their families had lived in the *haveli* along with the families of the servants who took care of the grounds and the house. All told, a good thirty odd people had lived in the *haveli* at any given time. Not anymore of course. Ever since Virat's grandfather had died the *haveli* had been locked up and left to disintegrate.

Virat and his mother had left Balpur soon after her wedding twenty years ago and never returned. Mili's husband had been so intent on avoiding her he hadn't even come back for his own grandfather's funeral. Not even to check up on the grand old house with its crumbling arches and verandahs. She had done everything she could. She had even bought a bucket of cement and patched up the roof herself when the rains made the kitchen flood. The thought of their family's heritage being left to rot like that made her so incredibly angry, so sad, she could hardly bear it.

When she and Virat were finally together the first responsibility they would fulfill as a couple was taking care of the *haveli*. Who else would do it? She had heard there was a half brother but her grandmother never talked about him. In fact, no one in Balpur ever spoke of him.

Samir gave her one of those *help me* looks as the auntie in the sari the exact green of an Indian parrot pulled him to the middle of the dancing crowd. Another three white-haired women surrounded him, bopping their shoulders and throwing their hands in the air. Mili was about to help him when Ridhi swung her around.

"Have you eaten anything?" She took a bite of the samosa she was holding and then stuffed the rest of the flaky, potato-filled pastry into Mili's mouth before dragging her toward the sweeping staircase, which of course was straight out of a Bollywood film.

"It's the *sangeet* today. You're my best friend. You can't possibly be wearing *that*." She made a face that suggested Mili needed to be fumigated. "Come on. Let's see if we can fit you into something of mine." She dragged Mili upstairs.

Ridhi's room was another union-sized spectacle with pink sequins, baubles, beads, and shimmering chiffon everywhere.

"I was in this Bollywood phase," Ridhi said sheepishly. "I wanted a room that looked like a Bollywood dance number, so Mummy had an interior designer cousin ship all this stuff over from India." Ridhi threw herself on the huge circular bed in the center of the room with yards and yards of filmy fabric hanging from the ceiling like a royal canopy.

"*Was* in a Bollywood phase?" Mili teased.

Ridhi made a face and pulled Mili into a closet the size of their entire apartment. Mili's mouth dropped open.

"Mummy likes clothes," Ridhi said, riffling through the rainbow of silk and chiffon. "She wanted to be a Bollywood designer before she married Daddy and moved here."

Saris, *salwar kameezes, ghaghras* in every color, every shade, and apparently every style covered three entire walls.

"Ridhi." Mili stood frozen in place. "How did you ever live in our apartment?"

"What do you mean?" Ridhi pulled a few hangers out and placed them on a dress-stand contraption.

"I mean look at this." Mili swept her arms around the veritable clothing store around her.

Ridhi pulled two *kurtis* from hangers and slung them on the contraption. "You know what it feels like to be in love, Mill. None of this matters. I didn't want any of it when Mummy and Daddy wouldn't let me be with Ravi. It totally drove them nuts when I didn't take their money, when I worked at Panda Kong. And see, they learned their lesson." She held a *kurti* against Mili and frowned. "You are like exactly half my size."

Ridhi was more than half a foot taller than Mili. She didn't have an inch of pudginess on her, but she had wide shoulders and lush curves that made her look exactly like those Amazons from Greek mythology.

"I have an idea." Ridhi turned back to the clothes. "And by the way, what's the story with this Samir guy?" She slid hangers back and forth, searching for something.

"No story. He just moved into our building. He knew someone from my village, so he stopped by to say hi and we . . . we became friends."

"Interesting." Ridhi pulled out two stringy chiffon blouses and pushed them toward Mili. "He doesn't look at you like you're a friend." She wiggled her brows.

Mili crinkled her nose. "Don't be ridiculous. Some mental stuff happened after you left. He's just been really helpful." Talk about understatements.

"Helpful?" Before Ridhi could say more a loud buzz pierced the air.

"Shit." Ridhi ran to what looked like a hi-tech radio mounted on the wall and jabbed a button. "Ya, Mummy?"

"Ridhika Kapoor, do you have any sense at all? It's eight-thirty. Your guests are sitting around twiddling their thumbs and wondering where the bride is." Ridhi's mom was back in full drama mode. Did she even have another mode? "Where are you? Ravi's here. The poor child has been sitting here waiting patiently."

"The poor child?" Mili mouthed at Ridhi. Talk about change of heart.

Ridhi rolled her eyes so far into her head, Mili giggled.

"I'm changing, Mummy. I'm coming. Two minutes." Ridhi ran back to the closet and thrust a blue chiffon blouse at Mili.

Mili stared at the ball of strings in her hand. "You can't be serious," she said to Ridhi. Where was the actual fabric that made up whatever this piece of clothing was supposed to be?

"Hurry up and try it on. It's a short top on me but I think it will be the perfect *kurta* length on you, and I'll give you *churidar* pants and you'll have a full *churidar* suit."

"But this doesn't have sleeves. Actually it doesn't even have shoulders. It only has strings." Mili held the thing up and shook the strings at Ridhi.

"And you will look lovely in it. Come on, Mummy will kill me if I'm not down in two minutes." She started pulling Mili's T-shirt off. "It's my wedding, Mili. I don't think you're allowed to argue with me."

"Yeah, because otherwise arguing with you is so very productive."

"I don't understand why everyone keeps saying that. Now take your clothes off or you'll get me skinned alive."

Mili laughed and pulled the strappy concoction on. She had to admit the blue-green was rather lovely and the fabric slithered like cool liquid over her skin.

"OMG!" Ridhi slapped her hands to her cheeks. "So beautiful." She fanned her face as if she were trying to stop herself from crying, looking exactly like her mother.

She turned Mili around to face a mirror.

Mili swallowed. *Beautiful* wasn't quite the word that sprang to mind. "There's too much skin showing." She adjusted the bodice and tried to spread the mass of strings over her shoulders so they covered more. The most skin she had ever shown was in her sleeveless kurtas. And those her *naani* only let her wear because she was an officer's wife.

I suppose an officer will want his wife to dress like a city girl . . . I suppose an officer will want his wife to read those books . . . I suppose an officer will want his wife to . . .

It was Naani's excuse for everything. And Mili didn't feel even the slightest bit guilty for milking it. If it weren't for Naani's raging need to turn her into the perfect officer's wife Mili would never have studied past tenth grade, and she definitely would never have been allowed to go to Jaipur University. As for coming to America, with that she had given poor Naani no choice.

Ridhi slapped away Mili's hand when she tried to pull the neckline higher and started tying the strings that crisscrossed Mili's back and held the flimsy thing in place. When Mili was all tied up, there was one thing she was sure of: if her *naani* ever saw her like this, she would lock her in a room and never let her out until Virat himself came back and took her away.

"May I at least have a *duppata* or a stole?" Something to wrap around herself and make her halfway decent.

"Don't be ridiculous," Ridhi said, handing her a pair of tights. "If I looked like that in anything I would never cover it up and I would never take it off. What size is your waist, Mill, twelve?"

"How would I know? Who measures their waist?"

"Um, everyone with two X chromosomes."

"I'm not leaving this closet until you give me a *duppata*. The entire household does not need to see my chromosomes." Mili pulled off her jeans and pulled on the tights and inspected the results in the mirror. The tights fit perfectly, gathering around her ankles and snugly hugging her calves and her thighs. But she had to remember never to bend over as long as she wore this blouse.

"And you call me stubborn."

Mili gave Ridhi her sweetest smile and held out her hand for the *duppata*. The intercom buzzed again. Ridhi held down the button. "Mummy, I said I'm coming," she said so loudly Mili wondered why they even needed the intercom.

She shoved a chiffon *duppata* into Mili's hands. "Go find your Romeo. I'll bet he's looking for you."

"Ridhi, please!" Mili said as Ridhi pushed her out of the room.

Mili tried to wrap the *duppata* around herself but Ridhi, the traitorous sneak, had given her a thin skinny scarf. She tugged and pulled it around herself to no avail. What she should've been doing was holding on to the railing instead of struggling with the scarf, because with her first step onto the sweeping stairs two things happened. One, her ankle did a funny twitching thing and turned to rubber. And two, she caught Samir looking up at her and her knees followed suit. Her arms flew out like wings, flailing wildly for support, and her body lurched forward into free-fall.

She landed with a thud against his chest. Her breasts flattened against hard muscle. One powerful arm wrapped around her waist while the other arm grabbed the railing and kept them both from falling. She found her nose squished against the exact center of his chest, which meant her lips were also pressed against his warm cotton-covered skin. Rich magazine fold perfume filled her head. Her senses pushed past the smell, searching for that other scent she knew she would find. The scent of the desert, of hot sand and warm rain. She breathed it in as her fingers found the bulges on his arms, and held on to them unbidden.

He pulled away and swept her up in his arms as if she were a child. One arm under her shoulders, one in the crook of her knees. No, not quite like a child. Hot need cramped in her belly. A cheer rose from the crowd, followed by claps and wolf whistles. He spun around, refusing to meet her gaze. Color kissed his golden cheeks. With slightly dazed eyes he took in the crowd at the bottom of the stairs.

"Put me down," she hissed. "What are you doing?"

He glared at her. "What are *you* doing? If you fall with that ankle, you could damage it permanently. Did you lose your mind when you crashed your bike?" He carried her down the stairs. The crowd parted for them. He dumped her on a puffy bench in the hallway.

"Please," she said into his ear. "Please don't make a scene. Everyone is watching."

He took in the expression on her face. She must've looked mortified because when he straightened up and faced the crowd, he had plastered a cocky grin across his face. "She's fine. Everything's okay. She was just born clumsy. Nothing more to it."

The crowd laughed and murmured their concern. Hands patted Mili's head and everyone dispersed into the kitchen and the living room.

"Born clumsy?" Mili glared up at Samir. But color suffused her cheeks and her eyes did that bashful thing they did when she was pretending to be angrier at him than she was. The ache that had set off in his chest when he'd seen her coming down the stairs struggling with her scarf took on an intensified burn.

It had been hard enough when she wore those boxlike T-shirts on her un-boxlike body. The women he went out with routinely wore a fraction of the clothing her friend had obviously forced her into. But the last thing he needed to see, to know, was that she blushed with her entire body, that the glistening luminosity of her skin wasn't restricted to her face, to her arms. *Shit*, he was thinking about the skin on her arms. And he couldn't believe how bloody erotic the thought was. He felt like one of those lecherous crotch-scratching *mawalis* who hung around street corners ogling women for sport. How many of those fuckers had he punched in the face?

He sat down next to her and desperately stared at the substantial crowd of unattractive, out-of-shape aunties wrapped in all forms of gaudy silk. But it relaxed him only a little. What he really needed was to get out of here and get laid. Fast. It had been a month, and that was a fucking record. This asceticism thing wasn't for him.

She twisted around next to him and planted her hand on her waist. The memory of how perfectly that waist fit in his hands burned on his palms, on his fingers. The action made her breasts heave in that stupid top and the oxygen in the room thinned. Her breasts were exactly the way he'd known they'd be, right down to the rosy blush, the lush rise—not looking at those breasts like one of those fucking lechers was going to kill him.

She blinked those how-can-they-be-real lashes, adding innocence to the anger flashing in her eyes, and earned herself a glare of mammoth proportions. "What, now you're going to yell at me for saving your life?" Great, now he was growling like a Mogul warrior from a period saga.

"Oh, is that what you did?" Her tone was angelic. "Because I thought you were trying to"—here her voice changed to a hiss—"kill me."

"By leaping up the stairs like some superhero and preventing you from bouncing down the tower of terror on your bum?"

"No, by—by—never mind." She colored even more and looked at her toes, and he felt like a bastard beyond compare. It was a feeling he had quite enjoyed until recently. Now he never wanted to feel this way again as long as he lived. Not with her.

He softened his tone. "Is your foot okay?"

Her head fell forward until her chin touched her chest and her curls spilled around her mortified face.

"Yes, Mili, is your foot okay?" The horrible nasal twang of Ridhi's voice destroyed the tenderness bubbling in his chest. Horse-woman threw a suspicious glare at him. "What are you two doing here when everyone else is in the other room?"

Samir gave Mili's friend his hottest smile. "We were making out. And now you've gone and killed the mood." He got up and stalked away without a backward glance.

15

Mili found Samir in the most unlikely of places. After he had stormed off in the style of Prince Salim in the Mogul saga *Mugal-e-Azam*, she had expected to find him brooding in some corner. Instead he was standing at the huge kitchen island—the only man in the room—surrounded by women of every age much like Lord Krishna and the worshiping village belles who couldn't resist him when he played his flute. Ridhi's two grandmothers flanked him on either side. Ridhi's niece was sandwiched between him and the kitchen island, watching his hands deftly roll balls of dough into thin, perfectly round rotis with a rolling pin.

When Mili entered the room he did nothing more than throw her the most cursory of glances. "There," he said, lifting the rolling pin off the roti and letting the little girl peel it off the wooden block. He helped her lay it on a sheet of butter paper next to several identical rotis.

"Fifteen!" one of the grannies announced, staring at his handiwork with an admiration that bordered on reverence. All the women standing around the island clapped.

Three cousins somewhere between the ages of thirteen and twenty furiously stuffed balls of seasoned potatoes into the rotis Samir had rolled out and tried to fold them into conical samosas. And failed miserably.

"You girls should be ashamed. Samir is rolling out the rotis faster than three of you can stuff the samosas. A man can beat you at cooking? What a generation of girls we have raised, *Didi!*" the grandmother making the potato balls said to the grandmother making the dough balls.

"Beating them at sports and academics was easy enough, but cooking too?" Samir *tsked*. The girls huffed and then ruined the effect by giggling.

"Great, he's sexist too." Ridhi dragged Mili into the kitchen and inserted herself into the audience around the island.

"Yeah, I'm so sexist I'm rolling out samosas for your wedding while you watch," he said without stopping what he was doing. The rolling pin moved over the dough in clean strokes, spreading it into a perfect circle.

Ridhi glowered at him. He looked bored.

"Are you a chef, *beta?* Did you go to one of those cooking-type schools?" right-hand-side granny asked.

"*Culinary* school, Naani," the little girl helping Samir said.

"Ah, finally a competent girl. There's hope for *womanity* yet." He patted the little girl on the head. "No, Naaniji, I didn't go to culinary school, I just listened when my mother taught me things," he said in an angelic tone that hid all sorts of arrogance.

Mili met his gaze and circled the island to where the girls were failing so miserably at stuffing the samosas. "Oh, there *is* hope yet." She faced him across the granite. "But only for *womanity*. There is absolutely no hope for you, mister."

He tried to give her a bored look too but his eyes lit with amusement. Amusement and something far warmer.

The little girl giggled and looked up at Samir. "*Womanity* is not even a real word."

"Samir doesn't get reality, *beta*. Let's give him a lesson in reality *and* humility, shall we?"

His golden eyes met the challenge in hers. "And who's going to beat me, you?"

"Single-handedly." She waved the three girls away and they almost sank to the floor in relief. A cheer went up around the island. "Ready?" she asked him.

The smile he was holding back split across his face. Mili removed the scarf from around her shoulders, slung it across herself, and knotted it at her waist. The battle was on.

She picked one rolled roti off the paper, laid it flat on one open palm, and flicked her wrist to give it a spin. More cheering. Samir raised an impressed brow.

Good. Arrogant donkey.

He picked up a dough ball, spun it up in the air, then caught it and slapped it on the rolling board.

Both their hands started to fly.

Mili folded the roti, flipping the edges to make a cone, smacked potatoes in the center, pinched the edges together, and one perfect samosa was ready just as Samir finished rolling out another roti. His roti landed on the paper at the exact same moment as the perfect conical samosa joined the less skillfully put-together ones from before.

Everyone cheered. Samir joined them and clapped. Mili tightened the scarf around her waist and curtsied.

One of the grannies laughed so hard someone had to bring her water.

They went for another round, then another. Each time they finished at exactly the same moment.

One of Ridhi's aunts put a huge pot of oil on the stove and started to fry the samosas. Soon the entire house was doused with the smell of freshly frying dough. The samosas disappeared faster than they could fry them.

Samir and Mili continued to work together, their hands in perfect synch, their gazes measuring each other's actions and falling in step, the rest of the world a buzz of activity around them.

"Ravi makes really good *dosas*," Ridhi pouted, inserting herself between them.

Samir promptly volunteered Ravi to fry the samosas, much to the grandmothers' chagrin.

"For shame—what kind of household puts the groom to work?"

"I've been making dough balls for half an hour, Naani, why can't he?" Ridhi whined.

"Because you're a woman. It's your place," Samir said, and

Ridhi and Mili both picked up handfuls of flour and dumped it on him.

That earned them both a sound scolding from the grannies and exaggerated indignation from Samir. "Girls these days, Naani," he said, shaking his head dolefully. "No grace. No refinement. Would you ever throw flour on a guest?"

That earned him bigger handfuls of flour, until Ridhi's mom bellowed across the kitchen for them to stop.

Before long the samosas were all fried and gone. Bhangra music started to pump from the backyard. The DJ had finished setting up. Everyone including the grannies ran out into the yard to check out the dance floor that had been installed across the lawn.

Samir stood by Mili's side at the kitchen window and together they watched the excitement. Suddenly the entire backyard sparkled to life. Thousands of tiny blue and white lights twinkled across every tree, every bush, every retaining wall. Thumping bhangra beats started up and the crowd threw up its arms in unison and broke into dance.

"And here I thought the way they showed Punjabi weddings in movies was a stereotype. These people are loony." Samir spun his finger around his temple like a five-year-old and Mili had the strangest urge to ruffle his hair. And pull him close. She reached up and wiped the flour off his nose and cheeks.

"Thanks." His laughing eyes darkened to smoky amber as he watched her.

"You should clean up," Mili said, ignoring the look on his face.

"I like it better when you do it for me." He didn't touch her, but he looked like he wanted to.

Mili's hand froze on his cheek. She pulled it away and stepped back, but only a little bit. No point letting him know how much he rattled her. "I think we got some on your shirt too."

"Even better."

She whacked his arm and dragged him by the sleeve to the bathroom.

"Are you coming in there with me?" He was all innocence.

"Samir. Shut up."

"What? You need to clean up too." He picked some flour off his shirt and flicked it on her.

"Samir, you can't talk to me like that."

"Like what?"

He was impossible. But in this moment she couldn't muster up any real anger. She pushed him inside the bathroom and pulled the door shut.

"Don't start dancing without me," he said from behind the door. Then suddenly he opened the door and stuck his head out, his brow furrowed with concern, his eyes so soft—the real Samir, not the rogue he loved to play. "Mili, you're not going anywhere near that dance floor. You need to rest your foot, okay?"

She pushed him back in and slammed the door in his face. A smile glowed in her heart and spilled to her lips. She headed for the backyard and stopped dead in her tracks when she passed the hallway mirror. Who was that girl staring back at her? She dusted off the stray specks of flour from her nose. But she refused to meet her own eyes or acknowledge what she caught shining in them.

Samir made his way across the suddenly empty house to the backyard and found Mili watching the crowded dance floor. She was perched on a patio wall, her body bobbing up and down to the beat. It wasn't an obvious movement. In fact it was so subtle you wouldn't see it if you didn't know how she usually held herself. There was something lyrical in the angle of her spine, in the tilt of her head. The lines of her body had the grace of a classical dancer and yet she was the clumsiest person he knew. She fell and she fell.

He had no idea how she knew he had stepped outside but she turned around and looked for him. Her eyes searched until they picked him out of the crowd, her smile a torchlight, her eyes flash-bulbs shining a light into him. All on their own his legs moved past the tables and candles and chattering people and took him to the patio wall where she sat, her feet dangling a few inches above the grass. She patted the concrete next to her and indicated the dance floor with her chin.

"No kidding. They're dancing," he wanted to say. But there

was something so comforting about this silent communication between them he couldn't disturb it.

He dropped next to her on the wall and they sat there together watching the dance floor. One thing he'd say about Punjabis, they could dance. Even the ones who didn't dance well could dance. They threw themselves into it, completely unselfconscious even when they were miles off the beat. From the two-year-olds to the ninety-year-olds, there was a wild abandon to their moves and right here, right now, he didn't feel like making fun of it.

"You like to dance," he said. Somehow he knew she loved it.

She turned to him, her smile so bright it hurt to look at her. "Not this kind of dancing. But when all the women in our village gather for the *Ghoomar* at the Teej festival and for *Garba* at Navratri we dance all night until the sun comes up. I'm always the last to leave. My *naani* has to drag me away and even then I can't get myself to fall asleep. Sometimes after Naani starts snoring I get out of bed and continue to dance."

He swallowed. What could he say to that? Except that he knew exactly how she must look with the bangles jingling at her wrists and anklets tinkling at her ankles as she twirled and her *ghagra* skirt spun a perfect circle around her.

A flush spread across her cheeks, as if she couldn't believe she'd just told him what she had. She stared at her toes, then looked back up at him. "You don't like to dance." She tried to make it a statement but the subtlest hint of hope leaked into her voice and hooked a finger around his heart.

"Not always."

"Ah. So you like to *go* dancing, like they do here in the west." That wasn't a question either.

"We do it there in the east too." He flicked his chin as if "the east" were next door.

"Isn't it amazing, Samir, how we're both from India but our Indias are so different?"

An intense need to know what her India was like flooded through Samir. He wanted to know where she lived, where she ate, what her precious *naani* looked like. He wanted to know why a person this sweet, this guileless, would send a wounded man's family a legal notice to claim his family home. There had to be something that had driven her to it. She wasn't spiteful and she sure as hell wasn't greedy. Then what the fuck was it?

"So in *the east*, when you go dancing, how do you dance?"

"It depends. If you go with a bunch of friends it's pretty much like this." He waved his hand at the crowd bobbing and shimmying to the beat as one. "If you go as a couple, you generally go to a place with slower music."

She lowered her lids and her lush lashes splayed against cheeks that couldn't seem to stop blushing. "And what do you do to the slower music?"

Maybe Mili shouldn't have asked the question because Samir hopped off the wall and strode to the DJ. By the time he came back, the catchy beat of the bhangra faded into the lilting strains of a much slower song.

"Pehla Nasha"—the slow-burning flush of first love. It was one of her favorite songs.

Samir held out his hand. "May I?" His gaze sent a slow fire burning through her. She let him take her hand and lead her to the dance floor.

"I thought I wasn't allowed to dance." She smiled up at him.

"I have a plan," he said. His eyes glowed with that arrogant mischief she was starting to realize wasn't arrogance at all but absolute and utter comfort in his own skin. He raised his eyebrows the slightest bit, adding a touch of mystery to his words.

He must be a very good director, she thought out of the blue.

"Kick off your shoes," he whispered into her ear.

When she didn't, he stepped out of his own shoes and waited until she did the same.

He placed his huge hands on her waist. "Put your feet on mine." He lifted her up and off her feet.

Her bare feet landed on his bare feet.

"Oof," he said and she hopped off.

"I'm sorry. I'm too heavy."

He laughed. "You're lighter than my high school backpack." He lifted her up again and put her back on his feet.

She dug her toes into his feet. "You're horrid," she said in the Hindi of her village.

"Ouch. That hurt." He mirrored her dialect.

"Good."

He wrapped his arms around her and pulled her closer. "It might help if you held on."

She tried to reach around him, but she couldn't bring herself to be that bold. Instead she let her hands rest on his arms. He started to move and she had to tighten her hold. Her elbows hooked around his, her hands cupped the beautiful bulges of his arms in a perfect fit.

His body picked up the beat, soft and lilting though it was. He swayed with her in his arms, moving her feet with his in the tiniest gliding steps. Where her skin touched his she felt warm. Everywhere else she burned. But it was the softest burn, not a hint of discomfort in it.

"Is this comfortable?" he asked against her ear.

She nodded and looked down at their feet. Her size-four-and-a-half feet on his boat feet.

"Now what do we do?" She leaned back and looked up at him.

"We don't lean back like that"—he tucked her head against his chest—"or we fall over." His chin rested on her head.

"And then?"

"Then we listen to the music." He moved in time to the music, little bobs and sways. "We let the music pour into us." His feet lifted a little higher, moved back and forth, taking her with him. "We let the rhythm move us." He spun with her in his arms, little twists. Two this way, one that way. Two steps forward, two steps back.

It was the most amazing feeling. His shoulders, his hips, his arms, all of him carried all of her, his movements so subtle it was as if they weren't moving at all, at least not on the outside. On the inside they were each move, each beat, each vibration.

She was dimly aware of people dancing around her. One song

dissolved into the next. The slow songs stopped and the fast ones started up again. But they had found their rhythm and draped it around themselves like a cape and under it every little part of them danced.

Finally when Mili had lost count of how many songs had passed Samir pulled away. He lifted her off his feet and put her back on the floor where she continued to sway. Laughing, he took her hand and led her off the dance floor. She followed him but the music continued to beat in her heart.

"Is your foot okay?" he asked, picking up their shoes and leading her to a relatively isolated corner of the patio.

"It's great." She wiggled her toes. "Yours?"

"My feet are fine. They're very happy to meet yours." He smiled. Not his usual movie-poster smolder, but his little-boy smile. Then he squatted next to her and before she could stop him he slipped her sandals onto her feet. Sparks ignited where his fingers brushed her skin. He pulled away with a jerk.

Her breath heated and stuck in her throat. Her face flamed.

Thank God he didn't look up. Instead he turned to his own shoes and started lacing them up.

"Are your feet really a size fourteen?" she said, mostly to push the breath out of her lungs.

He looked up, surprised.

"You told me at the hospital, remember?"

"Oh yeah, that day."

His shoes were still discolored from being washed, the brown leather a shade darker where she'd thrown up.

"I'm sorry I threw up on your shoes."

He rose to his full height and she had to lean her head back to keep looking at him. "Don't worry about it. My feet do get in the way, given their size." He smiled again and relief washed through her.

"Seriously, fourteen *is* abnormal!"

"Abnormal?" He raised one eyebrow, then shrugged. "Guess you'd think that if your feet were too small to even hold you up."

"At least mine don't get in the way of throw-up."

"At least no one can tip me over with one finger." The hot-hero smile was back full force.

"No one can tip me over with—"

He tipped her over with one hand, then reached around and held her up with the other.

She glared at him. "You did not use one fing—"

He did it again. This time with one finger. Only this time when he held her up, he pulled her close.

She flattened her hands against his chest and pushed away, needing to put distance between them. "That was not funny, Samir."

"You're right. I'm sorry." But he grinned from ear to ear. Little boy, hot hero, all those Samirs fused into one.

"It's nice when you're this agreeable. And rare." How could she not smile back at him?

He sat down on the patio steps and helped her down next to him. "I thought you said I was the most decent guy you'd ever met." He beckoned to a passing waiter and grabbed two glasses from his tray.

"You have your moments. You were wonderful in the kitchen, by the way. I think all the aunties are a little bit in love with you."

"Not the grannies?" He held out both glasses to her, orange juice and burgundy wine.

"Oh, definitely the grannies." She took the orange juice and smelled it, just to make sure there was no alcohol.

He didn't tease her about it. He took a sip from his glass and watched her over the rim. "And?"

She'd never seen him like this. This wide open. "And you were amazing. Your mother is a really good teacher."

He put his glass down, leaned back on his arms, and stared up at the sky. "The best."

"You said you used to have a hard time leaving her when you were a child. Were you a shy child?"

"No, not shy. Terrified."

"Of what?"

He continued to study the shimmering blanket of stars. "Of everything. Of the dark, of crowds, of being left alone." He paused. His Adam's apple bobbed as he swallowed. "My birth mother dropped me off on my grandparents' doorstep and never looked back."

"Oh God, Samir. I'm sorry." She inched closer, but didn't touch him.

"No. It was the best thing that ever happened to me. Baiji took me in. In every way it is possible to take a child in. It was love at first sight, she always says." He almost smiled.

"And your father?"

"He was Baiji's husband. He left my older brother and Baiji to come to America to get his master's degree and never went back home. He met my birth mother here, in America. They had me. And then he died in a car crash. After his death she no longer wanted me. She took me to India, handed me off to my grandparents, and came back here."

Mili wrapped her arms around herself. "How old were you?"

"Five."

Her throat constricted. "Do you remember her?"

He was quiet for so long, she didn't think he'd answer, but then he spoke. "I remember her name. Sara. Sara Willis. And that we lived on some sort of farm with a big red barn in a place called Munroe, Michigan. Other than that I remember feelings. I remember how the house we lived in felt. How the open land around the house felt, and the open sky. I remember how she felt. You know, not how she looked, but how she felt."

Her tears made his utterly still form wobble next to her. "How did she feel?"

"Wet. She felt sad and wet. Watery and light, like mist, like—" But he couldn't say more. He reached out and wiped her tears.

She pushed her cheek into his palm. "I don't remember anything."

His thumb caressed her cheek.

"Not one thing. Not a smell, not a feeling, nothing. I've seen one picture. So, I don't even have those fake photo-inspired memories all children are supposed to have of their own childhood."

"How old?"

"I was two. My father had just got a job as a professor in Delhi University. My parents were coming home after the interview to pick me up from my grandmother's house and take me back to Delhi. Their train ran off its track and into the Yamuna river. Not a single passenger survived."

He wrapped his arm around her, gathered her into himself. She sidled into his warmth.

For a long time neither one of them spoke. They just sat there like that, pressed into each other, watching the dancing people under the endless foreign sky.

16

❧❦❧

Mili got absolutely no sleep that night. She tossed and turned on the daybed in Ridhi's room and listened to her snoring. It should've comforted her. Her *naani* was a veritable orchestra when it came to snoring. In fact, Naani's melodic nighttime whistles had put Mili to sleep most nights of her childhood. Ridhi's snoring was nowhere near as loud. Mili sent up silent thanks on Ravi's behalf. And Ridhi didn't usually snore. Tonight was probably from exhaustion. The way the girl had gyrated on the floor last night it would be a miracle if she even woke up on her wedding day. No blushing bride at this wedding.

Mili on the other hand was still blushing from the peck on the cheek Samir had given her before heading off to the hotel where Ridhi's parents had put up their guests. The memory of that touch, the tenderness of it, made her blush again now. There was such tenderness to him. In the way he touched her, in the way he spoke to her. Even his gaze was tender, as if he were tracing the softest feather down her skin. Only when he wasn't trying to mask it in that hot hero nonchalance of course.

Not that his hot and seductive gazes weren't the stuff of legends. Another warm blush crept over her wide-awake body. Heat gathered in her throat, in her belly, and lower still between her legs. Her hand traced the heat, skimming over her body to her most private part and hovered there. She lowered her hand, letting the warmth of her own fingers mix with the warmth of her body's response to the memory of his touch. Liquid fire slid wet and hot from secret places and moistened her innermost folds. She pulled her hand away, mortified.

Guilt buzzed like an electric current inside her. Guilt at the heat that swirled between her legs, guilt at the wild abandon he inspired inside her, guilt at how safe she had felt by his side. So safe, in fact, that she had shared something she had never let slip around anyone before.

I don't remember anything.

It's what she hated most about her life. Even more than being married at four. Even more than the endless wait her life had been, she hated that she remembered nothing about her parents. It had been a leaden burden on her heart, crushing something inside, until his arm had snaked around her and the words had finally freed themselves from her chokehold.

A friendship that gave you that kind of freedom could never be wrong, could it? Their friendship was clean, pure, wasn't it?

She tried not to think about where her hand had been seconds ago.

No. Despite that, she knew their friendship was something good. In the deepest part of her heart, in the clearest part of her brain, she knew without a doubt that Samir's feelings for her were something good. His friendship was guileless, selfless, undemanding. Surely, friendship like that was a gift. She would not darken it just because her body was being a traitor. She would not turn it away because of its treacherous response to him.

Hypocrite, a tiny voice in her head said.

Hypocrite.

She rolled over under the thick comforter and pressed her face into the pillow. Oh God, what was wrong with her? She squeezed her eyes and tried to conjure up an image of Virat. The only image of him she had came from a picture his grandmother had framed from a newspaper clipping. How many hours had she spent secretly staring at that fading picture? A smiling, handsome man in pilot's overalls surrounded by other smiling handsome men in overalls against the backdrop of a fighter plane. She strained to focus on his face, strained to hold his smile in her memory as she slid her hand between her legs again.

This time she let her fingers slip under the nightgown Ridhi had let her borrow. This time she let her fingers slip under her already damp panties. This time she found the swollen bud that throbbed in her sensitive mound. Crazed by her own body, she dug into it. Hunger hot and unbidden rose beneath her fingers, sensation clawed at her gut, jammed in her untouched folds, moistening her mouth, moistening her fingers. Her nipples hardened to darts and pushed into the mattress. Her breasts ached. All of her ached, stretched taut to breaking point, wanting, waiting to break free.

She strained to reach for it, but the strain of holding the black-and-white image in her mind pulled her away, pushed her back, tied her up. She struggled, bit her lip, and intensified her own caresses. The raw scent of her own need reached her, bringing with it the scent of the desert, of hot sand and warm rain. The memory of powerful arms, of her fingers digging into hard muscles made her fingers frantic. Eyes the color of honey, hair the color of chocolate, teeth white as snow. Warm lips on her cheek. His low gurgling laughter overpowered her, wrestled her resistance to the ground. She released. She shattered. She spasmed, then spasmed and spasmed again and bit into the pillow beneath her face, swallowing her screams, swallowing her guilt, swallowing everything except the sweet, sweet throbbing that continued to beat against her fingers.

Samir usually did a hundred pushups before breaking a sweat. But today he was already at two hundred, and nothing. He was still too on edge, still too wound up. What an idiot. He could not believe what a total fucking idiot he'd been. He had never told anyone about his parents. He had never even discussed it with Virat.

I remember feelings.

Fuck. Where had that even come from?

And she'd listened. Hell, she'd known exactly what he meant. He went down to another set of twenty. Then another. Then another. The carpet barely scraping his forehead, his nose, his chin, up again, down again. Then again, then again. Until his arms felt like they would explode and he collapsed onto his face on the carpet.

When was the last time he'd been this horny? He felt like a fucking teenager with his hands on a *Playboy* magazine, ready to explode. He needed to get nice and laid, fast. To have his brains fucked out of him because they had sunk down to his dick. Thanks a lot, Little Sam.

He flipped over and grabbed his head in his hands.

Her smell was stuck in his head. Her feel was stuck to his fingers. How the fuck had this happened?

Laid. He needed to get laid. And he needed some Alka Seltzer. His head pounded like a jackhammer. After coming back to the hotel, Ravi and some of Ridhi's cousins had wanted to drink. And boy, could these guys drink. Samir hadn't had a drink since, well, since the person he valued the most in the world had fallen out of the sky and ended up almost dead. Unless you counted the few sips of wine last night. The memory of the terror of believing his brother might die swirled in his head and intensified the headache. The words *dead* and *Virat* in the same sentence made it difficult to breathe. Fuck yeah, he'd needed to drink last night. He'd needed something to wash down his own incredible stupidity.

And no, he was not going to analyze why he hadn't moved on the blonde who'd been giving him the breast lean and the hungry eyes all evening. Finally, she'd taken off with one of Ridhi's cousins, but not without giving Samir a disappointed frown.

"Yeah, honey," he'd wanted to tell her, "you think you're disappointed?"

The phone rang. Samir sprang up and pulled it to his ear.

"Dude, you ready? You're giving me a ride back to Ridhi's house. Remember?" How Ravi could sound so rested, so wide awake after last night, he would never know.

"Be there in fifteen minutes."

"Thanks," was all Ravi said before hanging up. The guy had questionable taste in women, but he wasn't a total dumbass. For one, he didn't blast off his mouth when there was nothing to say. Good for him, because if he liked talking he was marrying the wrong girl. Plus he'd completely held it together when Ridhi's cousins had slapped last night's impromptu bachelor party on him. He looked, had some fun, but never touched.

Samir dropped his boxers and jumped into the shower. It was time to take the lamb to slaughter.

Samir watched Mili come down the steps. He didn't realize he'd changed his stance to catch her just in case she stumbled until she grabbed the railing and stuck her chin up in the air. He almost smiled, but curbed the stupid impulse fast enough. He had no intention of smiling at Mili today. In fact, his plan was to avoid her entirely. For one, he needed some distance until Little Sam settled down and stopped running his brain. For another, she looked far too calm, far too beautiful, far too—He just needed distance until he figured out how to get the upper hand in this again, fast. A plan that made him the hunter again, not the fucking hunted.

Mili put one deliberate foot on the hallway floor. "There. I can do this just fine by myself, thank you," her expression said, and he had to channel all his anger at her to keep from smiling.

She was wearing another chiffony, snugly fitted concoction. It was a golden sort of yellow and it brought out the glowing richness of her skin. This one was also a strappy number, not many little strings like the one yesterday, but fewer, broader straps with some sort of traditional threadwork on them. But those incredible collarbones of hers were still on full display, flying out from the center of her delicate throat to her perfectly curved shoulders. An absurdly desperate desire to run his fingers over those winged lines had haunted him all night. He had copped one quick feel when she had sidled up to him on the patio. Really bad idea because his thumb still burned from the feel of the softest skin over delicate bone.

She touched her shoulders and self-consciously adjusted her strap, and he realized he was staring.

"You look beautiful," he said without meaning to. *Fuck.* So much for the upper hand.

Her cheeks colored and her eyes went all wide and vulnerable. "Shut up," she said predictably. "Samir, you have to stop saying things like that."

"Okay." *That's exactly what I'm trying to do.*

She had pulled her hair back in a ponytail today. And her face was scrubbed clean, bare as the day she was born. This woman had the most beautiful skin he'd ever seen, the kind of skin that could bankrupt cosmetic companies. A hint of dark shadows circled her eyes and made her irises seem even larger. For some reason she was having a hard time meeting his eyes and it drove him crazier than it should've.

"Did you eat?" He was dying of lust and that was the first question she asked him.

He swallowed. "No."

"Aren't you hungry? It's almost lunchtime. Can I get you something?"

"I'm ravenous." *Shit. Shit. Shit.* He hadn't meant to say that either and certainly not in that lusty tone.

She blushed some more.

"I can get my own food." He took a few quick steps back, spun around and walked away from her.

Mili gnawed at her cuticles. Her fingers smelled like Ridhi's sugary vanilla body wash. God knows how frantically she had scrubbed her fingers in the shower. Even as she watched Samir's retreating back she wondered if he'd been able to tell what she'd done last night. Except that instead of his usual tenacious as a rash self he'd been only too eager to run from her.

Even now his feet were walking but for some reason she knew he was running.

"Why's Romeo in such a hurry today?" Ridhi asked, coming down the stairs. She was dressed in an ankle-length tie-dye skirt with a heavy embroidered border and a heavily embellished tube top.

"Wow, you look, um, stunning," Mili said.

It wasn't untrue, but it was kind of risqué for your wedding day, even for Ridhi.

"Look who's talking." Ridhi gave Mili a once-over and adjusted her shoulder strap. "Gold is definitely your color. And my clothes look really good on you. Who would've thought?"

Before Mili could respond, there was a loud gasp behind her.

"Ridhika. Sagar. Kapoor! Has your brain taken a complete trip to Timbuktu?"

"And good morning to you too, Mummy." Ridhi took one step down and came to stand next to Mili. Her hearing must've abandoned her because she didn't seem to register the volume of her mother's voice.

"Good morning? Good morning nothing! Your *in-laws* are in the house. Don't you have any brains at all?" Her powder-pink skin raged near violet. Spittle danced on her cherry-red mouth. She pulled off the *duppata* from around her own shoulders and draped it around her daughter, pushing Mili aside with such force she stumbled.

"Mummy!" Ridhi steadied Mili and glared at her mother.

"Sorry. Sorry, *beta*." She gave Mili a quick apologetic pat on the head. "But your friend makes me completely crazy. I gave birth to a birdbrain. Not a girl, a flamingo she is. Dancing around on one foot." She turned to Ridhi and smacked her soundly on her exposed shoulder.

"Mummy, have you gone completely mad? What are you freaking out about now?"

"Freaking out? You're wearing *that*? On your *wedding* day? Oh Lord, take me now."

"What's wrong with this? You told me to wear something casual for the henna ceremony. So, I wore casual."

"I said casual, not *Chandni-Chowk*-whore slutty! Brainless daughter of an oaf."

Mili smiled, but quickly covered her mouth when Ridhi glared at her.

Ridhi yanked her ankle-length skirt all the way up to her thighs and looked down at it. "How is this slutty? It touches the floor. You can't even see my toes."

Her mother pinched the half of her breast that pushed up from her tube top. "What about these? You want your in-laws to see your mangoes? Save those for the man who's going to eat them," she hissed.

"Mummy!" Ridhi screamed. "You're disgusting. Yuck."

"Disgusting nothing. Go up right now and change before they see you." She threw quick darting glances over her shoulder. "Go, you stupid cow. Go!"

Ridhi ran up the stairs mumbling words Mili had never heard before. Ridhi's mother slapped her forehead and turned to Mili. "Her in-laws are *South Indian*," she said as if being South Indian was akin to being an alien species. "Doesn't she know how old-fashioned those people are? Does she have any sense at all?"

Mili patted Ridhi's mother's shoulder. "It's okay, Auntie, she's changing."

It wasn't easy but she didn't laugh until Mrs. Kapoor walked away.

"What's so funny?" Samir asked as she entered the kitchen and walked up to the island. It was covered from end to end with food. Fluffy white *idli* rice cakes, rolled-up crepe *dosas*, round donut-shaped, deep fried *vadas*, huge tureens filled with steaming sambar lentils, red, white, and green chutneys of coconut and mint and cilantro. Stuffed naans and *parathas*, freshly churned butter, yogurt, cut fruit, and all sorts of cakes and donuts and cheeses.

She had to be dead, or dying or something, because really, this had to be heaven.

He laughed next to her ear and she turned around.

"You didn't even hear the question, did you?" He smiled as if she had done something truly amusing.

"Shush, don't disturb me. I'm in heaven right now." She looked back at the food, closed her eyes and inhaled. Her mouth watered. The aromas danced in her head, danced in her soul.

When she opened her eyes he was holding out a plate and watching her. But with all these aromas strumming her senses, she couldn't analyze his expression. She reached over and picked up one hot, perfectly crisp stuffed *paratha*.

She brought it to her nose and took a deep sniff before putting it on her plate. Then she added some seasoned yogurt, green chutney, and a shamelessly large serving of mango pickle. She broke off a piece of the *paratha* with her fingers, used it to scoop up some yogurt, dipped it in chutney, and then popped it in her mouth. The purest pleasure exploded in her mouth. She moaned and her eyes fluttered shut. She chewed, and chewed, and wanted to go on chewing for as long as she lived.

Just as the *paratha* melted on her tongue she picked up a piece of mango pickle and sucked on it.

Oh dear God.

Samir grabbed her elbow and led her away from the island, where for some reason a crowd was starting to gather.

"God, Samir, have you tried these *paneer parathas?*" She broke off a piece, dunked it in some yogurt and chutney, and brought it to his lips. He swallowed before he opened his mouth and took the food from her fingers.

His lips grazed her fingertips and the sensation stunned her so much she forgot to remove her hand fast enough.

But the smell of the food on her plate brought her back. "Incredible, isn't it?" she asked, and took another bite.

He nodded and chewed and watched her wordlessly with suddenly shuttered eyes.

"Did you know we have ten thousand taste buds in our mouth?" she said, trying to hold the flavors on her tongue as she chewed.

He smiled. "Of course you would know that."

She put another piece in her mouth. Then another piece in his mouth. "Wait, wait," she said as he started to chew. His wide, lush mouth froze mid-chew. She picked up a piece of pickle and pushed it between his lips. His honey-brown eyes melted to that smoky amber.

"See?" she said, popping more food in her own mouth. "I told you. You're in heaven, aren't you?"

Before she knew it her plate was empty. "What should we get next?" she asked him.

He grinned, dropping his guard for the first time today, and she felt so light she thought she would float away. She was about to ask him what he was so amused about when his phone rang.

He wiped something off the edge of her lips before he answered.

His fingers stilled on her mouth. "Yes, Baiji. Hold on just a minute. I'm right here. Don't go away." His voice turned soft and respectful. Mili had never heard him sound like this. He spoke in the dialect of her village and it made her so light-headed with homesickness she had to focus to hear what he was saying.

He pulled his hand away, raised a finger to indicate he needed a minute, and walked out of the kitchen and into the backyard. The last thing she saw him do was wipe his fingers on his jeans. Her heart twisted painfully in her chest. He was wiping away her touch.

"How are you, *beta?*" His mother's voice was exactly what Samir needed to hear after what had just happened. He had been feeling so restless and crazed in there he didn't know what was wrong with him. It wasn't like he hadn't seen a woman eat before. It wasn't like a woman had never slipped food into his mouth. He'd done some pretty creative things involving food and women. But having Mili slip food into his mouth was the most erotic thing he'd ever had happen to him.

He shook his hand out, wiped it on his jeans again, but his fingers still tingled. He switched his phone from hand to hand and dragged his fingers through his hair.

"*Beta?*"

"Baiji, I'm right here. Sorry. There was too much noise. I needed to get to a quieter spot. Can you hear me?"

"Very clearly, son. I haven't heard from you in a week. I was starting to worry."

"I'm sorry. I should have called. Is everything okay? How is Rima? Bhai?"

"Rima's fine. She's starting to show more and more every day." He heard the smile in her voice, then sadness. "She's still having cramps. I think the shock was too much. But Krishna is watching over us. Everything will be fine." She went silent for a moment, and he knew she was saying a prayer. "She's still not eating enough. And she spends all her time in the hospital with Virat."

The *paratha* turned over in Samir's stomach. "Baiji, she needs to be there. Bhai needs her there. Please don't—" He swallowed the lump in his throat. He should've been by Virat's side right now. "Have they said anything about—" But he couldn't ask the question.

"Samir-*beta*, your brother is going to be fine. We are all fine. We all understand that work comes first."

Samir and Virat had told Rima and their mother that Samir needed to work with some investors in America for his film.

Suddenly Baiji's voice turned guarded. "*Beta*, it's been three weeks. When are you coming home?"

"Soon, Baiji."

"Okay, but don't linger. Finish what you have to do and come home soon." She kept her voice calm but Samir knew exactly what was running through her mind.

He had no business putting her through this. Especially not now with Virat in the hospital.

"Baiji, I can't wait to come home. There's nothing for me here—absolutely nothing. If you want I'll come home today. You just have to say the word."

His mother was silent for a long moment and he knew she was actually considering it. She had lost her husband to this country. The thought of her being afraid of losing him too made Samir sick.

"Finish what you need to," she said finally. "But remember you are my whole life, Samir."

"I know, Baiji, I love you too."

"Blessings, *beta*. Hold on, Virat has some news for you."

"*Oy*, Chintu! How are you, little brother?" Virat sounded like his old self and Samir dropped back on the patio wall with relief.

"You sound good, Bhai."

"Not good, Chintu, I'm bloody fantastic! They're letting me out of here *and* . . . are you sitting down because this is huge . . . I'm going to fly again. It's going to be another six months. But I'm going to fly again! Can you believe that?"

"That's amazing, Bhai." Samir's hands were shaking, all of him was shaking, his relief was so intense. The idea of Virat never being able to fly his beloved fighters again was a thought so preposterous Samir had refused to entertain it. Now he knew Virat had been just as worried.

"*Oy*, drama queen, you're not crying, are you?" But it was Virat's voice that cracked. "Baiji, you and Rima need to go get something to eat. I'm fine. My baby brother is sobbing, I need to take care of him." Samir could imagine Virat hamming it up as he sent Rima and their mother off.

There was a beat of silence.

"What's wrong, Bhai?"

"Well, did she sign yet?"

Samir rubbed his forehead and forced himself not to turn around and look for her. "I'm working on it. She will."

"Of course she will. Which woman can say no to Sam Rathod?"

No woman. That was the fucking problem. "I've been a little distracted with finishing the script. I'll get it done and be back home soon. Bhai . . . I'm sorry I'm not there with you."

"Chintu, you'll never change. Bastard, you travelled halfway across the earth for me. You're doing something I should be doing myself and you're apologizing? You're everything to me, brother. You know that, right? Without you there's nothing. Don't ever apologize to me again. Got that?"

Samir couldn't respond. *No, Bhai, you're everything.*

And he was. All the other shit that had been going on meant nothing.

"By the way, there was another letter. And another legal notice from her lawyer."

Despair slammed like a fist into Samir's gut. Another letter?

"Bhai, I don't want you to worry about it. You focus on getting out of the hospital and getting back in the cockpit. Leave this to me. I'll take care of it."

After Virat hung up, Samir swung his legs over the patio wall he was perched on and faced the house. It was a crisp blue-sky day. Not enough sun for sunglasses, but just enough to warm the air. Across the patio, on the other side of the lead-glass French doors, Mili's petite form was waving at him. Or at least that's what he thought she was doing. The beaded glass broke her into little pieces and blurred her slender form into disjointed parts. Which one was the real her?

The girl who had gone flying into a tree to protect her friend of four months. The girl who had deviously worked her friend's family to save her friend's love. The girl who ate food like she was making love to it. The girl whose body beat out music in the exact rhythm as his. Or the girl who threatened a wounded man for his ancestral estate.

Looking through that crystal window, across that sparkling afternoon sunshine, Samir had to reach deep into his cynicism, into his disillusionment with the world, into his distrust of human nature to find his anger, to find the belief that Mili, like everyone else, was capable of greed and deviousness.

He was sure she had her reasons. He knew without doubt that they would be good reasons. But he couldn't concern himself with her reasons. He had a debt to pay. A debt to a brother who had jumped into a dark well and let his little brother climb onto his shoulders while he clung to the protruding well stones and waited hours to be rescued. A debt to a mother who had packed up her boys in the middle of the night and fled the safety of her home to protect a little boy from the beatings that had gouged the skin off his back, before the beatings that had killed his spirit took his body too.

17

All day Samir had blown hot and cold. Mili knew he was struggling with something. She also knew with absolute certainty that it had something to do with her. It was just as well. After last night she knew what she had to do. The time had come to tell him that she was married. This warmth, this friendship between them, she had no right to any of it. It was time for it to end.

"A lie has only one face," her *naani* always said, "but a liar has several." She had always had only one face. And now there were too many faces; some she recognized, some were entirely alien. And yet with him she had never been someone she wasn't. She was just all the things she never thought she could be, no matter how badly she wanted to.

"You've been spending an awful lot of time making eyes at Romeo recently." How Ridhi had the time to make useless observations in the middle of her own wedding Mili would never know.

"I see you changed," she said, taking in the sleeveless white *kurti* that fit Ridhi like a glove. "And it covers your mangoes and everything."

Ridhi grinned. "I can't believe Mummy said that. But I'm glad she did. Don't know what I was thinking. Ravi's parents really are conservative. Did you meet them yet? His mother is actually wearing one of those stereotypical orange-and-green silk saris with that huge gold border. I mean, I thought they only dressed like that in those calendars they hang at South Indian grocery stores." She lowered her voice and looked around to make sure no one was listening. "I mean, how did someone like *that* give birth to someone as hot as Ravi? Speaking of hot, I have some dirt on Romeo. Did you know he's a big hotshot Bollywood director?"

"Hotshot?" No, he wasn't. He had told her he was a small artsy-type director.

"Haven't you watched *Love Lights*? It was like the biggest hit last year and like the most romantic film ever!"

"Really? The one with the human bomb? Are you sure?"

"Of course I'm sure. My cousin Nimi is like a Bollywood encyclopedia." Ridhi waved to her cousin, who was standing with a group of giggling girls. "She's the one who told me. Nimi, hey, Nimi, over here."

The entire gaggle of cousins sauntered across the kitchen to the arched entrance of the family room, from where they had a clear view of Samir, Ravi, and a few other cousins drinking beer.

"Nice view, ha?" Nimi whispered, coming to stand next to Ridhi.

"No kidding," someone else said.

Samir raised a questioning eyebrow at Mili from across the room and she looked away self-consciously.

"Holy shit!" One of the cousins Mili had not yet met gripped her chest as if she were having a heart attack. "Is that who I think it is?"

"That depends on who you think it is," Ridhi responded.

"That's that bastard director guy." She said it so loudly all the guys including Samir looked at them.

"Reena, shut up," Ridhi said, and Mili wanted to hug her.

"No, seriously, you guys have to see this." She ran into the kitchen and fished a glossy magazine out of a big leather bag. "That man is wanted by the police for beating Neha Pratap up."

A collective gasp rose across the room. The guys turned to look at Samir. He took a sip from his beer bottle, his face an unreadable mask.

Reena started to flip furiously through the magazine. "Here, see here!" She held the magazine up.

Splattered across the page were several close-up shots of a

woman's face. She appeared to have been brutally beaten. One side of her face was swollen and purple, one eye was puffed shut. Her hair was pulled back into a ponytail and her eyes had a hollow, pained look that made Mili's stomach cramp with sympathy. Across the middle of the page was a larger picture of a very beautiful girl in a very short, very tight dress hanging on the arm of a heartbreakingly handsome Samir dressed in a dark suit with a crisp white shirt, his hair gelled back, his breathtaking face smiling down at the girl as if she were the only girl in the world.

Scrawled across the bottom of the picture were the words, *"Sam did this!" Neha admits to their love affair going violent.*

"See." Reena smiled like a smug cow.

Anger exploded inside Mili's head with such force she snatched the magazine out of Reena's hand and shoved her hard. "Shut up. Just shut the heck up, you stupidhead witch. What is wrong with you? This is a gossip magazine. A stupid, donkey-faced gossip magazine. They write whatever they need to write to sell copies. Shame on you for buying this nonsense. Don't you have anything better to do with your life?"

Samir leaned forward in his chair, but he didn't get up. The other girl was at least half a foot taller than Mili and exactly three times as wide. And yet Mili went for her, lunging at her and practically toppling her over. This crazy household was definitely getting to her.

Or maybe it was just who she was.

Ridhi pulled Mili back before she did herself some serious damage against the mountainous woman who looked so shocked Samir had to suppress a smile.

"Mill, calm down. Reena was just showing us what she found."

"What she found in that . . . in that stupidhead magazine?" Mili stuttered, so angry she was having a hard time speaking.

"What do you mean, 'stupidhead magazine'? It's *Filmfare*. It's India's best—" The "stupidhead witch" was stupid enough to argue.

Mili charged at her, knocking the wind out of her. She burst into tears.

"Mili, stop it. What's wrong with you?" Ridhi held Mili back. "Samir's not even saying anything. Why are you so angry? Let him defend himself." Bizarrely enough, Ridhi sounded like the voice of reason.

But Mili hissed and sputtered, turning on Ridhi, incensed beyond reason. "Why? Why should Samir defend himself? Why should he dignify this nonsense with an explanation?"

Samir stood. Time to fight his own battles. Although, he could spend the rest of his life watching Mili go to bat for him like this.

Ridhi and her nasal whine still had some wisdom left to go. "Mill, how do you even know it's not true? You've only just met the man, he doesn't even know—"

Mili shoved Ridhi. "Shut up, Ridhi. Just shut your mouth. I might have just met him but I can tell you this: I might beat someone up." She jabbed a finger into her own chest. "You might beat someone up." She jabbed a finger at Ridhi's chest. "But Samir would never, ever hit a woman."

Fireworks burst in Samir's heart. Sweet pain shot through his entire body.

Mili turned on her heel, saw the magazine lying on the floor, and swooped down on it. She grabbed it with both hands and tried to rip it in half. She struggled with it for a good minute, but the darned thing wouldn't give. Finally she flung it across the room and stormed to his side. Then, grabbing his hand, she dragged him out of the room, pushing Ridhi, Ravi, and four gaping cousins out of the way. And of course when she stepped up from the den to the kitchen she tripped.

His hand pushed into her back, holding her up. She straightened with the kind of dignity only she could muster and out into the backyard they went. They walked past the impeccable manicured lawn onto a wooden walkway that led into a wooded area. She was in no mood to stop and he was in no mood to question her.

They walked like that in silence for a while. Maybe it was an hour, maybe it was longer. Somehow he found her hand in his and he couldn't bring himself to let it go. The sweetest ache burned in his chest. He kept thinking of the gargantuan girl's crying face and wanting to smile. But Mili was still fuming and he didn't think this was a good time to annoy her any further. He was only too happy to stand by and watch her cool at her own pace, as long as he had her tiny hand grasped in his.

When they came to a wooden bridge that led nowhere, Mili turned onto it. She stopped at the highest point on the curving surface, pulled her hand from his, and rested her elbows on the stained wood. He did the same. His arm brushed hers. Her scent filled his lungs. Jasmine and sweet herbs. They stared out at the sprawling manicured yards laid out in front of them like a greeting card landscape. A profusion of blooms spilled from stepped terraces and gazebos. Looming mansions surrounded the clipped paradise like fortresses, protecting it from the outside world.

"Thanks," she said suddenly, turning her head to look at him. "It would've been very embarrassing to fall on my face after that." An impish grin bloomed across her face.

If he leaned just a little bit closer he could touch her lips with his. He would know what it felt like to taste that imp's smile, to drop kisses on that crinkled nose.

"Samir?"

He blinked and looked up from her lips into her eyes. They were dark and sultry as ever and sparkling with life. "You're thanking me?"

Embarrassment stained her cheeks. "Shut up."

"Does that mean I can't thank you?" He pulled her fingers to his lips. But she pulled them away before his lips could touch them.

"Can I ask you a question, Samir?"

God. "You can try."

"Who's Neha?"

"An ex."

She raised one confused eyebrow.

"My ex-girlfriend."

She punched him. "I know what an ex is. I meant what happened? What did you do to make her so angry she would say such awful things about you?"

"Long story."

"What, you have a wedding to go to or something?"

He laughed. "Well, she wanted a commitment, I wasn't quite ready, she got a little crazy, came after me with a vase, lost her balance, and fell down my stairs on her face."

"Shit."

It was the first time he'd heard Mili swear. As in a real swear. Not donkey, monkey, crow, witch, hot fudge, et cetera.

"What a bitch."

"Wow, you're really on a roll, Mili. Not witch. Straight out bitch."

She blushed. "But she is." She twisted her fingers together. "I'll bet you were terrified." She touched him then. Slow, soothing strokes on his arm. It took all his strength not to pull her to him. "I'll bet you were the one who got her to the hospital. I'll bet you sat by her side the entire time. And she does this to you."

"Well, I didn't exactly sit by her side. But yes. I—" God, how had she pinned it down like that? "I did get her to the hospital."

She watched his face. Then there it was again, the imp's grin.

"What now? Or should I even ask?"

"I'm going to call you Florence."

He squeezed his temples with his fingers. "What?"

"Florence Nightingale. You know the nurse who was obsessed with taking care of people?" She threw her head back and laughed. "Who would believe that?"

Only you, Mili.

She started back toward the house, dragging him in her wake. "I'd better make sure Ridhi's okay. And her bi—witch cousin. You think I was too mean to her?"

"I think you're being kinda mean right now."

She spun around, horrified guilt on her face. "I am?"

All he could do was laugh.

Mili should have known Ridhi would be there when she dragged Samir back into the house. It was the girl's wedding, for heaven's sake—didn't she have anything better to do?

Ridhi narrowed her eyes at Samir. "Ravi's been looking for you. For like two *hours*."

They had definitely not been gone that long. But what was Ridhi without her drama?

"Very nice," Mili said, pointing to Ridhi's hands before she launched into another inquisition-slash-lecture.

Ridhi held out her arms and Mili inspected them dutifully. They were freshly painted with henna paste from the tips of her fingers all the way to her elbows. Not as beautiful as the patterns from the Teej festival back home, but beautiful nonetheless.

"Look at your hair," Ridhi said, shifting her frown from Samir to Mili's hair. "What a mess."

Mili reached up and touched her ponytail. It had slid to one side of her head and her hair stuck out in all directions. Must've happened when she attacked Ridhi's cousin. She pulled off the band and shook her hair out.

"Why didn't you say something?" she asked Samir. She must've looked like such a clown.

He shrugged. "Didn't notice." He gave Ridhi one of those grins designed specifically to annoy, dropped a kiss on the top of Mili's head, and went looking for Ravi with the oddest bounce in his step.

"Come on," Mili said before Ridhi put that frown into words and pulled Ridhi into the family room.

Three henna artists sat by the marble fireplace that was so ornate it would have been perfectly at home in the Jaipur palace. The rest of the room was as riotously noisy as its occupants. Steel, glass, and carved wood furniture was strewn across the glossy black-and-white-checkered floor. Brass railings edged the upper-floor balconies overlooking the room. Floor-to-ceiling tapestries from every carpet-weaving nation in the world hung from the walls. There was one from Rajasthan, black silk with the most intricate mirrorwork and hand embroidery. It made the knot of homesickness that always lingered in Mili's belly tighten.

Mili joined the line of girls waiting for the henna artists, who swirled henna in intricate patterns across the palms of three smiling girls. One of the artists finished the hand she was painting and beckoned the next girl in line. She was no more than sixteen years old. The moment she settled into the pillow, she pulled the neckline of her *choli* blouse down and exposed the top of one very well developed breast.

A collective gasp rose across the room. A few of the older women clutched their own bosoms in horror. A large woman in a magenta sari flew across the room in a flash of color and smacked the breast-baring girl upside the head. "Shameless slut, must you cut my nose in public everywhere you go?" She shook the girl so hard her partially exposed breast popped all the way out of her *choli*, causing another collective gasp.

Ridhi's mother streaked across the room in another flash of color and grabbed the girl out of her mother's arms. Or at least she tried, because the mother refused to let go. The two women yanked the girl by both arms like a partially naked human tug-of-war.

"Pinky!" Ridhi's mother shouted at the top of her lungs. "*Hai hai*, let the girl go. What's the matter with you? She's a child. All these people, all this *tamasha*. Come come."

She finally managed to yank the girl free and plunked her down next to the henna artist right on the lap of another girl, who, seeing an opportunity, had inserted herself into the spot. Both girls shrieked, Ridhi shrieked, arbitrary women in the crowd shrieked.

Mili looked up at the group of men who had gathered to see what all the commotion was about. She caught Samir's eye and thought she was going to die. He looked exactly like she felt. Ready to explode. "I'll kill you if you make me laugh," she mouthed and looked back at the unfolding drama.

Ridhi's mother threw a panic-stricken look at the men and hurriedly squashed the girl's exposed breast back into her blouse. She yanked the girl's sleeve up. "Here, here, give baby a tuttoo on her arm. *Beta*, that's a better place for it. Come, there's my good girl." She pinched the girl's cheek, patted the other girl she had displaced on the head, and put a twenty-dollar bill in the bowl next to the artist. Then she turned to the rest of her guests. "Come come, there's food in the kitchen. Samosas are being fried hot-hot. Come, come."

She pulled Mili along and deposited her closer to Samir, whose shoulders were shaking uncontrollably. Mili glared at him, but her stomach trembled with laughter she could no longer suppress. He pushed his way past the few people between them, grabbed her arm, and dragged her out of the room.

The house was so big they had to run past several rooms before they came to the French doors that led to the backyard. Samir pulled it open and they ran across the patio and collapsed on the grass, laughing.

"What the heck was that?" Samir said, tears streaming down his cheeks. "Where did you find these people?"

Mili couldn't speak. She couldn't stop laughing.

"Pinky? That big, scary auntie is called *Pinky?*" His voice squeaked on the name and he fell back, pressed his arm into his stomach, and laughed.

Mili doubled over. Her stomach hurt so much she held her breath to stop laughing. Samir sprang back up and yanked her sleeve up. "Here, here, put that tuttoo here. *Tuttoo?* Holy shit." He burst into a fresh fit and Mili started to choke.

He rubbed her back, his hand shaking because all of him was shaking. "You okay?"

She nodded and tried to stop coughing and laughing at the same time but she couldn't manage any of it. He kept rubbing, and laughing, and wiped the tears from his eyes.

He had the most beautiful golden eyes. But she'd never seen them like this, crinkled at the edges, lit with life, sparkling with humor and something more, something that made her breath catch. His eyes changed. The way his hand stroked up and down her back changed. His hand slowed to a caress and came to rest at the small of her back, where all the nerves in her body suddenly converged, where he found the springy ends of her curls and tangled his fingers in them.

She felt the gentlest tug. Her head tipped back and his lips touched hers. It was a whisper of a touch, so tentative, the sensation so light, she wasn't sure she'd felt it at all. Before she knew what she was doing she reached up into it. He sucked in a breath and pulled back, just the slightest bit. His wild eyes searched hers.

Heat bloomed in her cheeks. Her wide-open heart drummed in her chest. A semblance of sense started to creep back into her head. Then it flew right out into the blazing afternoon. Because Samir gathered her hair, gathered her face, gathered all of her and claimed her lips with such force the world went up in flames around her.

His lips were soft, so very soft. And firm. And insistent. Without meaning to she pushed into them. He groaned deep in his chest and parted her lips. She gasped. Tongue and liquid skin slid and stroked and filled her mouth, her senses. He reached into her, tentative, then bold, touching sensitive, secret flesh, stripping every resistance, ripping a moan from the deepest part of her.

And she let him in. She let him jab into her, free her, tangle her. She tasted him, breathed him in. His smoky taste, clean and dark and hot. His tongue, hungry and probing and hot. His heavy shoulders under her fingers, firm and yielding and hot. Heat rose from him, from the back of his neck, from the raw silk of his hair, and burned through her. Fire blazed across her skin and down her belly. She pressed closer. His fingers molded her scalp, trailed over her collarbones, and reached lower to her breasts. She jumped. The electricity of the touch jolted through her. It was too much. It was all too much.

"No." She heard her own voice, felt her hands pushing him away. "No, Samir, I can't do this." Oh God, what had she done?

She had no right to this. No right.

She tried to scamper away from him. But one stray curl wrapped itself around his button and yanked her back. She tugged at it, twisting it desperately, her fingers shaking too much to pry it loose. He held her fingers steady and unwound the lock, setting her free.

She stood up and broke into a run.

"Mili." He was next to her before her name left his lips. He reached for her.

"No. God. Samir. I can't do this." She moved out of his reach.

"Why?"

"Because I don't have the liberty to. I have something to tell you. I should've told you this before. Because . . . Oh God . . . Samir, I'm married."

His face darkened, his eyes darkened, the air around him darkened. "No, you're not."

"Yes, yes, I am. I'm married." Her heart was beating so hard it was going to break free of her chest. "God, that was . . . that should never have happened."

Samir could not believe it. Could not believe what he was feeling. The earth, the wind, the skies, it was all shaking. Shaking with rage. What a royal fucking mess.

Mili's chest was heaving. She was panting as if she'd run a mile. Guilt and confusion spilled from her face like the tears she couldn't control and all he could think of was that kiss. The feel of her in his arms, her lips against his. Those collarbones under his fingers. They were heaving now. All of her was pulsing with sick, sick guilt.

"I should have told you." Her voice shook.

"Then why didn't you?"

"Because . . . because I didn't think this would happen. I didn't think you would do this. I didn't think someone like . . . like you would fall for someone like me."

"*Fall* for you? You think I've fallen for you?" Oh, this was precious. "And what do you mean 'someone like you'?"

She shook her head so violently he thought she might hurt herself. "It doesn't matter. None of this matters because I'm married. Married. I can't be with you. I mean, not that I want to."

"Why wouldn't you want to be with me?"

She laughed. An incredulous, disbelieving laugh. "You're, well. You're *you*."

"Thanks. That explains everything."

"Well, for one, you look like *that*." She pointed at him as if he had an extra pair of ears sticking out of his head.

"What's wrong with the way I look?"

"Wrong? You look like you stepped off a stupid billboard. You smile like you're in a toothpaste commercial. I mean, who wants to be with a man who's more pretty than them? Would you want to?"

"No, I wouldn't say that I want to be with a man more pretty than me." Had she really just called him—fuck, he couldn't even think it.

"See, and nothing is serious to you. Nothing is sacred. You're not even horrified that you kissed a married woman."

Was she crazy? "You are not a married woman."

"Stop saying that."

"Then where is this husband of yours? Where's your *mangalsu-tra?* Where's your wedding ring? Where's your *sindoor?*"

"It's not that simple. My husband, he's . . . I haven't . . ."

"You haven't what, Mili? You haven't ever seen him?"

"We were married when I was very young. And . . . it's really hard to explain."

His rage started to take everything else over. "Try anyway."

"No. I can't. I can't explain it. I can't be with you right now. Please. I just can't." She backed away, but no fucking way was he letting her go.

"How young, Mili?" Her arms were so slender in his hands, so delicate, he gentled his grip.

She squeezed her eyes shut. "I was four."

"That's not a marriage."

Her eyes blazed open. "Someone like you can never under-stand it. It is a marriage where I come from. It is a marriage for me, Samir." She struggled to free herself from his hold.

He didn't let her go. "What about what just happened between us? What do you call that where you come from?"

And the guilt was back. He wanted to shake her, to kiss it off her face, every last bit of it.

"That should never have happened. These past weeks, these past days. Oh, Samir, it should never have happened. You should not be holding me like this. Let me go."

She yanked her arm, fighting to get away, but he wouldn't let go. He couldn't.

"Hold still, Mili, you're going to hurt yourself. I'm not going to let you walk away from me. Not until you tell me everything."

She stopped struggling. "There's nothing to tell. Nothing more than what I just told you."

"If you're married, what are you doing here by yourself?" He tried to swallow but he couldn't.

"He's an officer in the Indian Air Force. And I . . . I have . . ."

"When was the last time you saw him?" He had no idea what he was doing. But he couldn't stop.

Tears started streaming down her face. "I haven't seen him since I was four years old."

"Then he is not your husband."

"He is my husband because I believe he is. Because I'm sworn to spend the rest of my life with him. It's what I've dreamed of for as long as I can remember. Because, because I love him."

Samir let her arm go. "How can you love someone you've never met?" He rubbed his hand against his jeans, but the feel of her wouldn't come off.

"You can. I can. I do. I'm sorry. I'm sorry if I hurt you. If I let you believe anything could happen between us."

"Could happen? What about what just happened?"

"That meant nothing."

He grabbed her arm again and stuck his face inches from hers. She didn't flinch.

"I've stuck my tongue into so many women's mouths I've lost count. And *that*—that did *not* mean nothing to you."

She looked horrified. Round eyes, open mouth. "You've lost count?"

"Oh, that's what you picked up from what I just said?"

She swiped her hand across her mouth, rubbed her lips, and made vehement spitting sounds.

"You're wiping away my kiss? What are you, two years old?" God help him, he had never wanted to shake someone so bad.

"Samir, I do not want to talk to any man who . . . who . . . yuck!" She turned around and stormed off again.

He was next to her in a second. "That's it, you kiss me, like . . . like *that*, then tell me you're married, then you run off."

"You've survived *countless* kisses, you'll survive this one." She didn't stop.

This was ridiculous. He stopped. "I am not going to run after you, Mili."

"Good. Just leave me alone."

This had to be the craziest thing that had ever happened to him in his entire godforsaken life. He was not going to run after this crazy woman. He sank down on the patio steps and dropped his head into his palms. Of all the . . . she had wiped off his kiss, spat it out. She had called it . . . God, the kiss was seared into his fucking soul and she'd said . . . *yuck?*

18

For the rest of the afternoon Mili refused to talk to Samir. She refused to look at him. She refused to so much as be in the same room as him. Fortunately, Samir was beyond ever being surprised by Mili again.

What kind of woman jerked you around like that? What kind of married woman kissed you like that? What kind of woman—He ran his fingers through his hair. God, he was losing his mind. There were so many lies flying around he was actually starting to buy all the crap they were handing out.

First, she was not married. Rima was married to Virat. Second, both of them would be widowed, not married, if Virat had died in that accident. *God, Bhai. I am so sorry.* How would Virat have handled this? He certainly would not have messed everything up by getting involved with the woman who was trying to illegitimatize his child and steal his family fortune.

Something stuck out from under the couch. Samir leaned over and picked it up. It was the *Filmfare* magazine. The one Mili had used to almost dismember someone three times her size. Why was irony such a bitch?

He tucked the magazine under his arm and found Ranvir at the dining table with a man tying a turban around his head. Samir told Ranvir he was leaving. It was getting close to the wedding hour. Everyone else, including Mili, seemed to be upstairs changing.

The wedding was going to take place in the backyard in a few hours.

"You're coming back for the wedding, right?" Ranvir peered at Samir through the turban that had slipped over his eyes.

"We'll see," Samir said and headed for his car.

It was a nice enough hotel, and it felt really good to be alone. Samir pulled off his shirt, and threw himself on the carpet. A hundred pushups later, he felt much better. He got up, stretched, and saw the magazine lying on the bed.

He opened to the article that had turned his tiny little adversary into an avenging angel.

Neha looked really bad, that much he would admit. It was time to put a railing on that staircase. He skimmed through the article. *String of innumerable girlfriends . . . Casanova image keeps him in the media . . . Neha was the brightest star on the Mumbai horizon . . . blah blah blah.*

Finally his eyes stopped on something. *She had filed charges . . . He'd fled the country . . . The police were on a hunt.*

What the fuck?

He pulled the cell phone out of his pocket and dialed.

"God, Sam, it's the middle of the fucking night." As usual DJ was a font of information.

"I'm sorry, I should let your lazy ass go back to sleep then."

"What's wrong?" Samir heard some rustling, then a few feminine mumbles as DJ got out of bed.

Great, now he was ruining everyone's sex life. "When were you going to tell me Neha filed charges?"

"Where did you find a *Filmfare* magazine?"

"I pulled it out of my fucking ass. How's she doing?"

"She's fine. She's been trying to reach you. I didn't think you'd want me to tell her where you were. She was just being a woman scorned. And she's withdrawn the charges. I've spoken to the cops. I would have called if there was anything for you to worry about. When are you coming back anyway? It's been close to four weeks."

"I don't know. And stop fucking babysitting me. If someone wants to talk to me, let them."

"Yes, sir. Anything else?"

"Yes. Thank you."

"You're welcome. Are you going to tell me what the real problem is?"

"No." Because a real fucking problem would by definition need a real fucking solution. "Women are insane, that's all."

"We aren't talking about Neha anymore, I'm guessing." His agent was a veritable Dr. Watson.

"Well, she's insane too."

"So the bitch won't sign? Why don't you just come back and let the lawyers take care of it."

She's not a bitch, you fucker. "No. She'll sign."

Fuck, he couldn't talk anymore. He mumbled a goodbye and jumped in the shower.

It didn't help.

He picked up his laptop. All this wedding drama meant he had not finished the script. Chances were he wouldn't be able to write, for obvious reasons that he needed to get the fuck over. If it hadn't been for Mili's little critique, which he hated to admit had been bloody brilliant, he would have been done by now. But she had hit the nail squarely on the head and everything made perfect sense. He knew exactly how it was going to end. He just had to put the ending down on paper. Story of his fucking life.

There was a knock on the door. "Who is it?"

"Room Service." Mili's husky voice punched him square in the gut. His heartbeat sped up. The blood rushing through his veins sped up. Even his breathing sped up like some teenybopper coming face-to-face with her crush. All those damned pushups down the toilet.

He pulled the door open a crack. Whatever droll line he was going to throw at her died on his tongue. She was wearing a turquoise sari. Her hair cascaded around her shoulders, spiral ribbons falling all the way to her exposed waist. Someone had outlined her eyes in smoky kohl. Her irises glittered like gemstones. So what? They always glittered.

She pushed the door and squeezed past him into the room.

"Come on in," he growled, much like the wild beast raging in his chest.

"You're in a dressing gown." She was standing too close to him. The passage leading into the room was narrow. Too narrow.

He could smell her once he got past the blast of perfume. "What did Ridhi spray you with, a hose?" Without meaning to, he leaned in to smell her. Great, she'd turned him into a lecher, that's what she'd done.

She stepped away. "Oh, good, you remember Ridhi. My best friend. The one whose wedding you drove four hours for."

"I didn't drive four hours for Ridhi." He tried to hold her gaze, but she looked away, that damned flush swept up her cheeks, maroon and pink tinting the deepest caramel, like a rose that needed its own name.

She took a breath, raised those glittering onyxes, and met his gaze. A head-on collision. "I'm sorry, Samir. Can't we put that behind us and go back to being friends?"

"No."

"Okay, so don't be friends. But get dressed. The wedding ceremony is less than an hour away. We have to get back to Ridhi's house."

"I'm not going to the wedding."

"Okay. But I have to be at the wedding. And you have to take me." Now her eyes went all pleading. If she joined her palms he was throwing her out.

"How did you get here?"

"I made Ranvir drop me off."

"Then make him pick you up." It's the least Pillsbury Doughboy could do for her.

"Samir, can you get dressed, please?" She pressed her hands together and he cursed.

"I already answered that."

"Listen, you owe me. Come on."

"I owe you? For what, for lying to me?"

"I did not lie to you." She looked around the room and found the magazine lying on the bed. "I protected you. From that witch. It wasn't easy. She's scary."

"Right." But he was stupid enough to smile. She took full advantage and blasted him with all one-twenty watts of her smile. And he wanted to kiss her sneaky lips so bad, he had to step away and push into the mirrored closet behind him. "You should not have come here, Mili. You don't just walk into some man's hotel room like this."

"You're not just some man. You're Samir." She pushed the cascading mass of curls off her face with both hands and he knew it was going to bounce right back.

"Okay, somewhere in there is a compliment."

"Of course it's a compliment. I feel safe with you. You're my friend. I know you will never hurt me. The list is endless."

Yeah, an endless pile of crap. He didn't feel safe with her. He didn't want to be just her friend. And he knew he was going to hurt her shitless. "So this is my married friend come to get me. Nothing more."

She nodded and her hair slid back around her face. "Nothing more."

He dropped his robe.

At least five shades of red rushed up her cheeks. "What are you doing?" It was no more than a squeak, but he was impressed she got the words out.

"I'm changing like you asked me to, why?" He had pulled on boxers earlier, but the rest of him was as bare as the day he was born. He turned away and threw open the closet with both arms, no point having those back muscles if he couldn't put them to good use when he needed to. He took his time pulling pants out of the closet. Then an even longer time bending over and pulling them on. He'd been a model for almost a decade. She had no idea whom she was messing with.

She made an incoherent sound behind him, something between a choke and a groan. He straightened up and caught her reflection in the mirror. She was straining to breathe. "Did you say something?"

She shook her head. "No. I—" She gulped air.

He reached into the closet and pulled a shirt off a hanger. What a stroke of luck to have just finished his pushups and a hot shower. His abs, his arms, all of him was pumped and photo-shoot ready.

"You have a tattoo," she whispered. Lust glazed her eyes as they locked on his back.

Little Sam raged to life in all his glory. It was a good thing Samir had pulled his pants on. Not that they did much. He moved the shirt in front of him and drew a steadying breath as she disappeared behind him in the mirror.

Cool fingers hovered over his skin, cutting through the heat radiating from her body. "They're wings." Her breath kissed his skin. Her finger landed on his back and traced the spine inked onto his spine, traced the wings that fanned out across his shoulder blades. "Like an angel."

He turned around to face her. "Not an angel. A coward—they mean I can fly away at will."

The lust fogging her eyes cleared. "Craving freedom doesn't make you a coward, Samir."

And he knew then that she knew what it meant to crave freedom. He knew how much she craved it in this moment. What it cost her. How much it hurt her to not have it.

He pulled on his shirt and stepped back.

For a moment she didn't move. Then she shook her head as if to clear it, as if shaking off everything between them were that simple. She reached for his shirt and started fastening the buttons, her brows knitted together in concentration, her shoulders slumped, her fingers feathers on his chest. She slipped one button in place, then the next.

He just stood there, his fists hanging like dead weights from his arms. The mirror before him reflected the mirror behind him, multiplying their tethered forms a million times over. Yearning coiled like springs in their bodies spun out in infinite succession, image after image for as far as he could see.

"Damn but these guys know how to throw a wedding," Samir said, leaning into Mili's ear. Gooseflesh danced up and down her neck. She closed her eyes. No. She had to stop reacting to him like this. This was just who Samir was. He did these things. They meant nothing to him. He kissed women, countless women. He touched them as if he owned them. It was his world. She had let herself get dragged into it. And now she didn't know what any of it meant. She was what her *naani* called the halfway dog, who belonged neither in the house nor in the yard.

She stepped away from him. He followed her, close, as though some invisible rope connected them. The backyard was lit up like the parliament buildings in Delhi on Republic Day. There must've been at least a million lights. Red and gold today, not the blue and white from yesterday. Also, unlike yesterday, they weren't sprinkled like stars across the backyard, instead they outlined everything. The perimeter of the yard, the patio, every edge of the house, every tiered flower bed, it was all outlined in light.

A liveried band played at one end of the wooden dance floor and a Hawaiian bar had been constructed at the other end where almost the entire guest population was currently gathered. At the far end of the lawn stood the most beautiful four-post altar Mili had ever seen. Roses and ivy vines cascaded from wooden trellises held up by columns draped in cream and gold silk.

"Drama Queen Alert," Samir whispered into her already tingling ear as Ridhi's mom rose out of the crowd like a golden phoenix and rushed toward them.

So much gold threadwork was crammed into her sari Mili couldn't tell the original color of the fabric. "Where on earth have you two been?" she hissed, even as she pulled Mili into a hug.

"Sorry, Auntie, Samir takes longer to get dressed than a woman. This is beautiful."

"Isn't it? The things these wedding planners can do these days. One week! Can you believe? I told them, here, take this money, make it happen. Boom. Done!" She surveyed the yard much like Naani surveyed her courtyard when Mili decorated it with a hundred lamps at Diwali time. "No less than one of your Bollywood affairs, no?" she asked Samir expectantly, and he nodded. Then suddenly her brows knitted together. "You don't think we need more lights, do you?"

Samir choked on his drink.

Ridhi's mom joined Mili in thumping his back. "*Hai hai, beta.*

Drink slow. There's lots, no hurry. The night is young, no?" Then
to Mili, "*Arrey*, but why are you still standing here? Your friend has
been shrieking for you. She's taken the entire household on her
head and she's dancing around screaming, 'Where is Mili? Where
is Mili?' That girl! Go, go. Go upstairs." And with that she swept
off and swooped down on a waiter. "Look at your tray, it's empty.
Go, go, we want trays full when you serve. People should not think,
'oh, no food.' "

The terrified waiter nodded furiously and ran toward the tan-
door-style oven where whole spiced chickens and colorful skewers
of kebabs spun over the raging flame.

Mili turned away from the sight and elbowed Samir, who was
taking a long sip of his drink. "*Hai hai*, drink slow. There's lots,"
she said, imitating Ridhi's mother's Punjabi accent.

"Not on your life." He chugged the rest of his drink. But at least
he smiled.

Which made relief flood through her. She hated it when he took
on his brooding avatar. "I have to go see what Ridhi wants." For
some reason the idea of leaving him right now set off a strange
ache inside her. An ache she had no business feeling.

He handed his glass to a passing waiter and grabbed another
two glasses off a tray. "Go," he said and headed toward Ravi, who
looked ridiculously glad to see him.

Upstairs Ridhi had been holding off her gaggle of cousins from
ambushing the hairdresser. Ridhi pushed Mili into a chair in front
of her. The poor woman, who already looked exhausted, took one
look at Mili's hair and groaned.

By the time the bride made her way down the aisle to the beat
of *dholki* drums, Samir was so happily buzzed he actually thought
Horse-woman looked quite the vision in her bridal finery, plus she
was quiet, praise the gods.

"Close your mouth, man," he said to Ravi, "you have an audience."

Ravi took one quick sip, handed his glass to Samir, and followed
Ridhi's dad to the altar. His eyes never left his bride, the pathetic
lost cause.

"What, one glass not enough for you?" Mili said, coming to stand next to him. He loved how she looked up at him. He loved that she had walked straight to him. He loved how the sari hugged her body.

"*Hai hai*, but there's lots," he said, making a Mrs. Kapoor face and waving both glasses at her.

That earned him a smile. Which, predictably enough, he loved.

He put Ravi's glass on the high table next to them. "You tied your hair."

She spun around to show him a complicated updo that was so large it doubled the size of her head. Lots of little pearls were woven into it.

"Very elaborate." He reached out and touched the pearls, slipping one out, rolling it between his fingers and hiding it in his palm.

"Apparently, it's called an 'updo.' And it's really, really heavy."

He pointed to his shoulder. "Glad to be of service." He slipped the pearl into his pocket.

She frowned at his shoulder. "I was thinking maybe we could sit down."

They eased into the back row of the auditorium-style chairs arranged around the altar. In a stroke of unexpected courage, Ravi had insisted on a short, no-frills ceremony—just seven circles around the sacred fire, a garland exchange, and that was that. And he hadn't budged in the face of some daunting opposition.

Mili sank into the seat, her tiny body gathered into itself. As the priest started chanting, her sparkling eyes went somber, her fingers twisted together in her lap. Samir reached out and placed a tentative hand on her back. She sniffed and squeezed her reddening nose with the end of her sari and her jaw worked to prevent the tears from forming. His heart twisted. What must it be like for her to watch someone get married?

"Amazingly, I remember it," she whispered, as if he had spoken his thoughts out loud. "Not a stark clear memory, but I do remember how that day felt." She turned to him and searched his face, making sure he didn't mind her bringing up *that* conversation. "Maybe I remember it only because my *naani* talked about it so much. Apparently, I cried a lot. Screamed and screamed until my mother-in-law asked the priest to rush through the ceremony so my *naani* could take me home."

A startling vivid memory of a screaming girl with huge cheeks and huge eyes flashed in Samir's mind. Along with the intense restlessness that her crying had set off in his chest. The memory was so out of the blue and so stark he felt as though someone had pulled the chair from under him. The memory that followed was starker still. The slash of the belt slicing his back, pain upon pain, going on without end. The taste of his own tears, the heavy shame of his screams. The relief of Virat throwing himself on top of him to stop the belt.

Mili's brow crinkled. Sweat trickled down his spine and moistened his scalp. He wiped his hand over his forehead. His fingers were ice.

"Samir, are you all right?" She took his hand. "Are you sick?"

This was bullshit. Fucking ancient history. "I'm fine." He downed the rest of his drink, his entire buzz gone. "You were saying?"

"Nothing. Just that I don't remember anything else from when I was that young. But I actually remember my wedding."

"And your groom. Do you remember him?" Even to his own ears he sounded harsh.

She swallowed and of course she colored, but she didn't answer.

"Do you even know what he looks like now?"

Pain flashed in her eyes. He felt it all the way in his gut. But he couldn't stop. "You have the right to file for an annulment, you know."

She looked startled. "Annulment? You mean like a divorce?"

"Well, technically it's not a marriage, so, it's not a divorce."

She slid her hand out from under his, but he refused to remove his hand from her lap. "My *naani* will kill herself. If she doesn't have a heart attack first." Her eyes shot angry sparks at him. "And stop saying it's not a marriage. It is. I believe with all my heart that we will be together, that he will come for me one day."

"What if you find yourself in a situation where you don't want him to?"

Sickening sympathy diffused the anger in her eyes. "I'll just have to stay away from such a situation then, won't I?" She put his hand back on his lap.

He gripped her fingers and held them in place. "What if you can't? What if it just happens? Would you give it a chance?"

She met his eyes, unflinching. "No. The truth is I can't imagine being married to anyone else. I know you don't understand it. But my marriage is very real to me."

"What if something else becomes even more real?"

She pulled her hand away. "Samir, please, can we not do this? Can we just be friends, at least for today, for just one day more, please?" She looked so tired, so beseeching, so certain he would do as she wished.

He grabbed her hand again and dropped a kiss on her fingertips. "Mili, we will always be friends. Whatever else we become we will always be friends. Will you remember that? If you ever forget, will you promise to remember that *this*"—he traced an arc between them with his finger—"this is real. Okay?"

Her brows drew together again. "Of course."

He was blathering like an idiot, but he never wanted her to doubt what her friendship meant to him. Even though she would never know what she had come to mean to him. Because suddenly he could see clearly where they were headed and how violently the shit was going to hit the fan.

She leaned her head into the back of the chair. "This updo is really heavy," she said as they watched Ridhi and Ravi take their last and final walk around the sacred fire, the last vow after which there would be no going back. Unless of course they decided to go back.

"I can help you get out of it, you know, if you wanted out."

She straightened up and glared at him.

"Relax, I was talking about the updo." He gave her his best bad-boy smolder. "What did you think I was talking about?"

The crowd burst into applause and everyone stood. Ridhi and Ravi exchanged garlands, then Ridhi threw her arms around Ravi and kissed him—on the lips. There were many gasps, but amazingly enough, no one fainted.

In perfectly sane families the time after the bride and groom ex-changed garlands was chaotic. What with everyone descending on the couple to bless them, congratulate them, and generally hug and kiss the hell out of them. So Samir wasn't in the least bit sur-prised at the insanity that ensued with the Kapoor clan. Everyone sobbed. Mrs. Kapoor wrapped her arms around her daughter and refused to let her go. Mother and daughter remained stuck to-gether until the bride's father pried them apart. "Come on, Lovely, come now. She's not going far."

"My baby, my baby, my baby," Mrs. Lovely Kapoor repeated, giving each rendition a different nuance, much like they did in act-ing class.

"Don't say one word," Mili warned when she saw his expres-sion. Tears streamed down her face. Unlike the Kapoor women her eyeliner was not run-proof. She took a deep wet sniff and smiled through her tears in Ridhi's direction.

Samir put his napkin back under his drink. Let her enjoy her moment. There would be plenty of women jumping on her when they saw the streaks running down her face. As far as he was con-cerned that wet streaky face flushed with emotion and bare of even a hint of vanity was the most utterly beautiful face he had ever seen.

He had to tell her the truth.

The realization came to him in a flash. Bhai was everything to him. But his brother and he had completely misjudged Mili. There had to be more to the legal shit than met the eye and he was going to find out what it was. And he was going to tell her every-thing and let her decide what she wanted to do. As soon as the damn script was done, he was going to tell her everything. No mat-ter what the consequences.

She smiled as Ridhi jangled her bangles over the heads of a bunch of girls who bowed in front of her.

"What are they doing?" Samir asked.

Mili pointed to the golden tassels with golden foil flowers that hung from Ridhi's bangles. "The elders tied those on Ridhi's bangles for good luck earlier. Now Ridhi is trying to shake them off over the unmarried girls' heads. If a flower falls on an unmarried girl's head, it means she'll be next in line to get married."

"Ah, that explains it. I think your witch has been under Ridhi's arms for a full five minutes," he said, making her smile.

"OMG, look at your face!" It was the first thing Ridhi said to Mili when they finally made their way to the newlyweds. She swiped Mili's face with a wet tissue and set her to rights. Then she squeezed Mili into a hug so tight Samir feared for her life.

Samir congratulated Ravi and bit back the ball-and-chain jokes. He was actually feeling a little envious of the bastard, which should've scared him shitless but didn't. Which in turn did scare him shitless. "You look great, Ridhi. Congratulations."

Mili, Ravi, and Ridhi all gawked at him and waited for him to say something to ruin it, but he didn't.

"Oh. My. God. That is just. So. Sweet." Ridhi threw her arms around him, kissing him squarely on one cheek, then twisting his face around with both hands and kissing him on the other cheek.

He squeezed his eyes shut and patted Ridhi's shoulder awkwardly. Mili beamed at him like a proud mother hen and the torture seemed almost worth it.

"Why didn't you tell me about the smudged eyeliner?" she asked as they walked away.

"What smudged eyeliner?" Shit, now he was making puppydog eyes at her.

She rolled her eyes, but she glowed and panic squeezed in his chest.

"You should've told me. I'm sure I looked like a panda bear," she said.

He pinched his finger and thumb together to indicate that maybe she had looked just a little bit like a panda. She smacked his arm.

What he really wanted to tell her was how very beautiful she looked, how being touched by her felt. "Sorry I didn't say anything," he said instead. "But there is something I want to tell you now."

She raised terrified eyes at him. "Samir, please."

"Hear me out, because later you'll ask why I didn't say anything."

"Samir, no. Don't say anything. Please." Her voice was a breathless whisper.

"Mili, you have a golden flower in your hair. Ridhi must've dropped it on your head when she hugged you."

19

Mili knew they were back in Ypsilanti when she saw the water tower with its unmistakably phallic shape.

Samir lifted his sunglasses onto his forehead and squinted at the obscene structure. "I know I've hardly slept all night but you won't believe what I'm seeing right now."

She laughed.

"No, seriously, there's a giant erection in the middle of the road. Tell me I'm hallucinating."

"You're not hallucinating."

"Then what the fu—heck is that?"

"That's what everyone in college calls the Ypsi-mmm . . . the Ypsi-dick." She mumbled the last word and pressed her hand to her mouth self-consciously.

He didn't tease her about it. He just twisted around in his seat and looked at the tower as they passed. She caught his eyes crinkling with laughter before he dropped his sunglasses back in place.

Mili pinched her own arm. Driving in a yellow convertible on this beautiful early-September day with Samir had to be a dream. This entire trip had to be a dream. She had never seen Samir like this. She had asked for his friendship and he had given it to her with nothing held back. He had talked and listened, his curiosity about her endless. She had never felt so safe, so free to share herself. She'd told him about growing up in her grandmother's house, about being teacher's pet, about playing cricket with the village boys until she was twelve, after which she wasn't allowed to anymore.

She told him about winning a regional essay contest in high school and getting on a bus to go to New Delhi. Seeing the parliament houses, seeing Fatehpur Sikri, Emperor Akbar's red sandstone palace complex. About meeting the president of India, and seeing the Gandhi memorial. About seeing young girls in pants and skirts shopping in the markets of Janpath. Soaking up a whole new world and yearning to come back to it someday. About applying to Jaipur University without letting Naani know and then convincing her to let her go.

"How did you convince her?" he asked.

"I showed her a film in which the hero was an Air Force officer. The women in the movie were stylish and modern and educated. I told her maybe that's what he wanted. How could he want a village girl when these were the women he was used to?"

"And she listened?" He was incredulous.

"You have to understand how desperate my *naani*'s situation is. She had four children, but she lost two boys, one girl, and her husband to a cholera epidemic. My mother was the only responsibility she had left. Once she had my mother married off, she thought all her duties were done. She thought my father would take care of everything. But instead, my parents died and she was left with me and she had to start over. The dowry, protecting my honor, raising me to be a good wife. She had to do it all again. Then my husband's grandfather offered for me. Yet again Naani thought she was done. But then my husband's mother packed him up and took off for the city. His grandfather squeezed everything out of my grandmother. He took the grain from our fields, demanded clothes and jewels for every festival. Every year he assured Naani this year they would take me home. I loved school so she kept letting me study. She thought it would please my city husband. She would do anything to see me in my own home, settled and off her hands."

Samir paled, his face strained with sadness. But she didn't want his sympathy. What she wanted was to keep talking to him in this borrowed time they had left together.

"And how did she let you come to America?" he asked.

"Well, with that I didn't give her a choice. I had just started working at the National Women's Center in Jaipur. My boss recommended me for the scholarship program but I still needed money for a ticket. I told Naani I was going to go see my husband so I needed my dowry jewelry. And I sold it. I didn't tell her I was here until I was already here."

It had been a terrible, unforgivable thing to do. But instead of being disgusted, Samir looked impressed.

"Why didn't you ever really go see your husband?"

She shrugged. "I'm not sure. Where I come from it's just not how we do things. Plus, I . . . I felt like maybe there was a reason he hadn't come for me. What city boy wants a village girl, right? But then I went to Jaipur, got a job, a scholarship, I made it all the way here by myself. And I'm the best student in my program." No, she didn't feel unworthy anymore.

Suddenly she was angry. Truly angry. And terribly sad. She had wasted so much time feeling unworthy. She was smart and accomplished. She had always been. And for the first time in her life she also felt beautiful. And she wished it didn't have anything to do with the way Samir was looking at her.

But Samir had that gift. No wonder countless women had fallen under his spell. She thought of the *Filmfare* magazine: *Bollywood playboy changes women like he changes clothes.* The strange thing was she could imagine him like that, running from involvement. But she could also see him as something more.

"What about you, how did you end up in Mumbai? A hotshot director with a girlfriend angry enough to accuse him of beating her up," she asked as he turned down their street.

"I have a gift for making women mad."

She smiled. "No! Really?"

He narrowed his golden eyes at her over his sunglasses, but they were smiling. "I grew up in Nagpur. But I went to Mumbai to go to college and got picked up on campus by a modeling scout my first year. Guess what my first assignment was?" He smiled that thirty-two-teeth smile of his. "A toothpaste commercial."

"I knew it!"

"Modeling led to a bit part in a movie. But I spent so much time behind the camera with my director, he signed me on as assistant director. And from then on I knew exactly what I wanted to do with my life."

He made a screeching turn and pulled into their pothole-filled parking lot. A thought poked at Mili's mind. "Samir, why didn't you tell me that your movies were such big hits?"

He shrugged. "You never asked."

She noticed the peeling paint on her balcony, the curling, discolored roof tiles, and the thought roared to life. She slapped her hand across her mouth. "My God, you were never going to live in my building, were you? You only moved there after I got hurt. Why did you move into my building, Samir?" But she already knew. It had to do with her being hurt and needing help. Her throat constricted.

Instead of jumping out of the car as soon as it stopped like he usually did, he turned to her and studied her from behind his sunglasses, his face more serious than she'd ever seen it. "You give me too much credit, Mili." He took a deep breath, his chest swelling under the stretched cotton as he measured his words. "Truth is, I had been struggling with my writing for almost a year. No matter what I tried, I hadn't been able to write."

"That's why you signed up for the workshop," she said.

He swallowed and removed his sunglasses. And the relief of meeting his eyes again was so intense it was absurd. "The night I met you I was able to write again. It was you, Mili. You gave me back my ability to write. And I was too afraid the words would stop if I wasn't around you." The gold in his eyes darkened with emotion, as though a great burden rested on his heart, and her heart sprouted wings and started fluttering about in her chest.

He jumped out of the car, jogged to her side, and held open her door. "Thank you."

She stood and leaned back to look up at him. "That's it? That's all I get, a thank-you?"

A smile crinkled the edges of those too-serious eyes.

"Sounds to me like I was solely responsible for you writing this multimillion-rupee script."

"Let's not get carried away." He tried but he couldn't suppress that Colgate smile. God, how she loved that smile of his.

"But you couldn't have done it without me, right? So you owe me."

He leaned past her and pulled the bags out of the car. "I just drove you to your best friend's wedding and you want more? A bit greedy, don't you think?" But he was looking at her like he would give her anything she asked for and the fluttering intensified.

"I want your hero not to lose the love of his life." She had no idea why it mattered so much that he believe in happy endings, but it did.

"Okay," he said with a casual shrug, "anything else?"

"Really?" she all but shrieked. And then she looked in his golden eyes and she knew. He had already changed his story because of what she had said. She pressed her hand into her heart. "It doesn't count if you've already done it without me asking. You still owe me."

He threw his head back and laughed. "What now?"

She smiled at him, a crazy idea popping into her head. "Finish your script first. Then I'll tell you. But you can't say no."

"Of course I can't." And he followed her up the stairs.

He helped her put the sacks of food Ridhi's mom had given them into the fridge. She asked him to stay for dinner and he sank down into the mattress on the living room floor while she went in to change. When she came out she found him fast asleep. She tried to wake him but he was dead to the world. With the amount of sleep he'd been getting between his writing and the wedding, waking him up was a lost cause.

Mili heated a plate of food for herself, sat cross-legged on the carpet across from him, and watched him sleep as she ate. He was definitely the most handsome man she had ever seen. The perfect full mouth, the strongly etched jaw, the subtle cleft digging into his square chin. But it was more than just his features. It was the determination in his jaw, the humor dancing in his eyes, even the cynicism that played around his mouth, that brought all his beautiful features alive.

Yes, he was arrogant and impatient and stubborn. But he was also self-deprecating and more gentle and generous than anyone she knew. And when all his contradictions mingled in his face, in his big muscular body, he was like a huge living magnet.

A huge living magnet that had totally sucked her in. She touched her lips. The memory of his kiss was as real as physical sensation. She was going to carry it to her grave. In fact, she was going to carry the memories of this entire month to her dying day.

What if something else becomes even more real? Would you give it a chance?

She pushed the potatoes on her plate with the roti. Dear God, what was she going to do?

His phone buzzed next to him. It must have slipped out of his hands when he fell asleep. She picked it up.

Bhai flashed across the screen.

She hit the Ignore button.

Within five seconds it buzzed again.

Bhai, again. She hit Ignore again. Almost instantly it buzzed again.

Apparently Samir's brother was not in the habit of being ignored by him. That or there was an emergency. When it buzzed for the fifth time, she panicked. She laid one hand on Samir's arm and gave him a shake. "Samir, it's your brother."

He didn't so much as budge. She answered the phone. "Hello?"

A beat of silence. She'd thrown poor old Bhai for a loop. "Who is this?"

"This is Mili. I'm sorry, Samir is sleeping."

Another beat of silence. Oh no, maybe that hadn't been the right thing to say.

"He was really tired." Good Lord, that came out even more wrong.

"*Mili*, did you say?" Samir's brother finally found his voice. He emphasized her name, as if it were in some way amusing. He sounded just as arrogant as Samir.

"Yes. Can I take a message?"

"Yes, *Mili*, you can. Tell Chintu that if he's done with his *tiring work* his big brother would like a moment of his time. After he wakes up, of course."

"Sure. I'll ask him to call you." What a strange man.

Had he called Samir *Chintu?* That had to be the funniest thing Mili had ever heard. The biggest, no, the most humungous man she knew was called "tiny." Oh, how much fun she was going to have with this!

She couldn't stop smiling as she put her plate away, left some food out for Samir, and cleaned up. But even after she was done, she found that she couldn't go to bed. She had some reading to do for school, so she grabbed her book and settled down to read across from his sleeping form.

It started slow. Hands dragged him and dragged him. He clawed the floor with his toes, trying to find purchase, trying to stop it at any cost. It came anyway. A quick swish in his ear before the belt sliced his back, his buttocks. He tried to scream but there was no air in his lungs. It came again. Then again and again. He choked on his own sobs. He struggled to catch a breath but wetness drowned him. *White bastard. White. Bastard.* He twisted around himself, sweating, cold, panting. The hands lifted him, bony fingers gouging out his skin. He hung from them for endless moments. The floor fell away from under him. His stomach leapt into his throat and he fell without end into a bottomless well. His own gasps tore at his ears. Hands rubbed his shoulders.

"Samir. It's okay. Wake up." Tiny hands shook him.

He looked at her.

"It's me. It's Mili. It's okay. Shh . . ." Curls spilled like midnight around her face, worry shadowed her eyes and lined her forehead.

Shame sprang in his chest under her fingers.

He sat up and grabbed his head in his hands. Holy fucking mother of God. Of all the places this could have happened.

She left him, then came back with a glass of water.

He took it wordlessly. He was never going to be able to speak in her presence again.

She rubbed his back. Exactly where the belt had hit. And instead of driving him mad with pain it soothed him. He took a deep breath and drank and drank. The shame in his throat turned each gulp into hard labor.

"Here, give me that." She took the glass from him but didn't remove the hand from his back.

He wanted to thank her. He couldn't.

He wanted to get up and leave her apartment. He couldn't.

This was almost as bad as crying in front of his entire fifth-grade class when the teacher had read a story about a mother elephant being killed by hunters, leaving the baby to fend for herself. No, this was even more mortifying than that.

"You're not going to start crying, are you?" The gentlest smile kissed her lips and made her eyes glow. "It's what I always did when my *naani* came to me after I had a nightmare. It was a ploy to get her to let me sleep with her."

He smiled.

She blushed.

"That's not what I meant," she stuttered, and just like that the clawing shame vanished.

"It would help, you know," he said, ridiculously relieved to find his inner cocky bastard again.

"Samir."

"Seriously. I need comfort."

"Sa-mir." He loved it when she broke his name up like that.

"You have no idea how damaged I feel right now." He patted his chest, all drama queen.

She blushed and covered her face with her hands.

"If I cry will you let me?"

"*Ugh*. You're awful." But she let him pull her hands away from her flaming face. She wrapped her arms around his waist and held him. And it felt like he had never been whipped with a belt. It felt like fucking paradise.

20

When Mili arrived early at her office in Pierce Hall she had no idea her life was about to change forever. Last night after Samir had left she couldn't sleep. She kept thinking of his face, white as a sheet, his golden tan gone, his eyes wild, unseeing. All of him slick with sweat. His shirt wet, his cheeks wet, his hair wet.

That must have been some nightmare.

Her big, strong, indomitable Samir had scars. And she had an inkling she knew where they came from. More importantly, she had an idea how she might be able to help him heal them. The idea had been poking around in her head ever since they'd talked about their parents that night before Ridhi's wedding. And ever since they got back to Ypsilanti, she hadn't been able to get it out of her head. It was time to turn the idea into action.

She slung her mirrorwork sack on her chair. She had two phone calls to make before she started making copies of the grant proposal that was due today. First she called Ridhi. As expected she got her voicemail and left a message. Knowing how Ridhi was going to react made her smile. But Ridhi's family was really well connected. If anyone could help her find a lost person, it was Ridhi.

Next, she called her grandmother. And the world slipped from beneath her feet.

Mili had never heard her grandmother cry like this, as if her heart was broken, her faith destroyed. A feeling of doom so dark sprang in Mili's belly, she felt suspended over a precipice while someone hacked away at the rope.

She jumped off the desk she was perched on and rubbed her icy palms on her jeans. "Naani, at least tell me what happened."

"Oh Krishna, what did we do to deserve such a thing? Oh my beautiful child. I should've known when your parents died that you were cursed. I should have known then that there was no hope for you. I should never have listened to that evil son of a witch."

"Naani, please, calm down. What could be that bad?" Suddenly the room spun. She knew what it was. "Oh God, something's happened to him, hasn't it? Something's happened to Viratji."

"Don't say his cursed name in front of me. Oh Krishna, what kind of people do you make? What kind of days do you show us? Oh my poor, sweet child."

Tears sprang into Mili's eyes. "Is he hurt?" Oh God, please let it be just that, nothing worse. Guilt rose in her chest and tightened her throat. She was being punished for what she had done with Samir. Please, *please* don't let him suffer for her sins.

"What hurt? He deserves to be gobbled up by venomous snakes. But he won't get away with it. He has to pay. Curses on him, the son of a rabid dog." She blew her nose into the phone and paused, collecting herself before spitting it out. "He's gone and made another marriage, Mili. Your husband has got himself another wife."

It was great to hear Virat's voice so strong again but Samir had no idea what his brother was so damn amused about. "You've been there for four weeks, Chintu, and you've already shacked up with some chick? Come on, brother, when are you going to grow up?"

"What're you talking about, Bhai?" Samir sat up on the lumpy mattress on the floor of his shit-colored apartment, closed his eyes, and tried to picture himself in his beloved Mumbai flat.

"Your girlfriend picked up the phone when I called."

Mili had answered his phone? Why would she do that?

"Apparently *Sa-mir*"—Virat did the worst imitation of the way Mili said his name—"was very tired. Apparently *Sa-mir* had been up all night." Okay, so it wasn't that bad of an imitation. She did kind of stretch his name out like that, as if it meant more than it did.

He rubbed his forehead. "Bhai, I really was tired. I had driven from Columbus for four hours. I really was asleep. It's not like it sounds."

"Wow. Sam Rathod getting all defensive about being with a woman? Who are you and what did you do with my cocky bastard of a brother?"

Shit.

"So what were you doing in Columbus anyway?"

"Long story. There was a wedding. Some friends I made here."

Bhai gasped as if Samir had just jumped off a cliff. "You went to someone's *wedding?* We can't get you to go to cousins' weddings here and you went to a wedding?"

"I have five missed calls from you. Is everything okay?" Not the most skillful change of topic but it would have to do.

"We got another legal notice from the girl."

"Legal notice?" How was that even possible?

"Yes, legal notice, you know, the things the girl's been sending us? It's the reason you're there, remember. Hello? Anybody home?"

"Of course. Sorry. I'm a little distracted."

"No shit. Your Mili seems to be really working you hard." Virat guffawed. "Now the girl's claiming abandonment and emotional trauma. Breach of contract. All sorts of legal bullshit. She's saying that the Village Panch Council can even grant the entire estate to her."

The phone turned heavy in Samir's hand. *I'll be late. I have something important to take care of.* Mili had looked distinctly guilty when she'd told him that this morning.

"You sure, Bhai?"

"No, I'm making this shit up on the fly. What's wrong with you, Chintu? I have the papers in front of me. I spoke with your lawyer. He wants to know if there's a marriage certificate. We don't have one but she might. Since we were underage it's still not binding but if the Panch Council ratified it after we came of age, then we might have a bigger battle on our hands if she refuses to sign the annulment. I know you're trying to finish up the script but have you even met Malvika yet?"

"Yes. I told you I'm taking care of it, Bhai. How's Rima?"

"She's still cramping." All the fight went out of his brother's voice. "The doctor's put her on bed rest."

"And you're telling me this now?"

"She's going to be fine. It's just a precaution. Just for a few weeks."

Then why the fuck do you sound like that? "I'm sure it is, Bhai." It had to be. "You take care of getting better. And you take care of Rima. I'll take care of things here."

The guilty look on Mili's face from that morning blazed in Samir's head as he walked down the passageway from his apartment to hers. He'd asked her a few times what she was up to but he had been so involved in finishing the script he hadn't given much thought to anything else.

"Finish your script," she'd said. "And don't forget your promise." Idiot that he was, anticipation had flared through him like a fucking teenager.

He turned the key in her door and found a yellow sticky note under the peephole.

Don't stand around reading notes. Hurry and finish up!

He peeled the note off the door and took it in with him.

There was a second note on the refrigerator. *Food on red plate is breakfast. Food on blue plate is lunch. Be back before dinner.*

The red plate had two *parathas* on it, one cup of yogurt, and mango pickle. The entire thing was wrapped in cling wrap with another sticky note. *The* parathas *are to die for. God bless Lovely.* And a smiley face.

He remembered her slipping pieces of *paratha* into his mouth and a thrill went down his spine. He stuck all three notes together and put them in his pocket. Something was very wrong. There was no mistaking that Mili had looked very purposeful, and very guilty that morning. There was no mistaking, either, that she was struggling to keep their relationship confined to friendship, determined to give her damned "marriage" a chance. No, this was not the time to think about the inferno between them. He put the food back in the fridge. If she had sent a legal notice over the past weeks, she had to have copies in the apartment.

There was only one way to find out.

He stood at her bedroom door, fully aware that he was about to do something entirely and indelibly irreversible. He was about to break every last ounce of trust she had put in him.

Every moment he had spent with Mili, every smile, every soft touch pulled him back.

I believe with all my heart that we will be together, that he will come for me one day.

Her heart was going to break either way. Samir had to protect what he knew for sure: Bhai and Rima had to be together. No one deserved it more than they did.

He crossed the threshold into her bedroom. Had it really been only three weeks since he had left her standing here, helpless and hurting, and she had crumpled to the floor without him? But she hadn't been angry, she'd been touched that he'd come back.

He looked around the room. Desolation crawled up his spine. The mattress on the floor was neatly made with the scratchy blanket and a faded sheet hand-sewn from an old cotton sari. The kind of saris Baiji wore to bed. The mattress was so tiny, so narrow, only a pin tuck like Mili could fit on it. Half his legs would hang off. Not that he would ever find out.

Other than the mattress there were precisely two pieces of furniture. One rickety metal desk and one set of dresser drawers that looked old enough to be from the eighteenth century. Except there was no cheap boxboard in the eighteenth century. He yanked out a drawer. It flew out of its slot and landed on his toe. *Fuck!* Everything landed on his feet. Boats, Mili had called them. Her onyx eyes widened to saucers in his head. *Good lord, what size feet do you have?*

How a question that mundane, that innocent, could turn him on this much he had no idea.

He jammed the drawer back in, steadied his hands, and pulled another drawer out. Underwear. Great, he was going through her underwear drawer. He slammed it shut. *Not going to think about it.*

Not going to think about the glimpse of black lace lying on white cotton.
She had black lace underwear?

There was nothing in the rest of the drawers. Not one thing.
Nothing in the closet either. Except three T-shirts and a single pair
of jeans on hangers. The nothingness of her closet squeezed in his
chest and made horrible restlessness churn inside him. No shoes,
not one pair. No scarves, no bags, no jackets, no saris, no *kurtis*.
Nothing but emptiness and the stale smell of old boxboard. What
kind of girl owned six T-shirts and lace underwear?

Not going to think about the underwear.

His own closet took up an entire room in his flat. He had motor-
ized racks that moved back and forth on remote-controlled tracks.
He spent so much time in his closet it was wired for sound. He
missed his Bose speakers. He had donated twenty-eight pairs of
jeans and forty pairs of shoes at the last Stars charity gala.

Would you want to be with a man more pretty than you?

He rammed his fingers through his hair and squeezed his head
and turned to her desk. Nothing except piles of books, all with library tags. More squeezing in his chest. The desk didn't even have
drawers. Even more squeezing.

Samir sank down on his knees and looked under the rickety
black metal frame. Pushed up against the back wall all the way in
the corner was a brown suitcase. He reached it easily and pulled it
out. It was the kind of bag you saw in old movies. Not the eighties
kind of old, the fifties kind of old. Brown cloth on cardboard with
metal latches that popped up when you slid the spring-loaded buttons aside. He slid, and the latch sprang up with a snap.

He pulled back. It wasn't too late to stop. He had done a lot of
awful things, but this felt worse than anything he'd ever done. Mili
had taken him in, shared everything she had with him, and for all
the meagerness of her possessions she had enriched him tenfold.
To her he had been nothing more than someone who happened to
know someone from her village, and yet that had been all she
needed. She had let him have everything, the use of her home, the
full force of her friendship and trust. And he had taken it without
thought, without decency. But this was crossing the line. Her closet,

the underwear drawer—at least those were right there out in the open. She wasn't *trying* to hide them.

Something about the way the brown bag was pushed against the wall told him it was private. Opening the bag was worse even than touching her underwear drawer. It was a violation. He knew that with as much clarity as he knew his own name. What he was about to do was unforgivable. For all her bravado, and her openness, Samir knew Mili hid entire worlds inside her she didn't share. He'd seen the tip but she didn't want him to see the iceberg. He knew the feeling well.

He couldn't do it. He couldn't go here uninvited. He started to push the little metal latches back in place.

If Rima isn't my legal wife that makes our child a bastard, Chintu.

His brother's first words to him when he came out of the coma.

His niece or nephew was wanted. The entire family was waiting with almost crazed anticipation. The injustice, the stifling pain of abandonment Samir knew only too well would never rest on the baby's shoulders. No one would ever call her or him a name that held the power to crumble everything.

White bastard. White. Bastard.

Samir gripped the hard edge of the suitcase and threw it open.

A stack of saris in vibrant colors sat wrapped in clear cellophane. The kind of saris women wore to weddings in villages, twenty years ago. He touched the one that lay on top of all the others. A bridal red with bridal gold. And bangles, bundles of glass bangles tied together with satin ribbon. He remembered how she had looked with an armful of bangles. And pearls in her hair. The pearl he had stolen was tucked away in one corner of his wallet.

He picked up a red velvet jewelry box and opened it. Her *mangalsutra*. Black beads strung with gold chain—her marriage chain. He closed the box and put it back. Under the saris, under the bangles, under the velvet box, hidden beneath all her most precious possessions, was a white envelope. He opened it and slid out the contents. Three pictures and a single sheet of paper in a plastic sleeve. A picture of a younger, smiling Mili sitting at the feet of a toothless old woman with silver hair, the cane in her hand giving her a regal bearing.

Mili looked happy—Mili's signature brand of happiness. She must've been ten in this picture and she already looked world-weary and wise. She had never had a childhood. He swallowed the painful lump that lodged in his throat. But he didn't stop. The other two photographs were black and white. One of an older couple—the man wore a huge turban and an uppity landowner expression, the woman was the same one from the other picture, only younger. The other of a much younger couple—the man dressed in a starched white shirt and pleated pants. The woman in a bright floral sari, her head covered, but her face smiling. The man held a baby and they both stared at the baby as if she were a miracle. This picture was the most worn. As if it had been handled a lot over the years. Touched and embraced and held close.

I remember nothing.

He put the pictures back in the envelope. He hesitated before picking up the sheet of greenish paper tucked into a plastic sleeve. It was almost in tatters, the paper of such poor quality it crumbled along the folds and frayed along the edges. The three-lion insignia of the Democratic Republic of India had faded to gray. Below the emblem in bold letters it said in three languages, *Certificate of Marriage.* Emblazoned across the bottom was a red stamp of the Village Panch Council of Balpur.

Samir tucked the envelope with the pictures all the way to the bottom of the bag. He threw another cursory glance around the room, but he knew there would be no copies of legal papers.

Back in the living room, he removed the three Post-it notes from his pocket and stuck them on the marriage certificate before he slipped it into his laptop bag. Then he opened up his laptop and threw himself into his story, allowing himself to think of nothing else.

21

Mili stormed into the computer lab. She probably limped, but ever since that phone call yesterday everything she did felt like a storm. A storm followed by a flood and then back again. Virat had married someone else. Amazingly, she hadn't cried. Not once. If there ever was a miracle this was it. But she felt as dry as the Gobi desert, as hot as the sun that painted mirages across the sand dunes. And in her heart was a sandstorm. The raging need to do something, anything, consumed her. She needed to have consequence, to matter.

Yesterday she had spent doing anything she could to keep from thinking, from going back home. She had stayed late at the Institute, thankful for the proposal they were sending out, and had almost spent the entire night at the library catching up on her assignments. The thought of going home to Samir was unthinkable. She wanted Samir to have no part in this. Good thing he was so lost in his script.

This morning she had gone home just long enough to shower. She had almost checked up on Samir but all she was able to do was walk up to his door and then leave without knocking. But today the ache inside her refused to be ignored, today her agitation was so bad, she had to do something to stem it. The foundation of her life was gone. But what was more horrific than the pain of losing something she had held so close, so long was the bleeding sense of relief. A sense of relief that tore out her heart almost as much as the guilt of feeling it.

She checked out a computer. Some girls from one of her classes came up to her, eager to chat. She was amazed at her own calm as she chatted with them for a few minutes. They wanted her applied sociology notes. She pulled out her notebook and gave it to them to make copies and they left.

She logged into the computer and, just as Ridhi had suggested, she Googled Sara Veluri. Nothing.

She tried every possible spelling of *Veluri*. Still nothing. She tried every possible spelling of *Sara,* every possible combination of the first and last name. Not one single Sara Veluri, not one Sarah Veluri. Nothing. She tried several other search engines. Still nothing.

She knew she was missing some crucial part of the puzzle. But she couldn't put her finger on it. She closed her eyes. Her head rested on his shoulder. *I remember how she felt. Not how she looked, but how she felt. I remember her name, Sara. Sara Willis.*

She typed Sara Willis.

Bingo.

Four Sarah Willises and five Sara Willises came up in Ohio, Michigan, and Indiana. She jotted the names down and took them to the office.

The office was empty. She turned on the lights, breathed in the old wood smell, and settled into her chair. Then, pulling out the sheet of paper, she started making calls.

The first Sarah Willis was a college student at Ohio State University, who sounded a little drunk at six in the evening and couldn't stop giggling.

The next two had no idea who Samir Veluri was.

The fourth one threatened to report Mili if she didn't take her number off her list.

Finally Mili got an older-sounding woman. She wasn't Sara. Sara was resting. Who was this?

"My name is Mili. I'm a student from India. I'm looking for a friend's mother. His name is Samir." Mili couldn't believe she'd had the guts to just come out and say it like that. But right now she felt like she could move mountains with her anger.

The woman went silent for a full minute. Mili's heartbeat filled up the silence while she waited.

"Honey, I need you to stay on the phone for me, okay?" the woman said finally, then she repeated it again as if she half expected Mili to run off. "I'll check if Sara is awake. Don't hang up, please."

In under a minute another woman whispered into the phone. "You're Samir's friend?" The voice was barely a rasp, as if the effort to get the words out took her last breath.

"Yes. Are you . . . Are you Samir's mother?"

"Is he there?" The words got stronger, an odd energy fueled them. "Can I talk to him?" Such hope filled the woman's voice, Mili found her throat closing up.

"No, ma'am, he's not here right now. But he is here in America. I was calling on his behalf."

Sara started sobbing and Mili's own nose started to run. She pressed it against her sleeve. *Not now, Mili.* She waited while the two women at the other end soothed each other; finally the sobbing slowed and Samir's mother came back on the line. "Please. I have to talk to him. I need to talk to him."

"Ma'am, he's not here right now, but I'm going to try to get him to talk to you. I promise."

"Thank you," she said, her voice wet with tears. "How is he?"

Mili clenched her jaw and pressed her face into her sleeve. She waited until she could talk without crying. "He's fine. He's great, actually." *He's perfect.*

That caused the woman to be overtaken with a fresh bout of sobs and Mili had to squeeze her eyes, her jaw, everything to keep from doing the same. "Ms. Willis, can I ask you a question?"

"Sure."

"When was the last time you talked to Samir?"

The sobs intensified. Another few moments went by before she could speak. "He was five years old. My little boy was five years old. Twenty-five years ago. And now there's no time left. Jesus. There's no time."

By the time Mili disconnected the phone, her sleeve was soaking wet and her heart felt bruised in her chest from the weight of what Sara had told her. She had no idea how she was going to keep a promise she had no business making to a woman she didn't even know.

She hadn't thought this through. But now she had no choice but to keep her word. Samir was going to kill her. He was never going to speak to her again. He was going to pack his bags and leave and never turn around and look at her busybody interfering face. And how on earth was she going to handle that?

"Anybody home?" Mili called as she entered her apartment.

It smelled of freshly cooked dal and roasting wheat flour. Her stomach gave a loud growl. Samir pulled the last roti off the pan and onto a plate and turned the flame off. "Hi," he said, his voice strangely distant.

"Hi," she said, wanting so badly to run to him and pull him into her arms. She put her bag away and looked at his closed laptop sitting on the mattress. "Is it done?"

That made him smile, a victorious smile. "Just sent it."

She did run to him then and flung herself into his arms. He lifted her up and spun her around.

"Are you happy with it?"

"Thrilled. It's fu—flipping brilliant, if I may say so myself." He put her down, smiling away.

She took his hand and touched it to the wooden cabinet. "Touch wood. Don't say that. It tempts fate."

His smile widened. His little-boy smile.

She looked at the dal and the rotis. "There's so much food in the fridge. Why did you cook?"

"I felt like doing something special. I figured we deserved a celebration." Was that sadness she saw in his smile?

And then it struck her. He was saying good-bye. His script was done. He didn't need to stay for the workshop. The restlessness she'd carried home with her flared. A gnawing craving hollowed her out. He looked away first.

She helped him carry the food to the table.

It took Samir a while to notice Mili wasn't eating. He never thought he'd live to see the day.

"What's wrong?" he asked, leaning forward in his chair. But he already knew what it was. He had just told her he was done with the script. She had just realized he would be leaving soon. For all her bravado, her heart was going to break to pieces when he left. He knew that like he knew his own name. What he didn't know was how she was going to react when he told her the truth about what he was doing here. But it was time.

She sat up straight and put a big spoonful of dal in her mouth. "Nothing. Why would you think something is wrong?"

"You're not eating." Well, not the way she usually ate.

She pointed to her mouth and chewed furiously. "What're you talking about?"

He wanted to say something light, something funny, but the sight of her face, unfamiliar lines of worry furrowed into her forehead, twisted in his belly. The piece of paper in his bag, the memory of her closet, the black lace, the white cotton, the colorful bangles. All of it twisted like a knife in his belly.

"Are you sure you're feeling all right?" She blasted him with the full power of those huge irises soaked in concern and that something else. Her eyes always held that something else when she looked at him now. When had that happened? Why? He didn't deserve it—whatever it was her eyes held, he wasn't worthy of it.

But bastard that he was, it swelled in his chest. "I'm fine."

They ate in silence for a while. It was a first for them. The last time he'd seen Mili this quiet was when she was passed out with all the medication. Was that really just four weeks ago? Then why did it feel like he'd known her a lifetime?

Suddenly she squared her shoulders and met his eyes. "You finished your script. So you know what that means." For the first time that day she sounded like his Mili.

He bit back a smile. "I have no idea what you're talking about," he teased.

"You can't go back on your promise, Samir." She looked equal parts fierce and tentative, a tigress on a hunt but with a little bit of the hunted doe thrown in.

"Fine. What do you want?" He leaned back in his chair, refusing to acknowledge how much seeing her like this excited him.

"Really?" All her bluster dissipated, leaving behind nothing but sincerity. "But you can't say no."

"Now you're scaring me."

"Samir?"

"Okay, I won't say no."

"I want you to go somewhere with me." Her voice was too quiet when she said it, far too calm, like she expected a storm to follow.

But it was the flash of sympathy that made panic explode in his chest.

No.

"Samir, I found her."

Fuck no.

"No," he said, pushing himself away from the table before she could say any more.

"I want you to go with me to Munroe. To see your mo—"

"No." He clenched his fists to keep from turning the table over.

"But you prom—"

He stepped back with such force, the chair behind him toppled over. He grabbed his bag and stormed out the door. She followed him into the corridor, then across the hall into his apartment.

"Get out," he said. He didn't look at her. He wanted her out, now.

She stepped closer.

He spun around and walked all the way to the other end of the room. Then back again. Crazed restlessness churned inside him.

"Samir, pl—"

"No. I want you to leave, Mili. Right now. Get out."

Anger hummed in his head, roared like a caged beast in his chest. He loomed over her. His hands shook with the effort of not pushing her out.

She didn't cower, didn't even budge. She wasn't going anywhere. He pushed past her and left the apartment, slamming the door behind him. With too much fucking calm, she pulled it open and followed him out all the way to the open stairway. He was halfway down a flight when he spun around, that horrible dusty-dank carpet smell burrowing into his nose, a terrible pressure building in his chest. She stood at the top of the stairs. Her face was placid, dripping with so much bloody pity he wanted to shake it off.

"My mother is in Nagpur, you hear me? Back home in India, not in this goddamned country."

She took a few steps down until they were eye to eye. "I know, and she will still be there when you go back home."

She didn't reach out and touch him, but he felt like she had. He took another step down. "You know what you are? The nosiest fucking busybody I've ever met."

She didn't even flinch. She just continued to stare at him with those damn eyes. He didn't care. Fuck. Why had he ever told her? "You think you know everything, don't you? But you don't know anything. Have you seen what a sorry pathetic mess your own life is? How can you try to fix my life when you don't have one single thing going right in your own life?"

One shot of pain jolted her eyes before ten shots of courage steadied her gaze. He wanted to shake her. He wanted to fall at her feet and apologize. What kind of person had so much to ask for but chose instead to use her leverage to mess up his life? An insufferable, nosy busybody, that's who. But she was a bigger idiot than he'd ever imagined if she thought he was going to dig up a past he'd buried long ago. He had no intention of going anywhere near a woman who had dumped him like rotting garbage without so much as a backward glance.

"Samir, I understand you're angry, but—"

"No. You don't understand anything. Who gave you the right to interfere in my life? How did you think this was okay? What did you even do?"

"It's only about an hour away," she said, as if he hadn't spoken. "We'll be home by night. Then you're free. I'll never ask for anything again. You can get on a plane and leave tomorrow, if that's what you want." Her eyes filled with sadness. Good.

"I said I'm not going. It's never going to happen. Didn't you hear me?"

"I heard it. All of it. You made me a promise. Now you want to break it. Apparently you aren't the man I thought you were."

"Damn right." He turned around and ran down the stairs, away from her and her fucking two paise's worth of underhanded psychoanalysis. She followed him.

"Stop following me. Leave me the fuck alone."

She grabbed his arm. "She's dying, Samir. She has cancer. This is your last chance to see her."

22

Samir stood there frozen, as if his feet were nailed to the concrete, so still Mili didn't think he would ever move again. She walked around him and faced him. His eyes were glazed over with such pain it took all her strength not to stroke his face, not to wrap her arms around him. He looked like she had taken an axe and hacked through to the center of his chest. All the color bled out of his bronze tan, all the life bled out of his limbs. They hung motionless by his sides. She slipped his laptop bag off his shoulder, reached into the flap, and removed his keys. He didn't move, he didn't even look at her, but he let her take his arm and lead him to the car.

At the best of times Samir drove like he was flying. But today he was racing something. Today he was trying to outrun each spot he was in. Get out, get away, get past. His entire being was focused on moving. Mili was sure it had nothing to do with getting where they were going and everything with just moving from where they were.

She had punched the address into his GPS, a routine they had fallen into on their drive to the wedding. They had driven for an hour and he hadn't looked at her once. He hadn't said one word to her since she had pushed him into the car and shut the door behind him and then fitted herself into the seat next to him. The waves of anger rising from him were as palpable as the silence between them. The pain on his face almost made her regret what she had done.

Almost. Because deep inside she knew what she had done was right. She also knew without a doubt that this was exactly what Samir needed and she wanted him to have it. She realized suddenly that she wanted him to have everything. From the deepest part of her heart she wanted him to be happy. She hated that he was not. It wasn't like he wasn't capable of happiness. It was almost as if he held himself away from it just the slightest bit.

He felt undeserving of it, mistrustful of it, and the unfairness of that made her want to shake some sense into his stubborn head. The kindness inside him, his generosity, was beyond anything she had ever encountered. Even after she had told him she wanted nothing from him but his friendship, she had leaned on him far more than any friend had the right to and he had let her. Her own hypocrisy, her stupidity, baffled her. What kind of idiot doesn't see what's right in front of her face? No matter what she felt for him. No matter how different their worlds were, one thing she knew was that she was done pushing him away.

Samir jammed his foot into the accelerator and sped along like the madman he had turned into. Next to him Mili sat in complete silence, her fingers clutching the leather seat. She was trying to not let her terror show on her face, but as usual the canvas of her face painted each and every one of her feelings in vivid color. Good. At least that fucking pity was gone. He wanted her to talk to him, so he could put her in her place, blow her to shreds, ask her to shut up.

Suddenly the most horrible thought struck him. "Mili?"

She sat up straight but she didn't respond.

"If you're lying to me about the dying thing, I'm going to kill you."

"What kind of person do you think I am, Samir?" She had the gall to sound hurt.

"Just the kind of person who would make up something like this to get me to do what she thought I needed to do."

She squirmed in her seat but even she couldn't argue with that. "You're right, I would. But I'm not lying, Samir. I'm sorry." She reached out and touched his arm. When he didn't yank it away like he wanted to, she wrapped her arm around his and sidled up to him. And he knew without the shadow of a doubt that she wasn't lying.

She held on to him like that until they pulled into a muddy farm lane that cut through fields and led to a small cottage.

Behind the cottage loomed a huge red barn.

Everything inside Samir went cold. He stopped the car right there in the middle of the gravel road, raising a cloud of dust around them. The entire sweeping sight in front of him: blue sky, red barn, yellow house, green grass—it was all washed in gray shades of twilight. But Samir's mind colored it in, painting it with colors from another time, colors that were buried under his skin. And the force with which they rose to the surface sucked everything out of him. He sat drained of all feeling, unable to move forward, his arms and legs numb with cold.

When Mili tightened her hold on his arm, he realized he wasn't alone.

"I can't do it, Mili. I don't want to. It doesn't mean anything."

She didn't respond. His words hung in the air. Her hand moved up and down, the gentlest strokes. He removed it from his arm, but he couldn't let it go. He held it in his lap, clutched it like his life depended on it. Stupid, weak bastard.

"You shouldn't have done this. You had no right." Now he couldn't turn around and he couldn't go in.

"Let's go in just for a few minutes. Then we'll leave. I'm right here with you. Turn the car back on, Samir."

He turned the ignition and put his foot on the accelerator. The little house grew and grew until they were outside the porch. A woman sat on a rocking chair. She was wrapped up in shawls and knitting under the bright patio light that made her silver hair glow. Her eyes hitched on Samir over her half-moon glasses, but her hands never stopped.

Mili waved at the woman as if she'd known her all her life. "Kim?"

The woman put her knitting down and stood.

Mili turned her wide eyes on Samir. Unconsciously, he stepped out of the car and went around to let her out. She laced her fingers through his and clung to his arm. They climbed the patio steps.

"Mili?" This Kim person walked up to them.

Without letting his hand go, Mili gave the woman a one-armed hug. "This is Samir."

He focused on Mili's voice, focused on how she said his name, focused on her fingers slotted between his.

The woman squeezed her palm against her mouth and looked at Samir as if she could not believe what she was seeing. His stomach turned but he knew this wasn't the worst of it.

"Kim, is he here?" A thin, faded voice called from inside. The urge to turn around and run was so overwhelming he almost obeyed it. But the voice dug into his head and held him in place. Mili squeezed his hand.

"She's been waiting for you," Kim said, stepping inside the house.

Mili ran her hand up and down his arm. He had to move. *Move*, he told himself. She tugged gently at his arm and he followed her.

"Sara, he's here." Kim spoke before they entered the room.

It was dimly lit, the air thick with the astringent smell of disinfectant and medicine. The bed was metal, one of those hospital beds you could crank up and down. A sickbed. A dull numbness spread through him.

He looked at the yellow floral stripes on the curtains, the powder-blue walls, the graying white sheets, the floral comforter. All those flowers to cheer the space up. He looked at the thin body on the bed but he could not look at the face.

"Samir." She said his name like a foreigner. Rolling the *r* around her tongue and extending it.

Mili moved toward the bed. He let go of her hand. "Hi, Sara. I'm Mili."

"Hi, Mili," the raspy voice said. "Kim, could you sit me up, please?"

Kim rotated a crank and the bed folded into a seated position with a metallic groan.

"How are you feeling, Sara?" Mili placed a hand on her foot. Such a familiar gesture.

"Right now better than I've ever felt in my life."

"She hasn't sat up in months," Kim said.

"This is Kim, my sister. Samir, this is your Aunt Kim. She's your godmother."

Samir didn't move. His godmother. The person responsible for his welfare if his parents died.

"How was the drive?" Kim asked.

Mili replied. Then Kim asked another question. Then Mili. They went back and forth. Their voices buzzed around Samir's head. He didn't hear a word, just the occasional mention of his name and the occasional expectant pauses.

The raspy voice spoke again. It wasn't wet like he remembered, but parched, scratchy and dry as sandpaper. "Are you two hungry? You must be hungry. Kim made chicken curry. I gave her my recipe."

"Mili's vegetarian." Finally he found his voice.

"I'm sorry. I should have asked on the phone. Kim can fix something else. Maybe some *da-hl*." She said the word like she had a right to say it but it sounded foreign in her mouth.

"We ate before we left. Please don't worry about it." Mili's voice fell calm and soothing on the festering, wounded feel of the room. Why wasn't she making her big admonishing eyes at him?

"Maybe Samir is hungry. Do you like chicken curry? Your father used to love chicken curry."

He felt short of breath. "I'm vegetarian too."

"Yes, of course you would be. How is Lata?"

Samir looked up at her.

She wore a black knitted cap. No hair stuck out from under it. Her eyes brimmed with tears, but she smiled when she caught his eye. "It looks like Lata kept her promise. You know what she said to me? 'I'll raise him like my own son, but I cannot let him eat meat.' "

"That does sound like something my mother would say."

She flinched. "She kept her promise, then?"

"No. She didn't treat me like her son. She treated me better than him."

"You have no idea how happy that makes me."

Samir turned away from her and walked to the window. It was dark outside, but the black-on-black outline of the barn loomed in his vision like a surreal painting. A sudden memory of the dank, cold barn flashed in his mind, blasting open the hollow inside him. This was bullshit. What was he supposed to say to this woman? He felt nothing for her. Nothing. What had Mili expected to accomplish by bringing him here?

"Kim, could I have a glass of water, please?" He wanted to be annoyed at Mili's voice, but it was the only thing that made sense. "I'll go with you to the kitchen and get it."

He turned on her. "No, Mili, I don't want you to leave. You wanted this. Now you can't bear to watch?"

"If you want me to stay, I'll stay." She sank into the chair by the bed. "I thought you might want some privacy." She tried to calm him with her gaze. She was insane if she thought that's all it would take.

"We have nothing private to talk about. In fact we have nothing to talk about." He turned to the woman on the bed. "You look like you need rest. I'm sorry Mili called and bothered you. We'll leave now."

"Why didn't you ever reply to my letters?" she said as if he hadn't spoken.

You mean the ones you never wrote.

"I must have written at least a hundred letters."

Since you dumped me and walked away. "Why?"

"Why did I write to you?"

He couldn't respond.

"Or why did I give you up?" She started coughing, a hollow hacking sound, like rocks in a tin can.

Mili rubbed her shoulder and offered her a glass of water from the nightstand. She pushed it away and tried to speak again.

He didn't want to hear it. "You're not strong enough. And it doesn't matter anymore. Mili, let's go."

Mili was at his side in a moment.

"Your father and I fell in love," she said, pushing back another coughing fit. "I knew he was married. He was always honest with me about it. We tried to stay away from each other, but we couldn't. We knew he would go back when he was done with school. I thought I had two years and I chose to take what I could get. He didn't want to but I didn't give him a choice." She stopped to take a breath. This time Kim offered her water and she took a sip.

Her chest heaved from the effort, but she went on. "I never expected to get pregnant. Everything changed after you were born. I was terrified of losing him. As the time for him to leave came closer, my mind started to close in on me. I couldn't handle it. I slit my wrists. It was the only way I knew to make him stay."

Kim, who was sobbing hard now, left the room.

Sara spent another five minutes coughing. Mili left him and went to Sara and held her as she sobbed between hacking fits that pumped nonexistent breath from her lungs. Samir couldn't move. He felt like someone had smashed him into the floor with a sledgehammer.

"He was not a drinker," Sara said finally, her voice stronger this time, more determined. "He got into his car drunk only once, just one time, and everything ended. You were four years old. I couldn't take care of you. I couldn't even get myself out of bed in the morning. Taking you back to Mir's family seemed like the best thing for you."

Samir couldn't listen anymore. He turned away and headed for the door.

"Once you met Lata you wanted nothing to do with me," she said to his back and he stopped. "You took to her like a fish to water. You were the most beautiful child, a spitting image of your father, who was the most handsome man I ever met, and the kindest. She couldn't keep her eyes off you. When I left, you didn't even leave her side to give me a hug. Years later when I wanted to bring you back, you didn't want me anymore."

He turned around. That hadn't changed. He wanted nothing to do with her.

She started coughing again, but this time her coughing wouldn't stop. Kim came back into the room and turned on a nebulizer. Liquid hissed from the plastic funnel into her nose and mouth and her chest stopped heaving.

She moved the nebulizer away and spoke to Mili instead of him. "One more day. Please stay just one more day."

Mili didn't answer. She didn't turn pleading eyes on him. She looked to him to see what he wanted. What he could take.

He wanted to say no. The house suffocated him. He was choking on all the things she had told him. And Mili waited for his answer. "Fine. But we leave tomorrow morning." As soon as he said it, he wanted to take it back.

Mili's eyes misted over. She looked at him as if he were some sort of fucking hero and he couldn't take it.

He looked away, furious. He would never forgive her for this.

23

The choice was between sleeping in his childhood nursery and the threadbare couch in the living room. It was a no-brainer. Mili took the nursery and Samir took the couch. It was hard to fit his body on the tiny thing but he didn't expect to sleep much anyway. All he wanted to do was get through this night, get through tomorrow morning, then drop Mili off and go back to his life, to his family and his work. All the things he himself had built, not the lot that had been shoved down his throat.

He didn't expect it to but sleep did come.

And with it came the nightmare.

The dark, bottomless well, darker than any darkness. He dangled over it. His feet cycling the air desperately, his grandfather's fingers fisted in his shirt his only lifeline. The collar choked him, made it hard to breathe, to beg. *Don't let me go. Please, Dadaji, don't let me go.* His stomach catapulted into his throat and he fell without end.

He sat up on the couch, panting. Water flooded his lungs, burning fire up his nose and into his head. Sobs echoed around him, bouncing off stone walls.

He wiped his forehead against his sleeve.

It's okay, Chintu, I'm here. Stop struggling, I'm here.

Bhai had jumped in after him, carried him for hours on his shoulders, until Baiji pulled them out. Bhai had put him in the bucket first, let Baiji pull him out first. But the darkness of those hours had blinded Samir for days afterward. Even in the harshest

Rajasthan sunlight the darkness had stayed with him. It wasn't just the slashing belt but that darkness that had woken him screaming every night of his childhood.

And now again. Here.

The old bastard might have been the one to throw him in that well, to shred his back, but it was the woman in this house who was really responsible for it. And now she wanted him to somehow absolve her, to be a son? Everything she had said twisted around his throat in a noose. The labored breathing that had fueled her words pulled it tight. Mili's face with her bleeding heart gave it the final tug.

He never wanted to see Mili's face again. He hadn't felt so helpless, so desperately lost, ever. And given the kind of wimpy, pathetic child he'd been, that was saying something. He was in hell. And Mili was responsible.

He pushed himself off the couch. He needed air. How had that woman wanted him to take *his* nursery for the night? It was the creepiest fucking thing he had ever heard. The idea of Mili in there was sick enough. Tucked under the quilts that had done nothing to keep out the brutal cold of his childhood in this house. He slammed his fist into the rickety screen door and stepped into the night. The humid summer air hit his face but he couldn't pull it all the way into his lungs.

He found a swing on the back porch and sank into it. The din of frogs calling to their mates was deafening. Despite the horny frogs, despite the sparkling fireflies, the night felt dead. This place felt like the end of the earth; there was nowhere to go from here. He hopped off the swing, so on edge his skin felt too tight around him. The nightmare had left his T-shirt damp. The sultry air glued it to his body. He grabbed the edge of the shirt, pulled it over his head and dropped it on the porch before stepping onto the damp grass. The yard was overgrown and deep, edged with thick, looming woods. His bare feet began to eat the grassy earth. The breeze hit his chest but did nothing to cool him down. The faster he walked the more restless it made him. Soon he was faced with the thicket of trees. One step and he'd be inside the unending darkness, be inside the well again. This time he wouldn't be afraid.

The woman had actually reached for him. She had expected him to let her take him in her arms. She had expected him to let her look at him that way. With a mother's eyes, heavy with hope, expectation, pride. And he'd let her. He felt soiled. Only one woman could look at him like that—only his mother, and she wasn't here. She was eight fucking thousand miles away, terrified of losing him to this, this dark place, the way she had lost her husband.

He moved to step into the darkness and heard a gasp behind him.

He spun around. Mili's slight form stood a few feet from him. The oversized white T-shirt Kim had given her caught the moonlight and slid down one shoulder like a Grecian toga. Her mass of curls exploded from a band at the top of her head. She wrapped her arms around herself. Even in this heat she was trembling.

"Please don't go in there, Samir. It's too dark. I don't want to go in there." Her eyes were pools of moonlight.

"Then don't."

"I can't let you go in there alone." Her look was classic Mili. Fierce with sincerity. Everything out there in the open.

His heart did an awful squeeze.

"I can't go back in that house." His voice came out a whisper.

She came to him then. Before he could move away, her arms went around his waist and pulled tight. She pressed her face into his chest, exactly where his heart throbbed out its painful beat. He wanted to untangle her arms from around him and push her away, but he stood there rooted, paralyzed, as she clung to him. For a long time he didn't do anything, he couldn't feel anything. Then the warm wetness on his skin seeped through his numb haze and burned a hole right in the center of his frozen chest, right where her cheek was pressed against his heart.

His heart began to pound; hot thrumming gushed through his veins. He lifted both hands and did what he hadn't stopped craving since that first time he'd done it. He grabbed fistfuls of her curls as they spilled to her waist. Silken softness tightened between his fingers. He tugged her head back and turned her face up to his. Her face was wet. Silver moonlight bounced against her tears—against her onyx eyes, against her spiked midnight lashes, against her lips, her cheeks. She was all soaked and soft and yielding. He leaned over and pressed his face into the wetness.

Mili sucked in a breath. For a few moments neither one of them moved, their wet faces pressed together. Samir was trembling in her arms, the pain inside him too much to bear. She stroked his back, his arms, the tight cords of his neck. She tried to make soothing sounds, but his name was all that came to her lips. "Samir."

He pressed his lips into her cheek and dragged sweet fire across her skin, her forehead, her eyelids, the bridge of her nose. Until finally, finally he found her lips. Hunger exploded in her chest. She dug her fingers into his hair, clutched the heavy strands, and tugged him closer.

He moaned her name. "Mili." The crazy beat of his heart slammed against her breasts, stinging sadness in every beat. She wanted it gone, she wanted to suck it out of his heart, wanted to grind down every harsh edge jabbing into him. She pushed apart his lips, and reached into his pain. The world went soft and hot. Everything inside her melted and slid down her body and pooled in the ravenous space between her legs.

His hands molded the globes of her butt. He yanked her up, straightening to his full height and lifting her molten body high against his. She flowed over him, draping herself around him. The entire length of her arms wrapped around his head. She devoured his mouth, nipped, licked, sucked. His taste so familiar it stole her breath. She dived into it, inhaling every sensation like it was her last. It was. It had to be. Her legs wrapped around him, flattening her wet heat against the solid muscle of his belly. All her blood, every fiber of awareness that held her together rushed to where their bodies met.

A raw moan rumbled in his chest as he slid her down his body until turgid hardness fit itself against aching softness. "Mili," he moaned against her lips. "God, Mili."

She pushed closer. "It's okay, Samir. It's going to be okay." She locked her feet around him. "I promise."

He spun with her in his arms and pushed her against the tree, shielding her back from the trunk with his arms. But he let nothing shield her body from his. Every inch of him pressed into every inch of her as he swallowed her moans, and shoved his own into the heat of her mouth. There was such desperation in his lips, in his hands, such hunger, it was as if he wanted to drown in her. Their hearts slammed against each other and found the same beat.

How had she lived without this? How had she lived without him? How had she ever dreamed of another man? Samir was part of her, wrapped around her like blazing sunshine and pouring rain, her breath and her blood, her every thought.

His lips traced her throat and found her collarbones on an indrawn breath. He dragged fire across her flesh, taking her to the edge of a chasm, pushing her toward it. His mouth dipped lower. Through the bunched-up cotton, he captured the peak of her breast. She screamed into the night, reeling over the chasm. He pulled away, and she whimpered a desperate plea. "Samir. Please." She clamped his head closer and pushed herself into his mouth.

His response was fierce. Teeth and tongue, he gathered her up, consumed her, tender one minute, ruthless the next, until she forgot his pain, forgot her own and sobbed for more, crazed, mad with hunger. From the very deepest part of her soul, she threw herself open, her arms, her legs, every last part of her open. Exposed. His.

Samir came up for air. It flooded into his lungs, her smell, her taste, her very essence flooded into him. She tore through everything he knew, everything he was feeling. She was a dagger that slammed into his heart and cleaved him in half, and settled at the very center of his being as if he was exactly where she belonged.

Except he wasn't. He wasn't ready to have her pour life into him. There was too much anger inside him and years of deadness. She started trailing kisses down his jaw, her panting breath fanning the sweet wetness her lips left on his skin. Her fingers clutched his hair, the trust in her hold kicked him in the gut. He'd already violated it beyond redemption. He pulled away from her mouth, away from the impossibly hard nubs of her breasts pushing into his chest, the taste of them imprinted on his tongue. She moaned and tried to pull his mouth back to hers.

"Mili," he said against her lips, "go back into the house. Go back now while I can still let you go."

Her dazed eyes heated with purpose. She wrapped her hands around his face and speared him with her burning onyx eyes. "No."

He searched through their wide-open depths, but there wasn't one shred of doubt inside her. "Mili, if you don't go now, I won't be able to hold myself back. I'm just not that strong." But, God, he'd crumble to dust if she left him.

"Don't," she whispered, pushing her soft, pliant body into his. "Don't hold anything back." She closed her eyes, threw back her head, and offered him everything. "Please."

All that kept him sane flew out of his head.

He found her lips again and shoved his tongue into her mouth, not seductive, not artful, but as clumsy as a teenager, every move-ment a movement he had to make. His hands searched her body, finding their way under her shirt, learning, touching, breathing her in skin to skin. The keys of her spine, the silken softness of her skin, the lush weight of her breasts. She pushed into his hands. Every inch of her screamed for more. Her mouth chanted his name. *Samir, Samir, Samir,* over and over as he kneaded and circled and stroked.

His mouth nipped at hers; he couldn't let go of her lips.

"Samir, please," she moaned. "Please."

He reached down between their tightly pressed bodies mean-ing to give her the release she craved. But his fingers touched soaking wet cotton hot against swollen flesh and the very last thought exploded in his mind and disappeared with a blinding bang. He had to have her around him, now. The cotton bunched in his hands as he ripped it off her legs. He wanted to trail kisses up her legs, down her belly, but all he could do was yank down his zipper and lunge for her mouth as he pulled down his pants. She grabbed his shoulders and squeezed her thighs around him, her groan so fierce the inferno inside him flared, consuming every ten-derness. He backed her into the tree and pushed himself into her.

She was too tight, too slight for how much his hunger had en-gorged him. He tried to stop, tried to slow, tried to ease into her. She whimpered and pushed into him. Her hot slickness clenched with need and he lost all semblance of control and drove into her like a crazed beast.

And for the first time in his life came up against a barrier.

Panic gripped his throat, an almost unbearable rush of tenderness burst in his heart. He tried to pull away, but she made a wild sound, tightened her legs around him and clawed his shoulders. It was more than he could take. One hard thrust and he ripped past the resistance. This time her cry was laced with pain. She went rigid in his arms.

"*Shh*, sweetheart. I'm sorry. It's going to be fine. Trust me."

"I trust you, Samir," she said through a sob.

He slid his tongue into her mouth, stroking her in the deepest kiss, shaking with the effort to hold still inside her. The tension melted from her body; she loosened against him and wiggled closer. That was it. He lost his mind, plunging and plunging until she sobbed into his mouth, and pulsed and squeezed around him. He slammed into her, mindless frantic thrusts until he exploded, and exploded and exploded without end.

When he found his mind again, Mili sagged limp in his arms, slick with sweat, and shaking. Her arms were still locked around his neck. Her face was pressed into his chest. Where their bodies joined, hot sticky sweetness glued them together. Her legs started sliding off him. He pushed them back up, spun around, and pushed his own back into the tree trunk.

He had just taken her standing up against a tree, out in the open. And this had been her first time. Every complication separating them, all the lies and deceptions, all the reasons why this was the very last thing he should've done came crashing down on him. "Shit, Mili. That was terrible. That should never have happened."

She stiffened, lifted her face off his chest, and slid off him. He wanted to stop her, but he couldn't move. She stepped away, her shoulders slumped, her head bowed, her legs unsteady. "I'm sorry," she said. "It was my first time. I didn't know what to do. I thought . . ."

What the fuck? "Mili, listen." He reached for her, but she skittered away from him like a dazed animal who didn't know it had just been hit by a car. He knew exactly how she felt.

"I shouldn't have—I shouldn't have brought you here. You're right. None of this should've happened. I'm sorry."

"Stop saying that," he said more harshly than he had meant to and she said no more.

Just waited. Seconds ticked by. She stared up at him, her huge eyes bewildered, and waited for him to say the words to make it better, to tell her not be sorry, to tell her what she'd just given him, what she'd made him feel. But he just stood there slumped against the tree, horrified at how he had hurt her. Bastard. *Bastard.*

When he didn't say anything, she looked away and started searching for something. Then leaned over and picked up her panties. Even in the moonlight, he saw her cheeks flaming. Awkwardly she bunched the scrap of fabric in her hands and ran toward the house. He was about to follow her, but her gait faltered, as if she hurt between her legs. And his limbs locked in place. Shame flooded him. He was a monster. A monster who'd hurt her and didn't know how to make things right.

When he could move again, he pulled on his jeans, walked back to the porch, and sank into the swing. His shock at what he had done made his movements slow and stiff. Mili was gone. The thought of her back against the tree trunk, her pained, indrawn breath as he rammed into her, clawed at his gut. He had gone crazy when he'd touched her. All these years of seducing women, and he'd lost all control like some starving animal. And then he'd sent her away feeling like she had done something wrong. Over the past month he had gone from being the kind of bastard he didn't mind being to the kind of bastard he would like to beat the crap out of.

If this is what being in love did to a man, he was essentially screwed.

Mili slung her hair across one shoulder, swung the porch door open, and stepped outside. Samir sat slumped in the swing, his head in his hands, his burnt-gold hair flopping across his forehead. The memory of those thick strands fisted in her hands as he claimed her body made heat spread across her skin. The desperate need in his eyes, in his touch—need for her—it's what had forced her to come down those stairs, to come back outside.

Samir lifted his head from his hands and started when he saw her. The huge white T-shirt Kim had let her borrow slipped off one shoulder. His gaze lingered on her fingers as she tugged it back in place before he met her eyes. Meeting those golden eyes made her entire body reach for him. The pain in his eyes when he'd called what happened between them horrible made her want to crumple to the ground and start crying again.

But she couldn't sit upstairs and sob anymore. She wouldn't. Not after what had happened between them. She hadn't meant for it to happen, not with the shambles her life was in, or his. Not when his mother lay sick in the house. A house he couldn't even seem to go inside without hurting. But no one could call what had happened between them horrible. No one. And yet he had. She had to know, just had to know, how he couldn't have felt what she felt. She sucked in a breath, and spoke before she ran out of courage. "Samir, I've never done this before. So I have to know." Her fingers trembled on the out-of-shape neckline. "Was it really horrible for you?"

His eyes widened, then narrowed. His molten gold gaze hitched at her heart in that way it always did. The swing creaked as he rose and came to her, traversing the five-step distance with a deliberation that made each breath an effort. He reached out and touched her cheek. Without meaning to, she leaned into his touch and closed her eyes.

He waited until she met his gaze again and held it. "Mili, from the first moment I saw you I've wanted you."

She blinked, startled.

"Ever since that first day, I've imagined making love to you. I've imagined being inside you, fantasized about how you would feel around me, dreamed about all the different ways I could take you." His finger stroked her cheek. "You've driven me completely insane with lust these past weeks. The expectations I had—nothing could've matched up."

Understanding dawned on her in a rush. Understanding and

crushing pain. She opened her mouth to speak. Although she had no idea what she could say.

He pressed his thumb to her lips. His touch always so tender, so possessive, it was imprinted onto her soul. "No. You don't understand. Despite that, despite my impossible expectations, how touching you felt, what being inside you felt like—I could never have imagined anything so . . . I had no idea such a thing was even possible. You made me lose my mind, Mili. Do you understand what I'm saying? I forgot myself. And I forgot to take care of you. Hell, I forgot how to speak. I hurt you. That's what I'm sorry about. Only that."

Stupid, dumb tears rose in her eyes. An even dumber smile blossomed in her aching heart. It must have floated to her lips because he stroked it with his fingers and gave her that half smile of his in return.

"Really? You mean that?"

"You have no idea how much."

"So, that was you *not* taking care of me?"

His half smile spread all the way across his face.

She reached up and touched it. Dear God, was it even legal for someone to be this handsome? "So it gets better than *that?*"

He squeezed his eyes shut and nodded. "For you, I should hope so. For me, I would die."

She stepped closer, until her entire body touched his. Joy and tenderness and fierce hope kindled inside her like a prayer lamp. She had no idea who she was anymore. But she knew exactly what she had to do. She went up on her toes. "Samir?" she whispered against his ear.

His smile pushed against her cheek and made sensation sparkle all the way down to her toes. "Mili?"

"Could you, you know, show me? Please."

He scooped her up in his arms and gathered her against himself. She snaked her arms around his neck and stared at his beloved face as he used his back to push the porch door open.

When he stepped into the house his stride was sure, not an ounce of pain inside him, and it made such joy, such relief burst inside her, tears spilled from her eyes even as laughter bubbled from her lips. He pulled her closer and carried her up to his childhood nursery, blasting through the demons of his past, taking her away with him, away from her own past to a place where her past could never touch her again.

"Sure, Mili," he said, sprinkling kisses across her lips as he went, "I can show you."

24

Usually when Samir had sex, once the deed was done, all he
could think about was getting off the bed. He always forced
himself to wait the polite fifteen minutes, just to make sure everyone came off their high feeling good about themselves. But that
was about it. Even if girlfriends slept over, they had their side of
the bed and he had his Lazyboy with inbuilt, noise-cancelling
Bose headphones. Tonight, however, he couldn't stop checking to
make sure that Mili was still tucked into his side.

Her cheek was pressed into his shoulder. Her fingers clutched
his skin. She was dead to the world, her exhaustion complete,
every inch of her body replete. Who could sleep with such a sight
to look at? He could spend the rest of his life just looking at her.
Her silken mocha skin, her midnight curls, her onyx eyes. Her dark
beauty sparkled like the night sky, as fresh as the glow of dawn, as
hypnotic as the glimmer of dusk, softer than moonlight and warmer
than the blue flames of a midnight bonfire.

An unfamiliar feeling of peace blanketed their intertwined bodies, lighter than the whispers they'd spoken into each other's ears.
Each time he'd entered her, each time she'd sobbed in release, the
crushing weight of the air in this house had lifted off his shoulders,
off his heart.

He tucked a stray curl behind her ear. She didn't move. He felt
like one of those head cases, poised to pull her back if she moved

even an inch away from him. But she stayed sprawled across him. And finally, somewhere in the wee hours of morning, he stopped worrying about losing her and fell asleep, grinning like the fool he was.

The sound of laughter woke Samir. Not nightmares. Not a cold sweat but Mili's laughter. Husky, unreserved. The spot next to him was cold. She was gone, but his arm was still curved around her missing form. She had remembered to pull the blinds and darken the room. But a stray ray of sunlight broke through the gap in the old blinds and poked him in the eye. She laughed again.

He sprang out of bed, a rampant yearning to see her tearing through him like hunger. He was starving for her. He pulled on his jeans and walked to the door, cracking it open to see Kim give her some clothes and go down the stairs. He opened the door and pulled her in, wrapping her in his arms and falling back against the wall. She fell against him, wet ringlets framing her face and sticking to his bare chest. She smelled like sunshine and night-blooming jasmine. He dug his face into her hair.

"Well, good morning to you too," she said.

Would he ever get used to her voice? "I don't want it to be morning."

He felt her smile against his ear. It was bloody hard to pull away but he did, just enough to look at her face and trace her collarbones with his thumb. "How are you feeling? Are you sore?"

She colored. In that way she had of coloring from the very depths of her soul, and it made him so absurdly happy he thought his heart had burst from its seams and seeped into his chest.

"I have no idea what you mean." She actually gave him a coquettish look. Talk about quick recovery.

"I mean, does anything hurt?" He ran his fingers over her breast, down her belly, to her warm mound. "Are you in pain?"

Her eyes fluttered shut. She moaned deep in her throat and pressed closer. "Yes. But only because you have terrible morning breath."

He smiled against her lips. "Too bad, because I have the most wonderful taste in my mouth and I'm not brushing it away."

She kissed him. Reached up, dug her hands into his hair, and pressed her lips full into his. Hard and soft. Fierce and yielding. She was going to kill him.

When he came up for air she was panting.

He lifted her up and started carrying her to the bed.

"Samir, are you crazy? Kim and Sara are waiting for breakfast. Put me down."

"Not on your life. You shouldn't have done that if you weren't going to follow it up. You have to put your money where your mouth is, woman." He put her down on the bed and climbed over her.

She kissed him again and rolled him onto his back. He went easily, putty in her hands.

"I don't have enough money to cover this huge mountainous body of yours," she said, before springing off the bed.

He reached out but she was already at the door. "Down in ten minutes?" For all her cool tone she looked so mussed, so vulnerable, he almost went after her. But she was right, the sooner he went down the sooner they could get out of here.

Samir stepped out of the shower, wiped down his smug, ridiculously satisfied body and pulled on his clothes. He ran his fingers through his wet hair and padded down the stairs in his bare feet. He felt fresh and clean despite the fact that he was wearing the same clothes from yesterday, despite the stubble he usually wouldn't be caught dead with. Despite where he was and what waited for him downstairs. Amazingly, he felt none of the anger that had engulfed him yesterday, the rough edges of his rage were gone. How could he hate these walls, this place, after what he had found here?

A tiny splinter of fear poked at his heart, but it had nothing to do with this house or the memories he had taken from here. He had to find Mili, had to tell her who he was, how he felt. Tell her everything. It was past time.

The smell of ginger tea wafted through the air. Mili was in the kitchen with Kim. He stood outside the mullioned glass door, unseen, and drank her in with his eyes. Her hair was still damp, her cheeks still flushed, and he knew every spot under that ridiculous blouse where her skin was marked with his love. She was wearing

Kim's oversized polyester blouse—white with pink roses, high fashion from at least three decades ago. It came down to her knees. It could've been a dress, but she wore it like a blouse over her jeans. She looked like she had just stepped out of a Renoir painting. She could've been standing in a meadow collecting daisies, with her curls flying like ribbons about her face. Minus the bonnet.

"I boil the ginger with the water first, then I add the tea leaves," she said, scooping a few spoonfuls from the jar and dropping them into the boiling water. She took a deep sniff before closing the jar and putting it away. "These are really authentic," she said. "They remind me of my *naani's* kitchen."

"Sara loves this brand. She's always used it since she came back from India." Kim took the jar from her and put it away.

"Did she like India?" Mili turned off the flame and put a lid on the boiling chai.

"She loved it. Even before she went, when she was with Mir it was like she was obsessed with it. She read every book about India, ate the food, she bought clothes that were made there. He used to call her a hippie for it, but she loved it. She was always like that. There was no going halfway for her. No matter what it was she went all the way without looking back. It always scared me. But I think that's what got to Mir. That's why he couldn't leave."

"Why didn't she go back to get him?"

"Who, Samir?"

"Yes."

"You have to understand how she became when Mir died. She had suffered from depression off and on for years, but losing Mir pushed her over the edge. Samir was five years old when he found her passed out in the barn. She hadn't eaten or talked to anyone for days. He ran back home through the snow and called nine-one-one. Social Services was all set to take him away. Sara and I grew up inside the foster care system. Sara would've done anything to keep him out. She begged me to take him but I couldn't. I was working as a housekeeper. I didn't even have a home. I was the one who suggested she take him to Mir's family.

"When she came back her illness only got worse. There weren't many treatments for manic depression back then. She struggled for a long time. Finally, about ten years back, she met her doctor and her life changed. But it was too late. Samir was already an adult and living in Mumbai. Lata told her he didn't want anything to do with her. It broke her heart but she understands, I think."

Mili turned and found him standing there watching them. Her eyes were soft with understanding and that something more that stirred his blood. She had known he was listening when she'd asked Kim the question. Something in the way she turned to him told him that. Now she challenged him to do the right thing.

Samir walked into the kitchen and took the tray from Kim's hands.

"I'll take her the tea, Kim, if you don't mind."

Tears sparkled in Mili's eyes as he turned around and walked out of the kitchen. Tears and pride.

If Sara was surprised that he had brought her tea she didn't show it. But her gaze kept darting toward him over her cup as they drank in silence. He had two women looking at him like he was God's gift to the earth. Based on what the magazines said, he should've been used to it by now. But how could you ever get used to this? He had done nothing to deserve their devotion, and it made him ache.

"You have your father's mouth, his jaw," Sara said, drinking him in with her eyes. "I could always tell what Mir was feeling from the set of his jaw."

"Samir is like that too," Mili chimed in from behind him and he turned to her. This he had to hear. "When I first got to know him that's how I knew if he was going to do something I wanted him to or not. If his jaw got all stubborn there was no way he was doing it. But if his jaw softened I had him."

"What did I ever refuse you?" he asked. "Who can ever refuse you anything, love?"

She blushed. "That's because I never ask for anything I shouldn't. I'm always reasonable. How can anyone refuse that?"

"Yeah, right. When I first met you all your behavior was perfectly rational."

She stuck out her tongue at him and narrowed her eyes.

"What did she do?" Sara asked, smiling. Her breathing was

more even today, and there was something familiar about the way her lips turned up when she smiled.

"Let me see, she jumped off a balcony, took off on a broken bike, ran into a tree, and landed upside down with her butt literally turned over her head."

Sara put one gnarled, spotted hand on her mouth and laughed. "Sounds painful."

"It was. He scared me so much I broke my foot and my arm."

"She *sprained* her ankle and *dislocated* her wrist, and all I did was knock on her door."

"Yes, but I had never seen a big-footed giant before. It was scary. Have you seen his feet? They need their own atmosphere."

"They did need their own atmosphere when you threw up on them."

To her credit she looked the faintest bit apologetic at that. "My *naani* says if you don't get out of the way, you can't blame the water hose. And I did make up by letting you write in my apartment. Samir writes and directs movies. According to my friend he's made the most romantic film ever."

Sara looked from Mili to him. "I know," she said cautiously. "I've watched all his movies."

He didn't know how to react to that. But she didn't wait for a response. She looked back at Mili and gave her a teasing grin. "I have no doubt about how romantic Samir is." Her look was so knowing Mili blushed even more. Samir found that he didn't mind that look at all.

"Where are you from, Mili? Where is your *naani* now?" Sara asked.

"I'm from Balpur in Rajasthan. It's a small village near Jaipur." Mili collected the teacups and put them on the tray. "I went to college in Jaipur. My *naani* still lives in Balpur."

"Of course I know where Balpur is. That's where Samir's father was from. Did you know Samir's name is a combination of both our names: Sara and Mir-Chand. Did Samir and you know each other from Balpur?"

"Samir's not from Balpur, he's from Nagpur." Mili shook her head and picked up the tray.

"No, Lata moved with Samir and Virat to Nagpur but the Rath-ods are originally from Balpur."

The teacups shook on the tray in Mili's hand. Samir's mouth went dry. Mili's startled, confused eyes looked up at him. He watched, helpless, as the crank went off in her brain and started to turn.

The first thought that hit Mili was the *Filmfare* magazine in Ridhi's house. That was the part of the puzzle she had been miss-ing and it sprang into her memory like a dragon baring its fangs. *Sam Rathod, the Bollywood Bad Boy.* She had been so livid at Reena for spreading lies that the name had completely escaped her.

If the full magnitude of what this meant had not been evident from the name, the look on Samir's face made it abundantly clear. Mili gripped the tray so tight the sharp edge dug into her palms. "I'll take these to the kitchen. Can I get you anything?" Her voice had to be coming from someone else.

"Thanks, honey," Sara said as she headed for the door.

Samir was standing in her way. His large, tense form loomed in front of her. She walked around him, her ears ringing. She didn't look at him. She had no desire to look at him ever again. His smell as she passed him brought back hot, wet memories and the horri-ble anger bubbling inside her flared. Once in the kitchen she put the cups down and squeezed her nose. Oh no, she wasn't going to cry. If she cried now it would all be over. If she collapsed now she would never get up. She rinsed out the cups, refusing to let her hands tremble, and put them on the draining board. When she turned around he was standing behind her. She couldn't face him. Not yet. Not ever.

She squeezed past him and up the stairs to his nursery. The thought of that room made her stomach cramp. This room, this morning, last night, it was all chiseled into her very being. How was she ever going to wipe those memories off? What was she going to do with them? She could never forget as long as she lived, not the night, not the room, not the full extent of his betrayal. It was all searing into her consciousness like an inferno, getting hot-ter and higher by the second.

He followed her into the room. She couldn't bear it. She couldn't be near him. She wanted him to leave, but she didn't trust herself to speak. She picked up her purse and quickly patted down the bed. Oh God, how was she going to get back to Ypsilanti?

"Mili." He said her name. It felt like an invasion, like a violation. "Mili, please, can you look at me?"

When the flames of hell burn me to ashes.

She tried to get past him. She had to get out of the room. He held her arm. She yanked it away with so much force her sleeve ripped in his fingers. She started shaking. Every muscle, every cell in her body started shaking. Kim had given her the blouse this morning. It belonged to Sara. Mili had loved the flowers. They were so beautiful. She had wanted to wear something beautiful. For him. Pain choked her throat. But she would not sob. She studied the tear on her sleeve. She could fix it. A needle and thread was all it would take. She could fix it.

"Mili. Please. I'm sorry."

"That's okay, it's a small tear. I can fix it."

He tried to hold her again.

She stepped back, pushing him away with as much force as she could muster in her shaking arms. "Don't touch me. Don't. Ever. Touch. Me. Again." Her voice cracked and she clenched her jaw tight. If she broke now she would never forgive herself.

"You have to listen to me. Please."

She spun around and faced him. "What is it you want to say to me? That your last name is Rathod? That your brother's name is Virat? That you knew all along that I was married? That you are . . . you are . . . my brother-in-law." Her voice shook again but she did not let it crack.

Oh God. Samir was her brother-in-law. She had just slept with her brother-in-law.

She had never felt so filthy, so used. Last night she had finally accepted that her marriage was over. In her past. A past she would never go back to for anything. She'd realized what she felt for Samir was not just friendship and even for just one day she had wanted to know what it would be like to be his, to let him be hers.

But what had happened between them. God, what could she even call that?

"I am not your brother-in-law."

"I am married to your brother. Where I come from it's called a brother-in-law. Where I come from, that's higher than a brother. More sacred. Oh God, Samir, I'm your *bhabhi*. And you knew. How could you do this?"

"Mili, listen to me. You were never married. That was not a marriage. It's not even legal."

"So you came all this way to tell me that my marriage isn't legal? And because I was so stupid you thought it would be fun to seduce me. And because your brother marrying me and never wanting me wasn't enough you thought you'd break my heart too? Two times over?"

She was not crying. She was never crying again. But her insides hurt so much, she wished for physical pain; she wished for a twisted foot, a broken wrist. Suddenly something struck her.

"Why did you come here, Samir? Did you come after me? Did Virat send you? For twenty years I waited for your brother to come get me. I fooled myself with hope. If he didn't want me, why didn't he just tell me? Why send you? Why? Was it a joke? Let's see how much we can pound the stupid village girl until she folds."

"Mili."

She flinched. She didn't want him saying her name. Having him chant it in her ear as she gave herself to him, as he changed her forever, it was too much, too close, too fresh in her mind. His hands on her, inside her, it was all too close. And filthy. It was filthy.

"Mili, it was not supposed to turn out like this. Can you at least give me a chance to explain?"

"There's an explanation?" How stupid did he think she was?

"Yes, damn it. There is. For one, there's the court case you started."

Court case? What was he talking about? What would she even go to court about?

He looked incredulous. "I know about the legal notices, Mili. You claimed half the *haveli*. We thought . . . I didn't know you, Mili. What would you think if you were me? As for the marriage, Baiji had sent your grandmother a notice annulling the marriage the year after it happened. Virat had no idea that you still thought you were married. Until the letter came he didn't even know. And Mili, Virat, he's . . . he's married to someone else."

It was a miracle she remained standing.

Shame in all its corrosive intensity roared through her blood. All the things she'd told Samir about Virat, he'd known. He'd known everything. She wanted to clamp her hands to her ears. But she couldn't move. He'd known even more than she had. She'd struggled with herself while he watched, while he played her, while he seduced her. God, he had known.

She had never hated anyone in her life, never been so disgusted with another human being, but his presence made her physically sick, the force of her loathing was so strong.

Mili opened her mouth but no words came out. The disgust in her eyes crushed Samir's soul and the pain in her eyes made him worthy of it. He wanted to go to her, but one step closer to her and she would break. Her eyes, her nose, all of her was tinder-dry. One match would burn her down to the ground. He had sucked her dry.

She swallowed and clenched her jaw. "Why did you come here, Samir? The truth. Nothing else. Just the simple truth."

It was too late to turn around now. It was too late to soften the blows.

"I came to get you to sign annulment papers and to drop the case."

"By seducing me?"

He couldn't bear the pain in her eyes. "That was not what this was."

"The truth, Samir. It was all part of a plan, wasn't it? You knew I wouldn't be able to resist your charm."

"Please, Mili, don't—"

"Why didn't you just ask me? Knock on my door, tell me who you were and give me the papers."

"Would you have signed?"

"Not at first, but if you had told me he's married to someone else I would have been happy to be free of him. I've craved freedom all my life. Now I'll never be free. Never."

"Mili."

"No. *No.* Don't say my name. Don't look at me. Please just—Oh God." She looked around the room, desperately searching for something. "How am I going to get home?"

"I'll take you home, of course."

She flinched but then straightened her spine as if she were bracing herself for another humiliation. She nodded without meeting his gaze, the slightest hint of a nod. "Okay. But you will not speak to me. Not one word. That's all I'm asking. I can't get in that car otherwise, and I need to get back."

Samir could never have imagined something hurting so much. But watching her like this, this helpless, it made him crazy and he could do absolutely nothing about it.

He nodded and followed her down the stairs.

"I can't leave without saying bye to Sara," she said, and he nodded again.

Sara looked worried when they entered the room. "Are you two all right?" she asked.

Mili didn't answer.

"I have to take Mili home, Sara. Something's come up." Samir stood aside as Mili walked up to Sara and took her hand in hers.

"Please take care of yourself, Sara. It was so nice to meet you."

Sara touched Mili's cheek and Mili's already-rigid back stiffened some more. But tears didn't form in her eyes.

"Is there anything I can do?" Sara asked. You would have to be a block of wood to not sense how much Mili was hurting.

She shook her head.

"Will you come back?"

She nodded. "I'll come see you as soon as I can. But you have to promise to be better when I come back, okay?"

"I'll try," Sara said, her eyes filling and brimming over. Mili pulled away, her eyes as dry, as desolate as the Rajasthan sky in the dead of summer.

Samir forced himself to move. He walked up to Sara. He still couldn't let her hug him. His heart was just not that big. But he did let her hold his hand.

"Will you come back, *beta?*"

He nodded.

"Thank you," she said. "If I don't get a chance to see you. Thank you for this."

He looked at Mili. She wasn't looking at him. "Thank her," he wanted to say.

Sara wept like a baby when she let Samir's hand go.

Kim wept like a baby when she held Mili.

And still Mili didn't cry.

25

The ride back to Ypsilanti was the longest and shortest ride of Samir's life. Silence stretched between them like an unbreachable chasm. If he didn't find a way to cross it everything would be over before it even started. What had happened between them yesterday still sent tremors through his body. She sent tremors through his soul. He could still feel her against him. She was under his skin, inside him, her softness wrapped around his sinew, his nerves. She'd made the most painful thing he'd ever done bearable. And he'd ripped her heart out. And he had to find a way to make it better. He just didn't know how. All he knew was that he wasn't going to lose her. He just couldn't go on if he did.

But she sat there, still and mute, her fingers clasped together in her lap, her body squeezed into the door. Her eyes dry.

He opened his mouth a few times to say something, anything, but he had promised and he couldn't break his word. From the moment they had got into the car his phone began ringing off the hook. First it was Virat, then DJ. He didn't answer. He could not speak to anyone right now. Finally, he turned the phone off. Mili didn't so much as move a muscle through it all. Not until they were back in the smelly parking lot.

It was garbage day again and the truck was scooping trash out of the huge green Dumpster. As he pulled to a stop across from her mutilated yellow bike, he wondered if she would ever throw it away. He had tried throwing it away once but she had threatened him with bodily harm if he dared to touch it. Before he could come around and get her door she opened it herself and headed for the stairs.

"Mili, can we talk now?" He ran past her and stood over her in the stairway.

She swallowed and forced herself to speak. "You promised."

"I promised not to speak in the car but we're home now. We have to talk."

She squared her shoulders and looked at a point slightly to the right of his head. "Come inside." Her tone was so defeated, so un-Mili-like, he wanted to kill himself for what he'd done. He opened her door and let her into the apartment.

The smell of old cooking hung in the air. Usually they opened the windows to let the smells out. But because they had been gone for a day the smell had sat and festered in the apartment and sunk into the carpet, the walls.

Mili entered the house and turned to face him.

"My keys." She held out her hand.

"Mili."

She left her hand out and he returned her keys. She withdrew her hand before he could touch her.

"Where are the papers you want me to sign?"

"Mili."

Every time he said her name she flinched. And it was like a knee to his balls.

"Can we talk first?"

"What's left to talk about?"

The fact that I'm in love with you. But she looked so disgusted with him, so heartsick, he couldn't get the words out. "What about us?"

"Us?" She laughed. Not her husky, sunshiny laugh, but a painful groan of a laugh.

"Which *us*, Samir? The *us* you created to end my marriage? The *us* you made up so your brother's betrayal would cost him nothing? Or the *us* where you made a fool out of a stupid virgin, where you let her expose herself in the most humiliating way, so she could have no recourse, no life after you?"

"Mili, you know that's not how it was."

"No. I don't know anything, Samir. After this I will never know anything for sure again. I will never trust anyone again. You've taken my trust, my honor, my self-respect. You've sullied me. You made me feel filthy. I'll never feel clean again. I was pure." She stopped talking and clutched a fist to her chest. "I felt pure. I know that means nothing in your world. But I was untainted. Now I'm a sinner, a slut. You robbed me of who I was."

"Mili. I didn't know."

This time her shoulders just shook, but no laughter came out. No tears either. "You didn't know that you don't sleep with your sister-in-law?"

"You are not my sister-in-law, Mili."

"Why, because you say so? Because your dishonorable, cheating brother says so?"

"Mili, this was not Bhai's idea."

"That's a relief. This was your idea then. I spent my entire life loving him, waiting for him, and he sent his brother to sleep with me. And I'm such an idiot, I—I—Tell me, Samir, was I easy? Was I at least a little bit of a challenge?"

"Mili, it wasn't like that."

"Oh my God, you didn't even have to try. I practically begged you to sleep with me. Was sleeping with me in the plan or just making me fall in love with you? Did you brothers sit down and plan it? Get her to sleep with you. These village girls are really easy and stupid."

"Mili, stop. Don't do this to yourself. You're not stupid and we didn't plan it. At least not the way you think. All we wanted was to get you to agree to drop the court case and sign the annulment."

"And you had to wait until now, until I—You've been here four weeks, Samir." Her voice rose, but she choked it back.

God, why hadn't he told her? Why had he waited? And he knew it wasn't the script. It was this. This look in her eyes. He'd known she'd throw him out and he'd been too much of a coward to face it.

She held out her hand and shook it. "Give me the papers. I'll sign whatever you want. Actually, wait, let me make it easier."

She went to her bedroom—he heard her moving around. It took

him less than a moment to realize what she was looking for. He pulled the marriage certificate out of his laptop case.

When he entered the room, Mili was squatting next to the desk with the brown bag open. She turned around, her forehead lined with confusion. When she saw the plastic wrapped paper in his hand he thought she was finally going to cry. She didn't.

He had gone through her things. He had lied to her. The full extent of his betrayal killed every last sign of innocence from her eyes. "Mili, I'm sorry." He held the marriage certificate out to her.

The heavy cover of the suitcase slammed on Mili's hands. The sting of pain registered in her brain, but she didn't feel it. She slid her tingling fingers from the sharp metal jaws and stood up. Samir held her marriage certificate out like an offering, as if he expected her to take it from his hands. Those long tapered fingers that had violated every inch of her gripped the piece of paper she had always treated with the reverence of a holy text. Bile churned in the pit of her belly. She wrapped her arms around herself. The pain in her fingers finally broke through her consciousness and spread through her.

"Send me whatever papers you want me to sign," she said to the tattered piece of paper, unable to look away from it.

Poor Naani. She had to have been the one who filed the court case. Mili was sure of it. And now all her machinations had backfired. Everything had backfired. Mili thought about the desperation in Naani's voice. *He won't get away with it. He has to pay the price.*

No, Naani. He wasn't the one paying the price.

"Whatever legal documents you're talking about, I didn't send them. It must have been my *naani*. I'll talk to her. You won't hear anything more from us." She tightened her arms around herself and forced herself to look directly at him. "But please, if you have any decency left in you, don't ever come anywhere near me again. I never want to see you again. I never want to hear your voice. Never want to hear your name. I find you repulsive, disgusting, and I want nothing to do with you. Ever."

Mili waited, but Samir just stood there like a statue who had been slammed into the ground with a sledgehammer. She couldn't ask him to leave again. She couldn't talk to him again. But she had to get away from him. She walked past him and out of her room, out of her apartment, out of the building. She kept walking. Across the stinking parking lot, across the green campus lawns, past the red brick walls, over the gray cement walkways.

She took the long winding roads, every hill, every steep climb she could find. Unseasonably cool wind whipped her face and made her torn sleeve flap against her arm. The sun was still up in the sky, flowers bloomed everywhere, but the only thing she could see was the look in Samir's eyes as he stood there clutching the marriage certificate he had stolen from her. Her eyes burned, her throat burned. Parched and dry. She yearned for tears, to wash away the pain, to drown the shame, but none came. And she knew with absolute certainty that her tears were gone forever.

When finally she reached Pierce Hall, she sat on the stairs for a long while, unable to go inside. But how many places could she avoid that she'd been in with him? She couldn't avoid her own heart, her own body. She felt him on her, inside her, tearing her open. Every gentleness turned to violence, every whisper he'd whispered in her ear turned to a scream. The most beautiful time of her life had turned into a nightmare. She had turned into someone she would never recognize and even the memory of happiness was gone. Gone with him, gone with the him she loved. A mirage in the desert. A promise of rain that would never fall.

Finally, she got up and went in. She spent the rest of the day working. When she went back home Samir was gone. Her marriage certificate sat on the dining table. The smell of stale food still hung in the air. Amazing how something that smelled so good two days ago could now stink like death.

26

"Listen, Chintu, my wife is going to kill me and it's going to be your fault." Usually Virat wasn't the dramatic brother—that was Samir's role.

I had no idea you city boys were such drama queens.

Samir adjusted the road sign one last time and jumped off the ladder he'd been perched on. The set technician gave him the thumbs up, but Samir still wasn't sure it was exactly where he needed it to be. He signaled the team to take five minutes until he was done with the call.

"Bhai, I'm working, did you need something?"

"You worked even before you went to America. But you never forgot to call your family. I haven't talked to you in two months."

"I spoke with you two days ago, Bhai."

"You call that talking? All I've gotten out of you these past months is monosyllables, Chintu, and frankly you're scaring the fuck out of me. Rima wants you to come home for Diwali."

"Can't do it."

"Really, that's your answer? This is your *bhabhi* we're talking about. She's going to need more than that."

"I'm shooting."

"On Diwali?"

"Early morning the next day."

"Have you told Baiji you're not coming home for Diwali?"

"Not yet. Listen, can you tell her for me?"

"No fucking way you're firing that gun off my shoulder."

"Then I'll tell her."

"Chintu, you know what Baiji's thinking, right?"

Samir said nothing. He walked to the other end of the street set and looked at it from where the third camera would be. It was still off.

"If you come back from America after spending two weeks with your mother and act like someone died, you know what it looks like to Baiji, right?"

"My *mother* is living with you right now, in Jamnagar."

"I know." At least Virat had the decency to sound sheepish. "I shouldn't have said that. Sorry. But I'm worried about you, damn it."

"Don't be. I'm fine. I'm just stressed about the film. There's still too much to be done." But first he needed to get off the phone.

"Don't you want to know what happened with the annulment papers?"

Samir's heart kicked to life in his chest. He couldn't speak.

"Malvika signed them. The property case is officially closed. That damn saga is finally over. Whatever you did, it worked like a charm. She even sent the marriage certificate and the *mangalsutra* back. And a box full of saris. Apparently, our grandmother had been sending her a sari for every Teej over the years. What the fuck am I going to do with twenty brand-new saris? They're all still in their packaging."

His family had sent her gifts on the Teej festival. His grandfather had used up her dowry. All those rituals. All the promises that went with them.

It is a marriage to me, Samir.

"Send the saris to the National Women's Center in Jaipur." How had she even paid for shipping? The memory of her empty fridge, her empty closet, her empty apartment squeezed his heart.

"Chintu, seriously, what is wrong with you?"

"Nothing. Why? They have a safe house for women who have nowhere else to go. These women need clothes. What else would you do with the saris?"

"Why the fuck would you know this?"

"It's one of the charities my accountant pushes for taxes. Sounds useful enough."

"Fine. And Chintu, call Rima. What they say about pregnant women being hormonal, it's all true. She spends half the day worrying about what's wrong with you and the other half driving me crazy about it. If you don't call her, she's going to be on a plane and then God help you."

"I'll call her." He should've said more, should've apologized for being such a bastard of a brother. He'd completely forgotten to call Rima and check up on her this week. The baby was coming. Their lives were about to change forever. How had he forgotten about the baby? But he forgot a lot of things these days. Except the one thing he could not forget, no matter how hard he tried. No matter how many twenty-hour days he worked.

Today he'd been on the set for over fourteen hours, working with the set designer and the technicians to get it exactly right. They had another week before the schedule started and it still looked like a set, not like the low-income housing in the armpit of Mumbai he needed it to look like.

"The street edging is still too perfect, Lawrence. We need more dust, more crumbling mortar."

His set designer looked exhausted. "Yes, boss. A little more yellow in the whitewash, what? You're right, in this light it's too much white."

"More yellow, more gray streaks too. If the water tank leaks down this wall, we need more water damage."

"Brilliant, boss. You want to do now? Tomorrow okay?"

The workers were sprawled across the lawn, smoking. They looked like he'd need a crane to move them.

"No, let's wrap up for today. Seven tomorrow?"

Lawrence nodded in his usual enthusiastic way. "Sam-Sir, you having dinner with us?"

"Thanks, boss, but I can't. I still need to check the lights and make sure the effect for the night shots is correct."

"I'll stay. No problem," Lawrence said. His set tech was a gem.

"No, Lawrence, I got it. You'll get the union up in arms if you make the guys work any more."

"Sam-Sir, for you the guys will stay. No union-*shunion*, not for you."

Samir patted Lawrence on the shoulder. "Thanks, boss. I'll need that another day. Not today. Today you go get some rest. Fantastic job so far, thanks."

The rest of the crew was already at the local bar. The set guys picked themselves off the grass and headed there. If they were offended he wasn't joining them they didn't say anything. Usually, he'd be the one buying the drinks for his guys, sharing some smokes with them. He wasn't a smoker but hanging out with these guys was fun. They had some great stories. They had the dirt on everyone. All the stars, all the producers. Maybe tomorrow.

He pulled out the set sketches and started to study them against the streetscape, trying to put his finger on what wasn't working.

"Looks really great, Sam." The practiced husky voice reached him before he saw Neha crossing the lawn. She appraised his set and looked sufficiently impressed.

"Neha, I didn't know you were shooting here." He let her air-kiss both cheeks so her glossy pout remained untouched.

"Well, you've given up on your old friends, but your friends still care about you."

Is that why you went to the press and accused me of bashing your face in? "Thanks," was all he said.

She ran her fingers over his cheeks. "What's with the depressed *Devdas* look? I thought you hated stubble. This one's almost a beard."

"I do. I just haven't had the time to shave."

She took a step closer and strung her arms around his neck, pushing herself into him. He didn't move but a terrible queasiness rose in his gut.

"I still have your razor in my toilet kit. What say you come back to my room and I can take care of it for you?"

"If you nick me can I go to the magazines with it and cry abuse?"

She unwrapped her arms from around him and stepped away, her pout pushed out in all its glory. "Come on, Sam, baby, don't be like that. You broke my heart. I was upset."

Plus it was really good publicity. DJ had told him that Neha was booked solid for the next five years.

"And I withdrew the case. I thought you liked messing with the press. I thought you'd get a laugh out of it."

He'd got more than just a laugh out of it. He'd got someone to go to bat for him.

Samir would never, ever hit a woman.

"Are you all right? You look ill. I'm sorry, I really didn't realize you would be so upset about it."

"I'm not. You're right, it's pretty darned funny. I've always thought it would be a hoot to be labeled an abuser."

Her pout turned gargantuan, taking over her entire face. Huge tears pooled in her eyes. He couldn't stand to stay and watch. He couldn't even get himself to say good-bye. He turned and walked away.

"Sam," she called after him, her voice rising in pitch. "Sam, come back. I'm sorry."

You have no idea what it means to be sorry, Neha.

Fuck, he really was turning into a drama queen.

Samir no longer woke up with nightmares. Now he woke up from erotic dreams with such intense pain in his heart he wished for the nightmares. But his dreams were the only time he got to hold Mili, to feel her against him. And it was so real, he fell asleep every night praying for it, the pain afterward be damned.

He clutched his pillow and sat up in bed, waiting for his heartbeat to slow. The guest rooms in the studio complex weren't half bad. The owner had done a good job with the place. He'd skipped the glitzy granite and glass and gone rustic. Lots of natural stone, wood, and terra-cotta. Samir walked to the balcony that overlooked the Matheran mountain. In the dark, only the gray outline of the mountain was visible against a moonlit sky, but during the day it was magnificent, all red earth and lush green woods.

Like everything else these days the silence made him restless, and he reached for the phone. There was only one person he could call at this hour.

"Hello, *beta*." Sara's voice didn't seem as raspy and tired as usual. There could be only one reason for her cheery tone.

Suddenly Samir wished he hadn't called. Then just as suddenly he was glad he had. He settled into the rattan rocking chair. "How are you, Sara?"

"Don't I sound good?"

"You sound really good." Over the two weeks he had spent with her after Mili threw him out, she had progressively gotten stronger and more cheerful. It had been the most hellish two weeks of Samir's life but he couldn't have spent it anywhere else. Sara didn't know him. Didn't question him. Essentially she had left him alone and been happy with whatever time he spent sitting next to her as she rested after her radiation.

"Mili was here with her friend today. They stayed and made lunch with Kim. Mili makes the best rotis, did you know that? But that friend of hers, she'd burn water."

"Sounds like you had fun."

"It's great that Mili comes to see me."

He had no idea why she did it. But he couldn't imagine her not doing it either. "How is she?"

"Why don't you call and ask her yourself?"

"How's Kim?"

"She's fine too. She didn't feel too good this week. It's hard on her taking care of me. She's the older one, you know. She gets tired."

"Someone should be taking care of both of you." They shouldn't be stuck like that alone, taking care of each other, waiting for visitors to cheer them up. Suddenly he had an idea.

"Sara, would you . . . would you come here to India? Come stay with me? Let me take care of you?"

She went completely silent for a long moment. "Are you serious?" He heard a sob.

"I'm absolutely serious." Why hadn't he thought of it before?

"Let me think about it. Let me talk to Kim. But Samir, just that you asked. Thanks, son."

"Sure, Sara. Think about it. I'll talk to my lawyers and see what paperwork we need if you decide to come."

*   *   *

"Mill, you're not seriously going back to the library. You spend all your time either at the library or at Pierce Hall. I never get to see you anymore." Ridhi pulled her shiny new car into the smelly parking lot.

"Ridhi, I just spent two hours in the car and four hours in Sara's house with you." Mili pushed her door open and got out of the car.

"Yeah, four hours of having a mother rave about her son." Ridhi followed Mili up the stairs. "Why don't you just tell her what a bastard her son really is? I mean, what kind of son leaves his mother to die by herself?"

Mili let them into the apartment and tried to muster the energy to respond. "Sara's not dying. She's actually responding to radiation beautifully. Her past two scans have been cancer-free." She didn't tell Ridhi that she believed it was because she was finally able to talk about her son. Talk *to* her son.

"I hope so. She has been getting better each time we go see her. Are you sure you don't want to come eat dinner with Ravi and me?"

Ridhi had moved back on campus to finish out the semester. Ravi lived in Dallas. They had an apartment there and they visited each other on weekends. Ridhi's parents had taken one look at the apartment she shared with Mili and bought her a condo in Ann Arbor a few miles away. Ridhi was well and truly over her rebellious phase and she had gladly moved out. Now if she would only stop trying to get Mili to move in with her.

Thanks to the paper Mili had coauthored with Dr. Bernstein she had won another fellowship and it had more than solved her rent problem. She was almost done with her course and she wasn't going anywhere until it was time to go back home next month. Plus the reason they had an apartment was so Ravi and Ridhi could have their privacy when he was here. Mili had no interest in being the bone in that kebab. Also, much as she hated her apartment, she wasn't ready to let it go.

"Not tonight, Ridhi. Tonight I have a lot of studying to do."

"Mills, at least come up with a new excuse. And when are you going to start eating again? Look at you. You're wasting away, honey."

"I'll pick something up at the union. I really have to study. Two papers due next week."

"Are you ever going to tell me what happened?"

"Nothing happened. Hey, can you call Sara and let her know we made it back safe and sound? So she doesn't worry."

Ridhi handed her the phone. "Here, you do it. And while you're at it, why don't you call her son and tell him to come fix the mess he's made."

Mili dialed Sara's number and went into her bedroom. Sara answered, all bright and cheery. Mili hadn't ever heard her sound this strong.

"Mili, I have wonderful news. You're not going to believe this. Samir's asked Kim and me to move to India with him. He wants to take care of me. Can you believe that?"

Mili's heart twisted so tight in her chest the pain made her breathless. Sara sounded so excited, Mili could not believe this was the same woman who had barely been able to talk on the phone two months ago. Two long, painful months. The parched pain of unshed tears tore at her eyelids, jabbed at her throat. She swallowed and forced herself to speak. "Of course I can believe that. He's trying to be a good son." And that wasn't a lie.

"Mili, he's not just a good son, he's a good man. Can't you forgive him for whatever he did?"

Mili squeezed her dry eyes shut. Her throat felt like she was swallowing nails. "There's nothing to forgive, Sara."

"Child, don't wait until it's too late. Lost time is lost forever."

It was already too late. Their time was never theirs. How could she lose what was never hers? Why, then, did it hurt like this?

"Sara, can I call you later? I have a paper to finish."

Sara let her go without another word. Mili stared out the window. Cruel sunshine pierced her tinder-dry eyes. Her yellow bike stood wedged between two other bikes in the stand. She had come home from school one day the week after he left and found it repaired. The seat replaced, the brakes fixed, the handle unbent. There had been no note, nothing to tell her who had done it.

One of these days she'd walk it to the Dumpster. One of these days when she could bring herself to touch it.

* * *

The studio complex was a two-hour drive from Samir's flat in a north Mumbai suburb. But his driver and he had been stuck in traffic for two hours and they were barely out of Karjat. Samir was so restless he couldn't sit in the car one more second. He had gone over the screenplay for the hundredth time, tweaked the dialog, called the dialog writer and ironed out every nuance of the Hindi translation.

He had called Lawrence so many times his set tech was no longer answering his calls. His AD wasn't taking his calls either. Neither was his executive producer. "Sam, this is my twenty-ninth film in Mumbai and I swear to God, I've never been more well prepared for a film. You cannot do anything more until shooting starts. It's Navratri. Everyone needs time to celebrate the festival season from now until Diwali. If you don't stop calling people, they are going to drop out of the project. I'm turning my phone off now. I'll see you on set first thing Monday."

And she really did turn off her phone. Because when he thought of something else and called her again in five minutes, she didn't answer.

As for his driver, Samir loved the man; he had been with Samir for seven years now, but Samir could not discuss the three girls he was three-timing one more time without strangling his scrawny, red-scarf-covered neck.

"Javed, I'm going to get out and start walking. Pick me up when the traffic jam clears." He opened the door and got out of the car, feeling like a swimmer breaking water and gulping air.

Javed stuck his head out of the car. "Sam-Sir, have you gone crazies? What are you doing?"

"I'm walking, boss, what does it look like I'm doing?" Samir threw over his shoulder.

"But we are one hundred and fifty kilometers from home." For some reason Javed pointed to his watch as he said it. Another time Samir would have made fun of him for it.

"I know. So hopefully you'll catch up before I make it all the way back." He held up his cell phone. "I'll stay along the road. Call me when you start moving."

Javed smacked his head with both hands and looked heavenward in response.

Samir had walked for two hours before Javed made it to him and picked him up. It was another two hours before they got home. The last person Samir expected to see when he let himself into his flat was his mother.

"Baiji? What are you doing here?"

"*Arrey*, what kind of question is that for a son to ask his mother? It's my son's house. I'll come and go as I please."

He quickly bent down and touched her feet and she pulled his face to her and kissed his forehead.

"I'm sorry." He hugged her and found it hard to let her go. "I didn't mean to be rude. Of course, you come and go as you please. All I meant was that you should've called me so I would have picked you up at the airport. When did you get here?"

"This morning. Your housekeeper let me in. Then that cook of yours tried to bully me into letting *him* cook. But I set him straight. He's going to do the cutting and chopping and cleaning. I will be the one doing the cooking. No way is some strange man cooking for you when I'm here."

Samir had tried to get his mother to come and stay with him for years. But she never visited him. She hated Mumbai. It felt like a foreign land to her. She'd been here only once five years ago when he'd moved into this flat and that was it. He was the one who went to see her. She found Virat's military cantonment housing much more restful. And since Rima had come into the family her preference for Virat's home had only doubled. "When you get married I'll come stay with you," she liked to say. "I need female company now. I've spent my entire life with you boys. Now I need some softness in my life."

"Don't you want to know what I cooked?" she asked, searching his face.

"Actually, Baiji, I'm not hungry. I already ate." He smiled. He really was happy she was here. He didn't want her to think he wasn't. But he couldn't bear the thought of food right now.

"Chintu, I have been waiting for you for dinner and I'm starving. You will eat something." She gave him a stern look but he saw the worry it masked and his heart squeezed.

He washed his hands and sat down to dinner.

His mother had cooked all the things he loved: dal and potatoes and spicy *kadhi*. He tried really hard to enjoy it.

"Are you going to tell me what the matter is?"

"Matter?"

"See. Usually if I asked you one question you gave me three different answers in one breath. Now I get 'matter?' What is that?"

He shrugged.

"And there's a beard growing on your face. And your cook was right. You've lost too much weight. *Beta*, what happened in America?"

"Nothing, Baiji." Nothing had happened in America. It had all just been nothing.

"Since when do you lie to your mother? Is it Sara? Are you regretting not meeting her sooner?"

He did feel bad that Sara hadn't been part of his life before and he felt guilty that he had spent so much time hating her. But he didn't regret not reaching out to her sooner. And that was because the amazing woman watching him eat had never let him feel motherless. Even now, Sara was Sara. In a weird sort of way he loved her. Finding her was like unwrapping a gift he had not wanted and being surprised by how different it was from what he had expected.

But his love for Baiji was alive, definitive. It was wrapped up in the edges of the sari she had used to wipe crumbs from his mouth, to dab tears from his eyes. It was wrapped up in the hands she had used to wash and bandage not just a tattered back but scraped knees, to roast rotis just the way he liked them. It was a real and tangible love, tied up in memories and experience, in a face so familiar it didn't have to speak its worry to communicate it.

"Baiji, actually there is something I want to discuss with you." He got off his chair and squatted next to her.

She pushed his hair off his forehead. He hadn't realized how long it had grown. "I'm listening," she said.

"I want to bring Sara and her sister Kim to India. Kim is too old to go on caring for Sara by herself. They have no one else. What do you think?"

She pulled his face to her belly and kissed his head. "You stole the words from my heart, *beta*. It's the best idea. It's the only idea. If we don't take care of her, who will?"

He laid his head on his mother's lap. Her warmth, her strength seeped into him and for a few moments the incessant raw ache inside him let up. "Thanks, Baiji."

She continued to stroke his head. "*Beta*, I'm so proud of you for having the strength to go see her. You've made me proud of how I raised you. Thanks for turning into this man."

If only she knew what kind of man he had really turned into. The kind of man who had to be threatened and dragged to see his sick mother. The kind of man who killed innocence and had no idea how to fix it.

"Samir, do you think they can get here before Diwali? Maybe we can have Diwali here this year. All of us, because if we go to Rima's home it will be hard to keep her off her feet. Let's have Virat and Rima come here instead. What do you think?"

"Yes, Baiji, let's do Diwali here."

She lifted his face off her lap and peered into it. "So what else is the matter, *beta?*"

"I'll try to get the lawyers to expedite the paperwork." It was all he could say.

People loved to rant about bureaucracy in India and how it was impossible to circumvent. But if you knew the right people things worked like clockwork. It took one phone call to his lawyer to set the wheels of Sara's visa in motion. She had talked to Kim and Kim had seen no reason to refuse.

"Sam," his lawyer said in his courtroom baritone, "since I have you on the phone, I need Virat and you to sign a few more papers for the Balpur property to finish executing your grandfather's will."

"Sure. Send them over." The sooner he had nothing more to do with the bastard the better.

"And you brothers still want to do a split, right? You get the *haveli* and Virat gets the lands?"

Virat had given him a choice. Something had made Samir choose the *haveli*. "Yes. And once the split happens we can do whatever we want with our share, right?"

"Of course." He sounded taken aback. "Were you interested in selling? I can look for buyers if you want to sell."

"No, I don't need a buyer. But there is something else I need you to do for me."

Ridhi barged into Mili's office and dragged her to the union for lunch. "I want to actually see you eating."

"Isn't there anything interesting on TV today?"

"Very good! There's some of that old snark. I miss you, Mills. Come back to me." She waved her hands like a Bollywood chorus dancer beckoning her audience.

"I'm right here, Ridhi. Stop being such a drama queen."

"You're not right here. You haven't been right here since your stupid Romeo left. I swear if I get my hands on him, I'll kill him."

Mili groaned. It was going to be a long lunch hour. They picked up their sandwiches and waited to find an empty table. The union was packed today.

"And speaking of your stupid Romeo, his lawyer's been trying to reach you on my phone. He said you could call back even if it was late."

Mili nibbled her sandwich. It tasted like cardboard. She thought all the legal stuff was taken care of. Why was the lawyer calling again? Her stomach wobbled. Would this nightmare ever end? She took the phone Ridhi was holding out and dialed.

"Hello, Ms. Malvika. How are you?" She always felt like she was in a courtroom scene in a film when she spoke to the man. It was a good thing he used her first name. Now that her marriage was officially "void," she no longer knew what her last name was.

"I'm fine, Mr. Peston, thank you. I thought the annulment case was closed. Did I miss something?"

"Oh no, no. The marriage matter is all very fine and done. This is about the *haveli* in Balpur."

Mili's stomach turned over. She thought she had made it perfectly clear to Naani that she was to drop that blasted court case she had started. Naani had tried to convince her to fight for her rights. But there were no rights because there had been no marriage. At least in that Samir had been right. Because if it had been a marriage then its loss should have hurt at least a little. And it wasn't the loss of her marriage that hurt.

Mili still couldn't believe Naani had done something so awful in the first place without even letting her know. If Naani hadn't sent Virat those legal notices, if she hadn't petitioned for Mili's share in Virat's property, things might have been different.

What about the court case, Mili, what would you think if you were me?

No. She would not hold Naani responsible for what he had done.

"I'm sorry, Mr. Peston. I'll talk to my grandmother. Ignore any notices you get from us. I'll make sure any new case she's started is withdrawn. I'm sorry for the trouble." The sooner the connection with the Rathods was severed forever, the better.

"Oh no, no. There's no legal case. Your grandmother dropped the case. Your grandmother is not involved in this matter."

"I'm sorry? I don't get your meaning."

"I see. I thought you were aware." His usual confident bluster slipped slightly. "You see, Ms. Malvika . . . Mr. Rathod—Sam— he's signed over his half of the property to you. The *haveli* is now yours."

27

Within the span of a month Samir's life had changed entirely. He no longer needed to use his keys to let himself into his own home. Just the sound of the elevator opening on his floor made someone yank his front door open for him. And it could be any number of people. Today it was Rima.

She glared at him. "It's nine. Your shooting ended at noon. Where were you?"

"Well, hello to you too. Why are you answering the door? Where's Lily Auntie? Aren't you supposed to keep your bottom squarely on the sofa or, even better, the bed?"

"I'm pregnant, not handicapped. My doctor was all right with me travelling to Mumbai and I'd like you brothers to get off my case." She took his laptop bag from him and handed it to Poppy.

His housekeeper's granddaughter took the bag and smiled her special shy smile at him. He patted her head and she ran off. He missed her smile. He still remembered bringing her home from the hospital, beaten to a pulp by her father just because she wasn't like other children. She had lived with her grandmother in Samir's home ever since. And last month she'd moved to Jamnagar to help Rima.

Rima's glare softened a little bit. "Go wash your hands. Everyone's waiting for dinner."

"Are all pregnant women this bossy or just her?" he asked the seven pairs of eyes he found focused on him when he entered his living room.

"I suggest you don't piss her off any further until we get some food in her." Virat walked up behind his wife and wrapped his arms around her very pregnant belly.

Insane relief still surged through Samir every time he saw Virat walking around without his cane. His brother looked like he had never so much as tripped on a rock, let alone ejected from a burning plane.

"How's my niece doing?" Samir asked Rima's pregnant belly.

"She'll answer when she decides to take a break from playing football." Rima's face melted into its proud mama avatar. She pressed Virat's hand against her belly.

Her stomach undulated under their clasped hands and a gasp of wonder escaped Samir. No matter how many times he saw it happen it still took him completely by surprise. "How does she do that?" he asked, feeling every bit like someone who had just experienced a miracle.

Rima took his hand and placed it on her belly.

"See, that's her foot. She's like her daddy. She kicks in her sleep."

Sure enough, Samir felt another kick and the wonder of it made him feel like a four-year-old at a fair. Rima ruffled his hair.

"You were a kicker too," Sara said from the couch.

"Was he?" Baiji said. "See, Virat didn't kick but he hiccupped a lot."

"He hiccups now too, after two large ones." Virat's wife patted her husband's cheek and dragged him to the dining table.

He obligingly demonstrated a drunken hiccup as everyone took their places around the table.

"Back in a minute," Samir said, and ran up the stairs to wash up. He could still feel the gentle push of the baby's foot against his fingers. Amazing how there was a real live person in there. Amazing how much he loved someone he had never even met yet.

"Of course you love her, she's your niece!" Mili would've said. And then she'd have followed it up with some silly saying of her *naani*'s. A shaft of pain so intense slashed through his chest he could barely breathe.

He hit his face with a cold splash of water but instead of calming him it just made it worse.

A chorus of voices called his name and he squeezed his eyes shut. He loved his family. But he couldn't go downstairs. He couldn't spend one moment with anyone but the one person he wanted to spend every moment with. He pressed a towel into his face. The ache in his heart was so strong, his loneliness so overwhelming, his entire body hurt with the force of it. Just one look at her face. He needed just one more moment with her.

It took all his effort to push himself out of the bathroom. He stood at the top of the staircase and clutched the brand-new tensile metal railing, willing himself to be man enough to pull a smile across his face and join his chattering family without imagining a hundred scenarios of how perfectly Mili would fit at that table. How she would take care of everyone. How she would soak up the affection. How she would look at him to make sure he was all right.

And that's where he was standing, on that top step, talking himself into going down, when the bell rang.

Virat jumped out of his chair and ran to the door before any of the servants made it.

"Is this Samir Rathod's house?"

Only one person said his name like that.

Samir's entire numb existence sprang to life with such force it locked him in place.

"Mili?" Sara was the first to react.

"Sara?" Mili flew into the room past Virat and threw herself at Sara. Even in her fierceness she was gentle with Sara, the way only Mili could be.

"Sara, look at you—you are sitting at the dining table. All by yourself." Her incredible, sweet, husky voice cracked. "It's so good to see you."

Sara held Mili's face in both hands. "How are you, Mili, honey? What are you doing here?"

Sam watched Mili look around the room. Suddenly she seemed

to register that she was surrounded by strangers. Her face flushed with embarrassment. She searched the room, skimming face after face and not finding what she was looking for. Finally she lowered her lids for the briefest instant, as if she were bracing herself before she looked up and found him standing motionless on the stairs.

Her eyes melted into intense pools of light, vulnerable and yearning. Everyone else in the room fell away. Samir tried to hold on to that look. But she closed her eyes and shut him out. When she opened them again with what seemed like herculean effort, they were wiped clean of everything but pain.

All her defenses were up again. There wasn't a hint of that soft burn left. Samir gripped the railing to keep from running to her, to keep from doing something, anything to bring that look back. But the Mili standing in front of him was the Mili he had lost, the one who had turned away from him.

You've sullied me. You made me feel filthy.

"Are you Samir's Mili from America?" Trust his brother to say the one wrong thing and to grin like a charmer while saying it. "Hi! I'm Virat. Samir's brother." He extended his hand, ever the officer.

If Mili had looked like she was in pain before, now she looked like she would implode with it. Blood drained from her face, leaving it ashen. Samir felt twenty years of longing spill from her as she took Virat's hand.

"What do you mean *Samir's* Mili? Samir met someone in America, and you never told me?" Rima stood up and glared at her husband, then turned the accusing glare on Samir.

Baiji pushed her back into the chair. "If you keep jumping up like that, I'm not letting you get out of bed. Now calm down." Then she turned to the housekeeper. "Lily, bring her bags in."

Lily patted the silver bun at her nape and rushed to the front door without taking her eyes off Mili and dragged Mili's old brown bag into the flat.

"Did you bring the bag up by yourself? You should have told the watchman," Baiji said to Mili, who looked so overwhelmed that Samir's heart gave another painful twist. "I'm Samir's mother, by the way."

Mili leaned over and touched Baiji's feet and finally found her voice. "*Namaste.* I'm sorry, I didn't mean to intrude." She joined her palms.

Baiji placed a hand of blessing on her head. "Bless you, *beta.* You're not intruding. This is Samir's home. His friends are welcome here anytime." She threw a questioning glance in his direction, prodding him to move, then looked back at Mili. "We were about to sit down to dinner. Join us."

Mili looked at the food. Samir held his breath. He would've given anything to see her eyes light up at the sight of the table. But her eyes remained passive. If anything she looked nauseated. He forced himself to ease his grip on the railing.

She raised those awfully guarded eyes to him. "Actually, I need to speak with Samir just for a moment."

All seven people in his household turned simultaneously to stare at him. He still hadn't moved off that step, hadn't said a word. He hadn't been able to do much more than stare at her.

"Usually it takes him ten seconds to come down those stairs. Today, it looks like he might need some help. What, Samir?" Rima, in all her delicacy, added a wink because her meaning wasn't clear enough without it.

"Anytime now he'll find his tongue. In the meantime, you come sit. There is so much we want to talk to you about." Virat pulled out a chair and patted it meaningfully.

Mili looked at the chair, then at the smiling, teasing faces, and her nose reddened. She squeezed it.

Samir wanted to shake his grinning clueless family. "She said she wanted to talk to me. Didn't you hear her? Why don't you just leave her alone?"

At the sound of his voice Mili folded inward. Her insides cramped into a ball of unbearable pain. The roaring that had started in her ears when she'd seen him standing motionless as a statue at the top of the stairs intensified to a deafening pitch. Everyone sitting around the table gaped at him, shocked, as if he had never used that tone with them before.

Her head started to spin. It had been a long time since she'd eaten. She'd been so sick on the flight, so anxious at the thought of seeing him again, she hadn't been able to touch food. Now the sight of it made bile rise in her throat. Strength drained in slow motion from her limbs. Dark pinwheels exploded in front of her eyes. She was going to completely humiliate herself and faint five minutes after entering his home. She reached out and gripped the chair his brother had just pulled out for her. Very slowly her legs gave beneath her, then the rest of her followed. The last thing she remembered before everything went black was Samir flying down the stairs.

He had her in his arms before she hit the ground. His heart beat so loud against her ear she thought it was going to explode. Her own heart refused to beat.

"Mili?" Her name on his lips fell like knife stabs on her body.

She tried to open her eyes but everything spun. She clamped her jaw to stop the darkness from swirling around her. She would not throw up on his feet again.

"Call the doctor." His arms tightened around her. The buzz of his family's voices swarmed after them like bees as he bounded up the stairs.

"Stay right here," he snapped and a stunned silence followed. "Don't you dare follow us up, you hear me?"

The silence didn't last. Everyone spoke at once. "What is wrong with you?" "Are you crazy?" "She just fainted!"

A door slammed on the voices and he laid her down on cool softness. It was like landing on a cloud. His arms slid off her, the gentleness of his touch gouging out a million memories. Her head still swam, but her dark wobbly insides spun mercifully slower.

"Mili?" His hand rested on her forehead. His voice barely concealed his panic.

She forced her eyes to open and found his face inches from hers. Damp strands framed his golden face. His perfect jaw worked. Despite the shadows beneath his eyes, despite the worry etched across his forehead, he took her breath away. And she hated him for it.

She pushed back, trying to put some distance between them, and realized she was on a bed, propped up on a pile of pillows. It was the most comfortable bed she'd ever been on in her life. It molded willingly to her body, cradled her every angle and curve.

Good Lord, she was in his bed. *Again.* She sat up and skittered away from him. The room took another spin around her head and she gripped the bed to steady it.

With quick steps he backed away and folded his arms across his chest.

She wiped her sweating forehead against the sleeve of the *kurti* she had bought at the airport. "I'm sorry. I didn't mean to do that. I've never fainted in my life. Oh God, your family must think I'm so stupid."

"When was the last time you ate?"

She swallowed.

She could not bring herself to meet his eyes. And the thunderous note in his voice didn't help matters at all. Why couldn't he do that Mt. Vesuvius thing now? He poured a glass of water out of a glass pitcher, thrust it into her hand, and walked to the door. He opened it only a sliver. "Lily Auntie, I need a plate of food up here—*dal,* roti, and potatoes," he called. "And Lily Auntie, you will bring it up alone. Just you, no one else."

He shut the door and stood there without turning around, one fisted hand on the beautifully carved wood, the other on his temples. His white shirt was beyond wrinkled. She had never seen him in wrinkled clothes. Everything he ever wore had always looked brand new and fresh from the store. His jeans hung low on his hips. Her eyes, which had stayed stubbornly dry for months, warmed behind her eyelids. Pain, embarrassment, and every other emotion she had ever felt danced to life in her heart.

He turned around so abruptly she almost dropped the glass.

"You didn't answer me. When was the last time you ate?" His hand continued to squeeze his temples. "What have you done to yourself? How much weight have you lost? You *fainted.* You can't—" He ran his hands through his hair. It was overgrown. His face was overgrown with stubble. He looked like an unkempt wolf. A heart-breakingly handsome unkempt wolf with tortured honey-gold eyes. Nothing like the always impeccable Samir she knew.

Suddenly his stormy eyes lit with understanding. "Holy shit! That's why you're here. You're pregnant."

28

The door to Samir's room flew open.

"She's pregnant?" Three women came rushing in. The pregnant one was first, her huge belly pushing in front of her, Samir's Baiji was next, and the woman carrying a plate of food must've been Lily Auntie, who was supposed to bring the food up by herself.

Mili's hand flew to her mouth.

Samir tried to get between her and their gaping faces. "Everyone out. You need to leave. Now."

The pregnant one grabbed his shoulders and bodily pushed him out of her way. "We will not. What is wrong with you?"

"Rima, you're supposed to be taking it easy. What are you doing?" He looked so helpless, Mili's heart twisted some more.

"She's pregnant and she just fainted in our home. You want me to stay down?" Whoever this Rima person was, she glared at Samir as if he were an imbecilic child. Despite herself Mili wanted to smile.

"Both of you be quiet." Samir's Baiji, who had the kindest eyes, gave them both a silencing look and walked straight to Mili. She took the plate from Lily Auntie and held it in front of Mili. The food smelled so good that Mili nearly passed out again.

"First eat something, *beta*. Then we can talk." She ran the gentlest hand over Mili's head. The look on her face was so affectionate, so filled with motherly concern, that for no reason at all Mili's stupid nose started to run and without a second's notice more her eyes flooded and tears started to flow down her cheeks.

Rima took the plate out of Baiji's hands and Baiji pulled Mili to her. Mili pressed her face into her shoulder, lost all semblance of dignity, and sobbed like a baby. The tears felt so good. For the past two months, the pain in her heart had been constant, unyielding, her loneliness ghastly and dark. These ten minutes, this past moment, it was more than she could handle.

Sobs rose from the deepest part of her and soaked through her dry, starving heart. She should have tried to stop herself but Baiji's soft muslin sari felt so good against her face, her arms so soothing around her, Mili couldn't bring herself to even try. Finally, she felt the wetness soak through Baiji's sari beneath her cheek and embarrassment took over. She pulled away, feeling so incomparably stupid she couldn't meet anyone's eyes. Her head hurt and her eyes stung.

Samir tried to get closer to her but Rima placed one hand on his shoulder. Mili couldn't tell if she was holding him away or trying to soothe him.

"Go downstairs," Rima said in a voice that brooked no argument.

"Not on your life."

"Samir, give her a few minutes. Listen to me."

"No, you listen to me. I'm not going anywhere. But you're leaving. All of you. Now."

Baiji wiped Mili's cheeks with her sari and turned to Samir.

"Are you telling your mother to get out?"

"No, Baiji, I'm asking. Mili and I need to talk. Please."

"What is there to talk about? You're going to be a father. Evidently you've done something to hurt this girl very badly and it's made you so miserable these past few months you've made us all sick with worry. Now she's here. You're here. Make it right."

For one brief moment Samir looked like he was going to smile. Mili felt like she was going to smile, but neither of them smiled.

"Baiji, I can't make it right if you don't give us two minutes to talk."

"So talk," Rima said, looking like she wasn't going anywhere.

"Virat!" Samir hollered.

"I'm right here." Apparently Virat had been in the room all along.

"Please take your wife downstairs. Or I'm going to pick her up and take her down myself."

"I think you've done enough sweeping women off their feet for one day, thank you. Leave this one to me." Virat leaned over, picked up his pregnant wife, and headed out the door.

"Lily Auntie, you too," Samir said. "Because I'll carry you down if I have to."

Lily Auntie scampered out of the room, giggling into her palm.

"Put me down, Virat. Baiji is watching," Rima hissed at her husband, but she seemed perfectly content where she was.

Baiji stood. "I just found out my son got a girl pregnant before marriage. I think I can handle watching the other one carry his wife down some stairs." She patted Mili on the head and handed her the plate. "Before any talking there will be eating. First she finishes the food." She gave Samir a stern look.

Baiji didn't get an argument from Samir on that. He herded them out the door, and watched until they were well and truly gone. He pulled the door shut and waited there for a few seconds, then quickly opened it to make sure no one had sneaked back up.

Finally he turned to her. "I'm sorry about that."

To keep from responding Mili forced a piece of roti into her mouth. And then couldn't stop. The food was delicious but the taste brought back so many memories of Samir cooking for them she had to keep choking back the tears, which apparently had decided they had stayed away long enough. And choking back the impulse to seek him out with her eyes.

He stood motionless, his hip leaning against a huge desk that looked like something out of one of those good-living magazines, all solid wood and polished surfaces. The entire room looked like something out of a very fancy film, only warmer and suffused with something far too familiar, someone far too familiar. But between the potent silence and the rich-people décor, he might as well have been standing across the earth.

"How could you not have told me sooner?" he said the moment

she put the last morsel in her mouth. He took the plate from her hands and put it on the nightstand. "How long have you known?"

"I am not . . . I'm not pregnant, Samir."

Her imagination had to be in overdrive because she could have sworn she saw disappointment dim his eyes. "Then why did you say you were?"

"I didn't. You asked me a question and your family—"

"Fu—" he trailed off and began pacing the room, his fingers in his overgrown hair.

She reminded herself how angry she was with him, how filthy he had made her feel. But the pain and loneliness of the past months had been like a sandstorm, eroding through the giant dunes of her anger.

He turned his molten gaze on her. That gaze with its wounded vulnerability had stolen her head once, made her fall on him like a hungry animal. Now it made rabid fear rise inside her.

"I'm sorry. They aren't usually so obnoxious. It's just that— Why did you pass out then? Are you—you're not sick, are you?" Raw panic flashed across his face. Tenderness and longing melted in his eyes.

She had been in hell because of him. She could not let that look take her back there. "I'm fine. I just hadn't eaten."

"You hadn't eaten?" Again that rawness in his voice, again that concerned caress of his gaze. She had to get away from him. Give him back his stupid *haveli* and just get away from him.

"Samir, please don't. I can't." The sound of his name trembled on her lips, made her voice crack.

He stepped back and schooled his features into a mask. Not quite Pompeii, but he tried. "It's okay. I didn't mean to . . . It's just that—"

"Why did you sign the *haveli* over to me? You can't do that."

"It's yours. Your *naani* was right to ask for it."

"No, she wasn't. You were right—there was never a marriage."

His eyes softened. No, they more than softened, they bled with understanding. "I'm sorry you had to see that. I'm sorry you had to see Virat and Rima like that."

Mili blinked. She had been startled when Virat had introduced himself. She hadn't expected to see him here. But it was the near physical impact of seeing Samir again that had taken everything over. She wrapped her arms around her knees and pressed her face into them. Twenty years of thinking she loved someone and she hadn't even registered meeting him. And Rima, so she was his wife—Samir's *bhabhi*.

You are not my bhabhi, Mili.

Oh God.

How many times was she going to play those conversations in her head? How many times was she going to relive that month? From the first moment she had laid eyes on Samir she had been able to think of little else. And for most of that time the pain had been blinding. And here he was, looking at her in that way that had put her in this situation in the first place.

She got off his bed. "I already told you, you were right. We didn't have a marriage."

Samir didn't respond. He just looked at her like he wished she would say more, like his life depended on her saying more.

She really had to get out of here before this went any further. He was too much of a slippery slope for her. "Please don't put me through this again. I can't have anything to do with you. Please."

His face softened even more, and she knew he could see right through to the horrible storm inside her. "Mili—"

"No, Samir. No." She put her hand up for him to stop, for him to stay away from her.

He stopped in his tracks. But he didn't move back. "Just tell me what you want. I'll do whatever you want."

"Take the *haveli* back. I don't want it. You can't just give me something that big."

Samir had never in his adult life felt this helpless. She was turning him back into the whiny pushover he'd been as a child. But he wasn't that pathetic child anymore. He could and would give her whatever the fuck he wanted. He had given her everything anyway. Everything that was his was already hers. It meant nothing without her. "I'm not taking the *haveli* back."

"You gave her the *haveli?*" This time Virat barged into his room with a bowl in his hands.

"For God's sake, Bhai, can you people at least knock?" He had never before raised his voice to his brother. Right now he had to fist his hands to keep from pushing him out of his room.

"You gave our ancestral property to a girl you got pregnant and you want me to knock?"

"Get out."

Virat skirted around him as if he weren't shouting like a madman and headed straight for Mili. He handed her a bowl of *kheer.* "Baiji sent me up with dessert. It's crazy good."

"Get out, Bhai, or God help me I will bodily throw you out."

"You've never talked to your brother like that. What's wrong with you?" Rima followed Virat into the room, one hand supporting her stomach.

Along with the anger already exploding inside him, terror gripped Samir in the gut. "Rima, you need to stay off your damn feet."

From the look on Virat's face he was on Samir's side on this one. Thank God. The two of them grabbed Rima and pushed her into a chair.

"Baiji!" She had the gall to call for help.

"What is going on, Samir?" Baiji was at his bedroom door in an instant. She had always been spry but this was ridiculous.

Samir grabbed his head, then grabbed Mili's hand and tried to pull her off the bed. "We're going for a drive."

Of course she didn't comply.

"You are not going anywhere. She's pregnant and she just fainted. She's not going anywhere until she sees a doctor." Baiji challenged him to argue with her and threw a protective look at Mili.

"You're pregnant, Mili?" Great, now Kim was up here too.

"Should we take this downstairs? Why leave Sara out?" Samir stood between Mili and his family and glared at them. He was too afraid to look at Mili. She had looked so fragile before they had all come barging in.

"Exactly what I was thinking," Sara shouted from downstairs in a voice that did not belong to a woman who hadn't been able to get a word out a few months ago. "Mili, you didn't tell me you were pregnant."

Samir grabbed his head and sat down on the bed next to Mili. He was about to let out another yell, but out of the corner of his eye, he saw Mili's lips quirk. Not a whole lot, just a little bit. And for a moment, just for a flash, her eyes twinkled. She caught him looking. A sweet memory of how things had been passed between them. But then it was gone and she looked terrified by what had just happened.

Samir stood up, shielding her from all those curious eyes. He didn't want anyone to see her like this, like a wounded animal. He faced his family. "Mili is not pregnant." Then he shouted it down to Sara. "Mili's not pregnant."

"I heard you the first time. Keep going," Sara shouted up.

Behind him he heard a sound. It was suspiciously close to a giggle. He spun around. Her hand was pressed into her mouth. Behind her delicate fingers hid the most beautiful thing—not quite her full-blast one-twenty-watt smile—but a smile nonetheless.

Samir forgot what he'd been saying.

"What are you talking about?" Baiji said behind him.

"Then why did you say she was?" Rima added.

Samir raised his eyes heavenward and her eyes sparkled. "I didn't," he said, soaking up her smile before turning around. "Anyway, the point is she's not pregnant and she doesn't need a doctor. What she needs is ten minutes to talk to me without having all of you violate every tenet of civilized behavior."

"But why would you give her the *haveli* if she's not pregnant?" Virat asked, ignoring Samir's rant entirely.

"Why would he give her the *haveli* if she *were* pregnant?" Rima asked.

"He's not giving me the *haveli*," Mili said behind him, and walked around him to face everyone.

"I am," Samir said.

"Why?" This from Baiji.

"Because her dowry saved it from being auctioned. It's hers."

* * *

Mili couldn't believe Samir had just said that to his entire family. The attention of every single person in the room focused on her. But Samir's attention was what stole her breath. "It's hers because she's done more for it than any of us."

Finally, there was silence in the room.

But it didn't last. "What is that supposed to mean, Samir?" Rima said. She tried to stand up, but she seemed to lose her strength and sat back down, her face suddenly as white as a sheet.

Virat was on his knees next to his wife in an instant. "Rima." Just that one word and Mili felt a lifetime of love wrapped up in it. Rima stroked his cheek.

"Rima, are you okay?" Samir pressed a hand into her shoulder and looked so scared that Mili wished she could go to him.

"Of course I'm not okay, Samir. I have no idea what you're talking about. And frankly you've been acting so crazy lately you're really starting to scare me." She pressed her hand into her belly and leaned forward with a pained hiss.

The blood drained from Virat's face. "Rima, *jaan*, let's get you to the bed. You need to lie down. Samir is fine."

Rima gave her husband a soothing look and turned to Samir. "What do you mean Mili has done more for the *haveli* than any of us? What's going on, Samir? Virat, do you know what's going on?"

Virat turned to Samir, then looked at Mili, then back again at Samir. "Bloody hell," he said as realization dawned on him.

Baiji looked from Virat to Samir. "Oh Krishna, what have you boys done now?"

Mili felt the weight of Samir's gaze, but she couldn't meet it. Not only did Samir's family know she had slept with him, now they all knew that she was the one girl who should never have gone anywhere near him.

Rima looked from face to face, her own confused face going whiter and whiter with every breath. She started to say something, but another gasp of pain escaped her lips. She pressed a hand into her belly and swallowed.

The collective anxiety of the room shifted to Rima. Her breathing became labored, her face scrunched up in pain. Baiji used the end of her sari to dab the sweat that beaded across Rima's forehead. "Samir, call the driver, we need to go to the hospital right now."

Before the words had left Baiji's mouth, Rima screamed and doubled over.

29

"*Oy hoy*, look at your faces, did someone die?" Rima sat propped up in one of those partially folded spaceship-style hospital beds. Despite the glazed, medicated look in her suddenly sunken eyes she was a stunningly beautiful woman, all delicate features and skin almost as light as Samir's.

Mili stood by the door and watched Samir wrap his arms around her, taking care to avoid all the machines and tubes spouting from her like an octopus. "Yeah, us. We almost died. Thanks for scaring us to death."

Instead of responding to Samir, Rima beckoned Mili over. "I hope you know what drama queens these brothers are."

Samir tried to catch Mili's eye, but she kept her focus squarely on Rima and took the hand she was holding out.

Rima was right. Samir and Virat had both been a mess last night when Rima had gone into premature labor. Samir had asked her if she wanted to stay home, but strange as it was, she had wanted to be at the hospital with them. None of them had slept, eaten, or talked while they waited all night for the doctors to stop the labor. The baby was still a week away from the safe thirty-week mark and it was imperative that he-slash-she stay inside for at least a few weeks more. Mili said a silent prayer and squeezed Rima's hand.

"Would you like your breakfast?" Samir picked up the green Jell-O from Rima's food tray.

Rima made a face.

"Put that awful thing away," Baiji said, smacking Samir's hand. "Lily is bringing home-cooked food."

"So, what's the story?" Rima raised a brow at Samir. "What's this thing about the *haveli* and Mili's dowry?"

Virat and Samir looked at each other.

"*Arrey*, what are you gaping around like that for? Why did the *haveli* have to be saved and why was Mili's dowry—Oh! Oh, Good God!" Rima's eyes popped to perfect circles. "Oh God, Samir, how could you not tell us? Virat, did he tell you?"

Virat swallowed hard and rubbed her feet. "Rima, I don't know what you're talking about, but can we talk about it later?"

"I'm right, am I not?" She turned to Samir. Samir's gaze bounced from Rima to Mili, then to Virat.

"Why are you looking around like a fool? No one's going to help you. First you run off and get married and then you keep it from us? What is wrong with you?"

It was a good thing the bed had rails because Mili had to hold on to keep from falling off.

Rima turned to Mili. "I don't understand what the big secret is? Why didn't you two just tell us? Was it because of the baby?" She touched her belly. "Did you meet in America? Oh my God, are you taking him back to America with you?"

"For someone who just put us through hell last night, you're just bursting with questions, aren't you? Why don't you rest for a while? We'll explain everything later," Samir said.

"*Arrey*, let Mili answer. Why are you interrupting?" Rima looked at Mili.

"Samir's right. We can discuss it later. You should rest now." Mili pushed her back on the bed and pulled the covers over her.

Baiji watched Mili with a curious expression and Mili gave up on trying to tamp down her stupid blushing reflex. Then Baiji turned her mother's curiosity on Samir. He looked away.

"But I'm not tired. What I am is hungry," Rima said.

As if on cue the door opened and Lily Auntie walked in with a carrier full of food and a worried frown on her gently lined face. Two other worried faces followed her into the room.

"We wanted to come and see you, Rima-*bhabhi*," Lily said tentatively. "Sam-Sir said it would be fine."

"Of course it's fine. Come, come." Rima smiled and waved them in.

Baiji took the food carrier from Lily and started laying food out on a steel plate. Mili helped her.

"Samir, why don't you introduce your wife to your staff." Rima put a spoonful of dal and rice in her mouth and gave the three new entrants a meaningful look.

Samir squeezed his temples.

He had a staff?

He searched her face with his too tired eyes, looking almost afraid of her reaction. "Staff?" she mouthed, eyebrows raised, and he relaxed.

"Sam-Sir, you made marriage and didn't even tell us? How like that?" The tall skinny man in a bright red shirt and meticulously slicked back hair threw a seriously offended look at Samir. Then flicked his head in Mili's direction with a camera-ready smile. "Sam-Sir, at least do intro, no?"

Samir let out a sigh. "Mili, this is Javed. Javed, this is Mili."

Mili couldn't help but smile. "How are you, Javed *bhai?*"

Javed flashed her another camera-ready smile. "Very fine. Very fine. Myself Sam-Sir's driver," he said in English, even though both Samir and Mili had addressed him in Hindi. "You from America, Mili-*bhabhi?*"

"We met in America, yes."

"Ah, so now I get!" Javed said, still in English.

"Javed." The warning in Samir's tone was impossible to miss.

But Javed missed it anyway and turned to Mili like an excited child with a secret to share. "Mili-*bhabhi*, Sam-Sir has been acting so strange-like since he came back from America. Full-on *Devdas* mode—total sad-song types. You know what he did today?"

"And Mili, this is Lily Auntie. You've met her. She keeps my house for me." Samir cut Javed off without a hint of his usual Samir finesse.

"Hello, Lily Auntie." Mili returned Lily's smile and turned

back to Javed. "So, Javed-*bhai*, you were telling me what *Sam-Sir* did today."

Javed got so excited he forgot his camera-ready smile. "*Arrey*, Mili-*bhabhi*, it was full-on drama. He just got out of the car in the middle of Mumbai-Pune highway and started walking." Javed pushed his arms out and did an incredibly accurate imitation of Samir's guy-with-humungous-biceps swagger. "This long the traffic jam was"—he motioned a great distance with his hands—"but Sam-Sir's face was even longer. I tried to stop him. But where was he listening? He just took off. Two hours it took before I picked him up. Still walking." Javed walked his fingers across the air in front of him.

Everyone turned to Samir, shaking their heads and laughing. But Mili couldn't breathe.

"Mili-*bhabhi*, Javed is right. Ever since Sam-Sir came back from America, he's been all down-in-dumps." Lily made a thumbs-down sign and smiled. "Usually, he's all tip-top. Clothes, room, everything doing shining. Now. Nothing. Everything all over the place." She shook her hands to indicate Samir's nothingness and tears pushed at Mili's eyelids.

Samir pulled himself to his full height. "Lily Auntie, let's save some of these fond stories for later, shall we? Rima needs rest."

Rima didn't seem to think she needed rest, because she turned to the teenage girl cowering behind Lily. "Mili, this is Poppy," she said in a softer voice, throwing the skinny girl a gentle look. "She's Lily Auntie's granddaughter. Samir's taken care of her since she was a little girl. She just moved to Jamnagar with us. Now she's going to help me take care of my baby. Right, Poppy?"

"Unless Sam-Sir needs me here. Then I'll come back," Poppy said with a debilitating lisp that made it hard to understand her. She gave Samir a look so worshipful, the mood in the room changed.

Lily dabbed her eyes. They mirrored Poppy's devotion.

Samir's entire body went utterly still, in that way it always did when he was overcome with emotion.

How had she thought she knew him so well? There was so much about him she didn't know. The Samir who had dragged her to the wedding. The Samir who had raced to make samosas with her. The Samir who had branded her body, lain prostrate under her in total surrender. The Samir who had taken all responsibility for what happened between them, absolved her of all blame, when really she had wanted him more badly than she had ever wanted anything in her life. That Samir she knew. It had been hard, but that Samir she had been able to shut out with the force of her anger.

But this Samir who stood before her with his staff and his family, whom he allowed to walk all over him with such ease, this Samir, whom everyone seemed to love with such fierceness, was far more dangerous than the one who had made her forget everything she had been before him. This Samir with his unkempt clothes and his desperately hopeful eyes was making her forget the agony of the past months. He was making it hard to go on believing that the incredible generosity he had shown her, his innate gentleness, had all been an act to get what he wanted.

He smiled at Poppy. And Mili knew without a doubt how wrong she had been. It hadn't been an act, none of it.

Mili turned to Poppy, her throat working to push back tears, and gave her a quick hug. "Hello, Poppy. Rima-*bhabhi*'s baby is so lucky to have a *didi* like you."

Poppy's face lit up with pride. She turned to Samir, clapping her hands, and he knew with absolute certainty that he was never letting Mili go. He would do whatever it took to make her see what she meant to him. He would follow her to the ends of the earth.

She searched his face, cocking her head to one side as if she were trying to gauge what he was thinking.

I love you. That's what he was thinking. He wanted to mouth it to her. He wanted to whisper it into her lips, into every secret place in her body. He wanted to scream it out in front of the entire world.

She didn't look away. For the first time since she'd come back she held his gaze. It was equal parts fear and hope. And that something else she saved only for him sparkled at the edges. He would bring it back. Whatever it took he would bring it back.

She leaned back into Rima's bed and suddenly everything disappeared from her eyes except horror. The beat of his heart stopped. Mili held up both hands. Her palms were completely red with blood. She spun toward Rima just as Rima's head lolled back and her entire body went limp.

Mili had never seen a grown man cry. Virat slumped on the bench next to his brother and wept like a baby. Not for long, just for a few moments, but it was the most heartbreaking thing Mili had ever seen. Samir sat there with his arm around his shoulders and said nothing until he stopped. When he finally spoke, his face was carved in stone but his voice crackled with hope. "She's going to be fine, Bhai."

Mili leaned against a wall across from them in the private waiting room and watched Virat wipe his eyes. She should have felt like an intruder but every time Samir looked at her she knew there was nowhere on earth she needed to be but here.

After Rima had started hemorrhaging they had rushed her into surgery. That had been three hours ago. The huge wooden clock ticked away on the wall. Baiji paced the room, a tattered copy of the *Bhagavad Gita* clutched in her hands as she chanted verses under her breath. Every few minutes she stopped and pressed a hand into Virat's shoulder.

Mili walked up to her and eased her into a chair. She sat down at her feet, took the book from her hands, and started chanting where she had left off. Her *naani* had taken her along whenever anyone in the village got sick and she had sat with the womenfolk and chanted the peace mantras for hours even when she was too young to know what they meant. The same peace she had felt back then settled over her as her voice sang out the familiar Sanskrit syllables.

Baiji placed a hand on Mili's head, leaned back, and closed her eyes. Virat and Samir joined her on the floor. Sitting cross-legged next to her they joined their palms and closed their eyes. The whispered sounds of their voices blended with hers. The strength of their joint prayers intertwined and wrapped tightly around them and shut out the ticking clock, shut out everything but their words and their hope.

Hours or maybe it was just moments later a knock sounded on the door. The heavy curtain to the room lifted and the doctor walked in. She waited for them to finish the verse before she spoke. "Rima is out of surgery," she said directly to Virat, who jumped up. "You have a baby girl. She's healthy and stable."

No one could breathe. They waited.

"Rima?" Baiji asked, and Virat made a pained sound.

The doctor patted Virat's arm. "We've stopped the bleeding. The next few hours are critical, but if she doesn't start bleeding again, she should regain consciousness. You can see her as soon as they have her settled in the ICU."

"Can I see my baby?" Virat rubbed his eyes with his fingers and Samir squeezed his shoulder.

The doctor smiled. "They're setting her up in the incubator. She'll need to be there for at least a week. But she is one strong girl with very strong lungs." Her phone buzzed and she glanced at it. "You and one more person can go see her now."

Virat and Baiji followed the doctor out of the room. The moment they were alone, Samir slumped into a chair and dropped his head into his hands. Without thinking about it, Mili sat down next to him and placed a hand on his arm.

That's all it took. He turned to her, dug his face into her shoulder, and started shaking. She wrapped her arms around him and pulled him closer. There were no tears, no words, only utter relief for his niece and absolute terror for Rima.

She cradled him, stroked his hair, his back. "Shh, Samir. She's going to be fine. They've stopped the bleeding. The baby is fine. You have a niece. A little girl to call you *chacha*. Samir-*chacha*. Or how about Chintu-*chacha?*"

He laughed and slowly the shaking stopped. His breathing steadied. For a long while he stayed right there in her arms, as she whispered nonsense words into his hair, soaking up everything she was pouring into him. How did he do that? How did he have the courage to lay himself out in front of her like that at every turn, knowing full well she could push him away? Had pushed him away. Hearing his voice, looking at him, touching him, it still hurt, but pain wasn't all she felt. And what she did feel gave her the courage to not push him away again.

Mili heard Virat enter the room and her eyes flew open. She was bent over Samir, her head resting on his. His face was pressed into her lap. They had fallen asleep like that in the waiting room. She straightened up and found his fingers entwined in hers and tenderness bloomed in her heart. Virat cleared his throat. Despite the shadows under his eyes and the weariness etched into his face he looked amused.

Mili withdrew her fingers from Samir's and he shifted awake. He sat up, his overgrown hair pushed into disheveled peaks, the embroidery from her *kurti* imprinted into his cheek above the stubble. He gave his brother a look filled with such hope, every remnant of resistance inside Mili crumbled to dust at his feet.

"Rima woke up," Virat said. "She's going to be fine. The doctor is with her right now. You want to go see your beautiful niece?"

Samir threw his arms around Mili and was out of the room before she could react.

Virat sat down next to Mili.

"How is she?" Mili asked.

"She's wonderful." His voice shook with relief and Mili's nose started to run. "You can go and see her when the doctor leaves. She asked for you, you know." Virat plucked a tissue from a box and handed it to her. "Mili, do you mind if I say something?"

Mili blew her nose into the tissue and nodded.

"When I met Rima, when I married her, I didn't know I was still married to you. If you hadn't sent that letter, I would never even have known. Baiji had filed a petition with the village council telling them the marriage was illegal the year after it happened. But our grandfather retracted it from the council and never told us about it. He was a real piece of work, our grandfather."

She remembered how terrified she had been of the man, with his towering height and his perpetual scowl under that huge snow-white mustache.

"Chintu's really the one who should tell you this but all I'll say is that the old bastard blamed Chintu for losing his son. And his means of punishment . . . well, let's just say if Baiji hadn't taken us away from Balpur my brother might not have survived to put that look on your face."

A pained sound escaped Mili's throat. The memory of Samir's sweating body writhing in the throes of a nightmare seared through her mind. She bit the inside of her lip to keep the sobs from slipping out, but it didn't work.

Virat plucked another tissue from the box and handed it to her. "My brother would do absolutely anything for me. And I would give my life for him. But the only reason he came looking for you, the only reason I didn't do it myself, was that my plane crashed. I was in a coma for a week and then flat on my back for months after that."

At least let me explain what happened, Mili.

Why hadn't she let Samir explain?

She could no longer keep the sobs inside. Virat let her cry, handing her tissues as she turned them into soggy blobs one after another.

"Poor Rima, how many months along was she when you had your accident?" she asked. No wonder Samir had wanted to do whatever it took to protect Rima.

Virat smiled. His eyes crinkled up exactly like Samir's did when he smiled. But his smile didn't have that earth-tilting quality to it. Then he laughed. "The only other person I know who would ask a question like that after what I just told you is Chintu."

He patted her head and pulled out another tissue. This time he used it to wipe the tears on her cheeks. Then he lifted her chin with his finger and looked her straight in the eye. "I'm sorry I wasn't the one who found you and set things straight the way I should have. But Mili, please don't punish my brother for my mistakes."

30

The huge glass window framed Samir's magnificent body. Sara had sent over fresh clothes with Kim and he was back in one of those T-shirts of his that always looked brand new. Right now, though, a blue hospital apron covered the T-shirt. A blue hospital cap held back his overgrown hair. Mili had helped him push the thick, freshly washed locks into the cap, and their silken imprint still made her fingertips tingle. The look in his eyes as he searched hers for how she felt had made her heart stutter and shoot sparks into her belly.

How did she feel? How could anyone feel with a sight like this to behold? A man this beautiful with a tiny, wailing creature in his arms. His entire body curved around his hold. Every cell spoke of infinite gentleness. Wonder poured from his eyes and the tiniest hint of astonishment kissed his smile as he mumbled words at the baby, who cared only about the sound of her own voice. The doctor had been right. This baby girl had some strong lungs.

He held her up so Mili could get a better look at her and winced when she screamed in his ear. Then he pulled her to his chest and started to sway to calm her down.

"It's a beautiful sight, isn't it?" Baiji too had showered and changed and looked renewed. Now that Rima was fine the new day did really feel like a new day.

Mili smiled but she was too shy to go on looking at Samir the way she had been. She hoped Baiji hadn't noticed the yearning tearing at her heart.

"He looks almost invincible, doesn't he? So big and indomitable. Not many people can see beyond that," Baiji said in that beautiful old-world Hindi of hers.

Samir turned around to show them that the baby girl had finally quieted in his arms and Baiji squeezed her knuckles against her temples to ward off the evil eye. "Believe it or not, I actually remember your face from the wedding."

Mili turned to Baiji and found her smiling—that at once firm and soft, wrap-you-in-her-sari smile that had her boys mesmerized.

"I wish I had been able to stop it. I know it's the way our people have done things for generations but you were even younger than I was. I was seven when they married me off. And unlucky enough to get my monthlies at ten. So I was packed off to the Rathods at ten. My only skill was to feed the cows and to count my uncle's money while he stared at my budding breasts. Virat's father was something I had never heard of. 'A scholar,' his family called him." She smiled a smile heavy with memories and tinged with regret.

"The villagers called him cursed by the devil. His brain saw the world in particles and numbers and strings of energy. It was all he was interested in. So I adjusted my particles to match his. And I let him teach me to read. I became an obsession. He burned with the fire to educate me. I hated it. I did it the way other women learn to cook, desperate to find a way into his heart. Other girls burned their fingers, I dulled my vision reading and memorizing. My glasses made the man as deliriously happy as a new sari on his wife would have made another man. Those glasses gave us Virat."

Baiji adjusted the glasses on her nose and her smile turned shy— the kind of smile Mili would never have imagined on her. "But who can fight fate? His hunger was greater than a doctorate. Greater than changing one girl's life. Going to America, seeing the universities, the libraries there, it exploded his mind. It was America who took my husband from me. At first I cursed fate, fought with my gods for their injustice, but for him to have died without seeing what he saw, becoming what he became, that would've been the gravest injustice of all. And if none of that had happened, I wouldn't have Samir."

She placed a finger on the glass window, as if to touch her son and her granddaughter, and Mili found her own palm pressed against her heart. "When Sara first brought Samir to Balpur, he used to follow Virat and me everywhere. I was feeding Virat one day and he was watching us from behind the kitchen door, so I called him over and I fed a handful into his mouth too and he crawled into my lap and let me feed him. I used to sing a lullaby to Virat before bed, and I found Samir standing by the door, listening, so I laid him down next to Virat and sang to him too. One day he fell off the courtyard verandah and split his knee. I bandaged it and held him when he cried. That's all it took. Three acts of kindness."

She held up three fingers. "Three acts of kindness and he was mine forever. He never left my side after that. He helped me with all my chores. The devotion in those big brown eyes has never dulled for a moment over the past two dozen years. He recognizes love and lunges for it. And once he holds on to you, he will never let you go. His love is fierce and utter. But it's not for everyone. Some people might find it overwhelming and turn it away."

Mili knew exactly how fierce Samir's love was, how utter. Four weeks with him, one night, and she knew she could never belong to anyone else. She placed her own fingers on the glass. This time she didn't try to conceal the rampant hunger with which her heart craved him. For Samir to not exist. For what he and Baiji had to not exist—Baiji was right, Mili could think of no graver tragedy.

"That," Baiji said, giving her a pointed look. "Whatever that thought was that just popped into your head. That's your answer. That's divine intervention, *beta*. The rest is all courage and choice."

"Did you really put her to sleep by yourself?" Rima gave Samir an impressed look from her hospital bed, her non-ICU hospital bed, he reminded himself, thanking all the gods in the universe. It had been horrible to see her in the ICU. Here, she looked so much more like his *bhabhi*, relaxed and in control.

"Yup, the nurse told me I'm the only one who can quiet her when she starts bawling. I think you might be looking at the world's best *chacha*."

Virat looked up from rubbing Rima's feet. "Oh, a nurse told you that, did she? Was that before or after you turned on the Sam-charm?"

"He's a *married* man now, Virat. Don't say things like that. Where's your *wife*, Samir?" Rima said with such teasing delibera-tion Samir turned to Virat, who was grinning like an idiot without a care in the world.

"You told her!" Relief flooded through Samir. Walking on eggshells around Rima had felt just wrong.

"Everything," Virat said. "Should have done it a lot sooner."

Rima gave Virat one of her caressing smiles and Virat slid up the bed and kissed her. With too much tongue for a hospital room, if you asked him.

An overwhelming urge to see Mili surged through Samir.

"And you're okay, Rima?" he asked. As okay as she could be with Virat cutting off her air supply.

She looked up with fuzzy eyes. "Of course I'm okay. They were kids and it's not like Virat knew when he met me."

"I worship you. You're a goddess. Did I tell you that?" Virat said, reaching for her again. "I told you, Chintu, luckiest bastard on earth."

"Undoubtedly," Samir said, pushing him away and giving Rima a hug.

"Go find your own woman, Chintu," Virat said, smiling, "this one's mine."

"Try and stop me." And with that Samir ran down the hall all the way to the Baby ICU.

He had switched baby-duty with Mili before going to see Rima. Now Mili was switching with Baiji. Baiji patted Samir's cheek and gave Mili a knowing look before she went to her granddaughter.

Mili blushed. Furiously.

"What was that about?" Samir asked, watching the color suffuse her cheeks and dying to trace it with his fingers, with his lips.

Mili narrowed her eyes at him. "You've been bribing your family, haven't you?" Her lips quirked and her tone flashed with her usual spark. And no, Bhai wasn't the luckiest bastard in the world. He was.

"I would if it put that smile on your face."

She looked away, still blushing, and watched Baiji pick up his niece, who usually was impossible to look away from. But with Mili in her bright white *kurti* over jeans, with her hair springing out of that stupid braid and framing her face, he was having a hard time looking at anything else. She waved at Baiji and Samir wondered what had happened between them.

"How's Rima?" she asked, and then raised a brow at him when he smiled in response. "Can we go see her? She wanted a baby report."

"She's a little busy right now. But I'm starving. You want to run down to the cafeteria? Javed said they have the best samosas."

Her eyes actually sparkled and anticipation reared up inside him like a fire-breathing dragon who'd slept too long. He took her hand and walked to the elevator. She didn't pull away and the dragon let loose another huge flaming breath.

She watched the elevator doors and rubbed her eyes. His heart squeezed. She hadn't left the hospital in two days. Hadn't left him. "I'm so sorry you had to go through this. You look exhausted."

She gave him a sideways glance. "You don't look so great yourself."

"Thanks a lot." The elevator opened and they entered. It was empty. He found himself praying for a power outage.

She smiled. "I don't mean that literally. Although, what's with the beard?" She threw a pointed look at his jaw and her eyes hitched on his lips.

Every cell in his body leapt toward her. He used all his strength to hold it back. "I don't know. I haven't felt like myself lately. No point looking like myself then, I guess."

She swallowed but she didn't look away.

"Mili, what you did for me, for my family—I don't know how I would have got through this without you. I don't know how I could ever thank you."

Her eyes flashed fierce one moment, soft the next. "Actually, I know exactly how you could thank me."

"No."

She blinked up at him and he almost smiled. "But you don't even know what I was going to ask for."

"I'm not taking the *haveli* back, Mili."

"You can't just give me something so big, Samir."

The elevator stopped and they stepped out. By some miracle the corridor was isolated. This was definitely his day. "Mili." He opened his mouth then closed it again, suddenly nervous. "What I did, I could never tell you how sorry I am. I understand that you can't forgive me. I can't forgive myself. But let me make it right. Please."

Mili waited for him to say more. She prayed. She held her breath.

He didn't.

Had she really thought she couldn't forgive him? Had she really thought she could live without him? "Is that what you want, Samir? My forgiveness? I don't need the *haveli* for that. I know now that you didn't mean for it to turn out the way it did." How had she ever thought he would knowingly hurt her? "Of course I forgive you. You're free." She stepped away from him and then instantly regretted it.

He stepped closer. "Mili—"

Three nurses came chattering down the corridor. They slowed down when they passed Samir and started giggling like schoolgirls. He didn't seem to notice. His gaze never left Mili.

Enough was enough. She reached out and slammed her palm into the elevator button.

The elevator doors slid open and she grabbed his arm and dragged him back into the metal cage. His only reaction was the slightest raise of an eyebrow. She took a step closer to him and looked him straight in the eye. "Samir, isn't there any other way you can think of to make this right?"

His eyes widened. She loved surprising him, loved the way he looked at her when she threw caution to the wind and did exactly as she pleased. She bit her lip and smiled up at him, feeling every bit of the power she had over him. She had no idea why he had given her that power but she loved it. It made her feel as tall as him, taller even. It made the fire burning in her heart flare and lick at every inch of her.

He reached behind her and pushed a button on the panel and the elevator bounced to a halt. "You got any ideas?" The heat was back in his eyes and it wasn't nearly as restrained as his voice. He was doing it again. He was laying himself bare in front of her. And for some reason she knew he always would.

She reached up and touched his face, his overgrown stubble as thick and silken as his hair. "Don't ever thank me for caring for your family. They . . . they don't feel like just your family."

"They don't?"

She shook her head. "And you don't feel like my brother-in-law."

He grinned, some of that wonderful arrogance returning to his face. He plucked her hand from his face and pulled it to his heart. It thudded beneath her fingers. "I'm not."

She closed her eyes. Suddenly too shy to say more.

"Mili, if there is something you're trying to say, say it. Please." The desperation in his voice was pure pain. And beautiful.

"I can't." Warmth rose in her cheeks.

"Okay. If I don't feel like a brother-in-law, what is it I do feel like?" A smile seeped into his voice.

"I don't know." She wanted to hide her face in his chest.

Samir lifted her chin with his finger. No way was she going all bashful on him now. "Let me give you a few choices."

She smiled. Eyes closed. Cheeks blazing.

"The best friend you ever had? Someone whose family would kill him if he ever let you go? Someone who loves you so much he doesn't know what to do with it? The answer to all your prayers? The person you've waited for all your—"

She opened her eyes and placed one finger on his lips. It was the lightest touch but his heart thumped like elephants parading across his chest.

"Do I have to pick only one?" she said.

Laughter trembled in his belly. He leaned over and dropped

kisses on her eyelids, on her wet cheeks. Her skin was the softest velvet and he had craved it for so long. She pressed into his kisses, her smile widening with each touch of his lips. His fingers, mad with hunger, undid the twisting strands of the fat braid hanging down to her waist and soaked up the silk that tangled around them.

She grabbed on to his shoulders and climbed up on his feet just as his lips found hers, the fit so perfect he forgot to think, forgot to breathe, and lost himself in stealing his life back from her lips. It raged back through him, everything he had ever lost. He plucked it from her lips, whispered it back into her mouth. When he finally pulled away he found her eyes glazed with the same ravenous need that raged through him and he had to remind himself where they were.

She didn't seem to care. She reached up and gave him that look, the one that asked him to bend to her. And he did because he could never refuse her anything. She dug her fingers in his hair, wrapped him up in her fierce warmth, and spoke in his ear, her whisper trembling with emotion. "You're everything, Samir. You're everything I ever wanted. And I choose you. You are my love, my freedom, and I choose you." She dragged her lips across his jaw and found his lips.

His world spun. He would have to get used to that. He pulled her body impossibly closer. Terror of ever having to let her go gripped his gut. "Screw freedom," he said against her lips. "I'm not ever letting you go."

Banging sounded from outside the elevator. "Hello? Anyone in there? Are you stuck? Hold on, we'll get you out."

He groaned and Mili threw her head back and laughed, her onyx eyes sparkling, her midnight curls cascading down her back, the smell of night-blooming jasmine flooding his senses. Oh yeah, he was well and truly stuck. And no fucking way was anyone getting him out. Ever.

EPILOGUE

A single wedding altar stood on the sandy beach rimmed by a sun-drenched ocean that disappeared into the horizon. The celebratory lilt of *shehnai* flutes piped from speakers and mingled with the gentle crashing of the waves. An auspicious pyre dotted the center of the altar like a scarlet *bindi*. By the pyre sat a chanting priest and one bride and her one and only groom. A kurta of the sheerest silk stretched across his humungous shoulders. A vermillion sari edged with the most intricate gold wound around her delicately curvy body.

Around them in concentric circles of color gathered their friends and family, sipping wine and munching cocktail-sized samosas.

Lata surveyed the scene from the very front of the chaos, where her sons had obtained the plushest of sofas for her and the bride's grandmother. Unlike the beaming grandmother, tears flowed in rivulets down the bride's velvet cheeks. Her chest hiccupped with sobs. The bride's brother-in-law dropped a kiss on his own wife's head and went to the bride. He switched out the empty tissue box next to her with a new one and winked at his brother, who stared at his bride's tears with almost absurd pride.

"Some things never change," thought the groom's brother.

"I still can't believe those lashes are real," thought the groom.

"Good Lord, he has the most beautiful shoulders in the world and I can't wait to get my hands on him," thought the bride.

"Please, God, let the poor fool get whatever she's crying for this time," thought the groom's mother.

And she did.

A BOLLYWOOD AFFAIR

Sonali Dev

ABOUT THIS GUIDE

The suggested questions are included
to enhance your group's reading of
Sonali Dev's *A Bollywood Affair.*

DISCUSSION QUESTIONS

1. Mili believes she loves Virat without ever having seen him. But when she feels things for Samir, she is unable to categorize that as love. Although Mili's situation is unique, do you believe conditioning by society influences whom we fall in love with? At a wider level does societal conditioning dictate our friendships and people we are drawn to?

2. Samir is still reeling from abandonment as a child and yet he puts himself in a position where Mili abandoning him is almost inevitable. Do you think we tend to put ourselves in positions where our worst fears come true? And if we do, why do you think that is?

3. Mili accepts her lot in life but she keeps working within the confines of her situation to change it. Have you ever been in a situation where you couldn't change the source of the problem but you worked around the problem to keep going and make it bearable? And does that ever really work?

4. Why do you think Samir never tells Mili who he is? Do you believe the reasons he gives himself—his script, her injury? Could he have told her sooner? What do you believe would have happened if he had?

5. Why do you think Mili never tells Samir about her marriage? Does her lie by omission make Samir's lie easier to forgive? Do you think that their relationship is based on lies or do you believe that the foundation of their relationship is outside of the lies?

6. Naani makes decisions for Mili she believes will benefit Mili. Baiji does the same for Samir. Do you believe families, by virtue of loving us, have the right to "do what is best" for us? What about your own family—how far would you go for those you love?

7. Why do you think the system of child marriages or even arranged marriages, for that matter, where the choice lies outside the marrying couple, ever started? What was the benefit to society? Apart from the obvious injustice of it, what other repercussions does a society suffer as a result of such a system?

8. Culturally, does the Indian community in the story seem like an isolated island? Do you believe it is more important for immigrant communities to assimilate and integrate into mainstream American society, or is holding on to their roots important and beneficial? Why?

9. Despite Mili and Samir being from India, their worlds are very different. One rural and traditional, the other urban and more Western. What do you think fundamentally attracts them to each other despite these differences? Do you believe a similarity in backgrounds/belief systems helps a marriage or is the opposite of that true?

10. Mili and her roommate, Ridhi, have both been raised in traditional Indian families but in two different countries. Both families believe the women should follow the path set for them. Both women maneuver their way around these expectations to get what they want. Do you think the burden of a set path to follow is unique to the Indian culture? Or is it something all cultures have to deal with? What kind of expectations have you had to work around in your own life? Can we ever be empowered enough to make decisions free from expectations?

11. Tradition and family values play a large part in the lives of all the major characters. How do you think traditions and family values help or hinder the characters? What is the place of tradition in today's world?

TELL THE WORLD THIS BOOK WAS		
GOOD	BAD	SO-SO